BEYOND THE MASK

A FICTION-ATLAS SUPERHERO ANTHOLOGY

C.L. CANNON   R.M. DEMEESTER

MATTHEW STEVENS   SARAH BUHRMAN

REBEKAH DODSON   K. MATT   BOB JAMES

MELISSA E. BECKWITH   DEVORAH FOX

C. M. LANDER

FICTION-ATLAS PRESS LLC

BEYOND THE MASK

A FICTION-ATLAS SUPERHERO ANTHOLOGY

FICTION-ATLAS
PRESS LLC

SUPERANNUATED

BY MATTHEW STEVENS

"There I was. The Dzopa Stones lying on tables in the middle of the room. Alarms blaring all around."

"Obviously, you escaped. But, how? What did you do?" Wilbur's jaw fell open matching his saucer-like eyes.

I glanced around the open space of Shady Acres Retirement Home's community room. Dozens of other residents were occupied with different activities, puzzles, watching television, or playing cards. Ethel's crew was in the opposite corner knitting away as usual. Wilbur and I enjoyed our quiet table away from the rest.

"I had to complete the mission. All 716 of the stones were right there in front of me." I'd told this story so many times I'd perfected the art of stringing my listener along.

"You didn't get them all, right? How could you?"

"I didn't need all the stones. The power and secrets contained on one stone would keep our top scientists busy for decades."

"How did you make it out with even one stone?"

"Very carefully, Wilbur. I retraced my steps."

"You must have killed dozens of soldiers."

"Nope. I made it out without harming a soul."

"Wow." Wilbur marvelled. He was entranced. "I can't believe that you really did all those things."

"Yep, I was just like America's favorite superhero. Of course, I didn't get all the pomp and circumstance. And, I'm real." The edges of my mouth tightened into a scowl. The captain was famous. They made movies about him.

"Captain Who?"

"You know...." I wasn't sure if this was part of Wilbur's Alzheimer's, or not.

"What did he do?" asked Wilbur, his brow furrowed.

"Not a damned thing." I huffed.

"So, you did all the work, and he got all the glory? What did you do about it?" Wilbur asked more questions than a toddler.

I fidgeted in my seat. "I couldn't do squat. It was best for myself and the country that my existence remained a secret. So, he got the credit for missions I completed." Anger I had tucked away bubbled to the surface. Of all the times Wilbur and I talked, this was the first time he'd hit on this chord with his questions.

Wilbur's gaze turned toward the window. He stared past the trees and parking lot, concentrating on everything and nothing. I could see the wheels turning and thought he was going to hit me with another barrage of questions, but then he lowered his eyes. When he raised them again, he extended his hand.

"Nice to meet you. I'm Wilbur. You are?"

I laid my head in my hands. I knew this was coming. It always did. But the further his Alzheimer's progressed the more I knew I could trust him with my secrets. Essentially, the sole reason I talked to Wilbur. He could remember his wife's birthday and what gift he gave to her every year, but that marriage ended almost forty years ago. Ask him what time he got up this morning and he'd look at you like a deer in headlights.

Sighing, I reached out to shake his hand. "The pleasure is all mine, Wilbur. I'm Eugene." I rose from my chair.

"Where are you going?" concern laced his inquiry.

"I'm going to head to my room before dinner." I didn't have anything to do, but I'd expended my patience. "I'll see you at chow."

Half-hunched, I reached for my walker. I hated the damn thing. I didn't really need it, but I had airs to keep up. If people knew I could get around, they'd probably toss my flabby, aging ass out on the curb. But I had a purpose in here. I was doing research, and I hadn't found my answer yet.

"Well, okay. I'll see you around," Wilbur replied dejectedly.

I started across the room. Lift the walker. Move it forward a few inches. Shuffle. Repeat. If nothing else could kill me, this game of charades might.

Big, bold, bright letters flashed on the television, catching my eye. Superheroes had once again managed to save a city, this time on foreign soil. Cities, states, and countries had boundaries, but superheroes were everywhere. And, when they saved the day, you had to be living under a rock to avoid knowing. The anchor glossed over the events and moved on to a more important story: how to make macaroni and cheese—on the grill.

Good Lord. The shit they come up with. The sad part is that people get paid to brainstorm, write, and produce this stuff. I continued my trek across the room, grumbling under my breath. Distracted by the mental assault masquerading as news I stopped paying attention to my feet, which caught the edge of the rug.

It all happened in slow motion.

The walker clattered to the floor. I followed behind. I tried to catch myself, but my hands got tangled in the walker. Twisted around I braced for impact with the tiled concrete floor. I wasn't as infirm as everyone believed, but I was still eighty-three years old. And, super-powers or not, my reflexes weren't what they used to be. A couple of nurses, always hovering like distracted bumblebees, heard the noise and bolted over. A few of the other residents gasped in horror.

The nurses arrived as my body settled awkwardly and painfully on top of the walker. "Don't move, Mr. Dalca. Where does it hurt? Lisa, go get Doctor Varma."

I knew nothing was broken. In connection with my power, my

body protected itself quite effectively, but, if I didn't groan or grab at something, flags would fly because every other resident of this place would have shattered multiple bones.

"I think I bumped my head. I tried to stop myself, but I'm not as strong as I used to be," I whined.

"Your head?" The nurses shared a confused look. "What about your legs? Can you feel them? Do they hurt?" They had seen too many broken hips to count and just as many stubborn old people.

Sluggishly, I extended each leg, grimacing for show when I stretched my left. Worst case, they'd take me to the medical center, check me out, and wheel me back to my room until dinner. Haha! That might get me there faster than my previous pace.

A dozen or so other residents continued to stare as the nurses slid their arms under my armpits and carefully helped me into the closest chair. Voices whispered around the room. I couldn't make out what was said, but I had a good idea. They were questioning, or jealous—how could I possibly get up after a spill like that? They'd be laid up for weeks.

The nurses checked my walker, which was neither bent nor broken. I tried mightily to convince them I was fine before the doctor could arrive. I just wanted to be alone in my room for a while. Not likely, having already mentioned my head. Damn. Here came the doc and the wheelchair.

The nurse rolled me up to my door. I braced my hands against the armrests to raise myself from the chair, but a firm hand on my shoulder insisted help all the way into the room. He reached around me and gave the door a gentle shove. It came to rest against the bumper on the wall as he pushed me through the doorway. Only then did he allow me out of the chair to situate myself on the couch.

My living room was simple, housing a couch, two large overstuffed recliners, with the rest of the space filled with bookshelves. My little safe haven.

The nurse said nothing as he left my unit with the wheelchair. It was better that way. I was in a mood, and if he felt obligated to be pleasant, I might have regretted my response. The door shut, and I took a few deep breaths as I leaned my head back. There was a knock at the door. Hrumph! I had no family and wasn't really friends with any other residents. That only left one person: my handler, Jessica. And she would enter whether I replied or not.

She did.

A perk of her also being a full-time nurse here at the home.

Before she could feign concern for my tumble, I hit her with some of the remaining anger and cynicism from my revelations in the TV room.

"Did they send you to make sure I hadn't actually hurt myself? Or was that secretly their hope? I can hear their petty little discussion in some poorly lit backroom in D.C." I alternated voices mimicking a stodgy suit and his crony. "'The report says that he hit his head. You think it might lead to something?' 'Can't say yet, sir.' 'Hope so. I'm tired of having to hide payments to nursing homes for a washed-up superhero that we just can't seem to get rid of.'"

Jessica chuckled next to me on the couch. "You're just a ray of sunshine. What was it this time?"

"Don't pretend that you care. I know this is a paycheck for you. Hell, you probably get hazard pay on a day like today."

"Eugene." She set her jaw and crossed her arms over her chest. "You're right. I do," she said with a sly grin.

I sighed and sunk a little further into the couch. I didn't need to take out my discontent on Jessica. "I know. I'm just frustrated, Jess. Besides, trust me, if I tried to off myself, I'd do a better job than wiping out in the TV room."

"I'm sorry. I'll never understand, but over the last seven years, you've become more than a job. You've seen so much. Done so many things. It's—"

"Okay, okay. I get it. You don't have to get all sappy on me. Remember, my whole point is to find a way out."

Jessica didn't say anything. She stared at me for a moment. Maybe she was hoping I'd do a trick, like phase into the couch. She was the only person in the home that knew about my powers and my struggle, especially of late.

When she was assigned as my handler, they had been intentionally obtuse. I'd already chased off the first two they'd sent my way. I wasn't keen on being watched like a puppy. The government started keeping a closer eye on me again after the friends I'd made during retirement died. The old folks' home was my idea. They weren't happy about the financial expenditure, a deal is a deal, especially when it's a signed contract.

I'd tried to off myself a few times after the Cold War ended and the government stumbled upon newer, more effective superheroes. But my body had a way of thwarting my best-laid plans. My power to phase was something that in many ways, I couldn't control. You don't know frustration until you try to slit your wrist and the knife continues to pass right through your arm. I'd have made one hell of a magician if I could count on my body doing the same thing every time. But I couldn't.

"I'm not doing it, if that's what you're waiting for," I offered.

In either resignation or boredom, Jessica began moving around the room absent-mindedly tidying up.

"I'm not. I know you can't really control it. Your body does its own thing."

"Yeah. Which occasionally was nothing short of embarrassing."

Atoms are mostly space; my ability takes full advantage of that. The cells and molecules that make up my body expand or condense as necessary to work around the atoms in the surface I press against. When I phase, the pressure initially feels like pressing a hand against a balloon. The air inside the balloon moves, but the surface of the balloon fights back, resisting and bulging. The difference with me is that eventually, the wall begins to give way.

My ability is controlled, for the most part, subconsciously. If I push too hard or too fast, my body reacts as if it is being attacked. Sometimes that means I slam into the wall, other times I fall through it. I've tried to control my abilities, but they don't work that way.

The first time I met Jessica, she came unannounced to check on me. I was in the restroom, using my walker to keep up appearances. I'd left the door to my room unlocked and didn't hear her enter. She snuck up on me in the bathroom with my pants still undone. Startled, by her knock, I tripped over my walker and tumbled backward. The end result was my body from the waist up phased into the wall while my lower half lay there, still exposed, on the bathroom floor.

"It wasn't the prettiest." Jessica winked and jabbed me gently.

The mortifying, but funny memory momentarily softened my cynicism.

"Uh-huh. So, tell me why you're here. They heard that I'd fallen, and you're here to check up on me. Am I right?"

"Come on, Eugene. You are America's first superhero. A couple of people in D.C. remember what you've done and want to make sure you're as happy and healthy as can be while you do this ... thing you're doing." For as long as she'd worked with me, I wasn't sure if she was being snarky or genuine.

"Jess, I don't know how much longer I can go on like this. I know that people live longer than me, but eighty-three years is enough. Especially when you consider all I've done."

"You survive because that's who you are."

"I've survived because my body won't let me do otherwise." I had faded into melancholy. "Too many people that I've known, trusted ... loved, are gone. All I want to do is join them."

"That's what today was? A sad attempt to finish the job?" She knew that wasn't true, but in our years together, Jess had become an expert at getting me to open up to her.

I scoffed.

"You know very well that if I wanted to finish the job, I'd try something a little more ... I don't know ... violent or dangerous. I couldn't even succeed in breaking a hip today. I don't need Kevlar to stop a bullet or deflect a knife. My body won't even let me swallow an object it senses to be harmful."

"Are you done wallowing?" she said matter-of-factly. "Can I walk you to dinner?"

"Yeah, I'm hungry. Starvation isn't appealing to me. Too long and drawn out. Not what I'm looking for."

"Quick and dirty, huh?" Jess winked at me.

"You're supposed to be helping me live, not helping me die." I shot her a look of confusion and mock contempt.

"The sooner you kick it, the sooner I get reassigned to something interesting," she retorted with a mischievous grin and a playful shrug. She was a fireball. It struck me that any child I might have had would probably have been a lot like her. But I couldn't burden a child with a life like mine.

"Fine. I'm done sulking. Take me to dinner."

The worst part about dinner at the home isn't the company. It's the slop that passes for food. I ate better in military mess halls, and that's saying something.

No one else seems to notice the sub-par quality of the food. Maybe everyone else is happy to be gumming food of any kind at their age, but I couldn't settle for that.

Jessica accompanied me to the dining room and even carried my tray to my seat.

I spooned the slop in front of me until my plate was empty. Not eating your food in the dining hall was an excellent way to attract unwanted attention from the medical staff. Better to force the sad excuse for food down my throat than listen to their fake sickly-sweet voices chirp at me incessantly.

When I finished, I caught Jessica's eye over at the nurse's table. They didn't eat at the same time as the residents. They had a separate cafeteria for themselves, not as large or fancy as ours, but with solid foods. I'd dared an expedition once out of curiosity while the food service staff was home overnight, but they didn't leave anything out. I had to go off the grounds for a proper dinner.

Jessica saw me back to my unit for the evening. Even as a regis-tered nurse, sometimes she paid so much attention to me, I worried that our secret could be exposed. But we'd carried our charade around to three other nursing homes so far, without anyone the wiser.

Safely returned to my unit, my walker tucked away by the front door, she turned to face me. All I wanted was to finish my book before lights out and my excursion beyond the walls for solid sustenance.

Mostly joking, I returned to my perturbed and cynical ways. "Why are you still here?" I threw in a little extra sneer.

She ignored my tone. "Thinking."

"Maybe you could think me up my slippers. They're in the bedroom." Jessica knew I was being snide for the sake of levity. She played along.

"How 'bout you think me up a magic word, you old coot?" She remained standing in the middle of the room.

"I can't stand you young 'uns anymore. No manners, no respect for us old folks." I shifted on the couch making myself comfortable and reached for my book.

We both stared at each other intently for a moment before bursting into laughter. She wandered out of the room and returned with my slippers. I wiggled my toes into the fuzzy foam caverns.

Jessica headed for the door. "Just stay out of trouble tonight?"

"Who? Me?" I feigned innocence.

She opened her mouth to counter but chuckled instead. "'Night," she said, pulling the door shut behind her.

Finally, getting some peace and quiet, I read for an hour before the intercom system beeped softly three times—the signal for lights out. As old as we were, they still treated us like kids at summer camp. At least at summer camp, we went swimming and then home after a few weeks. In this case, we weren't so lucky on either count.

I remained on the couch until the soft click of the lights turning off echoed throughout the home. I waited. The deafening silence grew louder, the screech from my tinnitus drowning out any other sound. A rumble from just above my waistband disrupted the intolerable mix of serenity and catastrophe.

Time for a real dinner. I made sure the door was locked, then crossed to the outside wall of my unit, which, by happy coincidence, was located on the first floor. Not that I couldn't still accomplish my late-night food rendezvous, but being on the first floor made it much simpler.

Phasing required a mental reset. I cleared a space against the wall and inched my toes up to the baseboard. I took a long, deep breath and thought about what I would order at Taco Mama's. I pictured the menu in my head. Then, raising my foot, I pushed it slowly against the wall.

I focused on clearing my head and pressed harder.

The atoms in my toes and feet began to rearrange themselves individually around the atoms that made up the concrete wall. I found the tipping point where the surface tension released, and the phasing began. My body temperature dropped as the atoms in my body expanded to work their maze-like magic around the concrete atoms, my body heat dissipating into the wall.

A chill buzzed through every molecule of my body, threatening to force me into thinking about my progress. Instead, I concentrated on listing the ingredients in the Mucho Loco Burrito. Tortilla, beans, rice, chicken, salsa, steak, fresh jalapeños, cheese, salsa verde, sour cream, guacamole, lettuce, and Mama Rosario's secret ingredient—the one she wouldn't confirm even if guessed correctly. Once, I guessed love, to which she replied with only a subtle wink.

My eyes remained closed the entire time every time. I'd never opened them, and I wasn't sure what would happen if I did. Sure, I was curious, but it seemed like a good way to leave a necessary part of me behind. Might be something to investigate. A means to an end? Likely messy, but not like I would be cleaning up.

The phase was almost complete. I could feel the coolness of the fall evening on my cheeks. Then, the cricket's music joined my perception. Finally, I felt a gentle pop at the back of my neck, as if someone had pulled a small suction cup away from my skin. That was the signal to open my eyes. I glanced around to make sure the coast was clear. Not a soul in sight. Taco Mama's, here I come.

After inhaling a tray full of food that widened even Mama Rosario's eyes, I leaned back in my chair, arching backward with my arms stretched over my head. I took a deep breath and felt myself sink slightly into the chair—literally. I bolted upright, stopping the phase so quickly, a tiny pop echoed through the empty dining room.

The clock confirmed, as I let everything settle for a few more minutes, that more than an hour had passed since lights out. I should probably head back. The longer I was away, the greater chance a nurse might stop to check on me, especially after my tumble this afternoon. If I wasn't there, all hell would break loose. You'd think a maximum-security prison break was happening the way they acted when they couldn't find a resident after lights out. Seriously, we weren't going anywhere. And if we were, we weren't going fast.

The walk back to the home wasn't long, only a few blocks. Taco Mama's was the only restaurant within walking distance of Shady Acres. I often wondered about its location, not that I was complaining by any means. When I arrived back at the home, all the lights were out except for a couple of emergency lights at each corner of the building. The nurses' station and welcome area were on the other side of the building, so I didn't have to worry about sneaking past anyone. I approached the wall to my unit and cleared my mind, settling my focus on my wonderfully full stomach. Phasing would be a little slower and more complicated, but well worth the trouble.

Back in my unit, I found everything as I left it, empty and dark. I headed for bed. I was in store for some crazy dreams, but I would sleep well.

Knock! Knock! Knock! There was a brief pause followed by a louder, more insistent trio of knocks. I rolled over and focused on the clock. 6:47 AM. Who would be banging so obnoxiously this early? The knocking continued. If truly a matter of life and death, the nurses all had master keys. I slowly and deliberately made my way to the door. I would get there when I got there. By the time I made it, I could hear keys jingling.

"I'm coming! I'm coming!" I shouted, coating my voice with as much old crony as I could muster. The keys stopped. I turned the handle and pulled. "What?" I grunted.

Jessica stood as close to the threshold of my unit as she could without actually entering. The color of her skin was a shade north of death, her eyes bloodshot and rimmed in red.

"Good Lord, child, what the hell happened?" I ushered her inside. My indignation evaporated. There was no one in this world that I cared more for than her.

She rubbed her hands over her face and through her hair repeatedly before she spoke. I rested my old bones beside her on the couch. Tears rolled down her cheeks. She leaned over and squeezed me so hard I thought I might phase into her.

"Now, tell me what in the world could possibly lead to this." I couldn't think of anything aside from the death of a close relative that would shake her. Her government training had toughened her exterior, but one hit to the right spot and she melted like snow indoors.

"I-I-I-" she stuttered through the tears. "I-I thought you were g-g-gone."

"Huh? Where would I go?" I held her. Sobs shook her body. The tears slowed, but they still left a half-dollar sized damp spot on my shoulder.

Jessica took a deep breath, dabbing her eyes with a tissue. "They found your wallet outside on rounds. I knew you went out last night, but I was afraid that-that, you'd ...." She trailed off, as the tears returned.

I hated crying. Crying of any kind, to be honest, was horrible. I just wanted her to stop.

"Look. I'm right here. Nothing happened to me." I patted my chest. "I went for a bite to eat. What was the worst that could happen?" The question wasn't rhetorical.

"M-M-Maybe your secret got out and they w- w- wanted you for tests. Or w-what if you g-got stuck?"

"First off, I'm pretty sure that I'm not a classified secret anymore. And second, I've never gotten stuck while phasing. I've been doing it since I was a teenager and even when distracted in the girls' locker room, I didn't get stuck." I chuckled at my own memory. I had almost been busted for sneaking into the girls' locker room when in an early attempt at phasing to escape, I momentarily lost to a wall. I was nearly spotted before I was able to back through the wall to safety.

Jessica regained a tenuous composure as the tears and blubbering halted. "Why mention that now?"

"No real reason. I was just reminiscing about nearly getting stuck and getting caught while phasing." I thought for a moment. "I've never been either stuck or caught while in the process. So, worrying about that is unnecessary."

She stared at me for a moment. Her brow furrowed; her eyes, usually warm and pleasant, were dark. "You know, this isn't just a job for me. And I'm not exactly sure what I'd do if you … if you … well, you know." Jessica's resolve faded, and tears welled up at the corners of her eyes.

"I do know. But you also need to understand that I'm here until I'm not." The direction this conversation was taking was not a place I wanted to go. She knew why I was here, and she knew that I wouldn't be around forever. At least, I hoped I wouldn't.

Jessica wiped her eyes, then honked her nose into a fresh tissue. No longer teary, she refocused. "Maybe … just maybe, you should be more careful." Loaded with indignation, she chucked my wallet at me.

"Isn't it time for breakfast?" I said, checking my pretend watch.

"Yeah. Should be ready," she replied.

Neither of us wanted to talk about the emotions that had just spilled over.

"Then let's go."

Jessica led me to a table, then wandered off to assist other residents. Best to keep up appearances, and while each resident had their favorite nurses and vice versa, if Jessica didn't spend any time with other people it would draw unwanted attention. Neither of us needed the hassle. So, another nurse, Marie, who I liked well enough, brought my tray of food. A side effect of my ability was an increased appetite. Most people my age ate a few spoonfuls of scrambled eggs, a few slices of apple, and a small glass of orange juice or coffee and they were full until lunchtime. Me? Not so much. Jessica had filled my tray and passed it off. An extra bowl, even. More mush. The unending variations were truly amazing.

"I'll swing back by in a few to see how you're doing, Mr. D." Marie didn't hover. She was pleasant but knew not to overstay her welcome.

My tray was over half empty when Ethel wheeled by the table.

"How's it going, hot stuff?" She winked. Ethel was sweet, and it was obvious that at a much younger age, she had been quite the looker. I'd seen a faded picture or two, and if I'd met her way back then, I might have rethought abstaining from marriage and children.

"What's cookin', good lookin'?" It was our typical exchange, but my line held a dual purpose. Ethel dealt in and dished out gossip.

"Well, in case you haven't heard, another soul left us during the night." Ethel was as serious as a heart attack when she shared news of those that'd passed on.

"Oh, no. Who?" I'd be lying if I cared as much as my tone implied.

"I think we all knew it was coming. Sooner rather than later; if you know what I mean?" She insisted on dancing around the details. I wanted a name.

"It's sad, but it isn't a surprise anymore, my dear." All too true.

"Wilbur, God rest his soul." Ethel lowered her chin and made the sign of the cross over her chest.

"How sad," I replied. Ethel looked at me expectantly, waiting for something deeper or more personal. "He was such a good listener," I blurted. That was true. Now I would have to make friends with another Alzheimer's patient.

She rested her hand gently on mine. "I know you two talked quite a bit. If you need someone new to listen for you," she winked, "you know where to find me."

Surely she didn't mean the wink in a romantic way, but for some reason, it came off like that. "Thank you, Ethel. Wilbur and I did talk a lot, so I appreciate the offer."

With that, she patted my hand once more and wheeled off toward breakfast.

Jessica walked up to the table, loaded with nervous energy. Her leg bounced, and her fingers tapped the tabletop.

"Now what?" I wanted to finish my breakfast.

Her response was to look down her nose at me. If I were drunk, her stare would have sobered me up. "I think it's time."

"Yeah, I know. I've been trying to find a good way to head where Wilbur's gone for years. And yet, here I sit."

"How'd you know? Pretty sure ESP isn't one of your talents." There was a hint of irritation in her voice. "I just came from the nurse's station, and Wilbur's favorite nurse is a wreck."

I didn't need to speak. She followed my gaze to Ethel, now stopped across the room at the edge of another table chatting it up with another decrepit fella.

"She knows? Wait … is Ethel …," her lips scrunched slightly. "Like you?"

"Huh? What the hell does that mean? Like me? Is she old? Of course she is." My ignorance was unintentional. I was busy thinking about my breakfast.

"No!" Jessica glanced around. Sinking to her knees, she lowered her voice, resting her elbows and forearms on the tabletop. Her voice dropped to match her body position. "Don't be dim." She checked over her shoulder. "Does she have powers?"

"Oh." What Jessica was asking about clicked. "Yep. She's got one that I don't have." I couldn't help but play along.

Jessica's eyebrows perked up, and her eyes went wide. "She does not!"

"Honest." She leaned closer and waited for me to spill Ethel's secret powers. "She has the incredible ability to be able to talk to any sack of bones on this planet. Alive or dead."

Jessica smacked me on the shoulder with the back of her hand. "Dammit, Gene."

I rubbed my shoulder in mock pain. I had been an ass about the situation, but there were times I couldn't help but play on Jessica's inability to see through my bullshit. "Come on, how the hell would I know? You're the one with high-level government top secret security clearance."

She snorted at me, perturbed, but came back around quickly. "You're right. If anyone here should know about another retired, aging, grumpy superhero, it would be me."

I laughed. Sometimes it was too easy to get her all riled up. "What were you saying before I got you all hot and bothered?"

"Huh? Oh, that!" She gathered her thoughts. "I'm going to check with D.C., but we might have to move again. Leave Shady Acres behind." Jessica didn't know it, but she had a superpower too. She could kill a good mood with two sentences.

Moments ago, we were all smiles and jokes, and now I was being packed, shipped, and shuffled around again like a crated weapon. "Why, because of Wilbur? That's absurd."

"We don't get to make the call, Gene. Besides, I heard some of the nurses talking about your fall and your lack of injuries. They notice when you don't bruise or complain about aches after things like yesterday. If too many people start asking questions …."

"I know." I didn't like it, but I knew what would happen. "In come the men in dark suits with their little thingies to erase everyone's brains." The very corner of my mouth twitched. Then it spread. I couldn't hold back my grin.

"That joke never gets old to you, does it?"

"Let me think … nope." I winked.

Jessica shook her head. "I'm going to clock out here and talk to D.C. I should know our fate by tomorrow. And maybe our new home."

I sighed. Moving had become an unforeseen side effect of my powers, one I never imagined. I can walk through walls and stop bullets, but I can't get over the fact that my body won't let me quit this life just yet.

"Just remember my requirements." I waited to make sure knew what I meant.

"We're not going to find another Taco Mama's. Ever."

My shoulders sagged. "It's disappointing. But there better be some damn good local fast food within walking distance. If I have to survive solely on food from one of these places, I'll go crazy before I kick the bucket."

"Gotcha, boss. I know they have your hand-written list of requirements. But I'll remind them to take them into account." Jessica stood up, kissed me on the forehead and walked away.

I was left with half a bowl of oatmeal. Cold, lumpy, and stuck… just like me.

ABOUT MATTHEW STEVENS

Matthew Stevens spent years dreaming about being a writer before he found time late at night to create characters and worlds and the stories for them to inhabit. His current projects find him dabbling in a wide range of genres from his drafted novel, a paranormal thriller, to numerous fantasy and sci-fi shorts, along with an occasional blog post examining his perspective on his own writing journey and any intriguing geeky topic that catches his attention.

He can be found online at:
theedgeofeverything.wordpress.com

facebook.com/matthewstevensauthor

twitter.com/matt_the_writer

instagram.com/matt_the_writer

TURNCOAT

BY C.L. CANNON

Ringing, ringing, why all the ringing? Shay glared at the red illuminated numerals of her alarm clock and cursed the person who dared call her at this hour. The sharp click of the call being forwarded to her answering machine cut through the dead silence of her apartment, followed by the insistent voice of her partner. "Tolliver...Tolliver? Where are you? We've got a situation."

She groaned, rolling to her side and patting the nightstand in a haphazard effort to find her cellphone and bring it to her ear.

"It's my night off, Merrick," she said, not bothering to conceal her annoyance.

"Heroes don't get nights off. Besides, you'll want to see this for yourself."

"If it's anything that involves me putting my pants back on, I'm... *really* not interested."

She could hear him sputtering on the other end of the line. "What? Gah, I..I did not need to know that."

"Oh, stop your fussing, I know you—" She was poised to tease him relentlessly when he cut her off.

"He's back, Shay. Gressler's back."

She felt her whole body tense, her breath stolen from her lungs. "Where?"

"I'm texting you the coordinates now."

Shay didn't bother with a reply. She dropped the cell on the bed beside her and tried to concentrate on her breathing. After all this time, Max was back, but what did he want? Could it really be him? There was only one way to find out.

She swung her legs over the side of the bed, jamming her legs back into her discarded jeans and lacing up her boots, tight. She shrugged on her leather jacket and fastened her weapons belt securely around her waist before disappearing out her door.

The coordinates Merrick had sent over were located on the south side of the city, a place notorious for all kinds of thievery, violence, and death. It didn't take her long to find the site of the disturbance. High atop the old cannery, lights flashed, and the clang of weapons shredding against one another sounded. Shay threw what remained of the doors open and took the stairs two at a time in a desperate race to the top, unsure of what she would find.

So many things had changed in the last five years. Her team had gone from a bunch of kids trying to do the right thing to a government-sanctioned task force with official assignments and the legal backings of the military and police forces. And while their numbers had grown, the sting of those they'd lost along the way, still ran deep, especially for Shay. Max was dropping back into a shadow of the world he had known.

As she broached the roof, she spotted Cerrie and Nathan facing off against a handful of Nick Faraday's goons. The evil mastermind himself was sparring with Fulton and seemed to be getting the upper hand. Automatically, Shay's body sprang into action. Her fingers deftly drew her blades from her belt before advancing upon Faraday.

"Nice of you to drop in," Fulton teased effectively blocking the energy blast Faraday had just thrown in his direction with a quick forcefield.

"A girl's gotta get her beauty sleep sometime," Shay quipped letting loose one of her daggers with expert precision. The blade dug itself into Faraday's left thigh, and the villain cried out in pain before snatching the weapon from his body and hurling it back at Shay. She side-stepped before twirling around in one fluid motion to catch the dagger.

"You should stick to what you're good at, Nicky," she teased, twirling the blade between her fingers.

"I don't know," Faraday began, doing his best to stanch his bleeding thigh with one gloved hand. "I thought I was quite adept at killing Tolliver girls. Maybe we should ask your sister her opinion."

Shay's eyes narrowed, and, ever so slowly, she backed the villain against one of the rooftop air conditioning units. She was mere inches from his smug face before she felt composed enough to speak.

"You only *wish* it had been you," she spat, disgusted by the man before her. "You could never take Elle down by yourself, and I'm going to find out who helped you if it's the last thing I do."

"It very well might be," Faraday mused, taking advantage of Shay's riled up state to blast her in the chest before hobbling to the opposite side of the roof.

Fulton fired a couple of shots after Faraday before stopping to help Shay to her feet.

"You okay?" he asked as they advanced to the back section of the roof.

"I could ask you the same question," Shay said, dusting herself off. "What are you doing on an op like this anyway?"

Fulton was more brains than brawn, and his powers were definitely more defensive than offensive. He was usually banished to the coms feeding the gang building schematics or remotely unlocking security systems.

"Believe me; it wasn't by choice. Me and Cerrie were kinda on a date when Nathan crashed it with news of a burglary in progress."

"Nice to see my night wasn't the only one ruined," Shay teased.

"Gee, thanks," he said, voice dripping with mock gratitude.

As she and Fulton rounded the back stacks of the roof, she felt herself freeze. There he was. The same signature red helmet covering his features, some updated leather gear, but the movement of his body hadn't changed. It was really him. She hadn't let herself truly believe it until this moment. Max Gressler was back. The boy who always promised to be there for her before promptly disappearing off the face of the earth for five years.

He seemed to sense her presence just as acutely as she had his. His back went rigid as he turned to face her. Faraday was close behind shoving what appeared to be a ledger of some sort into his coat.

"Gressler, I've got it!" the villain said, jumping from the building onto his waiting hover-bike.

Shay's brow crinkled in confusion. Why was Faraday talking to Max like they were old friends? Like they were…partners?

She thought she saw a sliver of concern in Max's eyes before he turned from her, throwing his skyblade down. The same one they'd worked on together all those years ago.

"Well, friends, as nice as this little get together has been, I must be going."

"Max!" She couldn't keep the desperate pleading from her tone. "Wait! Please…wait." Her voice cracked, the words falling on deaf ears as she watched him step on the blade and disappear over the side of the building at a breakneck pace. It was then that she thought maybe the concern she'd seen had, in fact, been guilt. He was working with Nick Faraday. He was working with the very villain that had stolen Elle away from them.

"What have you done, Max?" Shay whispered under her breath, still staring at the spot he'd just occupied.

Behind her, Nathan and Cerrie approached, joining an open-mouthed Fulton.

"What happened? Did they get away?" Nathan asked, looking over the edge of the roof then back at Shay.

"Yeah, I guess they did," she answered, crestfallen.

Cerrie opened her communicator to report their failure to headquarters. "Amani, we lost them. They escaped with a book of some sort. Any ideas?"

Nathan was studying Shay, practically staring a hole through her as they all awaited Amani's orders.

"Something on your mind Nathan?" Shay asked, already guessing his train of thought.

"Well, yeah. Out of all of us here, you're the one who was closest to Max."

"And, what's your point, or do you have one?"

Nathan's eyes narrowed, and he exhaled loudly, shaking his head from side to side. "You're telling me you have no idea who he really is? Wasn't your sister *engaged* to him? Surely you at least got a look."

"I'm telling you, he might as well have that helmet surgically grafted to his head. He never takes it off. I'm not even sure if Elle ever saw the real him," Shay admitted.

Before Nathan could form a response, Cerrie interrupted. "Boss says to report back to headquarters. Merrick's going through the archives to see if there are any long-lost urban legends about this place. Hopefully, we can figure out why Gressler and Faraday wanted that book so bad." She turned toward Fulton. "She wants you to help out with that. Scan surveillance feeds, dive into the deep web… you know, do your keyboard magic."

Fulton frowned wrapping his hand around the back of his neck to scratch an imaginary itch. He and Cerrie were in the first weeks of their relationship, and his awkwardness around the woman had not gone unnoticed by the whole team, and least of all her.

"Not exactly the magic I wanted to show you tonight, but I guess we'll have to raincheck?" he asked, hopeful.

"Oh, definitely," she replied, looking Fulton up and down, stepping uncomfortably close. "You know, you're kind of sexy when you're all sweaty like this." Her fingers grazed his temple, then grasped his chin, giving his head a little wiggle like an auntie who hadn't seen him in a long while.

Shay's gag reflex kicked in just watching them. "C'mon lovebirds, we've got work to do."

Headquarters was thrumming with the news of Max's return. Only a handful of operatives from the original team remained, but Max's legend was larger than life. And why shouldn't it be? He'd done great things. He'd even saved Shay, once upon a time.

"So, it's true? It's really Max?" Merrick asked as soon as she'd managed to drop into the seat opposite his mess of a desk.

"Yeah, it's him all right. I just don't know what he's up to. He was working *with* Faraday."

Merrick nodded. "That's what Amani said. But why? I don't get it. If anyone has a bone to pick with Faraday besides you, it's Max."

Shay shook her head, genuinely clueless. "No idea, but we need to find out, and fast. Have you had any luck figuring out what the book might be?"

She could tell by the smug look on his face that he'd found something.

"Does a bear crap in the woods?" he asked with a smirk.

"Ew, I don't know? Does it? Nevermind, just tell me what you've got."

The rapid *click-clack* of Merrick's keyboard filled Shay with both a sense of excitement and dread.

"So, the cannery, back in its prime, was actually a cover for an arm of the Galvatti crime family."

"Uh-huh. And this was how long ago?" Shay asked.

"About twenty-five years, give or take. Old man Galvatti finally got what was coming to him, but there were all kinds of back-alley whispers about a journal he kept."

Shay's head tilted as she considered this new information. "What's so special about a dead guy's journal? I doubt Max is chasing down Galvatti's secret crush."

"Well, let's say it was more like a record book. Information about every member of Galvatti's syndicate, every client, and every dirty secret was kept in that journal. The families killed each other in droves trying to discover its location, but no one was ever able to find it."

"And you think Max somehow stumbled upon this missing tell-all journal? Why would he even want it? Most of the criminals in there have to be dead, in prison, or retired by now?"

"What do I look like, a mind reader?" Merrick asked, hands shooting up in exasperation. "That's your job to figure out. I just get the maybes."

Shay rolled her eyes. Merrick had actually been very helpful. At least now she had a direction to go in, and she knew that was much more than she'd had to begin with.

"Thanks," she said, lightly kissing Merrick's cheek.

His cheeks flushed crimson as his hand absently rubbed the spot where her lips had just been.

"You're welcome," he said sheepishly. "Shay, are you all right?"

"I will be once we figure this out," she said, steeling herself against the emotion that threatened to consume her if she thought about the situation too much.

By the time Shay had managed to pry herself away from the investigation and her ever-growing list of suspicions about Max, it was nearly midnight. Her muscles ached from both the rooftop fight at the cannery and the constant state of stress she'd found herself in since hearing of Max's return.

She turned her neck from side to side and rolled her shoulders, trying to ease the tension. She pitched her keys in a dish by the front door and made a b-line for the shower. When she'd exhausted all the hot water, she slipped into an over-sized t-shirt and sweatpants, then collapsed onto her bed.

Just as she thought she might be ready to slip off into dreamland, a noise from the back entrance of the apartment startled her. She waited a moment, not entirely sure she'd actually heard anything at all when it happened again — a scraping sound, like boots across wood. Someone was on the back patio, which should be impossible five stories up.

Tiptoeing out of bed, she palmed one of her daggers and made her way to the back door.

"Who's there?" she called, sliding the glass door to the side.

Yellow light from the neighboring building illuminated half of the back patio, but she couldn't make out any sign of an intruder. She'd all but given in to the idea that sleep deprivation had been to blame for the noises when the small table holding her mostly-dead houseplant toppled over. Shay nearly jumped out of her skin, until she spotted Mrs. Penticoff's orange tabby fleeing the scene. She relaxed, breathing a sigh of relief when a raspy voice spoke behind her.

"A little jumpy aren't you?"

A man sporting a smirk and a shock of wild red hair appeared out of the shadows. His skyblade tucked neatly under one arm.

"Shay," he said, nodding, eyes trained on her features, no doubt trying to discern her mood.

She let out a shaky sigh. "What are you doing here, Max? And not here at my apartment, here in this city. And fighting for the bad guys no less. With Faraday?"

His smirk dissolved into a frown. "A means to an end, I assure you."

"Well, that makes me feel so much better, not only are you not loyal to us, you're not even loyal to them?" Shay asked planting her hands on her hips.

"And yet you trust me enough to keep my secret," Max accused. "You're the only one who knows my identity, so why haven't you told anyone yet?"

"Who says I haven't?" she challenged.

"Well, no one's busted down my door yet, and it's been a solid twenty hours…" He walked a step closer lowering his gaze to match her smaller stature.

"Maybe I was going to come after you myself," she said, closing the distance between them to stare directly into his eyes.

She'd meant to seem threatening, but Max merely smiled. "My, Bitsy, you have turned into a firecracker, haven't you?"

No one had called her by that nickname since Elle died. Hearing it spoken again, even by him, felt like a shard of glass had been stabbed through her heart. "Don't call me that. I'm not seventeen anymore, and we're not friends. Friends don't break promises."

Max lowered his head at this sharp reminder.

"You're right. I'm sorry. There's no excuse for what I did," he apologized.

"No," Shay said, shaking her head, "there's not, so why did you do it?"

He paused for a moment before responding with unbridled passion. "Because I couldn't let her go. Because I couldn't let her killers walk away scott-free. And I would do it again because it hasn't been a fruitless search, Shay. I'm closer than ever to finding out the truth. I just need you to believe me. I just need *someone* to believe me."

"What do you mean you're closer than ever? What have you found out, Max?"

His face twisted and he turned away from her to brace his arms against the railing of the balcony. "I can't tell you yet."

"I'm sorry, but that's not going to cut it. You can't disappear for five years, team up with one of Elle's killers to steal some drug lord's dear-diary, and then expect me to trust you. You're going to have to give me something," she spat, clasping onto his sleeve, urging him to face her.

He gently removed her hand from his jacket, clasping it between both of his own, but said nothing.

"What did you find in that journal, Max?" Shay pleaded.

He closed his eyes, swallowing the lump in his throat. Finally, he found his voice.

"It's bigger than Elle. It's bigger than us, and if I tell you, you'll be a target. The city's in danger, and I'm afraid it can't be trusted to the task force to solve this problem."

She could feel the blood boiling inside her veins — a traitor.

Someone inside their circle had betrayed them. Someone she trusted with her *life*, had been instrumental in stealing her big sister's.

Shay's jaw clenched before she grated out, "Who?"

"I don't have a name yet," Max admitted. "But it's someone on the force, isn't it? It's one of our…" Her voice caught as she fought to swallow the emotion down. "It's one of our friends."

"Yes."

"What's the plan? How do we figure this out?" she asked.

"I need you to get me into the facility. If I can gain access to the mainframe, I should be able to search the internal archives to look for a connection to my lead."

Was he crazy? She had to wonder. "And just how do you propose I sneak you into headquarters?"

"I never said anything about sneaking. We're going to go right through the front doors. There are some advantages to my anonymity."

"Okay, suppose I can get you in…past biometric security scans, armed guards, and over two dozen operatives…how do I get you to the mainframe without arousing suspicion. They're not going to let a newbie anywhere close to that level of information."

"Let me worry about that. I've been working on a lot of new projects since the skyblade." With a wave of his hand, she saw a flash of blue runes. They were stronger than she remembered, brighter.

"I think stealth is our best option, but I suppose we could get Merrick to create a distraction if need be."

Max shook his head, crossing his arm in front of him. "No one else can know. Not even Merrick."

"You can't possibly think *he* could be the traitor? We've been friends since the first grade!"

"I don't know anything for sure, but it's best not to take any chances."

"Fine, we'll do it your way, but for the record, I think this is a bad idea."

"Noted," he said, stepping up onto the balcony railing, throwing his skyblade our in front of him. It hummed to life hovering in mid-air, it's blue runes turning the yellow light lime green.

"It was good to see you again, bits…I mean, Shay."

She didn't know how to respond to that. Was it good to see him again? Only time would tell.

"Come back tomorrow, Max," Shay said, trying her best to fight off an enormous yawn. "I'm exhausted. I'm not going to be any help to your crazy little plan until I've had some sleep."

To Be Continued
(Look for the full-length novel Fall 2019!)

ABOUT C.L. CANNON

C.L. Cannon is a publisher, publicist, editor, author, designer, and lots of other occupations with the -er sound at the end!

She is a woman of many talents who never gives up or stops improving. She enjoys writing about love and friendship. She loves it even more when she can add fantasy and science fiction aspects to those themes!

She's a self-proclaimed Harry Potter freak (Slytherin Pride people), lover of anything Joss Whedon (Spuffy forever), Tolkien fiend (who enjoys second breakfast), an addict of classic literature (Social class struggles turn me on… literally ;) yah see what I did there?)

She spends her days trying to #bookstagram (and probably failing), helping other authors grow and succeed (I love my job), and loving on her two babes (velociraptors), Seth and Petey.

She's also sort of a social media enthusiast! You can find her basically everywhere on the net (man I just aged myself).

Or, you can visit her website for more content!
http://clcannon.net

facebook.com/clcannonauthor

twitter.com/clcannonauthor

instagram.com/cl_cannon

S.P.A.

BY SARAH BUHRMAN

Chapter 1

"You can't be serious! He's a villain!"

A gray-haired, ashen-skinned young woman snorted at the skinny, middle-aged guy who had spoken. "Not a super-villain, though," she said. "He's not enough of a threat for that, at least."

The half-dozen people sitting in folding chairs in a circle laughed. Trance put a hand to her head, rubbing at the bridge of her nose. She tried to ignore the petty jab and focus on her goal.

"Look, guys," she said. "I get it. I was skeptical at first, too. But he seems to really want to turn his life around. Who are we to say he shouldn't have that chance?"

The man who had spoken first – a fake-tanned, twitchy guy who went by the name Bug – barked out a laugh. "Not everyone deserves a second chance."

Trance took a deep breath, pushing her long dreadlocks back over her shoulder. "His file shows that he has never done any lasting damage to anyone. He has never killed or enslaved. At most, he was only associated with his younger brother's actions."

Ace, a younger, green-eyed ginger, sat forward. He fidgeted with several playing cards as he spoke, his fingers moving quickly through shuffling and sleight-of-hand tricks. "Feedback has killed. The fact that Mute can't be pegged with any deaths seems a bit convenient."

The others nodded, even as Trance sighed. "Why would he want to join us though? If he isn't trying to get away from Feedback, why would he ask to join a support group for minor super-powereds?"

The rest of the group shifted uncomfortably and exchanged glances.

"Let's just give him a chance," Trance pleaded. "We can keep an eye on him. Maybe do some real good."

She smiled as she recognized the signs of each of the super-powereds coming around to agreeing with her, however reluctantly.

Trance let her natural abilities loose, smoothing some of the tension that arose in the room as the black-haired man with too-pale skin lowered himself into the empty metal folding chair. Ace rapidly shuffled his cards, the quick movements giving away his feelings.

A loud pop drew Trance's gaze to a middle-aged woman who crackled as she shifted in her seat. Static was irritated, too, if she was throwing the tiny zaps of electricity off the ends of her blonde pixie cut.

Mute sat quietly, the tension in his shoulders belying his relaxed demeanor. He turned his head to watch Trance, ignoring the glares around him.

"All right, everyone," Trance said, starting the meeting. "We have a new member tonight. Mute, welcome to the Super-Powereds Anonymous of Hackensack. Let's start with the rules.

"First rule, all super-powereds will be known only by their chosen nickname. Second, the SPA encourages all super-powereds to abide by local and federal laws. Thirdly, we will not tolerate personal attacks, humiliation or vendettas during meetings, or at official or social events offered through the SPA."

"Fourth," Bug snapped. "We will not support the use of our abilities for what is commonly known as 'villainy.'"

Trance glared at the man. "Thank you, Bug. I was getting to that." She waited until Bug sunk back into his seat before continuing. "Fifth, this is a safe place to express any anger, frustration, or any other emotions regarding the unique hardships and joys of being a super-powered. I am Trance, your mediator for SPA Chapter #125."

Trance turned to the older Asian man beside her and nodded to him. He sat forward and smiled around the group. "I'm Unplug. I own a business, but it's hard to keep afloat with the extra insurance I have to keep as a super-powered."

"Just in case anyone isn't familiar, could you tell us about the insurance?" Trance prompted.

"It's a big expense," Unplug said, shaking his head. "Super-powered liability. Supposed to be in case I get upset and hurt someone or damage property or something. But it doesn't account for individual abilities. I'm technically telekinetic, but all I can effectively do is unplug things from sockets. I can't throw cars or people or anything like that."

"Wait," Mute said. "You can unplug things? That's it? How does that work?"

Unplug scowled, but Mute held up his hands. "Just curious, man. You don't have to answer."

Unplug glanced at Trance, but she could only smile encouragingly at him. It wasn't her job to force people to explain themselves or their abilities. Finally, the older man shrugged.

"It's like I can find a weakness in the line where electricity is flowing. I can feel where the break can happen and, if it's not held together too much, I can force it apart. It sounds impressive, but it pretty much only means I can pull plugs out of sockets."

Mute sat back. "That's still pretty cool," he said. "And it fits my theory. Thank you for sharing that."

"What theory?" Bug asked, jumping on Mute's words.

The new guy shrugged. "I have a theory that our abilities have an inverse correlation of power to complexity. Like, the more specifically you can do something, the less... well, impressive the power is."

Static snorted. "Well, I can disprove that," she muttered. "I create static shocks. Not very complex and not very powerful."

Mute shook his head. "Not exactly. Most powerful electricity-based abilities have to have a strong, outside source. You create it from the environment."

Static frowned and sat back, but she looked thoughtful.

Trance suppressed a smile and turned back to Unplug. "So, you find that the laws around carrying liability aren't considerate of SP's specific abilities to cause damage?"

Unplug nodded slowly, still watching Mute. "Yeah, they lump all SP's into the same overly-generalized group of risks."

"Like red cars and car insurance," Bug said.

"That's not true," piped up a small, thin brunette who was even more timid than she looked.

"Like you know, Sponge," Bug snapped.

Sponge swallowed and visibly gathered her confidence before she replied. "I underwrite insurance, Bug, so I do know."

Trance stepped in before Bug could go too far over the line. "Sponge, can you shed any light on this insurance issue for us?"

Sponge nodded and began explaining the insurance companies' decisions in her frail voice. Trance glanced at Mute, glad to see that he seemed to be fitting in as well as could be expected for his first meeting.

Chapter 2

"My brother and I were in foster care after our parents lost custody. It sucked, but it wasn't nearly as bad as the horror stories. Mostly just too many kids in a house. Not enough affection or consideration. That kind of thing."

Mute shifted in his chair, aware of the eyes focused on him as the story came out, particularly the deep, black eyes of the group's moderator.

"Since I was older, I naturally developed my ability first. It started with getting my brother and his friends to shut up when they were bugging me, always following me around and asking stupid questions." He shrugged his shoulders as if to dismiss the actions of his past. "It was harmless, but it made for a good threat. Just enough to make me a bit of an ass as a teen."

A few of the other SPA members laughed, remembering their own adolescent shenanigans.

"When Feedback developed his abilities, I was old enough to have grown out of most of my arrogance. Sort of." He sighed. "Actually, I was just pissed that his power seemed more useful than mine. But I could use mine to tone him down and keep him under control. At least, until he could control it himself."

"Then what happened?" Static asked.

Mute shrugged again. "Feedback was always the one who felt more like the world owed us for being in foster care and all. He decided to use his powers to take it. But it wasn't just that. He made it a competition between the two of us."

Ace snorted. "And that was enough reason for you to be a dick?"

Mute nodded. "Yeah, stupid reason. I know." He blew out a breath. "He was always going on about how he could do anything better than me, and I just kept trying to prove him wrong."

"But it's different now?" Ace asked. "Is that what you want us to believe?"

Mute shrugged. "Believe what you want. I did this crap for years. Then I woke up, facing middle age and still trying to keep up with my jerk of a younger brother. I got sick of being in an asshole pissing contest. It's not who I want to be. It's not even fun like Feedback says."

"Speak of the devil," Trance said. "What does Feedback think of you quitting? I mean, you were his right hand for more than a decade."

"Yeah," Mute said with a short, bitter laugh. "He wasn't happy when he realized I was leaving. Not that he could do much. I may not be as effective at being a villain, but I can still shut his fat, stupid mouth."

"So, you aren't worried about him coming after you?" Unplug asked.

Mute shrugged. "Doesn't matter to me."

"Hey, Mute!" Trance called to the man as he tugged a dark blue cap onto his thick, dark waves. She jogged up to him, slowing when he turned his head towards her. "I-I just wanted to say, I really appreciate you opening up like that. I think it helped the others understand why you... I mean-"

"Yeah," Mute said. "I get it. You all still don't trust me."

Trance shook her head. "No. I mean, yes. I mean, the others don't really trust you, or only trust you some. But I can tell you are sincere-"

The surly man barked out a sour laugh. "Oh, right. I forgot you're a 'pather. Oh, wait. No, you aren't." He smirked at her scowl. "You got some hardcore idealism working on my behalf. I'm grateful for it, make no mistake, but don't read more into it than that. I was a bad guy. I might still be a bad guy. You just don't know."

Mute turned on his heel and walked out the door, leaving Trance staring after him, her mind racing.

"Don't do it, girl," Static said, coming up behind her and intentionally jostling her shoulder in a playful move.

"Do what?" Trance grumbled.

"Don't fall for the bad boy," Static responded. "Or, in this case, bad guy."

The mediator pushed a handful of thick dreadlocks back over her shoulder with slender ebony fingers. The familiar gesture comforted her, and her emotional tension eased. She wasn't sure what it was about Mute that appealed, except that she'd known too many men in her life who ignored the opportunities they'd been given to change their lives. Mute had gone a step further and created his own opportunity.

Hopefully, she wasn't overestimating the former villain.

Chapter 3

Trance glanced around the group as they settled in. She was hesitant to bring up her concerns. After all, it was Super Powereds Anonymous, not Super Powereds Getting All Up In Each Other's Business. The problem was, even accounting for the usual ebb and flow of people missing meetings occasionally, or only showing up once in a while, it looked like a few were actually missing.

"Hey, guys," she said, clearing her throat. "I know this is unusual of me to ask, but has anyone seen Cobweb or Gypsum? They don't usually miss so many meetings."

The others looked around, shrugging their shoulders and shaking their heads.

"I know where Cobweb lives," Static said quietly. She looked uncomfortable. "I didn't stalk her or anything. I was just running deliveries for the dry cleaners and saw her come out of the apartment next door to the customer."

Trance bit her lip. "I'm gonna leave it up to you guys. Should we be worried? Should we check up on her?"

There was a lot of back and forth talk about "but privacy" and "looking out for each other" before there was an only somewhat reluctant consensus.

"Trance should be the one to go. We all trust you to keep confidences." Unplug nodded his head sharply and sat back after speaking for the group.

Trance nodded. "Static, if you could write down the address for me, I'd appreciate it."

That uncomfortable bit of business done, Trance moved the discussion back to SP discrimination with relief, even in the face of Ace's bitter rant.

Trance glanced down at the scrap of paper to recheck the apartment number, then looked back at the door in front of her. She wasn't about to knock on 5B now that she'd found it. The cris-cross of yellow crime scene tape was a pretty good sign that Cobweb wasn't going to be home. The metallic tang of blood and the nose-burning scent of cleaning products only reinforced that thought.

She stepped down the hall and knocked on the next door. An older Hispanic woman peeked out with the chain still hooked on the door.

"Can I help you?"

Trance put on her best public smile. "I hope so. I have an acquaintance who I was supposed to stop by and see. The address I have is for 5B, though." She dropped her expression into a worried frown that wasn't nearly as exaggerated as the smile had been. "Can you tell me what happened? Where I might find her?"

The woman frowned. "That SP girl? The gray one? You won't be finding her any time soon. She's dead. I heard her skull shattered." The woman glanced again at Trance's face. "Sorry for the bad news, honey. Don't know exactly what happened, but them cops filled up the hallway for hours investigating. Might contact them."

Trance swallowed hard and forced a weaker smile to her lips. "Thank you. Have a good night."

She turned and walked down the hall in a daze.

"Cobweb was killed last week. Gypsum was found four days before that. Now Laminate has vanished?" Ace snarled the words out. "What the hell is going on here?"

Trance shook her head. "I don't know-"

"It sounds like someone is targeting our little gathering, picking us off one at a time." The lean man flicked a playing card around his fingers like it was a weapon. He glanced over his shoulder at the rest of SPA-Hackensack as they milled around the box of donuts and the ancient coffee dispenser.

"Who-"

"We only got one villain in this group," Ace pointed out.

Trance shrugged her shoulders. She wasn't comfortable with how the man had maneuvered her into a corner before demanding to know what she'd found out about Cobweb. Since Gypsum's death had made the news, she couldn't think of a reason to keep another lost member a secret.

But now, he was leaning closer, biting out his words in barely controlled anger. Trance fingered one of her dreadlocks and exerted her power to take strong emotions down a notch or two.

Ace finally stepped back and blew out a heavy breath. "Look, I know you wanted to give him a chance, but I think we can safely say-"

"Say what?" Trance asked. "Say that, because he did some things and is now in the group, it has to be him? Say that his past has convicted him with not one shred of evidence to back it up?"

"Her skull was crushed," Ace pointed out. "Just like-"

"Just like Feedback's victims," Trance said. "Yeah, I know." She stared at Ace. "I get where you're coming from, Ace, I do. But this is so damn obvious. It could just as easily be a frame job. It's so obvious."

"A frame job?" Ace frowned. "I never thought of that."

Trance shrugged her shoulders. "If I were gonna take out some SPs, a guy like Mute joining a group like this would be the next best thing to Christmas, don't you think?"

Ace nodded slowly. "I guess..."

Trance put her hand on his arm. "Let's wait until we have some evidence - any evidence - before we start pointing fingers. In the mean-time, I need to make an announcement."

She walked away, raising her voice to get the others' attention. "Everyone! I'm sure you've all heard about Gypsum by now. If not, he was found dead. Cobweb was killed, too, and Laminate has disap-peared. Hopefully, she just had to work late again, but if anyone knows her..."

Sponge raised her hand. "We work in the same building," she said. "I'll ask after her."

Trance nodded. "Meanwhile, it looks very likely that someone is targeting this group. Buddy up, if you are comfortable with that. I'd be willing to hold onto phone numbers and addresses if you want us to

check on you. And keep your eyes open for possible danger. I hope we
are just being overly cautious, but-"

"Better safe than sorry," Static muttered.

"Yeah," Trance said. "Another thing. There is nothing to indicate
who is responsible for this, or if it is even anything more than a couple
of crappy coincidences. Please do not take this and your abilities as
carte blanche to try your hand at vigilante justice."

The group stayed longer than usual after the meeting, exchanging
information and leaving business cards pressed into Trance's palm.
Mute was the last to come up to her.

He stared at her for a long moment. "You didn't throw me under
the bus."

Trance smirked. "Yeah, well. Not my style."

He took her hand and squeezed it gently. "You have no idea what
that means to me." He looked down at their hands, pale fingers
wrapped around ebony. "I-I was hoping..."

He trailed off and Trance waited a moment, giving him the chance
to continue. Finally, she prompted, "Hoping what?"

Mute cleared his throat. "Uh, hoping that you... um, you might be
okay with- I mean, you might want to... Crap!" He looked up at her
suddenly. "Would you want to get a drink or something with me
sometime?"

Trance blinked in shock. "Um, like a-a date?"

He swallowed. "Not if you don't want it to be. I mean, we could
just hang out. Be friends. Whatever."

She smiled. "You up for coffee this late?"

Mute stared at her a moment, then shook himself. "Uh, yeah, sure.
That's fine. Great."

"I know a great cafe with the best pie..." Trance said, clicking the
lights out as they left.

Chapter 4

"Hey, we have a newbie tonight," Trance said, getting everyone's
attention. She felt her cheeks heat up when Mute winked at her. They'd

spent hours talking over pie and coffee, and she couldn't help but second guess her feelings. Hope could overpower common sense when the heart was involved.

"I'm Pulse," the new guy said. He was a middle-aged, middle-weight black man with a hairline in full retreat, turning white with fear at whatever it was running from. "I can sense a person's heart rate, which helps me to be able to tell when they are lying."

A few of the other's raised eyebrows and exchanged glances, impressed by the ability.

"It helps me with my job," Pulse continued. "And that's why I came here tonight. I'm a detective, see."

Ace shot to his feet. "You tryin' ta... whatever it is. Entrapment, that's it. You tryin' ta entrap us?"

Pulse got to his feet as well. Trance sat forward sending calming waves of energy out into the maelstrom of emotions.

"No, son," Pulse said, his voice calm and even. "I need your help."

Ace frowned, and Trance noticed he wasn't the only one agitated by the revelation. Trance wasn't too happy about it herself. Having someone spring this kind of thing on her in the middle of a meeting was not copacetic.

With a scowl on her face, she motioned Ace to sit down. Then she turned on Pulse. "This is extremely inappropriate, sir," she snapped. "If we didn't have so much going on, I wouldn't even be giving you this chance, but you have five minutes to explain yourself."

Pulse nodded and settled back on his chair. "I agree," he said. "I shouldn't even be here. If my captain knew I was an SP, I'd be under review so fast..." He blew out a breath. "But I've noticed a pattern in homicides lately. SP's getting targeted-"

"Yeah, we caught on to that," Static muttered.

Pulse nodded. "Good. You're not fools, then. How many have you counted?"

"Three," Trance said. "We have three members who have died suspiciously."

The detective pressed his lips together for a moment. "My count is seven in the county. I'd like to see if any of you recognize the victims." He pulled out a stack of pictures and passed them to Trance.

She looked through them, pulling one out, looking at it, then passing it around to the rest of the group. "This one is one of ours," she said, holding up a picture of an ashy-looking older man. "Gypsum, he called himself."

Pulse nodded. "A drywaller with one of the local contractors."

"This is Cobweb," Trance murmured, holding up the girl's picture. Another joined it - a middle-aged woman with a shiny complexion. "This is Laminate."

Trance handed the three pictures back to Pulse, while the rest of the photos were passed one by one around the circle. Everyone looked at the images carefully.

"Wait a minute," Mute said. "I know this guy." He held up a picture of a Hispanic man in his forties. Mute scowled and thumped his hand against his head a few times. "He... crap, he drove a city bus."

Pulse nodded. "Yeah, he did. How do you know him?"

Mute shrugged. "I took the bus to the city offices a while back to get some ID issues fixed." He stared down at the photo. "Didn't even know this guy was an SP."

He passed the image on and reflexively took the next photo as it was handed to him. He glanced down and went pale.

Trance felt her stomach roil as she watched him swallow several times.

"This woman lives two buildings down from me. I pet her dog while she was walking it. One of those pretty, fluffy little things." He passed on the photo and closed his eyes before looking at the next. "My garbage collector. I said hi to him a week or so ago." He heaved a breath. "This kid hangs out at the convenience store. I stop in for sodas and stuff a couple times a week. He was usually there. I guess, now that I think about it, he hasn't been there for a few weeks."

He passed the last photo back to Pulse. "I didn't know they were SPs," he said again. "I barely even knew them. I didn't..." He swallowed. "Is there anything connecting them? Any common threads?"

"Yeah," Pulse said. "You."

Mute sat with his head in his hands, barely responding to the voices rising in anger and fear around him. Trance watched him, carefully. He didn't look like someone faking innocence. His attitude was more of hopelessness. He also didn't look like someone trying to get away with something. He wasn't trying to escape or deflect or anything like that.

He just sat there, looking despondent.

Meanwhile, Ace was on full attack. Pulse took notes as people shouted information, mostly accusations against Mute or protests of circumstantial evidence. Static's blonde spikes crackled like sparklers on the Fourth of July as she shouted over Ace and Bug.

Finally, Trance walked over to Mute and leaned down to speak into his ear. He looked up at her with a frown and she nodded, patting his back in encouragement.

Mute stood, opening his mouth wide. He sucked in a huge breath, rotating his head around the room as he did so. Trance made sure to stay behind him as he worked.

Within seconds, the noise was gone. Nearly a dozen people stood mouthing words, holding their hands to their throats, and glaring at Mute. Pulse scowled and took a step towards the former villain, but Trance stepped forward.

"Now don't you people be getting mad at Mute," she scolded. "He only did what I asked him to. It'll only last a few minutes, right?"

Trance glanced at Mute, who nodded. "Maybe five minutes, max."

She turned back to the group. "If you'd have shut up instead of going crazy, I wouldn't have had to do this. Now sit down and act like you're older than your shoe size for a minute." Trance pointed at Pulse. "You, too, detective. You came here for help. Now you're gonna get it."

Mute plopped back down into his chair, and Trance paced around the circle, glaring at people. "You all have experienced the discrimination that comes from being a Super Powered. Each one of you knows what it's like to have people think you did do something just 'cause you have the power to do it. Or might have the power to do it. You know that those details don't matter to norms."

A few of the SPs ducked their heads, remembering those experiences and connecting the dots to what they'd been talking about.

"Some of you get it. For the rest, I'm gonna spell it out." Trance glared around at Ace and Bug, in particular. "Just 'cause Mute knew these people - and even saying that is kind of a stretch - that don't mean he offed them. That don't mean he's gone bad guy."

She paced back to her own chair and sat down. "We know a few things for sure." She lifted her fingers as she made her points. "SPs are getting targeted. All the vics have at least one thing in common - Mute. Mute is a reformed villain - 'cause nothing indicates he has gone back to the dark side with any certainty - but he has history with people who are still into villainy."

Trance sat back and folded her arms. "Got anything to add, Mute?"

The man frowned. "Detective," he said slowly. "You know how each of these people died, right? Was it all the same? Fractured skulls?"

Pulse nodded and opened his mouth as if to speak, but nothing came out.

Mute grimaced. "It'll only be another minute or so. Were the fractures similar to pressure cracks?"

The detective scowled and nodded slowly.

Mute sighed. "Crap. Crap, crap, crappity crap."

Trance tilted her head to one side. "Whatcha got?"

"It sounds like... dammit, it sounds like a sonic blow." Mute pounded his fists on his thighs. "I should have known he wouldn't let me get out so cleanly."

Static let out a sudden squeak, then cleared her throat. "Who did it then?"

Mute sighed as other people let out little squeaks and grunts. "Feedback."

The room erupted into noise once again.

Chapter 5

"I want to take him down," Mute said into a lull in the roar.

The lull faded into cricket-chirping silence. Ace's mouth fell open in shock. Static's hair snapped once, then fell limply against her scalp for the first time since Trance had known her. Sponge sucked in a breath as her coffee cup crumbled in her fingers, the liquid inside soaking into her flesh as quickly as if her skin was paper toweling.

Bug was the first to recover. "You-you're talking about Feedback, right?" he asked. "You want to take him down?" The gawky man looked around at the others. "You know he's got, like, minions and lackeys and other SPs working for him?"

Mute nodded. "Yeah," he said. "Same people I worked with."

"Most of them have stronger abilities than you do," Ace pointed out.

Mute shrugged. "One of the things I learned trying to compete with Feedback was that it isn't the power of your ability that matters. It's the creative ways you can use it."

Bug rocked his hips. "It's not the size of the boat. It's the motion of the ocean."

Static scowled at him. "Ew. Dude."

Ace howled with laughter, pointing at Bug while he scowled and sat back down sulkily.

"So, why are you telling us this," Bug grumped. "You could just go and do it."

Mute shook his head. "I am but one drop in the ocean," he said. "I need more if I'm going to make waves."

Static rolled her eyes. "Can we please get off the water analogy?" She glared at Bug when he snorted at her word choice.

Mute shrugged. "Fine. I need you guys to help me take down a super-villain who happens to be my brother and might be the one killing SPs off one by one. If he's targeting SPs that cross paths with me, it's only a matter of time before he comes after each of you."

Bug wiped his eyes as his sniggering finally faded away. "What the hell. I always wanted to be a real superhero."

Ace nodded. "Sure as hell beats talking about insurance." He shot a glance at Sponge. "No offense. I'm in."

Sponge sniffed. "You boys are gonna need someone with two brain cells to rub together. I'll help, if I can."

"Yeah, this boy's club BS isn't gonna happen," Static snapped. "You guys might need some real power." She wiggled her fingers as sparks snapped between them.

After all but a couple of the older SPs had volunteered, Mute glanced over at Trance who had sat silently, watching the whole thing play out.

"Well?" he asked her.

Trance lifted a single eyebrow. "You people can't even have a meeting without me holding your hand," she said. "Plus, you are MY people. No one takes out my people without getting on my shit-list."

"God, I hope we don't die," Static muttered.

"Woohoo!" Ace shouted. "SPA-Hackensack. Better than the League of Super-Powereds!"

"We're gonna die," Sponge assured Static.

Chapter 6

Trance stood between Mute and Pulse, trying not to pinch the bridge of her nose between her fingers. She could practically feel the exchanged looks the two men were giving each other over her head.

Bug had shown up in a neon green shirt straight out of the 80s, and an Islanders bomber jacket in blue, orange and white. It even had a reflective safety strip across the shoulders.

Ace, on the other hand, looked like an extra from Black Hawk Down in full desert camo military gear. He had straps and pockets everywhere, and he kept double-checking contents. Trance had even spotted the tan Mylar of an MRE in one thigh pocket.

Sponge was wearing dark colors at least, but she'd left her longish hair down, and it kept getting in her face, especially when Static stepped too close and made every strand lift and separate around her shoulders. Static had gotten a hold of some black grease paint and was swiping haphazard lines under people's eyes.

Trance stepped in to stop her when she'd moved to glop a handful on her own sparking blonde hair. "Hey, Static. Maybe not grease paint, huh?"

Realization dawned on the woman's face and she flushed. "Yeah, good call."

"Okay," Mute said. "Here's the deal. We can get to the main building pretty easily. Feedback doesn't have a lot of external security. Says it draws attention.

"Once we get to the building, there's a double-coded door lock. Bug and Static, with your powers combined, you should be able to get us through."

Bug offered his fist for Static to bump. As she reached out, he muttered, "Activate!"

Mute glared at the man. "Our best offense is to not offend. We sneak in with as little conflict as possible. Trance." He turned to face her. "You are Operation: Calm AF, okay?"

Trance nodded.

"Booger?" He turned to a kid of about 18 years. "If we do get rushed, you will lay down the snot. Slip 'em up, okay?"

The kid threw back his shoulders and nodded his copper-red head once.

Mute eyed the rest, including a portly young guy with a magnificent beard whose name he couldn't recall. "We stay in a tight formation, close together. When we get to Feedback's offices, that's when things get hairy."

"Why's that?" Ace asked.

Mute shrugged. "Feedback liked to add new traps and stuff all the time. His more personal defenses were always rotating and were usually based on nothing more than his mood at the time. I have no idea what we might be facing, so everyone is on deck for that."

Pulse cleared his throat. "I'll be the first responder. That'll keep the other cops off of you for a bit, and I'll be on hand to take Feedback in once you get him." He hesitated. "Just try to get me some evidence, too, will ya?"

Ace put his hand down in the center of the rough circle the group had formed. He looked around at everyone else. "C'mon. We need a 'go team' moment, right?"

Static rolled her eyes and Mute shook his head. Pulse was the first one out the door to the unmarked cop car and generic black cargo van sitting outside the community center.

"Fine," Ace called from the back of the group. "I'll just do it alone. Go-o-o-o-o SPAH!" He emphasized the "H" sound at the end of the word, making it sound like a breathy retreat with mud masks.

Static and Sponge spoke up in stereo. "Gonna die."

Trance was impressed with how easily the first part of the infiltration was. Of course, all they'd done was find the building, get out of the van without too much racket, and make their way in ones and twos to a small door along the industrial side-road. It helped that only a single light reached the small door, and the late hour meant that very few people were roaming the streets.

Still, the handful of SPs clustered around the door, barely making a sound. Bug reached for the panel and hovered his hand over it. The displays wavered and the lights flickered.

He nodded to Static and whispered a few words to her. She frowned, holding two fingers out toward the panel. Sparks crackled on her fingertips for a moment, then a tiny arc of electricity shot into the keypad. The lights flared, then went dead.

Mute tried the door and cursed. "Dammit. It stayed locked when it shut down."

The portly, bearded young man stepped up. "Is there a security camera just inside?"

Mute frowned. "Yeah, one of those rotating numbers."

The man nodded. "Everyone turn around."

"Who are you, again?" Mute asked.

"Call me Schrodinger. I can be in two places at once, so long as there is no observation."

Mute frowned. "Wait. What?"

The guy shrugged. "It makes sense if you know Heisenberg's Uncertainty Principle. Just turn around and don't look."

Everyone turned their backs to the door and the portly guy and waited. And waited. And waited.

Finally, Mute said, "Um, is it work-"

The door popped open, and Mute spun around. A skinnier, clean-shaven version of Schrodinger grinned at him, holding the door open from the inside. "C'mon."

The SPs filed in. Mute made a gesture like stroking a beard on his chin. "What happened to the-"

Schrodinger looked at him, a confused expression drawing his brows together. "What? Did I use to have a beard? That happens some-times. Wave functions mixing up when they collapse upon observation."

Mute gaped at him for a moment. That explained why he'd had trouble remembering the man. "I need to study more quantum theory."

Schrodinger laughed. "It just gets more confusing. Just roll with it."

Trance moved towards the front of the group, standing just behind Booger as they swarmed silently down the hallway. She focused on a carefree, anti-paranoid feeling, sending the waves of calm ahead of them.

They found the stairs and moved up to the fourth floor. They had just reached the landing between the third and fourth floors when a door below them banged open.

Chapter 7

Trance and Mute both gestured everyone against the wall and away from the stair railing where they were more likely to be spotted. Booger leaned over just enough to peer over the edge. His eyes widened, and he mouthed "dammit" before standing up, hawking up a loogie, and spitting it over the rail.

Trance leaned forward to follow the glob's decent. It splattered out on the stairs in front of the climbing trio of Feedback's minions. When it hit, the tiny bit of phlegm expanded to cover three steps from wall to railing.

The first two minions stepped onto the mucus and went flying back, tumbling down the stairs heavily. Several loud cracks practically felt painful to hear, and a few of the SPs cowering on the stairs flinched at the sound.

The third minion paused, looking up at Booger. "Who the hell are you? Banana?" He laughed maliciously at his own lame joke and leapt over the mucousy steps.

He advanced on Ace, holding out his hands. An odd wavering aura surrounded them, and he slapped his hand on Ace's face, barely hitting his chin.

Trance gasped as water flowed over Ace's head, encompassing him in an unbreathable blob. Sponge stepped forward and clapped her hand on Ace's head, reaching for the man with her other hand. The water soaked into her flesh faster than the man could produce it.

Ace gasped for breath as his face cleared of fluid. He lurched backwards and stumbled on the steps, crab-walking up them to put some distance between him and the lackey.

Trance stared as Sponge's flesh filled out. Her normally anorexic appearance swelled with the absorbed fluid, puffing out her skin and filling out curves that no one had known were there.

With a final gasp, the man, cheeks and eyes now looking sunken and dry, lurched away, tumbling down the steps to join his fellow minions. Trance's mouth curled in disgust as he slid through the phlegm on the slimed-up steps.

Sponge turned to face the others. A few eyed her up and down, and she flushed. "I'll go back to normal in about an hour," she murmured.

Mute nodded. "Good work. Quick thinking."

Ace stood up. "Yeah, thanks."

Before the awkwardness could continue for too long, Mute had the group moving again. They reached the stairwell door and cautiously opened it.

Booger peered through. Then he stuck his head out of the door to look the other way. "Looks clear," he hissed.

They tiptoed out into the hallway, dimmed with deep gray tile flooring and dark blue walls that absorbed most of the fluorescent lighting. They made it only a few feet when the frosted glass double doors at the end of the hallway sprung open.

A younger, blonder and more muscular version of Mute strode into the hallway, flanked by four people. All five of them wore identical outfits - a kind of futuristic-looking military pantsuit in gray and blue. Feedback's suit differed only in that his had silver stars, two on each side, lined up where his collarbone would be.

Feedback grinned as Mute stepped forward. His eyes gleamed with hate. "Brother, dear. You've returned to me. And you've brought me presents!"

Mute scowled but didn't respond. Trance could see that he was preparing to use his power, and she side-stepped until she was against the wall. The other SPs did the same, opening up a space around Mute.

Feedback continued. "You remember my four horsemen?"

Mute snorted. "Still haven't come up with anything more original than that?"

Feedback frowned. "Now, dear brother. Even originality must give way to the classics."

The four henchmen stepped forward, moving slightly in front of Feedback. Trance frowned. Mute would have a hard time using his power on Feedback if these guys got in the way. Which was, she supposed, the point.

She glanced at Mute and began sending waves of calming towards the quintet. She shot a look at the other SPs, trying to catch their eyes and indicate that they needed to be ready to help however they could.

The front two henchmen, a sallow-looking man and a very muscular woman, rushed forward. A grating noise sounded near Trance's ear, and a glob of phlegm sailed past her head.

The mucus splattered across the floor, sending both henchmen sprawling. The woman snarled and reached out a hand blindly, clenching it into a fist.

Sponge squawked as a psionic fist grabbed her and began squeezing. She cried out, struggling. Suddenly, liquid began to ooze from between the fingers of the energy hand. Static stepped up and zapped the hand, using the water to carry the charge further.

The electricity arced between the water oozing around the hand and the energy of the hand itself, until it crackled like a plasma ball set on high. The hand disappeared and Sponge dropped to the ground, where Static pulled her to the side of the hallway. The muscular woman cried out and fell back with an oozy squish into the mucus, cradling her now-charred hand.

The sallow-looking man crawled to his knees. He reached out both hands, and ribbons shot out of his palms, like mummy wrappings, or streamers. The ribbons shot straight towards Mute and Static, but Ace stepped in front of them just as the streams of fiber reached them.

The streamers wrapped themselves around Ace, covering his body from head to toe, layer upon layer wrapping around his arms, torso, head... until there was nothing showing. Trance gasped, realizing it would be impossible to breath wrapped up like that. Before she or any of the others could move to help him, Ace's hands twitched.

Trance gaped at the sight as the wrappings disappeared, and hundreds of playing cards fluttered to the ground at Ace's feet. As the last of the wrappings vanished, he launched himself forward, clapping his hands down on the sallow man's skin. The man gasped, then screamed, then disappeared in another cloud of fluttering cards.

Ace snatched one of the cards out of the air and flipped it around his fingers. It was the ace of spades. "What else you got, noise-maker?"

Chapter 8

Feedback flushed with anger. He flicked out his fingers and snapped at the two remaining henchmen, "Take out the mouth and subdue my brother. I want him to see how I destroy what he wants."

The more muscular of the men beat his fists against his chest several times, growling and roaring. Hair sprung up along his arms and legs, and his canines elongated. His muscles bulged, growing as he flexed.

Trance's eyes narrowed and she focused her energy on him. He ran forward with a snarl, leaping over the puddle of mucus. Trance took a deep breath, reached deep inside for all the calm she could muster and shot it at him.

The man stumbled, and she hit him with another shot of calm. Over and over, she sent waves of soothing energy at him as his attempts to stand back up weakened. After a moment, she slumped against the wall, exhausted.

Unplug appeared at her side, supporting her as she leaned heavily on him. She shot a final glance at the raging man and nearly smirked when he snored, worn out from the energy he'd burned up with his transformation, but no longer driven by the adrenaline rush from his anger.

The last henchman slunk up the hallway towards the SPs. Mute gestured the others back. "Don't get near him," he warned. "He's a cyborg. His ability is that he can merge himself with machinery."

The henchman swung his gaze around to each person, dismissing them as he passed them by. He stood off with Mute, his fingers whining mechanically as he flexed them.

Then, Unplug turned his head towards the cyborg and stepped away from Trance's side. She bit her lip, not wanting a protest to slip out and draw the half-man's attention.

The older man quietly stepped up behind the henchman and held out his hand, not touching, just sensing. A flicker of a smile crossed his lips, and he furrowed his brow in concentration. The machine-enhanced man jerked and twitched a few times, then slumped over, lights in his neck and arms fading away.

Unplug rolled his shoulders and stepped back towards Trance. "Places where machine and man meet always have weak spots," he noted.

Trance smiled. "You unplugged him."

The man grinned, and they turned their attention back to Mute. He had stepped forward and opened his mouth, with the same sucking move he'd done in the SPA meeting.

Feedback, on the other hand, wore an expression that was some mixture of shock and rage. He actually seemed to be in such a state of disbelief that he didn't even run from Mute's power.

By the time he recovered from his shock and attempted to use his ability, Mute had sucked a full day's worth of sound from him. Ace and Bug converged on the younger brother and quickly pinned his arms down.

"Aww," Ace said with false sympathy. "His squeaker's broken!"

"You'll have to go with him," Pulse told Mute. "Once he's convicted, we should be able to get an order to surgically remove or modify his vocal cords, but, until then, you'll need to keep him quiet anytime someone needs to interact with him."

Mute nodded. "I understand. His computer should have most everything you'll need for a conviction. I'll give you the last passwords I knew about, but I can't guarantee they'll work."

Pulse shook his head. "If they don't, that's why the feds have their own hackers." He moved towards the other officers. "I'll give you a moment."

Mute nodded and looked at Trance. "With my statement, the police shouldn't be able to identify you or the others as being involved. Pulse will help make sure they don't need to."

Trance smiled and nodded. "Yeah, thanks." She looked at the cruiser with Feedback glaring out at her and Mute. "When will you be back? Or will you...?"

Mute shifted his shoulders. "I don't know. I'm not sure it would be a good idea to come back-"

"What the heck, dude?" Ace yelled out the van's passenger window. "You gotta come back. I have a rep now, and you are my wingman. And, besides, how else you gonna hook up with Trance?"

Static zapped Ace in the back of the neck. "Seriously, man? What is wrong with you?"

Ace grinned at her. "Nothin' a good woman wouldn't cure."

Static and Sponge exchanged glances, then said again in stereo, "No thanks!"

Mute rolled his eyes as Ace bemoaned his lot in life. He looked back at Trance. "I guess I could come back for some coffee or something."

Trance smiled. "You should. I know a place with the best pie..."

ABOUT SARAH BUHRMAN

Sarah is an AuthorGoddess, one who embraces the divine honor of creating worlds with words in the hope of inspiring others. Sarah has been writing for more than 25 years, starting with poetry before moving on to non-fiction and fiction.

She lives in the Midwest with two monsters (the kids), an ogre (the hubby), and whatever drama-llama is coming to visit this week. Sarah is the author of the Runespells series: Too Wyrd, Fluffy Bunny, and The Chains That Bind.

She has short stories in several anthologies, including Counterclockwise: A Time Travel Anthology, A Twist of Fate: A Collection of 11 Twisted Fairy Tales, and Whispers of Hope: A Lexis Infinitum Charity Anthology.

Sarah also has a blog via Patreon and makes funny videos about writing on her vlog, Practically Writing.

facebook.com/AuthorSarahB

twitter.com/AuthorGoddess

instagram.com/authorsarahbuhrman

SUPER SAM

BY REBEKAH DODSON

"With great power, comes great responsibility." – Stan Lee, 1922-2018
May you rest in peace.

Chapter 1

What's going on? I struggled to open my eyes to a world of starkly bleached walls, a worn crimson chair sitting in the corner, and the thundering sound of something wet dripping next to me. *Where am I? Was that me, screaming?* I tried to sit up, but the IV in my arm restricted me to the bed, the oxygen mask firmly seated around my mouth prevented me from calling my child's name.

The images of the car crossing the other lane into mine flooded my vision. It was coming straight at me. It was raining so hard, and the wipers on my husband Tracy's car weren't working right. I couldn't see a thing. My children, Cassie and Cary, were in the back seat with headphones on when we were hit. Cassie was reading quietly on her tablet, and Cary's bass-loaded music thumped through his phone. I had hummed to the classical harp playing on the radio. I never had time to stop. I'd have had enough time if I'd taken the SUV today to drop the kids at school, but the battery was dead, again. Tracy had promised to fix it, but he had been too busy at the lab.

I didn't even remember my head hitting the windshield. Thank God I'd been wearing my seat belt.

Where was my daughter, my son?

Oh, oh god. Had I … killed them?

I scratched at the oxygen mask, my arm sore where the needle protruded from the IV. I was encumbered by so many wires criss-crossing over my chest. Where were Cassie and Cary? No, wait, they were at school. Now I remembered: I had dropped them off. I was just stopping to get coffee before going home to finish cleaning the kitchen.

"Whoa, whoa, Samantha, take it easy."

Tracy's face floated across my vision.

"You've been in a car accident."

I nodded, silenced by this mask. I held up a finger and spelled a 'C' in the air.

"Cassie and Cary are fine. They're right outside." His face softened, but his eyes darted back and forth behind his thick, black-rimmed glasses, his forehead creased with worry. His normally perfect brown hair had tendrils escaping, framing his face, despite the large amount of product he applied every morning. "I'll get the doctor and the kids. They're worried sick." He hurried out of the room.

A couple minutes later, I could hear Tracy's muffled voice as he talked to someone just outside my door.

"Did you tell her?"

"There's no need." That was Tracy. But who was the other voice? I didn't recognize it.

"She has to know sooner rather than later."

"I know!" Tracy snapped, so unlike him. I frowned.

He said something else then, but I could barely concentrate on his last words. My head pounded, the pain arising so quickly I gripped both sides of my head. With a deafening roar, the room exploded with a cascade of noises. Shrieking wheels echoed around me, a phantom by my bedside. Chattering voices and a ciphony of laughter floated around the hospital room. The slow beep of some hospital machinery was so loud I pressed my hands to my ears and started screaming.

"Mom?"

I swallowed hard as I forced myself to focus on the face my four-teen-year-old son, who stepped up to the side of the bed and touched my arm. I didn't have the heart to tell him his small, shy voice came out as "*Mom*!" as it boomed in my head. Behind him, the hospital bed door flew open with a bang as his little sister, Cassie, and a doctor on their heels.

"Mom! Thank God!" He flung himself into my arms. "Cassie was so scared...."

I gripped him with one hand and held out the other Cassie, who burst into tears, her curly brown hair, only a shade lighter than Cary's, shaking around her face as she cried. "I thought you were with angels, Mama!"

Cary picked her up as always and held her to his hip. "Shh, Sissy, Mom's okay. Look, she's right here. She's fine, right doc?"

Dr. Grove nodded. "She'll be right as rain pretty soon." He smiled. "In fact, let's get this off you, Mrs. Willows."

The doctor looked at the beeping machine next to me, made a few notes on the computer beside it, then reached over and supported my neck. He slowly pulled the oxygen over my head and switched a button over my head.

I sucked in a deep breath, choking. "Easy, easy," the doctor said. "You've been unconscious for a few hours, so your body has to get used to repairing itself, now."

All their voices were so loud I felt as if my head would explode, I really hoped it would get on with the business of "repairing."

Cassie released her brother and curled up next to me on the bed. Her little fingers caressed the IV coming from my arm. "Mommy, maybe next time we should just be late to school and not take Daddy's car, okay?"

Cary smiled a little at that. "Dad's car has … had … better acoustics."

"Had?" I looked at him.

"It's a miracle you survived." Tracy was closing the door behind him. He exchanged glances with Dr. Grove, who nodded and stepped out of the room. "The Buick's a total loss, though."

"Jesus." I was still struggling to take deeper breaths. I wrapped my arm around Cassie.

Tracy sat got a bucket of ice water and poured some in a cup with a straw. "I wanted to get you coffee, but the nurse said no. This'll have to do, my love."

I took the cup and took a long sip. I couldn't take my eyes off Tracy, I couldn't stop thinking about what I'd heard—was I imagining things? Maybe Tracy and the doctor were just outside the door when I heard them talking?

Tracy seemed to read my mind. We'd been together so long; he always knew what I was thinking. He pulled out his wallet and handed a bill to Cary. "Hey, bud, why don't you take your sister down to the shop and get her hot chocolate?"

Cassie jumped off the bed, my near demise a thing of the past. "Yeah, let's go!" She grabbed Cary's hand and turned to look at me. "You want one, Mommy?"

"No, I'm good." I smiled at her. I knew why Tracy was getting rid of them. I knew it wasn't good.

"Sam," Tracy shut the door softly behind them. "Sam, I have bad news."

"Why are you all talking so loud?" I blinked at him.

"What?"

"Never mind." If I focused enough, I could make their voices quieter. I was very focused on this 'bad news' at the moment. I remembered the conversation he'd had outside my door with someone who wasn't my doctor.

"Tell me what's going on," I demanded. "Who were you talking to outside the door?"

"Holy shit, Sam," was all Tracy said.

"What?"

"Sam... we weren't outside the door." He took my glass of water and started to refill it.

"Huh? Were you in the hall?"

"We were two floors down. I went to get the kids in the waiting room."

I gasped and bit my lip. "Surely a floor vent or something carried your voice..."

"We were in the elevator."

"What?" I was starting to sound like a broken record.

Tracy's eyes widened, and he took a step back.

A split second before it happened, I saw a blurry vision of the cup falling from his hand. I shook my head, feeling dizzy, disorientated. I figured it was the pain meds they have pumped me full of. Then, as if someone had put an old VHS tape on fast forward, the cup of ice actually did fall from his hand and scattered everywhere like shards of glistening glass. "Sam, you took ... my car...."

"Yeah, the SUV was dead, I didn't have a choice. What's wrong with that?"

"Oh my God, Sam, no," he fell back into the chair in the corner with his head in his hands. "This can't be happening. Not you, not now. The formula wasn't even right. We didn't even have time to test it."

Chapter 2

"Tracy, what's going on?" I hit the nurse's button automatically, worried one of the kids would step on all the glass, and then I struggled to sit up. "What do you mean 'the formula'? Was there something in the car?"

Tracy was still mumbling into his hands. "I've been so busy at work. I should have changed that battery. I should have left the formula in the lab. But I just had a few things left to do. It was too precious to be left in the lab...."

"Tracy!" I yelled at him. If I could reach, I would have slapped him, but he was on the other side of the room.

He looked up at me then, his eyes wide and glossy. "I'm sorry, Sam. I have to go. I have to get back to the lab."

"Tracy, wait—"

He stood up and almost barreled into the nurse, who was poking her head in the door to check on me. The door flung open as he pushed past her, the flustered look on her face almost comical.

That was Tracy, scatterbrained most of the time, but how I loved him. He was a dedicated scientist, Chief of Operations at Bandon Industries on the outskirts of town. He'd been there for almost fifteen years and not a day went by he didn't fret about some experiment, meeting, or financing.

I'll never forget the time Tracy brought home an elixir for Cary after Cary explained he couldn't grow a mustache in the eighth grade. All the girls loved mustaches, and he needed one so badly. But all the purple liquid had done was given Cary acne. To solve the acne, Tracy made a blue paste that was supposed to be the permanent cure for blackheads. But it turned Cary's skin green for a week, and he couldn't go to school. That was when I put my foot down: no more experimenting on our kids.

So, was he now trying to experiment on *me*?

No, I wouldn't believe it.

He said it was an accident, I wasn't supposed to take his car today. It wasn't the first time he'd had a four-eyed rat in a cage in the back seat or a dead snake in a bag on the front seat. I had inspected the car, and it looked okay, but I never thought to check the trunk. God help me, I should have.

I frowned as I watched him rush out. What he said worried me, and how could he explain what I'd heard two floors down, through concrete and into an elevator? Okay, something was in the car when I crashed, and now, I had … super hearing?

I almost laughed. I could just imagine Cassie trying to tattle on her older brother, but I'd be able to hear everything. I'm sure it was nothing. Wasn't there some research somewhere that people woke from comas with super hearing, sight, or something? I made a mental note to check Google when I got home.

If Tracy had infected me somehow, I'd better keep quiet about it — I didn't want the doctors here or at Bandon's to think I was some sort of guinea pig, after all. Like most of Tracy's experiments, the results were temporary and never lasted more than a week. In the end, I knew I was going to be fine.

"Good news, Mrs. Willows! The doctor has said you're free to go." The nurse was saying. She stepped to my bedside and flung the stethoscope off her neck. As she began to check my vitals, she asked me if I'd like to go home soon.

"Sure," I said, smiling up at her, "but my husband had to, uh, get to work, and the vehicle I'm in isn't in the best driving shape."

The nurse smiled. "We have a medical transport that can take you and the kids home if you'd like."

"That'd be great."

"Okay, let's get this IV out, then."

I winced as she rolled the cart over and proceeded to remove the needle from my arm, taping a cotton ball covered in medical tape over the wound. "The doctor is working up your discharge papers now."

"Great, thanks."

"You can get dressed now. Your husband brought some clothes. I'm afraid yours were, uh, ruined?" I nodded as the nurse started to push the cart out of the room. She stopped at the door. "You're very lucky, you know," she said over her shoulder, "walking away from that car accident with only a few cuts and bruises."

"I'm beginning to get that idea." I was glad her back was turned, so she didn't see my frown, or the sense the way thoughts of Tracy's 'formula' swirled in my head.

"Going home the same day after a car accident? Double lucky. Sometimes this hospital surprises me." She chuckled and pulled the door shut behind her. I winced as she left, the squeaking of the wheels a deafening blow inside my head. I squeezed my eyes closed until the booming sound subsided.

I threw my legs out of bed and stumbled to the closet, throwing the door open. Someone had hung up an old Christmas sweater and a pair of jeans I hadn't seen in forever. My poor, sweet husband who never knew where things were. I dressed slowly; my entire body was sore – my hips twisted as I walked, my left knee screamed in pain, and my neck felt stiff as I rolled my head from one side of the other. I had cuts and bruises on my hands up to my elbow and a few on my shoulder.

I was slipping my shoes on when Cary appeared, Cassie in tow. He was holding a steaming Styrofoam cup, and she was dragging a bag of Cheetos behind her. I smiled as she ran up to me. Despite my aching shoulders and arms, I hoisted her onto my hip. Her little fingers were covered in orange cheese dust, her lips were ringed with orange as well, but she pecked me on the cheek anyway.

"Where's Dad?" Cary asked.

"He had to get back to the office." I forced a smile. I was still so worried about the way he'd rushed out of here moments ago, but I couldn't let my children see that. "The hospital has a cab we're going to take home."

"That's so cool, Mommy!" Cassie bounced up and down on my hip. I winced and set her down.

"How will we get to school tomorrow, if Dad has to go to work?" Cary downed the contents of his cup and tossing it in a nearby trashcan.

"Dad and I will think of something, a rental car, maybe," My brave smile was still firmly in place. Inside I was dying. Tracy wasn't the budgeter in the household, I was. He made good money that took care of us, but squeezing in a rental car fee, on top of the copay to fix Tracy's car. It would take some magic math, to be sure. My head hurt just thinking about it.

Luckily, the nurse arrived then with a wheelchair. She smiled when she saw I was dressed and up and about. "Well, guess we won't need this," she held out a stack of papers. "Sign the blue and yellow copy, and you're free to go, Mrs. Willows."

"Thanks," I took the papers and pen she pulled out of her pocket. I signed in triplicate and handed the papers back to her. I was still a little wobbly on my feet from the pain in my hip, but I didn't want the nurse to see that, so I steadied myself on Cary's shoulder. "Let's go, kids," I said to them both.

We didn't make it home until the sun was already on its way behind the hills; it was the middle of June, and later than I imagined. No wonder the kids had been hungry at the hospital. The minivan was gone from the driveway, of course, Tracy was still at work I supposed, but I couldn't wait for him to get dinner. It was still a school night, after all, and even my teenager had a strict bedtime of eight-thirty. I set about whipping up a quick dinner — standing was still difficult, after all — and surprisingly, the kids were happy with macaroni and cheese with boiled hot dogs. Not my best culinary achievement, but quick and easy at least.

Cary grabbed his basketball from the closet inside the front door.

I stopped him. "Hey, where are you going?"

"Shoot hoops at Rob's." He threw open the front door.

I knew Cary's best friend, Rob Matthews, lived just down the street. "Be back in an hour for homework!" I yelled after him, the slamming front door cutting off the homework bit. Cary was a good kid. I knew he'd be back when he was supposed to be.

Cassie helped me clear the table and load the dishwasher, and we cuddled up in Tracy's recliner to read a story. After we finished the story, I told her it was time for bed. "Okay, Mommy. Don't forget, tomorrow is soccer practice!"

I groaned inwardly but smiled at her. "Off to bed with you. Goodnight!"

She skipped up the stairs to her bedroom.

Soccer? I forgot tomorrow was her first practice of the year. This was her second year playing, and she loved it. In my current state, I didn't know if I'd feel up to it. Maybe I could convince Tracy to take her instead.

Where was Tracy? I picked up the phone next to the chair and dialed his company cell. It went straight to machine, short and sweet, "Dr. Willows, leave a message." I hung up and considered dialing the office number, but at eight at night there would only be an answering service. I cursed under my breath and panicked as I looked toward the stairs, praying Cassie hadn't heard me.

Speaking of running late, Cary still wasn't in yet. It was creeping closer to nine, and he knew he had to be in. He'd never been late before.

As if he knew I was thinking about him, the front door opened, and Cary came in, bouncing the ball once until he saw the look I gave him. His eyes were drooping shut, and his hair was a mess.

"Sorry, Mom, Rob and I were talking."

"You look exhausted," I said with a sigh.

He tossed the ball into the closet. "It's been a long day, Mom, at the hospital and all…"

"Go get your homework done and get to bed," I opened my arms. He gave me a one-armed hug like always, and to my disgust smelled like sweat and teenage boy rather strongly. "Ugh, scratch homework, go get a shower instead!" I laughed.

He took the stairs two at a time. "Aw, Mom."

"Child," I warned. "Shower."

"All right. Night, Mom."

"'Night, Cary." I paused at the bottom of the stairs for a minute and focused on the new hearing skills I had. After a couple of minutes, I could hear Cassie softly snoring. Outside the house somewhere, I could hear an owl hoot and a cat screech in warning. I shut my eyes tight and focused, and I was able to shut it off.

Hm. This could be useful. I didn't know how, but it could be.

Exhausted, but too worried about Tracy to sleep yet, I sat at my desk to do some paperwork and bill balancing. I didn't even know what rental fees were, so it was a daunting task. After an hour, my eyelids felt heavy, and my head was pounding. I really should just go to bed; Tracy did this all the time; spending long hours at the office. I never had to worry about it. I leaned back, rubbed my temples, and set about finishing the last of the budget.

"Sam, Sam, wake up."

Tracy was shaking my bruised shoulder gently, but the scratches there made it hurt so bad I yelped. "Ow! Get your hands off me!"

"Sam, relax, you fell asleep."

I spun in the office chair and faced him, rubbing my eyes. I glanced at the clock on the wall. It was half-past midnight. "Late night?"

"Yeah." He pulled out a chair at the dining room table and sat down heavily. He pulled a kitchen chair our and sat backward on it. "Look, Sam—"

"Tracy, about our conversation in the hospital…." I interrupted at the same time. He motioned for me to continue. "This will wear off, right? Whatever this chemical is, right? Like my hearing will return to normal?"

"I ran the number three times, and I… well, would you like the good news or the bad?"

My eyes went wide. "There's bad?"

Chapter 3

My brain had trouble shutting off after what Tracy told me. The number of times he used "unsure" and "maybe" alarmed me more than the information he gave me. I finally passed out after midnight, my body and mind unable to handle anymore. Tracy was thoughtful enough to bring me a pair of earplugs from the office. Thank God – the barking dog three blocks over was keeping me awake.

I kept waiting for the side effects that Tracy had explained to take form, both dreading and hoping they would manifest to distract me from the pain. I actually felt energized this morning, though just three days after the accident, I knew at the very least I should be sore. I had come out of a car accident alive with some interesting side effects; not only the super hearing, Tracy had explained, but also some super healing, apparently. "You're like a goddamn Wolverine now," he had said with a chuckle I vaguely got the reference from some movie Cary had watched a few years ago. I laughed when he said I didn't get the cool claws, though. I couldn't even imagine. I was grateful that instead of a broken arm and a fractured skull, for all intents and purposes I was a hundred percent healthy.

Maybe, just maybe, I'd survive this. *Just a week or so,* Tracy had assured me, *and the drug will be out of the system. No harm, no foul.* I believed him of course; why wouldn't I? I felt *amazing.* In fact, I wanted to go back to the gym, but Tracy urged me to take it easy until we knew exactly what the chemical would do in my system. *Maybe nothing else,* he had said, *but only time would tell.*

The school year was almost over — it was a week of field trips, exploratory assignments, and ice cream parties, so the kids were up and ready on Friday morning before I was. It had been almost a week since the accident, and so far, no other side effects had surfaced. I was good —or so I hoped.

"What's on the agenda today, kiddo?" I asked Cassie, sitting next to Cary at the table, where they were both shoveling Cheerios into their mouths with gusto.

"We're going to a petting zoo!" she yelled, squirming in her seat.

"Cary, what about you?"

"Mr. Anderson is taking us to volunteer at the animal shelter."

"That's great!" I went through the motions of making coffee and some calls to arrange the carpool since we were left with only one vehicle until the rental places opened. I could hear the roar of my best friend Becky's Suburban a few blocks away, so I tucked lunches into my kids' hands and sent them to enjoy their day at school. My advanced hearing was getting the best of me at times, and it was often hard to control. Tracy said this was going to fade, but every day it just got worse.

"Love you, Mommy!" Cassie called as she piled into the car next to Becky's six-year-old, Alex. Cary and Becky both waved at me from the front as they pulled away.

Once they were gone, I realized I didn't have anything on my agenda. My days were packed with the gym, volunteering in Cassie's classroom, baking cookies, or shopping for some event. But today? I had nothing. I couldn't sit around idle and wait for the side effects any longer. I decided to take my mind off what was happening … and started cleaning. Because who doesn't clean when they are stressed? The problem was, my days were mostly filled with cleaning and running errands. So, my house was, unfortunately, spotless, despite the weekend I'd spent recovering.

But there was always the garage.

Tracy had promised he'd get in there and organize it so I could park the van in there, but that was almost six months ago. He worked so much I hated to remind him about it. That left it up to me.

As soon as I opened the door to the garage a disgusting odor hit me so intensely. I flung the door shut immediately. Shit, what was that? I had a fourteen-year-old; bad smells weren't new around here. Cassie wet the bed until she was four, and of course, there were the two rounds of diapers between them. Whatever was in the garage, was different. It was pungent. It was … completely revolting. Like molded cheese mixed with blood and … oh God. I felt my stomach turn.

I must be nuts. Was this a side effect? Was I slowly going crazy? I opened the door again, feeling nausea wash over me. There was just something so innately wrong with having a clean house, but such a disgusting garage. I pushed the button to open the wide electric door on the other side and set to work.

The garage wasn't full, but it was a mess. Broken bike pieces and wheels lay against one wall, and some forgotten tools were scattered everywhere. Boxes stacked on the right wall tilted precariously. Pieces of our abandoned camping equipment were separated into a tent here, a chair there, a Coleman stove on a shelf to the left. There was even a stack of lawn care equipment next to abandoned bricks covered in layers of dust. A hodge-podge of projects I never had a chance to complete. Even with both doors open, the fresh early summer air did nothing to kill that smell. I set to work organizing the boxes and stacking items together, distressed to find what was so awful in my garage.

That's when the next side effect hit me. I had super strength.

I could grasp an old TV with one hand, and some patio bricks from last summer's remodel felt like Styrofoam. In no time, I had completely shifted everything around in the garage.

"What the heck are you doing?"

I jumped, nearly tossing the two heavy boxes I was holding in each hand as I turned around. Tracy was standing behind me. I hadn't even heard the van pull into the driveway; I was so intent on shifting boxes, putting tools away, and stacking like objects together with my cool new power.

But still, that rotten death smell filled my nose.

"Do you smell that?" I said, lifting an old Bowflex out of the way with one hand.

"What the hell, Sam? That thing weighs a hundred pounds!" Tracy was staring at me.

I sat the Bowflex down with ease and dusted my hands. "Oh, yeah. Turns out super strength is a side effect. I thought you said this would wear off or something?"

"That's what the lab reports indicated." He crossed his arms. "And I don't smell anything except this terrible dust you've kicked up." He coughed and waved his hand to demonstrate.

"No, that horrible, rotting smell," I said, sticking out my tongue. "It's so gross. I don't know what it is, but I have to find it."

Tracy shrugged. "I don't smell anything."

"What are you doing here so early?"

"Sam, it's after one. I came home for lunch."

I looked at my watch. "Oh crapola, so it is."

"How long have you been out here?"

"Um, since eight."

Tracy surveyed the garage again. "Well, come take a break and eat with me real quick. I brought Indian from that place across the street from the office."

I noticed he was holding a plastic bag stacked with Styrofoam containers. The aroma of spicy curry mixed with tomatoes and tantalizing cream was so strong it made my mouth water. Were those cloves and cinnamon? A little garlic and some eggplant, maybe? The smells were so separate and distinct it was almost overwhelming. I'd eaten Indian for years but never thought about what was in it.

"I tried to call you, you know," Tracy said, pulling me out of my trance.

"I didn't even hear it."

"Seriously? This your super hearing?" Tracy peered at me curiously. I hadn't even heard the phone ring.

"Well, maybe the super strength cancels it out."

"Whatever it's doing," Tracy rubbed his smooth chin thoughtfully, "the garage looks fantastic."

The garage really did look ten times better. The boxes were neatly stacked, the bikes and their pieces in one corner, the camping gear all tucked into a couple of shelves, and there was finally an open space in the middle.

I couldn't even think about food until I figured out where that smell was coming from.

The one last thing I had to do was put the tools away. We had a tall, black tool chest, though for what I didn't know. Tracy had only touched it maybe twice since we bought it six years ago. He wasn't the tool type of guy, unless the tools happened to be a beaker and an eye dropper, that is. I opened the first drawer to put away the wrenches, and that's when I found it.

As soon as I pulled the drawer open, I knew that's what it was. That horrible smell.

There was a dead mouse in the drawer.

And then, of course, I did what any respectable thirty-six-year-old woman and mother of two would do upon finding a dead mouse that smelled like a hundred rotting corpses.

I screamed.

Tracy came running out of the house. "Sam? What is it? Are you okay?"

Shaking, I just pointed at the tool box's drawer. He went over and looked in, then picked up a wrench and poked it. Actually poked it. "Hey, little guy," he said to it. "What are you doing here?"

"I'm gonna puke, Tracy, just get it out of here."

He held it up on the end of the wrench. "It's just a little guy, but it looks like his heart gave out. Believe me. I know what that looks like, boy, do I," he mumbled the last part.

The smell was so overpowering I pulled my shirt over my nose and held my breath. "Just get rid of it!" My yell was muffled by my shirt.

Tracy shook his head at me like I was crazy. "It's been dead for maybe an hour, Sam, it's still warm." He walked across the street and tossed it into the creek that separated our property from the next.

"What the...," I shook as I watched him walk back toward the house.

Tracy slipped an arm around me. "Hun, I told you this might happen."

"You said...."

"I know what I said, but heightened senses for sure. I'm sorry, I know it doesn't help. I'm so sorry, honey."

I shook my head. "I should have never taken your car that day."

Tracy grabbed my hand and squeezed it. "I thought the Indian food would cheer you up, honey."

"I am hungry," I admitted.

"Come on, let's go inside," he said, reaching up and pressing the button to shut the door behind us. "The garage really does look amazing, sweetheart."

"Thanks," I forced a smile. "Well, maybe the good part will be my sense of taste, and that Indian food will be amazing to eat."

"You don't need superpowers to know curry is amazing."

I followed him into the house.

———

Unfortunately, my sense of taste hadn't changed, but the curry was still amazing as Tracy promised. After lunch, we stopped by and picked up the rental for him so I could have the van back for soccer practice that afternoon, then Tracy went back to work, promising to check with the mechanic on the status of his car. I picked up the kids and dropped Cary off at Rob's for their homework session while I took Cassie to soccer.

"Mommy!" Cassie was a bundle of nerves, I could tell.

"What, Cassie?"

"You have my water?"

"Yes, Cassie."

"Oh, no. Where's my ball? Mommy, where's my ball?"

"Right here, Cassie," I tossed it to her as we got out of the car.

It had been a long day of moving boxes and running errands, and I could feel a migraine creeping up my left temple. I threw shades on and got Cassie out of the car, making sure her shin pads were pulled up, and she had her water and ball. She ran off with reckless abandon to her team, many of which were little girls in her first-grade class. The field was a sea of blonde, brown, and black ponytails, and bright colored jerseys.

The small bleachers were crowded with a dozen parents, but my head was pounding now, so I didn't feel like socializing. I unfolded my camp chair on the edge of the field and shielded my eyes against the late afternoon sun to see who her coach was this year. Last year there was an amazing team of high school girls that volunteered their time and Cassie had loved them. She even picked flowers – mostly weeds – to give them before every practice.

The girls milled around a couple of parents, the parents who were looking at the parking lot much like I was. Where was the new coach?

A red truck, lifted at least three feet off the ground, careened into the parking lot and screeched to a halt next to my van. I winced, because I had this sick feeling in the pit of my stomach. That was him, that was the coach, I knew it. My heart raced, and I felt the sweat break out on my forehead. Why was I so stressed all of a sudden?

The man who dismounted from his truck looked more like he should be coaching football. He was wearing a sleeveless white shirt that clearly displayed bulging arms and black sports shorts over legs like tree trunks, with an orange reflective vest thrown over his shoulders. The sun reflected off his bald head, and his eyes were hidden behind sleek rainbow-hued sunglasses. He carried a bag full of neon and classic soccer balls.

The girl who jumped lithely out of the passenger side was every bit as athletic as the man I assumed was her father. She couldn't be more than six or seven since this was the first and second-grade team after all, but she was easily four inches taller than Cassie and impossibly thin. Her long, lean legs wrapped in professional grade brand-name shin guards and she was in a matching purple jersey and shorts. Even her brown ponytail was immaculate and tied back with a lavender ribbon decorated with soccer balls.

I sucked in a breath. They were nearly a football field away, and I could clearly identify the soccer balls on the little girl's ribbon. My sight was clearly advanced now, too. Oh, God, this was getting worse. Tracy had been right – it would be bad before it got better. I silently prayed this was the extent of the side effects.

"Lacy!" Cassie screamed, and a group of five girls broke out into a run when they saw the girl. I focused my hearing, and even from twenty feet away, I could hear the girls' squeals as clear as day: *Your dad's the coach? Awesome! We are gonna be so cool this year. We are gonna win that trophy this time! Oh yeah, your dad is so awesome!*

I had to admit I was digging this advanced hearing thing. The smell, not so much, but at least that wasn't working overtime right now, especially with all these different teams on the field. My head was still pounding as I tried hard to focus on my vision, which was floating between extreme detail, like a microscope on the zoom function. I felt dizzy.

Tracy had no idea if this would be permanent or not. The D2-40, the name of the chemical the lab had been testing, wasn't even out of Phase I – not only was I the first test sample, but I was the only one there would be for a while. Tracy would have to replicate the mixture in order to see what effects it would really have – which could take weeks, maybe months.

"All right girls, you ready to play some soccer?"

I snapped back to reality when I heard the coach's booming announcement. The girls cheered, which I didn't need my super-hearing for. The coach tossed them all a ball to start practice with.

I had to admit, the man was a little intimidating, but coaching six and seven-year-old girls was a daunting challenge. In fifteen minutes, he had them organized, and the girls were all working really hard, so I didn't give it a second thought he knew what he was doing.

I realized one of the girls on the team was Cassie's friend, Hannah, who was a bit overweight in comparison to the skinny first and second graders. Even Cassie, with her short and stocky build like her father, looked like a twig next to Hannah. I felt a little bad for Hannah as she struggled to keep up with the faster girls. A few times she stopped to catch her breath, and the third time, Coach yelled at her. A few minutes later she halted on one side of the field, breathing heavy, while the other girls were yards away.

The Coach threw down his clipboard and stalked over to her.

I felt my heart thunder in my chest, and the sweat dripped down the back of my neck.

Oh, no.

Hulking over the young girl, I focused my hearing, and what he said sent a shiver down my spine.

"Maybe you're too much a fat ass to be on this team. If you want this team to succeed, you need to lay off those cheeseburgers!"

Hannah burst into tears and covered her face, running to the sidelines.

Oh, crap. I leapt to my feet before I knew what I was doing. My heart pounded in my chest now, not just because I was livid a coach would ever talk to a six-year-old like that, but also because I spotted Hannah's father, Jose, wrap his arms around his daughter. Although short and thick like his daughter, Jose was a force to be reckoned with. I had gym classes two days a week, and our exercise rooms were just past the weight room. I'd seen Jose bench press close to three-hundred. I also knew he was a single father; Hannah's mother had walked away three years ago. So, he was a short, angry Hispanic man who was fiercely protective of his young daughter. This was not good.

Of all the soccer moms and doting dads on this field, he was the wrong person to call his daughter a "fat ass."

I also knew from the scuttlebutt from other moms he'd done a few years upstate for assault before Hannah was born.

I froze on the sidelines, knowing Jose was going to do what Jose knew best, and that was talk with his fists. Like the dozen other parents, we all watched, frozen as this scene unfolded as Jose crossed the field toward the coach, but I was the closest one. I wouldn't have to use my super hearing or advanced eyesight to know what was going to happen next.

The vision of Jose swinging his fist and the sickening crack of it hitting the Coach's jaw spread across my vision so quickly I wasn't sure what was going on. I could see the Coach fall to the ground, blood spraying from his split lip as the dust plumed around him. I felt dizzy, and stars exploded across my vision. I blinked once, then again, and my vision cleared to see Jose still a few feet away from the coach.

Without thinking, I jogged the distance to the coach before Jose could make it, suddenly thankful for all those spin classes. I put up my hand to hold Jose off; knowing full well if he swung it would hit me first. Did I even make it in time before that awful scene unfolded? Behind Coach I could see the girls were frozen on the field, watching the scene unfold.

"What's going on?" Coach blinked at me. "Who are you?"

I stood in front of the coach with my back to him. "Jose, Jose, you don't want to do this!"

"Out of my way, Sam! That coach has to be taught a lesson!"

Behind him, I could see Hannah on the bleachers, tears still streaming down her face.

Behind me, the Coach was panicked. "Hey man, I'm sorry, I didn't mean…."

"Think about Hannah for a second," I said to Jose, racking my brain for what to say. "She doesn't have a momma. You want her to grow up without a daddy, too? You know they will send you upstate again. Use your brain, man."

Jose stopped three feet from me, blinking. "How did you know…"

"Never mind, you wouldn't even believe me. Just take Hannah and go home, okay?"

"Yeah," Jose shook his head. "I think I will."

Once Jose was out of hearing range, I turned to the coach. "And you," I whispered, poking my index finger into his broad chest. Something like an electric shock shot up my hand, and I swore there was purple smoke coming from somewhere. I cleared my throat and focused on the coach's shocked face. "I have exceptional hearing, and I will be at all your games. You see my little girl over there with the blonde curls? That's Cassie. You can bet your bottom if you *ever* repeat what you said to Hannah, I'll make sure you *never* bench press or lift anything, *ever again*. You got that, *bro*?"

"Yeah, I got it," he said, blinking at me.

I turned and walked away from him, watching Jose and Hannah get in the car at the end of the parking lot. Coaches were bullies sometimes, and no one ever put them in their place. I wouldn't stand by and let a bully ever treat anyone like that, but at the same time, Jose had it all wrong. It wasn't about physical coercion at all. It was about making them learn their lesson.

Later that night, I realized one thing about today: so far, excellent hearing and too-excellent smelling were okay side effects I was dealing with. My vision zoomed in and out at times of high stress, apparently. Flashes of the future? I didn't know if I could handle that one yet. But if it meant I'd save someone from doing something dangerous, it was something I could get used to.

Chapter 4

"You seriously stopped Jose from punching the coach?"

It was Saturday morning, and the kids were still asleep. Tracy and I were stealing a few precious moments of solitude in the early morning on our back porch. We were still wrapped in our robes, even though the early summer air was already crisp and warm.

"Yeah, I did."

Tracy leaned back with his coffee and laughed. "Wow, Sam."

I blinked at him, cradling my own coffee cup. "What?"

"So, tell me again, what did you see, exactly?"

"The ribbon in Lacy's hair, or the glimpse of the future?"

Tracy waved his hand. "The vision side effect, we guessed would happen. The flash of future events concerns me."

"I told you, it was like something that was going to happen if I didn't stop it."

"Another side effect." It wasn't a question.

I nodded and took a sip. "I guess so."

"Don't go donning a cape and mask and leaping from rooftops," Tracy leaned forward and took my head. "Promise me?" I started to laugh, but then saw he was dead serious.

"I won't," I said solemnly, but still cracking a smile.

My smile was infectious, as he flashed one back at me. "And let's hope that's the end of the side effects." He stood and grabbed his empty mug.

"You think this is still temporary?"

He paused at the French door leading into the house. "I don't know, yet."

"How are the experiments going?"

He turned and looked at me, biting his lip, and shook his head.

"Oh, no."

"Sam," he said, coming to stand next to me. "I'm going to fix this, I swear."

"Okay," I pushed back the tears. I didn't mind hearing things, could do without smelling, but the flashes of the future were weird. And they were more frequent.

Like, right now. The vision was quick: coffee cup falling to the ground, Tracy reaching for the pieces, slicing his finger open. Then the world wavered back into stillness.

"Tracy, watch out!" I called, not wishing the vision to come true.

Before I could stop him, the coffee cup indeed slid from his fingers. I reached forward to grab it and found purple tendrils of energy shooting from my fingertips.

"Oh my god!" Tracy's mouth gaped open.

I was just as shocked as I lifted the cup with this strange energy and set it on the table behind him, then as I held my hands up the purple swirls sucked right back into my hands. I stared at them, unable to force even a single word from my throat.

"Sam, when did *that* start happening?" Tracy's arms were at my shoulders, gently shaking me.

I bit my lip. I didn't want to tell him I had felt it when I poked the coach. "Just now," I lied.

"That's ... not a side effect." He frowned and stepped back, crossing his arms.

"What?" I felt like I was going to cry. "Tracy, what's wrong with me?"

He held his hands out, helpless. "I'm sorry; I don't know."

"I hope you find the antidote soon," I said softly, sniffling back the tears. "Saving the coach from a punch is one thing, but tingly purple energy stuff is *super* scary."

"Sam...."

I floated over to my desk and sat down, my head in my hands. I suddenly didn't want this anymore. It was too much. The pounding headache spread across my forehead stabbed painfully. "Just find me that antidote," I said to Tracy as he approached me.

He turned and headed toward the stairs. "I'll get right on it—you're my highest priority. Maybe it's best if you stay inside today?"

I nodded. I couldn't agree more.

"Cary, where are you headed?" I called as I heard the front door open downstairs. Tracy was at the lab again, trying to squeeze more hours into finding an antidote. Cassie was in her bedroom getting dressed, and we were planning on going to the gym so I could get back into the swing of things. Cassie loved the daycare center there.

"Out," was all he said.

"Where?" I was leaning over the banister on the second floor, where Cary paused with the front door cracked open.

He shrugged. "Rob's, maybe shoot some hoops?"

"Okay, check in by lunch, all right?"

He shrugged again and then pulled the door shut behind him.

He'd been spending a lot of time at Rob's, but I figured with summer quickly approaching, he was just fighting the impending boredom. Cary was a good kid—did well in school and chose the right kind of friends. Tracy and I never had to worry about him.

"Let's go, Mom. I don't want to miss snack time there!" Cassie flew past me and down the stairs.

I grabbed my gym bag, and we set off for the local YMCA. When we got there, Cassie was excited to get to the daycare center. She brushed me off and ran toward the swings on the far end of the enclosed center.

I shook my head and smiled, trudging up the stairs to the front door.

"Sam!"

I spun and saw Becky, who like usual, was a bundle of energy. Her long, blonde hair was pulled into a messy bun on the top of her head, and she was wearing a tight pink halter top shirt over black yoga pants.

"Hey, Becky. Thanks for giving the kids a ride yesterday, I really appreciate it." I held the door open for her.

She waved her hand. "Anytime. Your kids are great."

"Where's Alex?" I looked around for her six-year-old son.

"At his dad's for the weekend," she said as we pushed open the door to spin class. "It's just me this weekend, yay."

The way she said the last word made me think she wasn't too excited about it. Considering her recent bad divorce that strung out for over a year, I couldn't even imagine. I pulled out my water bottle and filled it up at the fountain just outside the door. When I came in, she was stretching with her long leg pushed high up the wall. "You look great, considering the, uh…"

"Accident?" I supplied.

"How long has it been?"

"A week."

"Jesus, you're like super mom. Not a scratch on you."

I held out my bare arm and examined it. Even the scars were gone.

I swallowed hard. I didn't want to talk about this. "How are you handling the … you know…?"

"Oh, the living alone thing without my cheating bastard of a husband? It's been okay, I guess." She shrugged, stretching her arm across her chest. She sighed. "I'm lying."

"Yes, you are."

"It's terrible, and I hate it."

"I'm sorry." I craned my neck in a stretch. I meant it.

"I just wish I had mind reading powers, ya know? I could have avoided all this bullshit ages ago."

I choked on a laugh. "Superpowers don't exist."

She chuckled. The room was filling now, so we chose our bikes, next to each other at the back of the room. She lowered her voice as she spun the bike to life. "If they did, it would be pretty awesome though."

I didn't answer and focused on pedaling.

"Hey, we should go have drinks this weekend," Becky whispered.

"Oh, I, uh…" I didn't really drink – Tracy and I didn't even have any alcohol in the house. And I couldn't even imagine what it would be like if I put it on top of all these weird side effects.

"Oh, come on, Sam," Becky urged, a little pout on her face. She crossed her arms.

I didn't really feel like it. Part of it was the heightened senses—a bar scene seemed like too much of a disaster if I couldn't control it. The other part was the feeling this was all too good to be true. What would happen if it occurred while we were out having fun?

"You've been cooped up in that house for weeks. I only ever see you at the gym anymore," Becky whined. "Come on. You'll have fun."

I sighed and took off my light jacket, throwing it over my gym bag. "All right," I said, "I'll get Cary to watch Cassie if Tracy is still at work."

"Hell, bring Tracy, I don't care."

"I know it's terrible, but you're a lot more fun since your divorce, ya know that?" In the last year, Becky had transformed from a mousey boy scout mom to a newly single woman who was firmly in grasp of her sexuality. Finding her husband with the babysitter was possibly the best thing that ever happened to her. She had emerged from her shell like a bat out of hell.

"And pushier, but hey, who gives a shit?" Becky peddled faster as if all her anxiety was pumped into the spinning wheel.

I laughed. "I think that's why we're friends."

Becky turned and looked at me. "Holy shit, Sam, what have you been doing trapped in your house? You're ripped as hell!"

"Huh?"

"Look at your arms! Oh my god, what is your secret? Personal trainer? New program? Tell me!"

I extended my arm in front of the mirror that covered one wall, and I gasped. My biceps were bulging and huge, nearly putting Cassie's soccer coach to shame. Under my tight shirt, I could even see my abs rippling.

"Jesus Christ," I breathed. I probed my stomach gingerly. How had I not noticed this this morning?

"Is this like a cool accident side effect?" Becky called over the other cyclists who were getting into their routine. "What did they give you in the hospital, because I want some!"

"I don't know." I turned back to her. *It's definitely a side effect of something, all right.*

Our instructor, Iliana, skipped into the room at that moment. Short and thin with perfectly bronzed skin, she was always excited to see her class. She stretched for a few minutes, and then hopped on the bike at the front of the room. She zeroed in on me. "Wow, Sam, you look amazing! Class is really paying off!"

Becky was frowning at me. Jealousy had always been her weak spot. "Yeah, you look great," she mumbled and stared at the wall behind Iliana.

I popped one earbud into my ear and shook my head. "I won't be for much longer," I said softly, hoping no one could hear me. I wasn't exactly sure if that was a good thing or a bad thing. How in the world could this potion "grow" muscles in just four days? I made a note to mention this to Tracy later, that is if he didn't just notice it. And what would happen if those muscles just evaporated? I winced, focusing on the crooning country blasting in my ears.

The rest of spin class was uneventful, but after we were done, I noticed I hadn't broken a sweat or even felt tired. In fact, I felt more energized than before. Maybe this drug had sped up my metabolism? If that were true, as I remembered from my brief days in college training for medical school, then maybe it would burn up the drug before it could do any real damage? Cary's arrival had put an end to my college days, but I vaguely recalled something about a fast metabolism being a cause for healing. If that were true, maybe this nightmare would be over soon.

"So, how's soccer going?" Becky asked as we left the building and made our way to the daycare center.

"The coach is Adam Wells, Lacy Wells's dad," I said.

"Is he single yet? Because he looks so much like Vin Diesel, I could show him a thing or two...."

"Wow, Becky." Her side effect of divorce was slightly compromised morals, which I already knew, but sometimes she blew me away.

"He's also a volunteer firefighter, I heard, which is H-O-T."

I shook my head. She was bad.

A car whizzed past us, going way too fast for a parking lot beside a daycare.

"Slow down, asshole!" Becky lifted a middle finger high in the air.

I felt my heart pounding in my chest; a few more inches and he could have clipped us both. What a jerk.

"Mommy!" Cassie called as we approached. She was hanging on the gate, which was normally locked while the kids were out in the playground. The gate popped open this time, and Cassie, in her six-year-old reckless abandon, bounded toward us.

My vision turned black, then, and I saw an image of Cassie laying on the pavement, blood running from her ears and her head misshaped on one side. Her brown hair was matted with blood, and her arm was bent upwards, clearly crushed. Her eyes were closed, and I just knew she was ... dead.

"Cassie. No!" I screamed before my vision even righted itself, as the same car that had sped in front of us before circled back around the front of the playground. I realized something was wrong then—he hadn't been speeding but must have some kind of brake problem.

Cassie was too far for me to save her, even as I reached out toward her.

I felt my hands start to burn and I threw my gym bag off my shoulder, looking down. Just like when I had poked Adam a few days ago, little purple tendrils rose like steam from my fingertips, crackling like a strange form of miniature lightning.

I had no time. The black car was mere feet from my precious daughter.

I stepped toward the speeding car, vaguely aware of Becky screeching behind me: "Sam, *what are you doing?*"

I raised my hands toward the side of the car and pulled it toward me. It was a few tons of metal, so I had no idea what I was doing, but I had to save my daughter! My vision couldn't come true. It just couldn't! I couldn't lose Cassie!

The purple energy arched against the metal side of the car and cracked the air. I could feel the cool metal under my fingers. At first, I closed my eyes, knowing what I did was useless; Cassie was going to die right here in front of me.

But then I pulled back, and I felt the car change direction. I leaned back as it spun past me, and I pushed my hands out.

The car went barreling to the side, missing Cassie by inches. I opened my eyes to see it crash into the raised flower bed outside the gym, the front-end crumpling with a sickening twist of metal and a hiss of steam.

"Cassie!"

Chapter 5

My beautiful daughter stood frozen in the parking lot, tears streaming down her face. "Mommy?"

I raced forward and scooped her into my arms. "Cassie, baby, you scared Mommy so bad, are you okay?"

"Mommy, what did you do?"

Becky was right behind me. "What the *fuck* did I just see?"

"Becky, language!"

She blinked. "Sorry, Sam, I know you hate swearing, but, holy shit, you just moved a car!*"*

I gaped at her. "What did you see?"

She took a step back. "I, uh, I'm gonna go pick up Alex from the ex. Gotta go!"

I watched her retreat to her car, throw herself behind the wheel, and back out faster than if hell was on her heels. In the playground in front of me, the three volunteers and a dozen children were gawking at the crashed car.

I couldn't focus on them; an Asian man, at least ten tears my senior, stumbled out of the front seat, pressing a hand to his head. He was impeccably dressed in a three-piece suit. He blinked at me with glossy eyes and shook his head.

"Call 9-1-1!" I shouted at the daycare volunteers, one of whom had already flipped her cell phone out of her pocket and had it pressed to her ear.

"Cassie, Mommy's gotta make sure the man is okay, okay." I pushed a strand of hair behind her hair. "Go stand right beside Miss Becky, okay."

She nodded, tears still streaming down her face as I sat her down. She ran to Becky and grabbed her hand so tightly I saw Becky wince. I didn't dismiss Becky was staring at me.

"Are you okay? I know first aid," I jogged over to the car.

"I, uh," he mumbled, shaking his head again. "I must have passed out. My brakes…." he looked at me, blinking. "You stopped my car?"

"You must have lost control of the wheel." I ignored his last statement. "I'm sorry about your car."

He slumped down into a sitting position, leaning crookedly against his car. "My head feels like it's going to explode."

Both you and me, I ignored the pounding in my head. I knew the sirens blaring in the distance weren't that close, but the sound was like speakers blaring directly to my brain. I knelt down next to the man. "An ambulance is on its way, okay." I was probably shouting. I tried to focus on my hearing ability, but my brain was going too many directions at once.

He nodded, but his eyes rolled in the back of his head.

I shook his shoulder. "Hey, what's your name? I'm Sam."

"Kei," he shook his head and tried to force his eyes open. "Kei Hitcharo. There was a little girl...." His eyes popped open, and he searched the vicinity. "Oh god, I didn't hit her, did I?"

"No, my daughter is safe. You didn't' hit her." *No thanks to me.*

"Oh, thank God," he sighed.

"Do you want me to call someone? Your wife, maybe?"

"No, it's just me," he said, "but I need to call my boss. I have a board meeting I'm late for."

"All right, where do you work?" I pulled my cell phone out of my pocket, the sirens blaring louder and louder.

"Bandon Industries."

I had to strain to hear him over the sirens exploding in my hearing, but finally, I gasped. It wasn't a large town, but most of the employees there commuted from the nearby metropolis. In the six years Tracy had worked at Bandon, I had only met a few other people who worked there, mostly wives with kids Cassie's age, all who hated our small town and didn't last here very long. Tracy had told me once that Bandon, while on the cutting edge of chemical invention and distribution, mostly employed young graduates in the field who didn't have families.

Of course, with dangerous drugs like the D2-M2 floating through my system, it didn't surprise me Bandon preferred to hire single professionals that presented less of a risk.

"Ma'am? My cell phone is in the car, can you reach it?" Kei was saying to me.

I stood and pried open the bent front door, which only opened a few inches. A blackberry lay on the floor of the driver's side, and I snatched it up, handing it to him. "You work in the lab at Bandon?" I asked without thinking. I just had to know if he knew Tracy – if he knew about D2-M2 my cover would be blown.

"Yes, but I'm with the manufacturing field of fuel conservation." His voice was a little weary as he pushed out each word slowly. He looked down at his phone and started punching in numbers.

No sooner had he dialed a number than a bright red ambulance had swung into the parking lot, screeching to a halt ten feet from the car. Down the street, I could hear a fire truck barreling up Madison. Two paramedics in blue uniforms with yellow patches on their arms were running toward us.

I backed up and let the paramedics treat Mr. Hitcharo.

Becky, Alex, and Cassie, gripping each of her hands, trotted to my side. "Sam," she said in a hushed tone. "Sam, I have to go." I took Cassie's hand as Becky picked up Alex, hoisting her gym bag higher on her shoulder. "Call me later, okay." Under her breath, she added, "We need to talk about what happened."

I nodded without looking at her. I didn't even want to think about what Becky saw, and I made a mental note to try to explain it away later. The paramedics were trailing a small flashlight in Mr. Hitcharo's eyes to check for a concussion as a sleek black, and white police car rolled into the parking lot.

Cassie tugged on my hand as Becky and Alex made their way to their car. "Mommy, can we go? Please?"

I looked down at her. Her face was dirty from playing, and her tears had woven crooked streaks down her face. I noticed she was shaking a little, and her small hand had a vice-like grip on my own. The police officer was getting out of his vehicle and locked eyes with me. He was young with black hair protruding from his hat, his deep blue eyes sweeping the scene. I knew I couldn't leave yet, even though Cassie was clearly still terrified.

"In a minute, honey," I tried to smile but failed. We took a seat on the curb a few feet away and watched the paramedics help Mr. Hitcharo into the ambulance.

Finally, a police officer approached me. "What happened here?"

"Kei, Mr. Hitcharo, lost control of his vehicle," I reported slowly, rehearsing in my head what I would say. "He said his brakes went out."

The officer flipped open his notepad. "I see," he jotted a few things down. "And what is your name?"

"Sam Willows," I said.

"This your daughter?"

"Yes, Cassie."

Cassie pressed her head into my side.

"Look, officer, I don't mean to be rude, but he almost hit my daughter, and she's pretty scared. Do you mind if I take her home?"

He looked at the car and then at me, narrowing his eyes. "What do you mean, almost hit her?"

"She ran into the road, and he pulled away at the last second, but hit the curb, as you can see." I knew I was safe—Becky was gone, the only witness to what I had done, the car had blocked any of the playground volunteers from getting a clear view of my powers. I knew I had to talk to Becky about it, but that was another issue entirely.

The officer nodded finally and pulled a card out of his other chest pocket. "I will probably need to contact you in the future, but I agree you should probably take her home."

I nodded and took the card. "Thanks. I'll call you if I think of anything else."

He paused and looked at Cassie. "Is she okay? Do you want the paramedics to take a look at her?"

"No," Cassie whimpered and looked up at me.

"We'll be fine, I think," I squeezed Cassie closer to me.

"Okay, you're free to go." His face twisted with concern, as if he really didn't want to let us go but didn't have much of a choice.

As soon as we got to the car, I let out the huge breath I was holding. My headache was subsiding quickly, and for the first time since my accident, I felt completely drained. I cranked the engine to life.

"Mommy," Cassie said from her spot in her booster seat behind me as we pulled out of the parking lot.

"Yes, honey?" I peered at her through the review mirror.

"What was that purple light? How did you stop that car, Mommy? How did you save me?"

I realized Becky wasn't the only witness I'd have to worry about. I panicked for a moment; I didn't want to lie to my daughter, but I didn't know what else to say. I couldn't have her telling her friends at school what I had done. On the other hand, if I lied it would confuse her, and her questions would be endless.

In the end, I realized to a six-year-old, sometimes the truth was just the better option.

I turned and smiled at her as we sat at a red light. "Don't you know Mommy has superpowers?"

She seemed to accept that, nodding with a wisdom beyond her years. "Cool, Mom." A few minutes later, she piped up. "Does Daddy know you have powers?"

"Uh huh," I said, figuring the less she knew, the better.

"That's so epic, Mommy."

Oh, to be six years old and think that everything supernatural was "cool." I turned up the radio and Cassie hummed along to the song on our drive home.

As I drove, I focused instead on the strange results. So far, heightened senses, healing powers, muscles—okay that part was pretty badass, even I had to admit—and some weird ability to move cars, not to mention weird premonitions and visions of a future I could change. I felt trapped between the mental powers of Phoenix and the physical powers of Wolverine and Rogue from those comics Cary left in the bathroom.

I didn't know what was going on, but I knew the first thing I needed to do was call Tracy. This energy stuff was definitely a side effect we hadn't discussed, and it scared the crap out of me.

I couldn't shake the feeling of being grateful for this new power, even if I didn't know what it was. That car would have killed Cassie— she was so small, and he was going too fast. I saw her laying on the pavement, and my heart was broken. Side effect, though it was, it had saved my daughter's life.

Don't go donning a cape and mask, Tracy had said this morning.

That was ludicrous. I was just a housewife who cooked dinner, went to the gym, and ran the kids around to events. I mean, really, Tracy was crazy if he thought I was something out of a comic book for children.

I mean, right?

Things got even weirder that evening. "Mommy, there's a delivery truck in front of our house," I heard Cassie call from outside. I was in the back of the house, carefully pulling a piping dish of chicken pot pie out of the oven.

"What?" I wiped my hands on a towel and went outside. Tracy ordered supplies online all the time, but they rarely came to our house. He was so absent-minded lately with everything going on; I just figured I'd have to go correct the mistake. What could it be this time? A crate of beakers, a supply of rubber gloves, or maybe even a hundred microscopes he'd accidentally had delivered home instead of the lab like last time?

I pushed the screen door open. Cassie was sitting in the yard surrounded by her dolls and a rainbow array of fingernail polish, a plastic doll foot in her hand that was coated in three streaks of pink polish. In the driveway, a huge moving truck, white and unmarked, idled.

"Is it for Daddy?" I asked her.

She shrugged and went back to her dolls. "They said it's for you."

"Weird," I muttered.

A round man in gray coveralls was opening the back of the truck. "I'm looking for Sam Willows?" he said to me, an eyebrow raised.

"Yeah, that's me," I said.

He shook his head. "Good god, you're a woman."

I put my hands on my hips. "How nice of you to notice," I said with no small amount of sarcasm. "And?"

He sighed. "This is a weird delivery for a woman, is all." He shoved a clipboard at me. "Sign here."

I took it and immediately noticed Bandon Industries on the yellow carbon copy sheet in front of me. "I think there has been some mistake. This must be for my husband, Tracy. He works there." I tried to shove the clipboard back at him, wondering what in the world could be so large it required a delivery truck.

"No mistake, ma'am," he said. He began cranking down the ramp on the end of the truck and yanked on a chain to his left. I heard a mechanical whir as a large, black vehicle with two ... wheels? ... slowly lowered to the cement in front of my house.

"What the heck is this?" I took a step back, my heels hitting the curb. There was no doubt it was a motorcycle, but it looked like it was from a strange science fiction film. Solid, shiny black paint coated every inch, even where the wheels were supposed to be. It had all the elements of a motorcycle, from the steering handlebars to the leather seat and even a satchel thrown over the side. Yet it was the strangest thing I had ever seen. In place of wheels, there were studded black balls in the front and back, bigger than a wheel. I couldn't imagine why they were *cylinders*. The seat was doubly strange—a spherical cage covered the black leather with a glass-like substance, though it was frosted and translucent. Crap, this was like some kind of superhero vehicle or something.

Housewives *definitely* did not drive cool motorcycles like a terror that flaps in the night!

"This has to be a mistake," I said slowly and softly. I had never seen anything like this before. I looked down at the clipboard again and saw a business card was tucked into the corner of the clip. I ripped it out and turned it over. A short note was scribed on the blank side in a neat, flowing hand: "*A small thank you for saving my life, Mrs. Willows. Please accept this prototype – it will keep you and your daughter safe from dangerous drivers like me. –K.H.*"

KH. Hitcharo. Kei Hitcharo, he said his name was. The man in the black car who almost killed my daughter.

"I can't accept this," I said to the delivery man, who was busy removing the straps on the motorcycle contraption.

"I'm sorry, ma'am, but my job is to deliver this," he said as he pulled off the last strap. "I can't take it back. You'd have to contact the company if you'd like to issue a return." He rolled the motorcycle to the curb, where it stood without any kind of kickstand, despite the spherical wheels. He pulled down the door on the back of the truck and stood there, waiting.

I looked down at the clipboard. Tracy could fix this, I decided. I already had so much to tell him, what was one more thing? I sighed and scrawled my signature across the bottom. The man handed me back the yellow portion and hopped in the front seat of the truck.

"That bike is way cooler than mine," Cassie said, and I jumped to realize she was standing right next to me. "Is that Daddy's? Where's mine?"

"It's not Daddy's, and we aren't keeping it," I said to her. "It's almost time for dinner, why don't you get your toys picked up."

"Can we just go for a ride, real quick? Please?"

I looked into my daughter's big blue eyes. I'd do anything to give her the world, but this contraption looked unsafe to me, somehow. "I don't think so."

"Where are we gonna put it?" She looked back at the white minivan.

Even the six-year-old knew it was weird to leave it out here on the sidewalk. I grabbed the handlebars, expecting it to be heavy, and found it was light as a feather, even lighter than a bicycle. Could this get any weirder? "Go push the button to open the garage for me, baby?" I was suddenly glad my heightened senses had forced me to clean the garage this week. So much for parking the van in there now.

"Okay, Mommy!" Cassie ran off into the house, abandoning her dolls in the yard.

I wheeled the super light motorcycle up the driveway as the garage door creaked open. It was hard to manage at first, but then I realized what the round wheels were for. Briefly, I thought about taking Cassie up on her request to take it out for a ride. I stepped away before I could convince myself to keep this thing. There was no way I could accept a "prototype"—an expensive one like this? No way, at all.

After all, didn't Bandon owe me something for what these chemicals had done to me? I loved Tracy too much to blame him. It was an honest mistake he left it in his car. It could very well be Tracy had these side effects, and he wouldn't have been there today to save our daughter or save Cassie's friend that was being yelled at by that awful coach. Fate had decided to give me the superhuman issues, and while I convinced myself I was the better recipient, I couldn't shake the feeling that there was a chance, a small one, Tracy said, this was permanent.

Tracy would know what to do. He would fix it. But maybe he didn't have to know about it, just yet. Maybe I'd need this motorcycle at some point.

"Come on, time for dinner," I told Cassie, and she gathered up her toys and followed me in the house. "Where's your brother, it's late."

"I saw him down at Rob's house." Cassie shrugged and pushed me aside.

"Doing what?" As if I expected her to answer me.

"Smoking," Cassie replied from the hallway.

I froze in the dining room entrance, overwhelmed by the intense smell of my pot pie, my hearing out of control. My son was doing … what?

Chapter 6

Cassie hadn't been wrong. Cary had stumbled in last night reeking of cigarette smoke and something else so pungent and earthy I had no idea what he was doing. His eyes were bloodshot, and he mumbled he'd already eaten at Rob's as he headed straight up to his room. A few minutes later Tracy had arrived home, and though I tried to talk to him about it, he was too busy asking me about Hitcharo's accident. Not only had he seen it on the news, but it was all over work.

Before I could tell him what happened, Cassie appeared for dinner. No sooner had we finished our plates than Tracy announced he had to get back to the lab. Any hope I had of discussing my new powers with him promptly flew out the window.

Becky's invite for drinks couldn't have come at a better time. With Cassie tucked into bed, I shouted to Cary I'd be back in a couple of hours, and he answered with a tired, "Yeah, whatever."

"I'm a little worried about Cary." I took a sip of the cocktail in front of me. This bloody Mary was some weird thing with a sprig of asparagus and shrimp, combined with a pearl onion and a green olive, and topped with a hot wing. I let Becky order it for me, since she always knew her way around a bar, more so since her divorce. Whatever this thing was, it was very spicy, tomato-y, and delicious as heck.

Becky took a sip of her green, salt-crusted margarita. "Forget about Cary, what did Tracy say about what happened at the gym?" She lowered her voice, despite the bar being basically empty. It was a Thursday night. We were celebrating the last day of school on a Thursday. We tried to hide our obvious exhausted motherhood behind short black dressed and heels, literally our only fancy clothes, but if someone looked close enough, they could tell by our tired eyes, messy ponytails, and crooked eyeliner.

I paused, glass lifted to my lips. "I haven't told him," I murmured around my sip. I left out the part about the motorcycle thing. It was bad enough Becky had seen everything.

Becky's glass hit the bar so hard I feared for the skinny flume. "What do you mean you haven't told him?"

"When I got home, I made dinner, and then I got this …" I bit my tongue before I had to explain the motorcycle. "I got busy. And he came home from dinner and then disappeared like he always does."

"Sam!" Becky shouted, and the couple at the next table turned and looked at us. She scooted closer to me. "Seriously, how can you forget to tell your husband, the scientist, that you can… move things with your mind?"

I downed the last of my drink, wincing at the harshness. I wasn't used to drinking. "It wasn't like that it was … like some kind of energy."

"You have to tell him." She held up her hand to the bartender and ordered two more drinks. I hoped one of them wasn't for me.

"I'm still worried about Cary," I said again. My mind kept going back to his bloodshot eyes. Was this what the crack cocaine looked like? Did smoking lead to this? I had no idea! The very thought of my innocent son getting involved with crack was unthinkable.

Becky took her drink off the napkin, something blue with a pink hue on the top this time. She slid an identical one across to me. "AMF," she said, "though the real name isn't an appropriate name for company."

I took a sip slowly, choked, and pushed it away violently, nearly toppling it. "Becky, are you trying to kill me? How much alcohol is in this?"

"You need it after the accident," was all Becky said. She leaned back with her drink in her hand and crossed her slender legs. "Now what about Cary?"

"He came home late," I ordered water from the bartender. Becky waited. "Well, I told you we got the report cards, and Cary's looking at summer school. All Fs, with a D in physical education. Cary loves PE, and he's very smart. What could be going on?"

"Did you confront him about it?"

"I couldn't, he went to his room, and then you called," I finished my water.

Becky's eyes went wide. "I thought Cary's curfew was ten?"

"It is. He's fourteen, Becky. He's never been in later than nine without calling."

"Has this happened before?"

"I—" In the last two weeks since the accident, I hadn't paid much attention to Cary. I'd been so busy with Cassie and trying to deal with what was going on with my own body. It was tough enough keeping super hearing and weird visions at bay. "I don't know," I admitted. "We haven't talked much; but he's a good kid, Becky. Do you think … maybe he's smoking that marijuana stuff? You know they said when we made it legal all the kids would have it. Or maybe it's crack cocaine or something." I bit my lip, fearing the worst. "Pastor Dave said once they get on Lucifer's lettuce, it's all downhill from there…"

Without saying a word gulped down the rest of her glass and looked at me, rolling her eyes. "Calm down, Sam. Pastor Dave is an idiot. So, what if he had a joint or two? He's a teenager. They all do that." Before she could order another drink, she shifted in her seat and froze.

I turned around to see a tall, dark, and handsome man at the other end of the bar, locking eyes with Becky. Not my forte with shaggy black hair and green eyes, a red polo shirt that barely hid bulging arms and khaki shorts that revealed heavily muscled legs—he looked like a coach or a PE teacher. Becky had the strangest taste, especially since her ex was an accountant.

It was my turn to roll my eyes at her back. I flipped a few bills out of my clutch and stood up. "Look, I'm really worried about Cary—I left him with Cassie, and I need to check on them. Think I'll get a cab."

Becky nodded, paying her drinks as well. "Well, don't check on me later," she winked as she whispered, breezing past in a beeline for Mr. Handsome at the bar.

I shook my head with a smile and pulled my phone out to call a cab. Before I had a chance to dial, I noticed a familiar number on the screen—my home phone. It was silly we even had a home phone, and we really only used it before the kids were too young for phones, and Tracy…

I answered the call, panic seizing my throat suddenly.

"Mommy?"

"Cassie?" I had put it on silent, so I didn't realize she was calling. Usually, I heard it vibrate, even with my new sensitive hearing. Was the alcohol numbing my superpowers? God, I hoped not.

Cassie's voice was high pitched and cracked, and she burst into tears. I could barely make out what she was saying. "Mommy, something's wrong with Cary. He's sleeping on the floor and shaking a lot."

"Shaking?" I nearly screeched into the phone. A few feet away, the bartender paused and glared at me.

"Yeah, and there's white stuff coming out his mouth! Mommy, please help, I'm so scared!"

"Call 9-1-1, ok, honey? I'm on my way. I'm gonna call Daddy, too. Don't touch your brother, just call 9-1-1 like we practiced, all right?" All the while I was talking, motioning for the bartender to call me a cab, pulling a pen from the bar and writing "9-1-1" on a napkin to show him. The bartender's eyes were wide as he reached for a phone behind the bar.

Cassie cried heavier, but I made out an "okay." I hung up and punched Tracy's cell into my phone.

"Everything okay?" Becky said behind me. "Who was that?"

"Something's wrong with Cary, maybe a seizure," I said to her, as the phone rang and rang in my ear. *Come on, Tracy, pick up!* My brain was screaming.

"Did you call a cab?" Becky was saying. I waved her away, nodding.

Tracy picked up on the fourth ring. "Oh, thank God!" I nearly screamed into the phone. I threw my purse over my shoulder and pushed out the door, leaving Becky to her own devices. "Tracy, Cassie called me. Cary's having a seizure of some kind."

"What? He doesn't have seizures! Did she call 9-1-1?" Tracy's yell was filled with alarm. I heard a clink in the background as I paced in front of the bar, pleading for the cab to hurry.

"I told her to. I called a cab. I'm leaving the bar now."

I should have never come here – I should have never left them alone. I choked back a sob. My baby!

"I'm leaving work now. I'll meet you at home. Call 9-1-1, too, just in case."

"I will."

A cab pulled up at the curb then, and I hopped in the back seat. I gave my address, told him my son was sick, and it was an emergency. The cabbie gunned it so hard I fell back against the seat, dropping my cell.

I reached for it, and another flash floated in front of my vision before I could wrap my hand around the phone. Cary was laying on the floor in the living room of my house, blood running from his nose, white foam dripping from his lips. His hands curled into claws as they wrapped around his chest in a convulsion. Cassie was screaming, tears streaming down her cheeks as the seizure subsided. Tracy was there, too, yelling, "Son! Son, stay with us. The ambulance is on its way!"

The vision faded as quickly as my son's chest stopped rising. I snatched my phone from the floorboard and punched in three numbers.

"Nine-one-one, what's your emergency?"

"I left my six-year-old home with my son, and she told me he's having seizures! Send someone to my house now. He's dying!"

Chapter 7

"I don't understand, what kind of drugs would do this?" I demanded of the doctor, while Tracy paced the pristine hospital floor. "My son doesn't do drugs. He's never touched them in his life!"

"The good news is, we were able to fill his lungs with air and get him to a detox unit," the doctor said, flipping through the notepad in his hand. "We don't know what this drug is, but in my opinion, it's something laced with methamphetamines. A very high dosage."

Tracy paused and slumped into a nearby chair, his head in his hands. "My son, my son," he whimpered. Cassie was on the chair next to him. She got up and crawled into his lap. "Daddy? What's wrong with Cary?"

"Will he be okay?" I asked the doctor, twisting my hands in front of me.

The doctor glanced at Cassie, then took my elbow and escorted me a few feet away. "We don't know yet," he said. "If he makes it through the night, maybe."

"'Maybe'?" I shouted at him. "You mean my son is going to…."

The doctor nodded, shushing me. "You need to be prepared. This is a very serious overdose, and it's going to be touch and go all night."

With that, he turned and walked down the hallway, disappearing around the corner.

I fought back the urge to cry. The images ingrained in my brain were already too overwhelming. My vision had come true, and with all my powers I wasn't there to stop it—my son had died on my living room floor, and Tracy and I had been powerless to stop it. The paramedics had arrived within minutes, and all I could do was stand there, frozen, watching the constant compressions and mouth to mouth as they tried to save my first born.

I plopped down heavily onto the seat next to Tracy, hugging myself and rocking. I knew Cary had been at his friend Ron's house earlier that day. Did Ron give him drugs? My fists curled around the worn wooden edges of the chair arms. If Ron was giving my son drugs, I would kill him with my bare hands.

Cassie's warm hand wrapped about mine. "Mommy, is Cary gonna be okay?"

I turned to her. I was so livid I couldn't even answer. I wanted to assure her, bundle her in my arms, and tell her it was all right. She was only six for God's sake; she shouldn't have to witness any of this!

I squeezed Cassie's hand and stood up. "He's going to be fine, honey." She seemed to accept it and released my hand, still clinging to Tracy's folded arms. I turned away from my little family and started toward the ER exit.

"Where are you going?" Tracy looked up at me. He hadn't cried, but his face was filled with rage as much as mine must have been.

"To fix this." I left my husband and daughter outside my son's hospital room. I'm sure watching me go with shock on their faces. I didn't look back.

I knew where to start, and it was with Cary's friend. I would find who did this to my son and take care of it.

I couldn't sit by and let this happen to anyone else's baby.

My first stop was home. I didn't have a plan for what I was going to, but I ran over a few scenarios in my head on the drive back. Safe ones, of course. Go talk to Ron, convince him to tell me where he got the drugs, call the police. It'd be over and done, and I could go back to the hospital. Maybe, just maybe, Cary would be awake, and I could tell him justice would be served.

I got back to my house, parked, and walked down to Ron's. I paused just short of his house. He was a fifteen-year-old kid, and his parents would probably be home. I couldn't just bust in there like some kind of vigilante, right? As I got closer, I could see no cars in the driveway even this late of an hour, close to midnight, but the light at the end of the house was on.

I froze at the end of the driveway. Crapola. I couldn't interrogate someone—I didn't even have the foggiest notion how, anyway—looking like this. I was still dressed in my black dress from the bar and wearing heels. I was in no condition to go kicking anyone's behind.

My resolve was fading quickly as I trudged back to my own house. I was a housewife with weird glimpses of the future and some heightened senses with wicked sweet muscles. I could use a weird purple energy I didn't even know how it worked. I was very far from someone powerful and in a different world from badass altogether. God, the height of my physical knowledge was some Zumba steps from the gym.

"Worst superhero, ever, Sam," I muttered as I let myself into the house. I stopped on the doorstep, glancing over at the garage door. I didn't even tell Tracy about the motorcycle yet—everything had been such a swirl of chaos lately. But there it sat, quietly waiting, silently biding its time.

I slammed the door behind me and fled to the bedroom. What I was about to do was dangerous, terrifying, but the thought of it was exciting and filled me with adrenaline. I donned the darkest outfit I had —black yoga pants, a long-sleeved Under Armor shirt of Tracy's—and zipped up my only pair of calf-high boots without a heel. Deep in the closet, I found Tracy's black skull cap, from that one time he'd tried hunting a decade ago. I dusted it off and tucked my blonde hair under it as well as I could.

As soon as the garage door opened, I was breathing hard, and my heart was beating so fast I couldn't think straight. It was so late. I didn't have to worry about the neighbors seeing me and the motorcycle. This was the suburbs, which meant lights out by eight at night for most of the hard-working residents. I also knew there was an alley that ran behind the houses on this block, exclusively used for garbage pickup, some nonsense the Neighborhood Association had agreed on years ago about keeping curbs clean. I was particularly thankful for the nonsense right now.

I wheeled the motorcycle, still reveling in how light it was, to the end of the block opposite Ron's house. The cage opened easy enough with a latch, but as I threw my leg over the side, I realized I had no idea how to start it. I looked around on the dash, filled with the normal dials. Finally, I found a red button inside a plastic lid. I flipped up the lid and pushed it. The engine roared to life, but it was so quiet I had to press my head to the engine to figure out if it was running.

My father had a collection of bikes when I was a kid, so riding it was no problem. I gunned the gas and put my foot up. The bike took off with only a tiny bit of throttle, and I zoomed around the block to the alley.

Ron's light was still on, so I parked the bike and jumped out of the plastic cage, praying they were stupid enough to leave their back door unlocked. Sure enough, the screen opened easily, and I let myself into their kitchen. Ron's parents were accountants and friends of Becky's ex, so I'd been to quite a few cocktail parties over the year and knew the layout of the house quite well. The kitchen led into the living room, and to the left was a hallway where the three bedrooms and bathroom stood.

I felt comical, awkward, and strange, creeping around a dark house. My shin hit a chair at the dining room table that was sticking out too far from the table, and I winced, clapping my hands to my lips to avoid crying out. I probed the hallway with my sensitive hearing, and I could make out the muffled sounds of thrumming bass filled music, the same kind Cary listened to. It was so muffled I knew it wasn't just behind a closed door, but likely pounding out of headphones.

Oh, my goodness, this was too perfect. I pulled the ski cap down over my face and let my hearing guide me down the hallway to Ron's door, the last on the right. The vision of Cary's near death was still vivid in my mind.

I thought about kicking the door open but realized it would make too much noise, and I didn't even know if anyone else was there. Instead, I turned the knob slowly and opened the door.

Ron sat at his desk with his back to the door, large red wireless headphones plastered to his ears. He was completely oblivious to my entrance, his head bobbing up and down to the rhythm.

I stood in the doorway for what seemed like forever. I hadn't got this far in my plan. My hands were tingling, and I looked down to see the purple energy on my fingertips, the adrenaline flooding my veins. I knew it wouldn't work without energy in the room, without motion, and there wasn't any I could see. I flexed my fingers and wished I had something threatening, like a knife or something, so I could make sure Ron wasn't lying to me.

What? No! I wasn't out to hurt him. *A knife? Sam, what the baby Jesus are you thinking? Just ask him and get the heck back to the motorcycle!*

To my surprise, a blunt butter knife materialized into my hand. It was purple like the energy, with tendrils of purple smoke around it. I closed my fist around it and felt the weight of it in my hand. This was too weird—another power to add to the list. How could I ever tell Tracy about this one? *Sam, what are you doing?* I quieted that little voice and snuck up behind Ron, pressing the knife to his neck, and praying he wouldn't call my bluff on it being just a materialized butter knife.

"Ahh!" Ron cried out, yanking the headphones off his ears, and pushing back from the desk.

"Tell me where you got the drugs," I said softly, trying to make my voice sound as graveled as possible.

"What? Who the fuck are you?"

"The drugs you gave my ... that boy, Cary. Where did you get them?"

"I have no idea what you're...."

I pressed the knife a little harder, knowing it wouldn't cut him. "I don't have time for this!" I could feel him shaking underneath me, and I knew it was working.

"Okay, okay, okay." His voice squeaked higher than Cassie's. "I'm sorry, I'm sorry! It was our first time. He swore it was just a little pot. He swore! We just wanted to have a little fun!"

"Who!"

"Michael! I only know his name is Michael!"

"Where can I find him?"

"I don't know, okay? It was dark!"

I pressed the butter knife as hard as I could. "Tell me!" My nostrils filled with a pungent smell that rivaled the one in my garage a few days ago. I looked down and saw the lap of his pajama pants dark with wetness.

"You little shit," I said, nearly gasping when I swore, "you want me to tell your mommy you pissed your pants?"

"Union Avenue! It's apartment four-oh-five! Union Ave! Oh, God, please don't kill me!"

I laughed, hoping it didn't give away my identity. I pulled the knife away, snapping my fingers as it dematerialized. *Cool,* I thought, careful not to say it out loud. *I could get used to this!*

"Wait—"

I slammed the door behind me, ripped the hat off my head, and raced out the back door, breathing heavy.

Oh God, oh God, oh God. Crapola. Did he know it was me? Oh God!

I spun the bike out of the alley, throwing up gravel behind me, and drove a few blocks away to the empty playground, across from Cassie's school. It was still pitch black, normally I would have been frightened, but everything around me was so *alive.* I could hear the grass growing, the crickets booming in my ears, and even my eyesight was keener than normal. I pulled my cell out and dialed the police station.

"Non-emergency, how can I help you?" a tired, bored female voice answered.

"Yes, my son was given drugs that almost killed him, and I'd like to report the drug dealer's location."

"Ma'am, how do you know he's a drug dealer?"

"I…" Oh, crapola, I couldn't tell them I just terrified a fifteen-year-old kid into giving me that information. I also wasn't stupid; I knew they'd trace my call. I'd seen enough TV to know that. "His name is Michael, at four-oh-five Union Ave." I hung up and turned my phone off. I was worried about Tracy and Cassie, but the worst thing that could happen would be Tracy calling me right now.

I should have parked the motorcycle back in my garage and changed my clothes. I should have headed back to the hospital and sat beside my unconscious son. I should have done a million other things besides what I did—I started the bike and raced out of the playground toward downtown.

Union was easy to find. It was over the railroad tracks behind the train station, just under the bridge for sixteenth street. It was a seedy part of town, with three-story apartments lining the street which were often in the news for drug busts. I could park under the bridge and use my super hearing to know when the cops arrived, and make sure 'Michael' got what was coming to him. Dealing deadly drugs to kids—to my son—how dare he? Cary would get a strong tongue lashing when he woke up, but for now, I just had to stop this from happening again, happening to someone else's baby.

I waited under the bridge for so long. I turned my phone back on to check the time. It was after two in the morning, and I was exhausted. I couldn't see the apartment from where I was perched, but it had been over an hour since I left Ron's, and still no sirens in the distance, flashing lights, or even sounds of a battering ram smashing the drug dealer's door down. I had no idea if they used a battering ram, but it seemed appropriate.

I dialed the non-emergency number once more.

"Hi, I called about the drug dealer?"

"Ma'am, we don't just send people out to random addresses. I've notified an officer in the area and—"

"It's a bad part of town; he's obviously a drug dealer!"

"I'll send a uniformed officer over there in the morning," the voice said, and the line went dead.

I stared at my phone as "call ended" blared up at me. She'd hung up on me! Me, going to great lengths for doing all I had done for my son. What was this world coming to?

It was a punch in the gut that nearly took my breath away when I realized I could be arrested, and spend several years in jail, for what I had done. Was it worth it?

Who would find out? I was wearing a mask, I left no trace of a weapon, and Ron was so terrified he had no idea who I was really was.

I shut the bike off and dismounted. It was then I realized that the cops weren't coming.

There was no justice for Cary, or the countless other children this guy had given drugs to.

I had to handle this myself.

Chapter 8

I paused outside the apartment. What exactly was I going to do? My face was securely hidden, but I was shaking. Terrified, I realized I didn't know anything about drug dealers. Did they really have guns? I wasn't sure what I could do, but if I could stop a car and materialize weapons with a thought, then I could take out a couple of drug dealers. As a last thought, a green garden hose lay abandoned on the front walk. I picked it up, wrapping it around my shoulder.

As I crept up the front walk, the front of the apartment was dark, but my super hearing detected at least three voices inside. My hand trembled around the garden hose, but I couldn't stop thinking about my son, lying in the hospital bed, a tube down his throat and his precious eyes closed. The machines were keeping him alive in his coma until the doctor could figure out what exactly was in his system.

It hit me like a ton of bricks that my son could be *dead* right now.

Dead, and no one cared. The cops didn't care. They weren't coming.

It was up to me.

I took a deep breath and turned the front door handle. To my surprise, the door was unlocked. I shook my head. What kind of drug dealer left their door open?

The stupid kind that gives drugs to kids, I realized.

I was embarking on something that would probably land me in jail, but I didn't care.

For Cary! The voice in my brain shouted.

I burst through the door, the purple energy tingling at my fingertips. I looked down to see a knife, no bigger than a large steak knife, materialize in one hand, and a small, absolutely weightless cast iron skillet in the other. Like, a full sized one. I flipped it in my hand and swallowed a laugh.

I shrugged. I was running with it. Inside the apartment was a hallway, with no one in sight, but I could hear raucous voices in the other room, and blaring rap music. My blood boiled; they dared have a party after nearly killing my son? Of course, they probably didn't know about Cary, but I was still livid. My heart beat so fast I felt it would burst from my chest.

I crept down the hallway slowly, swirling the knives in my hand, hoisting the hose higher on my shoulder. The voices grew louder as the hallway opened into the kitchen and beyond it, I could see partially into the living room. Two men in baseball caps were slumped on tattered leather recliners, their backs to me. I paused, knowing any minute they would turn and see me. I focused my hearing and could make out four distinct voices.

Four! What are you thinking, Sam? You're going to take down four grown men—you, five-foot-three, hundred and fifty pounds, take them down?

I had taken down a car. Four men were nothing.

I jumped into the living room, and the two men leapt to their feet, but their motions were slowed.

"Who the hell are you?" One of them shouted. He brandished a rainbow-colored vape in his hand and exhaled as he talked, nearly filling the room with a huge cloud of nicotine vapor.

"What the—" yelled the other man by the recliner.

Two more were huddled around a coffee table in the middle of the room that was spread with more drugs than I had ever seen on any cop shows. White piles that looked like powdered sugar, and green piles of some kind of herb, next to small crystals packaged neatly in baggies next to three different scales, along with a stack of charred, broken light bulbs were scattered on the table.

They looked at up me but made no motion to move. One of them chuckled around a mod in his mouth. "All right, who called the stripper?" He laughed, turning back to the white powder on one of the scales.

On the love seat behind them, a young girl about Cary's age lay motionless, in nothing but a tube top and very high shorts, her feet and legs bare. Her arm was thrown out to her side, and I could clearly make out a dozen track marks from needles.

A TV with rabbit ears crackled in the background.

"Which one of you is Michael?" I yelled, trying to disguise my voice but failing horribly.

"Who wants to know?" The man in the blue baseball hat to my right threw his vape into the leather recliner and flipped a silver switchblade into his hand.

"Me. I'm your worst nightmare!" I almost wanted to laugh. Why would I say such a thing?

The smirk behind my mask disappeared immediately.

"I think you picked the wrong party, bitch!" He advanced on me.

I didn't know what to do, but I knew freezing wouldn't be ideal. I remembered a side step from Zumba and tucked my left leg behind the right. He lunged at me, and I realized he must have been high, because he stumbled, and his knife dug straight into the closet door behind me. While he was yanking on his knife, I smacked him on the head with the frying pan, then as if the muscles in my arms took over with their own brain, I reached down and stabbed him in the back of the knee with the energy knife, and he fell to the floor with a scream. The knife de-materialized as soon as he touched it, but I had clearly done damage with it as I saw the back of his jean-clad knee sport a dark red stain. I snapped my fingers, and the pan disappeared as well.

"How cute, you brought a knife to a gun fight." Baseball Cap Two said. I noticed he had a gun in his hand, and I swallowed hard, trying not to panic. To my left, the two men at the coffee table struggled to stand but were having a tough time. I focused on the gun. If I could use the energy of the car, I could use it from the gun.

If I was fast enough not to get shot, that was.

I heard the click of the trigger and realized I had no time to waste. Completely weaponless now, I threw my hands out to stop the bullet, flinging the hose into my hand as I did so. The bullet glowed purple, and I managed to shove it at the closet door, narrowly missing Baseball Cap One, who was still screaming at the top of his lungs and clutching his knee.

The two men from the table were finally closing in on me fast. I felt their hands dig into my left arm and tear at my shirt.

The energy from the bullet was, surprisingly, ten times more active than the car had been. I pulled it toward me and felt the intense sensation of everything in the room slowing down. I blinked and saw everyone was frozen. Frozen, or was I moving too fast? Their mouths were open, and everyone was completely still, cemented where they stood. I grabbed one end the hose and rushed around them, kicking the table over and hitting the recliner with my shin. White power, green buds, and clear crystals flew all over the room like sick party favors.

Once the hose was wrapped around all three of them, I tied it tight into a fisherman's knot like Dad had taught me when I was little. As soon as I released the hose, the energy dissipated as fast as it had come. They re-animated, and the room filled with a din of profanities. Baseball Cap Two was screaming so hard at me that spittle flew from his mouth.

In the distance, I could finally hear sirens. Better late than never. "This is what you get when you sell drugs to kids," I barked harshly.

The girl on the couch was stirring, her red-rimmed eyes barely open. "Wha … wha's goin' on?" She slurred, struggling to sit up.

I put my arm under her and helped her stand. The three tied-together men and the one stabbed in the knee were blocking our access to the front door, so we escaped out the back sliding door. "What's your name, honey?"

"Leslie," she mumbled, rubbing her already smeared mascara on her face.

"Come on, hon, let's get you somewhere safe."

"Where's my…?"

I could barely understand her. "Never again, you understand?" I demanded, "I bet you have parents who are worried about you some-where when you're here doing the smack." She nodded at me and started sobbing. It was a pitiful moan, and my heart broke for her. This poor teenager, I wondered what her mother would think.

She half limped, half walked with me dragging her, all the way around to the front of the two-story apartment building. I left her sitting on the curb just outside the apartment, with the sirens wailing so loud, I knew I didn't have much time.

I jumped on my bike parked next to the bushes and gunned the throttle. The fewer people who knew I was here, the better.

On my way back to my house, I realized it might have been a mistake to rescue the girl. Part of me hoped she was too high to remember anything about me, especially since I'd made no effort to disguise my voice at that point.

Risky, you were risky.

I urged it to shut up as I urged the throttle faster down the block and whizzed across town faster than I had gone to druggie central.

Too late, I spotted Tracy's black car in the driveway.

As the sun poked over the hills behind my house, I could just make out the outline of my husband standing on the front porch. His arms crossed over his chest.

Busted.

Chapter 9

"Sam, what were you thinking?" Tracy's voice was so loud I cringed.

I pulled the ski mask off my head and threw it on the table. "You'll wake Cassie," I said softly. "You know she's had a hard night."

"She's had a hard night?" He pulled a chair out and plopped down angrily. "What the hell have you been doing? Running around at night, on a motorcycle? Where did you get that, by the way?"

"I tried to tell you…" For all my badassness, why did I feel like I wanted to cry?

"No, you didn't."

"Remember when Cassie almost got hit by the car yesterday?" I paused as he glared at me. "Well, I didn't tell you the car was owned by Kai Hitcharo."

He sucked in a breath and leaned back. "Oh my God, Sam. Do you know who he is?"

I shrugged. "Someone with a powerful prototype motorcycle that is apparently bulletproof with balls for wheels?"

"He's the head of engineering – he makes the tanks we supply to the military and the new stealthy uniforms…."

"Wait, the what?" My arm was aching, so I clutched it toward me.

"Forget I said anything." Tracy leapt to his feet. "Sam, you're bleeding! Wait here." He disappeared into the bathroom around the corner.

I looked down. A gash about four inches long, flayed fabric of my shirt open around it, was bleeding profusely, dripping onto my pants and a few drops rolling to the white linoleum of the kitchen floor. I watched without any surprise as the gash slowly closed of its own will, leaving only a pink scar behind.

Tracy reappeared a minute later with the first aid kit. "What the … oh, I forgot." He dropped the kit on the table.

"There's blood everywhere," I whispered. "What will the kids think if they see this?"

"Listen to you," his voice was low, restrained. I knew he wanted to say something else. He sighed and pulled a bandage from the kit. "At least let me wrap it, so it doesn't get infected, all right?"

I let him. In his frustration, he wound it around so tight I thought it would cut off my circulation.

"Ow!"

"'Ow' she says," Tracy mocked me, "after running around like a goddamn superhero who could have gotten killed!"

"No one else's baby will be hurt." I declared matter-of-factly. I looked him directly in the eye.

He sighed and took the seat next to me. "Seriously, Sam, what if you'd been hurt?"

"Well, I have this new side effect...."

"Yeah, you said something about it with the car, but I was on my way out the door. Show me?"

"I can't," I said, leaning back, and hugging my arm. It was throbbing painfully now. Why didn't it just heal like everything else did? "Just before the gun went off, I was able to absorb its energy, I think...."

"Sam! There was a *gun?*"

"Yeah," I said, looking around the room at everything but him. "Don't worry though. I used the energy to tie up the drug dealers. With a garden hose."

"Drug dealers?" Tracy pressed his hand to his temple. "You tied them up? With a hose? And there was more than one?"

"Four," I told him, then relayed what happened at the apartment.

"Oh my God. Sam, this is crazy." Tracy buried his head in his folded arms on the table. He turned and looked up at me. "You could have been killed."

"Don't worry. I was armed."

"With what, a spatula?"

"No, actual knives," I couldn't help but get excited, "like I can just snap my fingers and they appear."

"But you can't show me?"

"No, I think I have to be stressed or something—it only happens when something bad is about to happen."

Tracy nodded at me, leaning back in the chair now. "So, kinetic potential energy manipulation and manifestation," he said softly, shaking his head. "Jesus, what else is going to happen now?"

"I could get massive boobs like Jean Grey," I said with a smile.

"How do you know who that is?" He glared at me, but a smile poked at the edge of his lips.

"I watch TV!"

"I suppose that's how you knew how to fight drug dealers, too? From TV?"

I shrugged. "I love crime dramas."

"This is ridiculous, Sam." He pinched his nose with two fingers.

"How's Cary?" I was almost afraid to ask, though his presence here meant there was at least some good news.

Tracy ran a hand through his hair and pulled his glasses off, throwing them on the table in front of him. "He's still under," he said, "the doc told me to take Cassie home, she was exhausted." He slid his glasses back on and glanced at his watch. "Speaking of which, I have to be at the lab in four hours. I need to catch some shut eye." He pushed back from the table and stood, holding out his hand to me. "Coming to bed, super wife?"

I glared at him. "You should be proud of me. I took a drug dealer—and three accomplices—off the street!"

"You're going to get yourself killed." He shook his head.

"After tonight, I've had enough action, I think."

He nodded. "Good. Tomorrow, call Mr. Hitcharo and return that bike. I want it out of my garage before anyone at Bandon figures out it's here."

I frowned. "Really? It's so much fun to ride."

Tracy looked at me over his glasses. "Yes."

"Okay," I lied, knowing full well I'd hide it before I'd give it back. What woman didn't want a bulletproof badass motorcycle?

I followed him to bed, hoping I wouldn't have to use it again. I'd had enough excitement, and injury, to last a lifetime.

Tracy let Cassie and I sleep when he rolled out to work the next morning. A few hours after he left, I got a phone call. Cary was awake and asking for me.

I called Becky to arrange to drop Cassie off—I knew she was too young to handle the stress of the hospital again. Becky asked how Cary was, and I decided to give her the details, leaving out drug overdose. Amazingly enough, she didn't even question it. Becky was quick to agree to watch Cassie, mentioning Alex would be home from his dad's that afternoon.

I got Cassie out of bed, still groggy from her late night, put her in the bath and made her breakfast. She chattered over scrambled eggs about Cary, hoping he'd be awake.

"You're going to hang out with Alex for a while," I told her as I cleaned up the dishes.

"Yay!" she said, but immediately frowned. "Really? I want to see Cary, Mommy. Is he okay?"

"He's awake, honey, but super tired. I'll take you over in about an hour, okay?"

She seemed to accept that and scuttled off to retrieve toys to show Alex.

I rolled up to Becky's just over an hour later, and she was still dressed in her robe, Alex clinging to her leg. She came out to the car and took Cassie's hand. "You ready for some SpongeBob?"

"Yes, Aunt Becky! I love SpongeBob!" Cassie and Alex took off toward the house.

"So, I'll be back in a couple of hours?" I told Becky.

She leaned in the open window. "Yeah, whatever, just like me know, 'kay?"

"Okay. Thanks, Becky."

"Anytime."

"Sam! What did you do to your arm?"

I pulled my shirt sleeve down over the bandage, which I knew by this point I didn't even need. "Didn't see a knife in the sink while I was doing the dishes," I said, trying to sound nonchalant about it.

Becky narrowed her eyes at me, crossing her arms. "Really? Or more purple energy stuff?"

"Nothing," I said, and I pushed the button to roll up the window. "See you this afternoon!" I threw the van in reverse and peeled out of her driveway before she could interrogate me any further.

At the hospital, Cary was propped up against a half-dozen pillows, eating a plate of Jell-O, chicken mash, and rice with gusto. He waved when I came in. The TV, hanging on a white bracket by the bed, was on some news channel showing the latest crime in the area. The volume was turned down nearly all the way, but I could clearly hear the weather report with my enhanced hearing. A nurse in blue scrubs was busy taking his blood pressure and smiled at me as I shut the door.

I waved back at Cary. "Almost done," the nurse said, taking his temperature and putting the thermometer in her cart. She wheeled it past me. "He's still tired," she whispered to me, "so try not to upset him, okay?"

"Okay," I agreed.

Once the nurse was gone, I pulled up the crimson armed chair next to the bed. Cary finished his plate and pushed the wheeled tray aside. He looked at me, frowning. "Mom…."

I patted his IV-laden arm. "It's okay, Cary."

He put his hand over mine. "Mom, I'm so sorry. Ron and I, we didn't know … we were … oh, shit. I'm so stupid, Mom."

"How long have you been doing this?"

"Just that one time," he said, looking down at his hands. "I was so upset about the grades. I knew you and Dad would be angry with me. I just didn't want to come home. And Ron had this joint. I figured one time wouldn't hurt … Are you mad, Mom?"

"No, son," I said, "just…"

"Disappointed?"

"Yes."

"I'll never touch drugs again, Mom. That was horrible. I really thought I was going to die. I don't ever want to feel that way again. How's Cassie?"

"You scared her, but she'll be fine," I said, "she's at Becky's now."

Cary nodded. "I hope she can come later."

"She really wants to. Dad, too," I said.

He glanced at the TV, then reached up and turned the little volume wheel on the side. "Check this out, Mom, I saw this earlier. Look what someone did down on Union."

Before I could even look at the TV, I heard the report loud and clear with my new hearing. I tried to keep my face straight.

"We're here on the scene of a bizarre assault," an Asian woman was saying into her wide microphone. She put her finger to her ear. "Larry, are you seeing this?"

"I am," said Larry from the studio. "What is going on, Amanda?"

"From where I'm standing, Larry, it looks like one of the biggest drug busts this county has ever seen. We're hearing a report there was a prostitution ring being run from this very location," the reported said, taking a few steps toward the wide-open door.

Prostitution ring? I had no idea about that, but I was now doubly glad I had done what I did.

The broadcaster continued. "As you can see, Larry, this is where the attacker smashed open the front door, where they apparently tied up the victims with a garden hose."

"Can you believe that, Mom?" Cary said, staring at me in shock. "Someone just busted in and tied up those guys. So cool!"

"It's not cool to hurt people," I told him sternly, fighting off a smile as hard as I could. "Whoever did this must have been very angry, but it's not okay to hurt anyone."

Cary peered at me. "How did you know anyone was hurt?"

I blinked. "Um, I…"

"Was anyone hurt, Amanda?" Larry was asking.

"Well, we have a report one of the victims was stabbed, and neighbors reported a shot fired, but other than that, the details are still unclear."

Larry gave a low whistle. "I hate to say it, but it sounds like some justice was served here."

I grinned, while Cary was still glued to the screen. *Of course, it was.*

Amanda was nodding, her voice emotionless. She pressed her ear again. "Larry, we have a witness on scene here, a Miss Leslie Whitcomb." The camera panned, following Amanda to the right, and the edges of an ambulance came into view. "Leslie? Tell us what happened here last night?"

I gasped as I saw Leslie, the girl I had wrapped my arm around, huddled in a gray paramedic blanket, still shaking as she was early this morning. "I don't exactly know what happened," she said, rocking slightly, her speech still slurred. "I remember someone helping me, but not what they looked like or anything. He was super-fast though, like a —*beep!*—Batman or some—*beep!*" she shrugged. "Wearing a mask and—beep!"

Cary laughed a little when they bleeped out the swearing.

The reporter looked at the camera. "Well, there you have it, Larry, this terrible assault at least ends in a happy story, with the rescue of Miss Leslie Whitcomb and nearly a hundred thousand dollars in drugs seized. The police are reporting this as one of the biggest drug seizures in the last ten years."

The camera focused on Larry at the news desk. "What an amazing story folks. And to think, we have some masked avenger on the loose. State police are asking any resident with information on this vigilante to call…."

I reached around Cary and dialed the volume down. "That's enough of that."

Cary was eyeing me. "You still didn't tell me how you knew they were hurt, Mom."

"I heard it on the radio on the way over," I said, and realized my stomach was rumbling. In my haste to get Cassie out the door, I realized I'd skipped breakfast. I stood and pushed the chair away. "I'm gonna go find some food in the cafeteria, do you want anything?"

Cary narrowed his eyes at me, but then his face softened. "A Coke, Mom?"

"Sure thing, Son."

No sooner had I left the hospital room than my cell rang. I pulled it out of my purse, and seeing it was Tracy, answered as soon as I could.

"Have you seen the news?"

"Yeah."

"Jesus, Sam."

"Well…."

"Look, I have good news. Are you at the hospital?"

"Yeah, I was just headed to the cafeteria. Why?"

"I'm in the parking garage. Meet me out here."

Shady, I thought, then dismissed it. It was just Tracy, after all. "Okay." I rounded the corner, away from the cafeteria toward the elevator that led down to the parking garage under the hospital.

A thought jumped into my brain suddenly. "Do you have the anti-dote?" The elevator doors swung open, revealing three doctors, a nurse, and an elderly gentleman hitched over a cane. I stepped in.

"*Maybe,*" he teased me. "I'll see you in a minute, yeah?"

The doctors and nurse got off on the second floor, the older gentleman at reception. No sooner had the doors whizzed open on the parking garage than I skipped forward into the dimly lit concrete. The lot wasn't empty this late in the afternoon, but it was after five, and most of the regular staff had gone home. The garage hid most of the bright summer light, and we were shrouded in just dim bulbs from the ceiling.

At the far end of the lot, Tracy leaned against the trunk of his rental car, looking as dashing as the day I married him. In another life, he could have been the straight version of Captain Jack Harkness, a sexy time traveler I always loved from Cary's favorite TV show.

Tracy held a vial between two fingers and smirked at me.

I broke into a jog, snatched it from him and held it up to view the pale purple liquid against the fluorescent lights. It glimmered, shimmering like the energy I could invoke from my fingertips. Would this really take away my sense of smell, my hearing? The ability to heal at a moment's notice? And what about my energy powers and premonitions? As much as I hated the latter, they had come in handy and saved both my children.

From the back of my mind, I recalled a quote: with great power comes great responsibility. I didn't know who said that; I only vaguely recalled it from one of Cary's comic books. Whoever said it, it was the truest statement of them all. If taking this antidote meant I'd never be able to save anyone ever again, well, did I really want it after all?

"Well?" Tracy asked expectantly. "Are you going to take it?"

Instead of answering, I tossed the vial high in the air.

"Sam, no!" He lunged forward, hands out in front of him.

"Relax!" I shot a tendril of energy forward and caught the vial, pulling it safely into my hands again. I shoved it in my pocket.

Tracy steadied himself against the car. "What are you doing?"

"I'll take it … eventually," I told him, turning toward my monstrous SUV, parked a few spaces down. "But for now, there's someone else's baby that could be laying in that hospital bed just like ours is, and I'll be damned if I'm going to let anyone else get away with dealing drugs to them ever again."

Tracy's hand reached for my shoulder, and he spun me around. "So that's it, you're just going to become a vigilante, now? What on God's green Earth are you thinking, Sam? You think you can just troll the streets at night, looking for bad guys?"

"Yes." I chuckled and pulled my black ski cap out of my pocket and pulled it tight over my curly blonde head. "You can call me Super Sam."

ABOUT REBEKAH DODSON

Rebekah Dodson is a prolific word weaver of romance, fantasy, and science fiction novels. Her works include the series Postcards from Paris, The Surrogate, The Curse of Lanval series, several stand-alone novels, and her upcoming YA novel, Clock City. She has been writing her whole life, with her first published work of historical fiction with 4H Clubs of America at the age of 12, and poetry at the age of 16 with the National Poetry Society. With an extensive academic background including education, history, psychology, and English, she currently works as a college professor by day and a writer by night.

You can visit her website or follow her on social media for more info.
https://rebekahdodson.com/

facebook.com/realrebekahdodson

twitter.com/AuthorRDodson

instagram.com/author_rdodson

TRAVESTY

BY K. MATT

A slow day at the comic shop was all it took for chaos to stroll on in. The shop wasn't even fully staffed that day. Add to that the fact that nobody had come in since ten that morning… Leo had checked the sign about ten times to confirm that they were, in fact, open. It was just him and Travis for the day, it seemed. He almost wished he had been dog sitting for that one family again, with the most rancid-smelling dog food he'd ever encountered. The last time that happened, they'd all made a bet that Travis wouldn't eat it. Not only had their coworker done it, but he managed to keep from vomiting afterward. They had all lost twenty dollars each that day, but it was well worth it.

For the time being, he switched on the TV in the corner just to the back-left of the counter. Might as well just see if there was something on. At that hour, there was probably some cheesy soap opera on. If nothing else, that might be good for a laugh.

But as it turned out, there was nothing like that on. No, it was just an infomercial. Something about some brand-new anti-aging method that would make doctors hate this single mom from Peoria or something. Ugh, did an infomercial and a clickbait article have a baby or something? He rolled his eyes hard enough that it almost hurt, but with nothing better to do, he kept watching this train wreck.

"So, what's goin' on?" asked a voice.

He looked over to see Travis walking out of the room the shop had specifically for manga, anime, and related merchandise, a finger between two pages of his current reading material to keep his place. Leo couldn't help but notice that it was one of the most recent adaptations of *Journey to the West*. Travis was one of his more unusual coworkers, at that; his hair was what many would consider too long, extending past his ankles while down. His DNA was severely altered, giving him a long monkey-like tail and feet with opposable toes. But strangest of all was the regenerative factor. The guy could recover from just about anything, from what they'd all seen.

Leo spread his hands, gesturing to the nothing going on around them. "What do you think's going on, Trav? Still no customers. And we've still got six hours on the clock."

Travis let out a whistle. "All that, huh?"

"Yep."

"Well, damn..."

Travis hopped up on the counter, sitting cross-legged. His tail twitched a bit, as he returned to his reading.

"Ugh...almost wish someone would come by and rob the place," Leo sighed after a few minutes. "At least that'd inject a little life into our day."

The half-monkey raised a thick eyebrow, glancing over his shoulder to Leo. "Dude, are you high?" he asked. "Who in their right mind wants that?"

Leo rubbed the back of his neck. "It's not like they'd succeed! I mean, not if we sic you on 'em."

Travis just laughed. "You're kiddin', right? I'm the first one they'd point a gun at!"

"You're also the closest thing here to one of the heroes in these books we sell," he replied. "And that's kind of in these guy's wheelhouse: stopping people like that!"

Realizing that he wasn't likely to finish reading while this conversation went on, Travis grabbed an ad for a locally-created comic series, slipping the postcard into the book and keeping his attention fully on Leo. His tail quirked somewhat, and he crossed his arms.

"I'm still pretty sure I'm not qualified for that kind of thing..."

It was then that a smirk crossed Leo's face. He rubbed the scruff on his chin, his dark eyes lighting up.

"...Are you sure?" he asked.

Travis narrowed his green eyes at him. "What're you thinking here, Juarez?" he asked.

Leo's grin widened, as he poked a finger into Travis's chest. "You think you'd suck at being a hero. I think you're wrong. So, Travis Isaac Malone...I hereby officially dare you to be a superhero! Like, costume and everything! I mean, you already have powers, right?"

Travis's shoulders slumped. He was not necessarily a smart man. Everything told him not to take this dare. In the back of his mind, he was telling himself: "No, Travis, this isn't a good idea! Don't do this!" But Travis had never turned down a dare in his life. And he wasn't about to start now.

"Bring it," he said.

And that was how the idea came forth. It was already known just what his superpower was, of course. So now it was a matter of his alter ego and a costume. They could always attend to this after work was over for the day. But given how slow of a day it was, there likely wasn't much harm in getting started now. Of course, it might not have been a terrible idea to get permission from their boss.

Sloane West was generally a reasonable woman, but she took her comic shop very seriously. It had taken her a while to work up the nerve to seek out funding for it in the first place. And if she learned that her employees had buggered off for the rest of the day so that one of them could play superhero... There was a chance she might not be okay with that.

Both of the young men working Hell Bent Comics that day knew this. But after a few moments of debate, Travis had decided to take the initiative and put in Sloane's number. Not wanting the others to feel left out of the conversation, he put his phone on speaker.

"Heya, Sloane," Travis greeted.

"This had better be important, Malone...I have a jury pool to get back to."

He'd forgotten about the jury summons, the half-monkey blushing as he realized this.

"Right, right, sorry. Uh, listen...Leo and me? We're thinking of taking the rest of today off. Leo dared me to become a superhero, and nobody's been in today anyway..."

There was silence on the other end before they heard her snickering. "I-I'm sorry...he dared you to *what*, now?"

Travis wasn't sure how he wanted to take that. Did she think he couldn't handle himself in a fight? Couldn't help someone if they needed it? She knew as well as anyone else that he could recover from the vast majority of injuries, injuries that might otherwise be fatal. Sure, that ability had led to trouble on more than one occasion. But all her derisive laughter had done was convince him that this was the right path for him.

"That's right. I'm going into the superhero biz. I was dared to do it, and it sounded like fun, so...is it cool if we take the rest of the day off to get some stuff figured out about this?"

Silence again.

"You...you do know how dangerous that is, right?"

The half-monkey shrugged. "I've been in plenty of dangerous situations before, boss-lady. I've got this."

A sigh. "Is there any way to talk you out of this?"

"Nope!"

"Fine...you can take the rest of the day off to figure out superhero stuff on one—*one*—condition. We're using this as publicity for the shop. Got that?"

In all honesty, none of the three had intended for this dare to turn into a marketing gimmick. Anywhere else in the world, a monkey-human hybrid on their own would be gimmick enough for a comic shop. Not in Hell Bent, where genetic experimentation was normal enough to not really raise many eyebrows.

"I guess I can work with that," Travis said. "So...we're good, then?"

"Yeah. Go forth, Monkey-Man."

She hung up the phone, as Travis did the same on their end. Pocketing it, he looked to his coworker, his tail twitching and a slight grimace on his face. "Yeah...just so we're clear, I'm *not* going by *Monkey-Man*."

"In that case," Leo began. "What are you thinking of going by? I mean, a superhero's name is kinda crucial, especially when they want people to know who they are."

Travis thought about that. *Monkey-Man* felt a bit too obvious. He was sure that his first thought, *Onslaught*, was already taken by a different comic character. But then he thought of one, a word his father had called him a couple of times. It was one of the nicer nicknames he'd had for him, and he did sort of like the word, in spite of that.

It was time to put a more positive spin on it.

"I'm thinking...*Travesty*."

Leo stared at him, wondering if he had heard that correctly. He cleared his throat, head tilted to the side in confusion.

"Are you absolutely sure you want to go with that?" he asked, leaning forward. "You sure you don't want something that inspires a bit more, well, *hope*?"

The half-monkey shrugged. "It rolls off the tongue, I think. Besides, you have any better ideas?"

The other man thought on that for a moment, wracking his brain for any better names than Travesty. After thinking, and thinking, and thinking some more, he had nothing.

"I think I can see that working," said Leo after a long pause. "Say you end up fighting someone, some kind of really hardened criminal...and then you can devastate them, therefore turning their plans into a *travesty*."

"Yeah, let's go with that," Travis chuckled.

Having already established his powers and name (and having gained permission from Sloane to take the afternoon off for this endeavor), it was on to creating Travesty's overall look. While Travis did know someone that was handy with a sewing machine, he knew that Yvette was not currently an option. There was an incident a few months prior which had resulted in her being taken from her family and friends. They still had not managed to track her or her abductor down. But they were trying!

Which meant that it was off to do some shopping. The guys would check any clothing shop they could find for something suitable. Leo knew of a few places that sold spandex garments of all sorts. But Travis had turned that down. He preferred more loose-fitting clothing. Spandex made him somewhat itchy.

"So, what, you're just gonna go out there in a shirt and pants?" Leo scoffed, eyebrow cocked.

Travis shook his head. "Of course not! Hm...wonder what we can find at the thrift store."

Thus, began their epic quest to peruse every thrift store between Hell Bent and its neighboring city of Philadelphia. If absolutely necessary, they could enlist some help from Travis's mother, Serena. She wasn't a seamstress by any stretch of the imagination, but she did know a thing or two about metalworking.

It was decided, as they moved from shop to shop, that the color scheme would be a deep, dark red. It wasn't so bright that it'd look horrible with Travis's red hair, but at the same time, the color could grab one's attention.

Though finding red clothing that fit Trav's vision was becoming increasingly difficult with each shop they went to. Most didn't have anything that really appealed to him, and his monkey traits got a few rather odd looks in the Philly shops, leading to him telling the half-truth of "Don't mind me. I'm just a cosplayer!"

They were both ready to throw in the towel when Travis saw the long, blood-red coat hanging in a window. It looked to be made of leather, its collar high, stiff, and flared. And it was only ten bucks. All he needed was to see if it'd fit, and he was golden. His tail flicked happily, as he pointed it out to Leo.

"I think I see something I want for it...!" he said.

Leo appraised the coat from a distance, stroking the scruff on his chin. "Hm...that could work...I mean, the badass long-coat look does have a certain flair to it... And it looks like the color we were talking about. I say we try it!"

He started nudging Travis toward the door, though the half-monkey was more than willing to head in. After speaking with the clerk for a moment or two, the coat was handed over to him, and he could try it on. The coat was, indeed, a thick leather, complete with that rich leather smell. It felt smooth in his hands, and not too heavy. Yes, yes, this would make for an excellent part of his costume!

Entering the changing room, Travis removed his olive army-style jacket, pulling the red coat on over it. It did not fit exactly as he had hoped it would. He could not close it over his chest, a four to five-inch gap between the two sides. The coat hung to his knees, though, which he definitely appreciated. The sleeves were a bit too short, and a bit tight along the arms, though at least the gussets were large enough to account for his arms, if just barely. The collar reached to just below his chin, and while he was disappointed that he couldn't close it, he did rather like how it looked on him.

Stepping out, he turned for his coworker. "Well, what do you think?" he asked.

The other man looked him over, carefully scrutinizing the garment.

"Well...it's a good look for you. Though it might actually look better without the sleeves, those look a little snug along the arms."

Flexing his arms a bit, Travis saw that he was right. And that couldn't be good for his dexterity. Ah, well; they could make adjustments when they finished shopping. He removed that coat, put on his other jacket, and continued the search. In that same store, he found a pair of dark red fingerless gloves along with a pair of baggy dark-red cargo pants. An image was already starting to form in his head of how he wanted this outfit to look. He would have to ask his mother about one part of it. But the rest of it? He could handle that himself. He wasn't an expert tailor, but he did know a thing or two about alterations and embellishments; a perk of being an experienced cosplayer.

The purchases made, the pair began to head back to their hometown. Travis made a call to his mother along the way. He didn't go into detail about the dare, knowing that she'd have questions. And those questions were bound to be plentiful. He asked if she had any scrap metal lying around that she could make into a pair of bracers for his arms. His timing could not have been better, as she was between projects at the moment. The plus side of being adopted by the city's foremost name in cybernetics: the only payment he owed her for this was sushi.

On some level, Travis felt like she should learn eventually. She was, after all, responsible for his powers in the first place. After Dr. Serena Taylor had taken him and his sister in all those years ago, she had given them the option of becoming something a bit more than human. In addition to her expertise in cybernetics, she had also picked up a thing or two thousand about genetic engineering. She didn't do a thing without their consent, of course.

But Travis still couldn't help but feel like she might worry if he told her about his intentions. He knew that his sister almost certainly would, as well as his brother-in-law.

He would figure out how to break it to them all later. Right now, he had to get home and make some alterations to his purchases. Leo headed there with him, ready to offer any advice he might need. Plus, he was sort of excited to see the finished product.

The trip to Travis's house wasn't a long one, but the anticipation made it feel that way. It didn't help that they seemed to hit every DON'T WALK signal along the way. The one consolation was that it was a lovely day, with only partial cloud cover.

When they arrived, Travis unlocked the door, holding the door open for Leo before joining him in the living room. From there, they headed to the kitchen, Travis laying the outfit out on the counter. The sleeves were the first to go, along with a good seven inches from each of the pant legs. The leftover fabric from the pants was repurposed to make a belt and a few straps for the coat. The monkey-man had a clear plan for what he wanted this outfit to look like, making the intended alterations to his coat. His coworker stood back, watching him work.

"So...what about a mask?" Leo asked at some point in the process.

Travis looked up from attaching one of the straps, his green eyes trained on him.

"What about one?"

"Wouldn't you want to, y'know, conceal your identity a bit?"

Travis raised an eyebrow. "You're kidding, right?"

A sigh. "Look, Trav, since we're actually committing to this whole thing, it might not be a horrible idea for you to try and keep your secret identity...well, a *secret*."

"Tell me something, Leo...how many people do you see running around Hell Bent with monkey feet and tails? I can't really hide my tail...that comes in handy when grabbing onto stuff! And do you wanna try stashing all of this hair under a wig? And there is no way in hell I'm cutting my hair, so don't you even think about *considering* suggesting that."

Leo held up his hands, realizing he had lost that argument. "Fair enough...but couldn't we find some way to alter your general appearance? Hell, even an eye color change might be good!"

Travis was about to ask how he was supposed to go about that when a third figure entered the kitchen. He glanced over to see Spencer there, the doctor pushing up his glasses. He set down the needle and thread, charging toward the other man and hugging him.

Spencer meant the world to him. The pair had been best friends since Kindergarten. As time went on and they experienced a whole host of events together (such as Trav's first breakup, college, that unplanned trip to a Russian lab...), they only grew closer. Spence had even married Travis's younger sister, the couple welcoming Travis to come live with them. Spencer may have married Travis's sister, but these two were the walking definition of *soulmates*.

The tall, slim doctor returned Travis's hug, before glancing around the kitchen. He waved to his brother-in-law's coworker, then glanced at the counter, his brown eyes narrowing.

"What's going on in here?"

Spencer was then subjected to the full explanation of the dare, of Travis's new alter ego, of Serena's involvement...all of it. As he listened to the tale, he shook his head, chuckling. But after a few moments, it dawned on him that they were quite serious.

"Are...are you sure this is a good idea, Travis?" he asked. "I know you can handle yourself in a fight. And I'm more than well aware of your regenerative properties. But I also know that you're trouble-prone."

Not that Spencer was much better; he had been in almost as many horrible situations as Travis over the years, prompting him to start learning magic. While that had led to a bit more trouble, it was hard for Travis to deny that Spencer had become a rather skilled mage in a relatively short period of time.

The half-monkey shrugged, his tail flicking. "Honestly, man? I'm not sure anything I do's really a good idea. But this is a chance for me to help people out. That's all I've really wanted out of life, anyway. Even if my means of helping someone is to get more people to the comic shop, so Sloane doesn't have to file for bankruptcy eventually, that'd be good enough for me."

Spencer nodded, running his fingers through his short sandy-brown hair. "Right. Just please be careful, okay?"

Travis was about to ask him when he wasn't careful...but then his college years came flooding back to him, and he thought better of it. Instead, he simply gave a nod.

"So, we're waiting for one last piece from Mom. Any suggestions you can think of?"

The doctor strode to the counter, looking over the costume in progress. "And you've already turned down a mask?"

"Right. Leo said something about doing something else to alter my appearance, though..."

Spencer thought for a moment, rubbing the back of his neck. He chewed his lower lip, thinking. Until he finally had an idea, charging out of the room. The pair watched him rush off, almost afraid of what he had in mind. But they waited for his return anyway.

As he re-entered the kitchen, Spencer carried with him a small box, containing a set of never-before-opened red contact lenses. He had initially picked them up for a cosplay last year but never got around to using them.

"Maybe try these?" the doctor suggested. "They'd go with the look."

Travis looked over the contacts. They would, indeed, go well with the look. But he wasn't sure how to put those in. Thankfully, Spencer offered to help him with that, the pair heading off to the bathroom to get the contacts in place. Leo would wait behind in the kitchen, pulling out his phone as he did so.

A news story caught his attention as he scrolled through, about a local string of fires. It was suspected to be arson, but nobody had a clear picture of the guy. The first place to burn was a chemistry lab, the next few also being labs. A couple of apartment buildings had also been hit. A male figure could be seen at the scene of each of the fires, but there wasn't a good picture of his face or hair or any of that. It just seemed to be obscured by flames each time.

"Hm. Weird," he murmured, continuing to scroll through the page.

In the comments, he could see misspellings galore, the occasional trolling comment about how those displaced deserved it, and a few offering thoughts and prayers. But what really caught his eye was the odd comment that suspected the arsonist to be a fire elemental, with fire as his head. Leo almost laughed at that, before he remembered that they were in Hell Bent, the Lab Capital of the U.S. There was a good chance that this guy was, in fact, a fire elemental that was created in a lab. That might explain the lab attacks. And as for the apartments, there was a good chance that scientists lived there.

But he felt that telling Travis was a terrible idea. On the one hand, a warning would be a good plan. If he knew, then he could avoid the arsonist. But on the other, Travis was the same man that had taken on more than one dare from Leo. He wasn't one to back down from a challenge, either. If he was warned away from it, that might make him want to pursue the arsonist even more. Neither of them was entirely certain how Travis's regenerative properties would deal with fire, and that seemed like a horrible way to find out.

Travis returned after a few minutes, but Leo hadn't noticed as of yet. His shadow fell over the phone as he leaned in, curious as to what the other man was reading. Leo jumped, pulling the phone to his chest. He looked his coworker in the eye, recoiling a bit.

"...Holy *shit*, your eyes look so freaky now...!" he informed.

Travis grinned, staring at him with his currently-red eyes. "What? You don't like my eyes, dude?"

Leo ran a hand through his messy dark hair, sighing. "Sorry...it's just that you get so used to the green, y'know?"

"Yeah, I get it."

Three hours went by, as they waited for the final component to Trav's outfit. In that time, Spencer had to head off for his shift at the hospital, and the guys decided to watch the news, seeing if there was anything that the local police could use some help with. Leo held his tongue on the arsons he'd read about earlier, not wanting to incite his curiosity. So far, there wasn't anything noteworthy: a couple arsons here and there, but mostly nationwide incidents and human-interest stories. Travis, much to Leo's surprise and delight, wasn't sure about investigating the arsons, thinking it might be best for him to start with muggings and the like.

Eventually, they heard the door open, as Travis's mother arrived. Her long black hair was pulled back into a thick ponytail, black cat ears poking out. She pushed up her light blue glasses with one hand, her other arm holding a wrapped bundle that Travis could only assume was his bracers. Her tail flicked as she handed the bundle over to him.

"So...let's get the whole effect, shall we?" she asked, an eager grin on her face.

Hmph. So much for not telling her. He raised a thick eyebrow, and she waved a hand dismissively. "Spence told me about the whole thing. So, I made sure to use a bullet-resistant material. The color should go with the rest of it, as well."

Travis should have asked Spencer not to tell anyone, but the fact that Serena wasn't freaking out on him was a good sign. Of course, he figured that of anyone he knew, Serena would be quite supportive of this entire endeavor. She was proud of her work and proud of her boy.

If there was anyone she could trust to use his powers for good, it was Travis. And he knew this. Somewhere deep in his soul, he knew this.

He hugged her for a brief moment, before taking the bracers and the rest of the outfit and leaving the room. There was a certain bounce to his step, his tail twitching. Clearly, someone was all too eager to suit up for the first time.

But after a minute or two, the change was complete. He had walked into that bathroom as Travis but had come out as Travesty. His coat and cargo pants were tattered in just the right way. His hands were clad in those fingerless gloves, the bracers covering his forearms. The straps across his coat were arranged in three x shapes. The belt cinched around his waist. He wore no shirt underneath the coat and had cut a hole in the back to accommodate for his tail. His now-red eyes glanced around, and his long hair flowed behind him like a cape.

By the time he emerged, Leo and Serena were engaged in conversation. Something about where to find some really good catnip. But when they did see the full look, Serena took out her phone and snapped a pic of him, sending the photo to Spencer. Leo did the same, his recipient being Sloane.

And Travis took a deep breath. Was he actually ready to do this?

The first patrol happened that night. Leo and Serena had set him up with a small body-cam, complete with an audio hookup so that they could monitor his every move and make sure he got out of this all in one piece. His willingness to go through with this dare so thoroughly was...concerning, to some extent. They were all for seeing some action but didn't want him to be in actual danger.

Right now, Travesty was perched on a rooftop, his hair and coat billowing in the gentle breeze of the night. The full moon shone just above him, bathing the half-monkey in its reflected light. He hoped that someone got a picture and that he looked just as majestic as he felt at that moment. He blinked a few times, still getting used to the contacts. While he had no issues seeing out of them, they still felt a little odd to him. Having never needed glasses, the redhead had also never needed the use of contacts.

The night was calm, for the most part. Nothing really going on aside from the hustle and bustle of the Hell Bent nightlife. Hell Bent didn't really see a lot of crime, so Travesty was having some second thoughts about taking on this dare. He looked the part, sure...but was there really any point to being a superhero if there was no crime to fight? Nobody in need of protection? Though he supposed that he could still be good for publicity. Or going around to hospitals and visiting sick children. They could always stand to see a friendly face.

A shout cut through the relative stillness of the night air. Looking in the direction of the scream, Travesty could see two figures in the nearest alley: one was an older gentleman with a thick white mustache, his hair mostly white, with a bit of gray here and there, and a much younger man with a long snake tail in lieu of legs. The snake man was demanding that the old guy hand over his wallet, but the man was telling him to back off, glaring at him from behind his large tinted glasses.

But even if he didn't show much fear toward his attacker, he could still be seriously injured. And there was no way Travesty was going to stand for that. He backed away from the edge of the roof, before getting a running start. He hopped off of the roof, landing right on the snake man's tail. His target turned his human half toward Travesty, his eyes narrowing.

"...Sherman, what the hell are you up to this time?" Travesty sighed.

He knew this snake man all too well. Known as Sherman Pataki, he was the city's best-known petty thief. He'd even had a few run-ins with Travis on occasion. While he preferred not to harm those he robbed, he was still ready to do whatever it took to get his loot. And the only reason he wasn't behind bars now was because he knew a guy who knew a guy that could work the system.

"You again?" Sherman groaned, the tip of his tail curling around Travesty. "What's with the getup, monkey-boy?"

Travesty tried to pull out of his grip, but the tail soon held him tightly, pinning his arms. "Hey, never mind what I'm wearing. Just leave the old dude alone, all right? Let him go about his night in peace!"

Sherman crossed his arms, hissing in annoyance at Travesty. "How about you leave *me* alone before I do something we'll both regret?"

His eyes narrowed, his forked tongue flicking out of his mouth for a moment. Travesty thought on that before he shrugged to the best of his ability.

"Nope."

He lashed out with a foot, kicking him as hard as he could in the torso, causing Sherman to drop him. With the snake-man's attention fully on Travesty, the old guy took the opportunity to make a break for it. As the man scurried off, Travesty could have sworn he'd heard him mutter something about this being something straight out of a comic.

Travesty threw an elbow strike at Sherman's face, screeching at him. The snake man took the hit, hissing again, before snapping at his arm. Travesty shielded himself with a forearm, Sherman biting down on one of his bracers instead of humanoid flesh. At that point, he moved to try and get him into a headlock, relieved that Sherman was only half-snake as opposed to a full one. The human half was much easier to fight.

The two wrestled for a while, Travesty having a firm grip on Sherman's human half and Sherman's snake tail having curled around Travesty's waist, attempting to pry him away. But Travesty had a plan, as he bit down on Sherman's neck. The snake man yowled in pain, releasing his grip. However, Travesty just kept clinging to him, growling. He may not have been a smart man. But damn if he wasn't a stubborn one!

But eventually, Sherman gained the upper hand, slamming Travesty into a wall. The half-monkey was stunned, causing him to lose his grip. And with him no longer trying to stop him, Sherman slithered out of the alley as quickly as he could. Trav watched him leave, groaning as he pushed himself upright. He watched as Sherman's half-serpentine form disappeared, raising a middle finger in his general direction.

"Hey, Trav, you okay?" Leo's voice crackled in his ear.

"All good here, Leo," he replied. "Broke up a mugging. Sherman was at it again."

A chuckle. "Yeah, I saw that...camera, remember?"

Travesty sighed, rubbing the back of his head. "I almost forgot about that part."

" Fair enough. But either way, I told yah you wouldn't be as horrible at this as you thought!"

Trav scoffed, making his way back up to the roof. "Please. It was one dude trying to take an older dude's wallet. Not like I just stopped the murders of Thomas and Martha Wayne."

"No, but you still may have saved the guy's life all the same. How're you feeling?"

He reached the roof once more, looking out on the city. "Pretty good. Just not sure what other crimes would be going on...I mean, that kind of thing doesn't happen as often as you'd think around here. And the worst ones end up getting taken out by my aunt and her friends. Or at least they did. Y'know, before we lost one of them..."

Travis's aunt was an assassin, one of a team of three. Known as the Slaughter Angels, they were one of the better assassin groups to come out of Hell Bent. Of course, they also tended to limit their targets to those deemed too dangerous for society, those that lashed out with malicious intent. One of the trio, Ivy, had been in a relationship with him for a while, and her twin sister Yvette was a close family friend. But a few months prior, an enemy of the family's had attacked. Before disappearing to who-knew-where, he managed to take Yvette with him. Beast and Ivy had been doing everything they could to locate her and had been forced into retirement, for the most part.

And that meant that the city was missing a few potential defenders. Trav knew that just him, just the one difficult-to-kill monkey-man didn't really amount to much, in the long run. But he would do what he could to help out around there. He may not have been particularly bright most of the time, but Trav knew that he had a good heart.

"Ooh, yeah, that's rough," Leo said, the grimace clear in his voice.

Trav had discussed the whole ordeal with his coworkers after it'd happened. He had come into work with a bit of a cough, which led all sorts of questions and concerns. He described to them a battle, in which he was subjected to a live burial by the enemy. By the time it had ended, everyone was quite disheartened. Ivy was not taking things well at all with the loss of her sister. So, things were a bit tense at home at that time. *Rough* may have been a slight understatement.

But that was months ago, and Travis/Travesty had more patrolling to do. He hopped to the nearest roof from his current perch, very nearly losing his grip. But he clung to the edge of that roof, hoisting himself to the top and running toward the other side to watch there.

In the distance, he saw a bright light. A bright light and smoke. Well, that looked concerning. From there, he felt that the best course of action would be to jump from there to the next roof, and then each one after that until he got a better look. The half-monkey had to do this for two blocks before he could see what was going on. There was an apartment building on fire.

People were evacuating the building as quickly as they could. Some were in tears, some shakily trying to catch their breath. But all seemed to be afraid. Of course, that made sense. At least fifty families had been displaced, future entirely uncertain. The fire department had not arrived as of yet, from what he could see. To be honest, he had no idea just how well he would recover from getting burned. But there wasn't time to think of that right now.

"Is there anyone else in there?" he asked a woman.

She was hesitant to answer, clutching her baby to her chest. "W-well...yes..."

"Which floor?"

She shook her head, gripping his wrist. "Please don't. I think he's the one that started it!"

So, this was an arson...

Travesty hadn't intended to get involved with the rash of arsons lately, but he had just sort of stumbled upon it. He had seen some of those impacted by the latest incident. All the more reason for him to get involved, wasn't it? The half-monkey took to all-fours, charging into the burning apartment building. He knew this was probably a bad idea, but if he could find this arsonist and bring them to justice, wouldn't that make it worth it?

He rushed forward, eyes scanning the area for any sign of life. But the apartment felt completely empty. He was ready to head back, figuring that the arsonist had probably gotten away. He got ready to turn back, starting toward the door when he heard humming behind him.

Wait...

Humming?

Slowly, the half-monkey turned, seeing a pair of reddish-brown boots. The legs attached to those were clad in a pair of deep red trousers. His coat had a mantle on it but was roughly the same length as Travesty's own. But the part that really stood out to him was his face. His eyes were a solid red, his hair appearing to be made of fire. On his face was a long bushy mustache, which also seemed to be comprised of flames.

He stepped back, his eyes widening for a second before he stood at his full height and growled. Time to hide his fear and put up that much-needed wall of bravado.

"Who the hell are you, and what is your problem?" Travesty demanded.

The fiery man chuckled, his voice carrying a brimstone quality the likes of which Travesty had never heard before.

"That depends...what are *you* supposed to be?"

Ooh, a challenge. His tail flicked in irritation, and he put his hands on his hips. "They call me Travesty, and if you're the one causing all of the arsons and all that around here? Yeah, I'm gonna have to ask you to stop that."

His opponent laughed heartily, wiping a small flame-tear from his eye. "Oh, that...that's adorable. But I'm not about to stop now. Oh no...not by a long shot, *Travesty*...you see, I'm Uncle Nero. And all I want is to watch the world *burn*."

"Uncle...Nero? The hell kind of name is *that*?" Travis laughed.

That was honestly the most ridiculous name he had ever heard. But his laughter stopped when a piece of burning debris slammed into the floor by his feet. He backed away, slightly embarrassed at the surprised squeak that escaped his lips.

"You'd do best not to screw with me, monkey-boy," Uncle Nero stated. "Because these prior attacks? Those weren't specifically targeted. You get off my back, or they may become a bit less random. Understand?"

"Yeah. Yeah, I get it," Travesty replied, taking to all-fours once again and leaving the building.

He moved backward, knowing better than to turn his back on an enemy. No, he kept his eyes on Uncle Nero the whole time as he backed away. By the time he got out there, the fire department had finally arrived. He had gone back to the rooftops, letting them get things sorted.

But Travesty was *not* pleased with that little encounter. Not at all. Turning tail and running from an opponent? That just stood out as inherently wrong to him. He muttered to himself about things he wanted to do to this guy, Leo disrupting his vengeful thoughts.

"Okay, I heard that whole thing..." said Leo. "I'm gonna do some research, but that guy might very well be a fire elemental."

Travesty grinned. "All right, cool...so how do I kick his ass?"

"Don't! Seriously, Trav, I'm begging you, just let the police handle that one, okay? Or your aunt or girlfriend...just someone more qualified for someone that dangerous!"

Travesty growled. "Yeah, he'd like that, wouldn't he? I'm not giving him what he wants, Leo. See, I don't believe in giving people like him that kind of satisfaction. Besides, what's to stop him from deciding to get more focused on choosing targets, anyway?"

"Ugh, *Dios mio...You're* what's stopping him! When someone like that says that they just want to watch the world burn, it's not because they're trying to deceive you, man! It means that they're likely to tell the truth because they're sure nobody can stop them!"

Travesty cracked his knuckles. "Good. I can prove him wrong. Bring him down a notch or two."

"No, Trav, please, just reconsider this! If you're going to go after him, at least find some backu-"

Travesty switched off the wire and camera, not wanting to continue this argument any further. He had an Uncle Nero to bring down. He would have contacted Ivy for backup, anyway, were she not still dealing with the loss of her sister. When she was upset, Trav knew better than to pry.

And so, he watched as the blaze was extinguished. It was a total loss, but all of the apartment's occupants had managed to get out unharmed. The area cleared out after a bit more, and Travesty watched for Uncle Nero to emerge.

A few flames traveled along the sidewalk, and that humming had returned. Watching them, Travesty could see arms, legs, a torso...

There he was.

He didn't want to make the fact that he was watching him known. Not immediately. Carefully, he hopped to the next rooftop, and then the next, following from above. The monkey-man kept leaping along, confident that nothing could stop him now. He *would* catch up to Uncle Nero...

What he failed to do was pay attention to the rooftops themselves. The eighth one he had landed on during his run? It was one of those that'd been hit by Uncle Nero earlier in the week. The interior was entirely gutted, but the frame and the roof were still intact. Intact save for the glass skylight (which had burst), and Travesty had found some of that broken glass with a foot.

Screeching in pain, he fell on the area next to the broken skylight. He very nearly ended up getting a shard embedded in his hand, as well but managed to avoid that. Well, this was going to be a minor setback. But it wouldn't be too much of an issue for him. The only thing about it was the pain. Gripping the shard of glass, he took a deep breath and yanked it out of his foot. The blood flowed freely for a half second before the injury faded entirely. Backing carefully away from the rest of the glass, he continued along his way.

He couldn't lose his target. Not now! Muttering a few curses under his breath, he moved to another rooftop, then the next. After a few minutes, he had a lock on Uncle Nero again. The fire elemental had come to a stop, opening a door to a cellar.

Travesty smirked as he disappeared into the cellar. That was where he'd get to him. Cautiously, he climbed down from the roof, stalking toward the cellar door. His tail twitched as his mind swam with thoughts of fighting Uncle Nero and getting him put in prison where he belonged. He would pay for his crimes!

Going to open the door, Travesty frowned. Locked. That was a slight obstacle...

But it wasn't a complete roadblock. He pulled the piercing from his tail with a grin, using that to pick the lock. Uncle Nero had no idea just what he was messing with, here. He didn't know what was coming for him. It was vengeance, and tonight, vengeance stood at 5'10" and had obscenely long hair.

The half-monkey had the cellar door unlocked in a couple minutes, not even noticing how much noise the piercing made as it turned in the lock. Pocketing the piercing, he opened the door and descended into the darkness of the cellar. The plus side of Uncle Nero's hair: it made for an excellent source of light. Travesty figured he would be able to sneak up behind him and catch him unawares.

But as he reached the bottom of the stairs, he noticed an added glow to that of his flames: his eyes. Crap, he was looking right at him! Upon realizing this, Travesty got into a hunched position, growling. He was ready for a fight, and no way was he going to let Uncle Nero go anywhere without inflicting some pain on him. His tail lashed back and forth, his teeth bared.

"Did I not tell you to back off?" Uncle Nero demanded, arms crossed.

Travesty grinned. "Yeah, you did. But here's the thing, I make it a point not to listen to people like you. Just what do you gain from, as you said earlier, 'watching the world burn'? What'd it ever do to you?"

Instead of an answer, he got a fireball lobbed at his face. Trav managed to dodge, but just barely. He could still feel the heat against his skin. The fireball hit the wall closest to him, and he let out a relieved sigh. That could have been disastrous. From there, he charged toward the fire elemental with an ear-splitting screech, his opponent stumbling back in surprise. He clutched his ears at the sound, barely reacting as Travesty's fist met his chest.

The half-monkey punched him a few more times before the fire elemental's hand gripped his wrist and squeezed, before giving it a little twist. Travesty hissed in pain, bringing up a knee to smash him in the groin. Uncle Nero responded with a headbutt to the forehead, his flames licking the skin. Travesty backed away from the hit, muttering a string of curses under his breath.

He reached up and lightly touched the point of impact, wincing at the soreness. He raised his middle finger at him, ready to attack him again. But Uncle Nero attacked first. He hurled another fireball at the half-monkey, and Travesty scrambled to dodge it. He ducked and made a charge at the elemental's legs. If he could tackle him, that would be ideal.

What happened instead was that his opponent grabbed him by the hair, slamming him into the wall a few times until he lost consciousness.

———

"Huh...well, this *is* interesting, now isn't it?" was the first thing Travesty heard as he woke once more.

With a groan, he opened his eyes. Along with the glow of Uncle Nero's hair and eyes, he could see the whitish-blue glow of a computer screen. But he couldn't see anything on the screen itself. The next thing he noticed was the post against his back. Looking down, he saw a few chains wrapped around him, securing him to what he assumed was one of this place's supports.

Well, this wasn't what he would call ideal. His stomach was also growling, nagging at him for food. He tried to piece together how much he'd had to heal thus far today. His forehead was still sore, and the back of his head was mildly achey. Did one of those strikes to the head kill him? His abilities usually required that he eat something after a major healing, and lethal injuries definitely counted under the category of *major healing*.

Uncle Nero turned to face him, smirking. "Welcome back, *Malone*," he greeted.

Travesty worked the name over in his brain for a moment or two, before it dawned on him that he knew who he was. His eyebrows shot upward for a moment, but he soon regained his composure, glaring.

"How do you know…?" the half-monkey demanded, trying not to freak out.

Trav accepted that he would be recognizable, yes. But when did this guy learn his actual name?

The fire elemental moved closer, crouching down to his eye level. His fiery mustache lightly brushed Trav's face, just barely singing the skin. A wicked grin crossed his face, and his red eyes flashed.

"You do know that everyone that's been through a lab ends up in a database, right? A publicly-searchable one. I ran a search for those with monkey traits. And you know how many people came up there? Five. And only one of them looked at all like you."

Trav took a breath, trying to keep his pulse from racing. It was always likely that someone would figure out who he was, but this guy had already threatened him. Knowing who he was, knowing that he was one Travis Isaac Malone, that could lead him to attack people he loved, people that had nothing to do with this!

"And…and what's your point?" he spat, doing all he could to keep his fear in check.

"I did a little more poking around online. And I found something *very* interesting…I won't say what, exactly. I'd rather it be a surprise. But help me decide: yoga studio or hospital?"

Trav kept up a calm front. But on the inside, he wanted to rip this Uncle Nero bastard to shreds. His sister owned and taught at that yoga studio, and the hospital… Spencer was still on his shift for the night, wasn't he?

"What, exactly, are you asking me?" he asked.

"Should I visit the yoga studio tonight, or the hospital?"

He thought on how to answer that one. The yoga studio was one of his sister's favorite accomplishments. She had gone to so much trouble to get the space and the funding for it. If anything were to happen to it, she'd be devastated. But at this hour, nobody was even there. Even if the structure was gutted, at least there would be nobody harmed, unlike with the hospital.

"I'm not choosing..."

"It's one or the other, Malone. If you don't choose, I'll go for both. And then your mother's home, and finally your house. And I'd want to watch your reaction anytime I bring you the charred remains of one of your loved ones. Now choose!"

Trav hated himself for what he said next. But he sighed. "...The yoga studio," he said.

Uncle Nero chuckled, giving him a little pat on the head. "Good monkey-boy...I'll be back in a bit."

He headed out of the cellar, humming again. And with that, Travesty was left in the darkness, only the glow of the monitor to break up the pitch-black surroundings. He needed to find a way out of there, and soon. For a moment, he recalled the wire he'd had on him. Maybe he could ask Leo for help?

But then he recalled his last conversation with Leo, and how he'd switched off the monitoring equipment. So, his coworker probably didn't know he was there. Serena might, though; she had her means of tracking him, having given him that tail piercing when he was a teenager. With any luck, she might be able to find him.

Trav sighed as he thought about that last conversation. He was pretty sure that after that, he deserved any pain that came his way. What kind of hero was he, anyway, getting into that kind of debate? And now, because of him, his sister's workplace was going to burn, then the hospital, his home, his mother's home, the comic shop...

All of it. And something told him that Uncle Nero would not hold off just because someone happened to be inside of each target. If he couldn't get out of there, he would only have himself to blame for the widespread destruction.

He knew that he would *not* let this happen. No way in hell could he let it happen. Not like this! With a growl, he tried to get at one of his pockets. He had a hard time getting to it with his hands, but he noticed that his tail had been left free. Chuckling, he started rummaging through his pocket with the tail, eventually managing to find the piercing with it. And once he had it, he managed to bring up a leg, feeling around for a lock with a foot. Sometimes, he loved the enhanced flexibility that came with his monkey traits.

It took a few moments of poking and prodding before he located a small padlock with his toes. To pick that lock would be a bit of a stretch, the lock being almost out of his reach. He could still swing this, though, and he transferred the piercing from his tail to his foot.

The lock itself was difficult, to say the least. Several times, he nearly dropped the piercing. He missed the lock a few times, jabbing himself with his improvised lockpick before finally finding the keyhole. He grumbled the whole time until he heard a soft click. The lock undone, he could work his way out of the chains and out of that cellar. He shrugged them off, once more pocketing the piercing.

Free of the restraints, Travesty scrambled up the steps and rushed out onto the sidewalk. He tore off in the direction of the yoga studio, weaving through throngs of people. Travesty did his best not to shove his way through, but for the most part, he was laser-focused on stopping Uncle Nero before he started another fire.

He had to stop for a light at one point, waiting impatiently for it to change. As he waited, he could see smoke not far from his current location. He chewed his lower lip for a moment, trying to determine which building was in that direction. He could have sworn that that was where the hospital was, but he could have been wrong, too. It wouldn't shock him if he were.

Turning on that block, he sped toward where he saw the smoke. As he rushed along, he switched the body cam and wire back on. Before Leo could get a word in, or so much as ask the half-monkey what his problem was, he was subjected to a rapid-fire apology and a request for backup. And the sooner that backup arrived, the better.

The night shift at Hell Bent General had never been known for its peaceful nature. That was usually when the more bizarre medical cases came in. Dr. Abbot was just thankful that he didn't have the exact credentials to work in the E.R. He was perfectly content as a basic physician. Normally, he didn't even have to work this late. But there had been an illness going around lately, and it never hurt to have as many hands-on deck as possible.

Things were slow for him right now, but Spencer was honestly okay with that. Slow meant safe, and there just wasn't enough of that going around these days. He could deal with safe. Safety allowed him time to enjoy his book.

Of course, the universe had other plans, as his evening was about to get rather heated. A voice came over the intercom, announcing that there was a Code Red. Spencer blinked. A fire? He knew about the string of arsons but didn't quite think whoever was behind it would be brazen enough to hit a hospital.

Would they?

Chances were, it was a small fire. Nothing that would constitute an actual emergency. It was probably just confined to one floor.

But then the next code was called. Code Orange.

Evacuation.

Well, that wasn't ideal. Maybe the arsonist actually *was* callous enough to attack a hospital. He got up, speed-walking from the room. Everyone's help would be needed to move some of the worse-off patients to safety. He tried to remain as calm as possible, of course. Best not to cause a panic. Or more accurately, cause more of a panic than the evacuation probably was. In all actuality, his heart pounded in his chest.

He reached one of the patient's rooms, checking for anyone that might require his assistance. The room was empty, thankfully.

No…

No, wait, not quite empty. A man was standing by the window. His head looked like it was on fire, and he wore a dark red coat. He looked right at Spencer, his red eyes boring into his very soul.

"Dr. Abbot, I presume?" he asked.

Spencer's breath caught in his throat. This fire guy was here for him? The hell did he do?

"Who wants to know?" Spencer asked, his brown eyes narrowed.

Uncle Nero chuckled, sending a fireball at Spencer. In a panic, the doctor put his arms in front of him. Bluish-green energy shot from his hands, before forming a magical shield around himself. The fireball hit his shield, dissipating upon impact.

"Huh...the monkey never said anything about his friend being a magic user..."

This entire situation already made Spencer uncomfortable enough as it was. But he had no idea what condition Travis was in right now. He dropped the shield for a moment, firing a small series of ice shards at him. Uncle Nero seemed unfazed, merely enveloping the shards in flames. With a snap of his fingers, flames rose up to block the door. The fire elemental himself was between Spencer and the window. And Spencer was certain that turning his back for even a second would result in a fireball to the back.

But Spencer was not about to back down tonight. He was terrified, of course. Unlike Trav, he couldn't heal from stuff. He instead threw every bit of himself into his retaliatory attack, generating two hands made of pure ice from the floor to grab hold of the elemental. The hands melted within moments, Spencer hurriedly trying to figure out his next move.

As Uncle Nero was about to attack once more, he was attacked from behind. There was a screech as his attacker clung to his back, fingernails digging into his neck. He yelled in pain, reaching up to try and pry Travesty off. But Trav just wasn't ready to let go, biting at his neck. He slammed his back into a wall a few times, trying to knock him loose.

It took a few minutes for him to successfully get the half-monkey off of his back, chest heaving. He grabbed him by the arm and hurled him at Spencer, knocking them both toward the flames. Upon landing, Travesty pushed Spencer ahead of him, and a little out of the way of the fire.

Both stood once more, facing Uncle Nero.

"Who the hell is this guy?" Spencer demanded.

His half-monkey friend shrugged. "Well, *he* calls himself Uncle Nero. I just call him an a-hole of the highest caliber."

Flames surrounded the pair in an instant, Spencer throwing a shield of magical energy around them both. The heat could still penetrate the shield to some extent, but it wasn't overwhelming. But Spencer wouldn't be able to keep that shield up indefinitely.

"So, any ideas?" he asked.

"I contacted Mom and Leo on the way over here," said Travesty. "They're looking into some backup."

Through the slight haze of the shield, they could see the fire elemental circling them. He was laughing at them.

"Afraid to come out and face me, you two? I'd have thought the monkey would be all over me!"

The pair looked at each other. They needed a plan, and they needed it fast. If they took him on head-on, he would just wreck them both and move on to destroy the rest of the hospital. If they did nothing, he would do the same thing. What they needed right now was to keep him from being a threat to the general population.

"Wait...could you turn him to stone or something?" Travis asked.

Spencer shook his head. "I haven't gotten to that point yet. I may know a thing or two about magic, but that's a bit above my current skill set."

Travesty ran a hand through his hair, growling in frustration. "Work, brain, *work!*"

It was then that his brain, for once, decided to listen to him, as an idea came to him.

"I'm thinking we should cut off all access to the room," Travesty said. "I'll stay in here and fight him, you get out of the room and create a barrier."

Spencer nearly dropped the shield in shock, as he stared at his friend. He shook his head.

"You can't be serious. What if he kills you?"

He considered this. On the one hand, he'd never encountered something that could kill him. Not on a permanent basis. But he hadn't healed from the prior burn. What if fire was the one thing that could do it?

"It's a risk I'm willing to take, Spence. Just let me out of the shield and get out. Please. I don't want anyone here to die."

As the pair debated, Uncle Nero chuckled and circled the shield. "I'm getting bored out here...should I just come back to you later?" he taunted. "Because I could always just burn this place around you two."

Travesty glared at Spencer. "Let me out of the shield so I can go deal with him and you can create the barrier. Please!"

Spencer nodded, soon shifting the shield to cover just himself. He headed toward the door, leaving Travesty to deal with Uncle Nero. The half-monkey got into a defensive stance, gesturing for his opponent to attack. As he watched through the haze of his shield, Spencer pulled out his cell phone, putting in his wife's number. He had hoped he would never have to make this sort of call to her, but this was a situation he had never anticipated finding himself in.

"Hey, Gemmy...," he began, struggling to keep his tone calm. "I know you're probably not going to get this message until morning, but I might not make it home. Please know that I love you and Daniel more than anything in the world, and I sincerely hope that this call becomes unnecessary, in the long run."

In a way, he was relieved that she didn't pick up. If things came to their worst possible conclusion, he didn't want to have to explain the situation and cause her to worry even more. Once the call was made, he dropped the shield entirely and cast a barrier spell around that room of the hospital, keeping himself inside with the two combatants. There was absolutely no way he was leaving his best friend behind with someone like Uncle Nero.

Back with Travesty, he had pounced on Uncle Nero and started biting at his neck, hissing, and growling. The fire elemental's mustache brushed against the back of his own neck, but he didn't particularly care right now. He fought through the burning. Neither of them noticed Spencer in the corner, starting to summon a sphere of pure liquid water. The water ball was almost large enough to contain a small child, and he lobbed it at the pair. The flames that comprised the fire elemental's hair and mustache were extinguished, and he screamed. Travesty took the opportunity to punch him in the face several times in a row, relieved that he could now get a few hits in without getting burned. He'd already have to have his forehead and neck checked out.

What he didn't notice was that the flames were beginning to form again, the mustache grabbing hold of his hand. He tried to pull away, but his opponent was determined to keep him there. The leather of his fingerless glove burned, and the bracer was beginning to melt. Travesty tried his best to hold back, but he couldn't help but scream. The rest of the mustache returned, as did Uncle Nero's hair.

He grabbed Travesty by the neck, hurling him across the room and returning his focus to Spencer. Spencer moved to throw a shield around himself and Travis just as Uncle Nero launched another attack at them. He managed to get the shield up, but not before the newest fire attack hit Spencer right in the leg. He hurriedly patted the flame on his pant leg out, the shield still up.

The fire elemental stalked toward the shield, kicking at it. "You can't keep hiding behind a shield forever, doctor! You'll need to drop it sometime. Might as well do it sooner rather than later. Face your fate now. Because you know what? I am a fire that will never be extinguished! I need no food. I need no water! I will outlive the both of you, so you may as well die now!"

Travesty pulled himself upright, glaring at their opponent. Even though it hurt him even to move the hand, and though it was burnt to nearly black, he still managed to lift it a few inches, turn the palm toward himself, and raise his middle finger at Uncle Nero. In turn, Uncle Nero summoned a hammer made of pure fire, smashing the shield with it. The vibration of that hammer against Spencer's shield was nearly enough to make the doctor lose his focus. It certainly caused Travesty to lose his balance, the half-monkey landing on the floor.

He looked up to Spencer, mouthing three words to him: "Open the shield." Given that Uncle Nero was so preoccupied with trying to smash the shield open, he hadn't noticed that it had opened up just a bit toward the bottom. It opened just enough for Travesty to reach out with his leg, sweeping his legs right out from under him. He attempted to pull his leg back into the shield, but he wasn't quick enough, the fire elemental pulling him out by the leg.

Spencer dropped the shield, trying to use water against their opponent again. He would trap him inside of a water bubble this time and then maybe freeze that. If nothing else, it might buy them some time to think of a different plan.

A loud crack filled the air just then, and Spencer fell to his knees. His head ached like it never had before. His barrier had just been shattered. Clutching his head, he looked around for a cause. Was it his worry over his best friend? No. Even stress *that* intense couldn't break his focus so. He saw another figure entering the fray, pulling herself through the broken window.

Her messy black and brown hair hung past her hips, and her one visible turquoise eye was narrowed, a dark circle underneath it. So, backup was finally here, in the form of Ivy. And she did *not* look pleased.

Wordlessly, she stormed toward Uncle Nero and Travesty, her eye glowing and a hand stretched in front of her. The fire elemental, currently in the middle of burning the half-monkey's leg, didn't even notice something was amiss until some invisible force gripped his head, beginning to twist it. He began to struggle, but that force was too strong. And within moments, he went entirely limp.

Travesty pulled himself upright, wincing at the burns on his hand and leg. His tail twitched as he noticed that Ivy had joined them, a grin forming on his face. That grin faded pretty quickly when he noticed that she was glaring at him. Tail drooping, he gave her the most pathetic look he could, pouting with wide red eyes.

"Did...did I do something wrong?" he asked her.

In all honesty, he knew exactly what he had done wrong. He pursued this threat, even when others told him not to. He let his temper get the better of him again. He'd been working on not letting that happen over the years, but sometimes, lapses happened.

"Oh, you know damn well what you did, Trav," she spat. "You could have gotten yourself, and Spencer killed! Have we not been through this before? Don't pull this kind of crap by yourself!"

He cast his eyes downward. "Yeah, I kinda forgot, and I'm sorry..."

She marched over to him, putting her arms around the half-monkey. "Please don't do that again, okay?"

"I'll try."

The hospital was soon cleared to bring doctors and patients in again, the overall fire damage being minimal, outside of Exam Room 3B. Before the two could be examined, Spencer took a moment to use a couple of healing spells on Travis's hand, leg, and forehead, clearing those up within minutes.

Travis's stint as Travesty had set a record for superhero careers. Having begun and ended in the span of twelve hours, it was on record as the shortest one ever seen. He would still bring the costume out for comic shop-related purposes on occasion. But as far as active field-work? He was done with that.

For the time being.

END

ABOUT K. MATT

K.Matt is an author and illustrator. Her main body of work is the Hell Bent series of graphic novel/prose novella hybrids. She can be found in Upstate New York, in pretty much the middle of nowhere. She's a fan of comics (and especially the movies based on them), and is an unrepentant workaholic. Her story "Travesty" is a culmination of her love of superhero media (and her love of making her characters suffer).

facebook.com/HellBentBookSeries

twitter.com/MarieTwixie

instagram.com/kmatt666

LADY BLACKWING GETS HER MONIKER

BY DEVORAH FOX

Mercedes jogged down the sidewalk along Lemon Tree Street and smelled bacon frying. She glanced over her shoulder and narrowed her eyes, sharpening her X-ray vision. The brick wall of the single-story residence vaporized, revealing a harried mom standing at a stove cooking breakfast for two youngsters. They chomped at the bit, no doubt impatient to go out to play, to squeeze the most out of what remained of their summer vacation before school started.

Mercedes too dreaded the new semester. She enjoyed classes and was eager to earn more credits toward a degree she hoped to achieve in this lifetime. But she didn't look forward to days crammed with class and homework as well as her job at the Kaffeteria.

She jogged on. The next house she passed exhaled a "springtime fresh" breath. Mercedes' eyes bore into the home where a senior lady in her laundry room folded linens scented by a dryer sheet.

Mercedes chuckled. If only she did possess X-ray vision instead of an overactive imagination. She didn't have superpowers at all.

Unless what occurred when she wrote counted. She didn't want to think about that. It was part of her misgivings about the new school year. Her assignments would require writing and who knew what would happen?

Though she had plenty of time over the summer, she had been afraid to do any creative writing. Mercedes told herself she needn't worry. She wrote plenty of shopping lists, emails, and online posts without any surprising consequences.

The difference was that the spot behind her ear hadn't itched.

Months ago, she accidentally stabbed herself in the head with a pencil. Not any pencil, a Blackwing pencil, the same brand used by renowned writers like John Steinbeck and Vladimir Nabokov. The wound didn't become infected, but the jab nevertheless left her with baffling side effects. Every now and then, the *Lead in Her Head*, the graphite point embedded in her skin, would burn. The only way to soothe the irritation was to grab that pencil and her special notebook and write about what was on her mind.

It seemed a simple remedy. The problem was the repercussions. She didn't know what to do about those.

Mercedes crossed to the other side of Lemon Tree Street and jogged back to Pulaski Avenue.

Three people gathered at the bus stop. Mercedes recognized two of them; she passed them most mornings. Though they stood close enough for conversation, like people in an elevator, they each gazed off into the distance. She caught a whiff of the perfume the young woman wore. It smelled like the cosmetic counter of the discount store from which she likely bought that drab budget suit. The man by her side was in a tie and shirt sleeves and held his jacket slung over his shoulder. Mercedes picked up the scent of his aftershave. *On his way to a job interview?*

Mercedes figured the teenager was taking the bus to the mall to hang with his other deadbeat friends. She scolded herself for her judgmental profiling, but his attire raised her suspicions. Those oversized cargo pants with the knee-level crotch might be a fashion statement, or they could provide ideal places to stash shoplifted merchandise, like those pricey athletic shoes of his. The bandana tied around his forehead could serve to soak up sweat, or it could be a gang insignia. His ball cap pulled low over his forehead threw his face into shadow. And he wore a hoodie although the waning days of a Yankee August were unseasonably hot.

A city bus approached the stop and slowed, its air brakes releasing with a signature fart. Mercedes chirped "Good morning" as she passed the waiting riders. The woman and man smiled and nodded in acknowledgment. The teen was far too engrossed in his cell phone conversation. "Gonna do it tonight," he told his listener.

Mercedes woke from a sleep that was more tossing and turning than actual rest. The area behind her ear flamed, and there'd be no ignoring it.

She got out of bed and in the dark and padded across the bare floor to the cluttered chrome-and-Formica dinette table. She shoved aside a plate dotted with the crumbs of her evening meal, a peanut butter-and-pickle-sandwich. She flipped on the overhead light. Blinking in the glare, she rummaged in a stack of mail, newspapers, and magazines for the writing tools she avoided all summer, a deluxe Moleskine notebook and what she came to think of as a magic pencil, both appropriated when discarded by a customer at the Kaffeteria.

Mercedes didn't believe that using them endowed her with any genius writing ability. She did like feeling connected to the literary giants who used the same brand of notebook or pencil, part of their elite circle if only on the outside looking in.

But the magic part ... it was hard to argue with what happened after she wrote with them.

She bit her lower lip. *Was she ready to unleash their power?* Ready or not, she didn't have a choice. The *Lead in Her Head* was on fire.

The scene at the bus stop called to her. *How about a character study of one of the waiting bus passengers?* That seemed harmless enough. *What could go wrong?* She sharpened the pencil and opened to a clean page.

Dink crouched behind an oleander. The new moon did little to lighten the low hanging overcast sky. The street lamps cast dense shadows. Still, he needed to work fast. He was close enough to the street that the headlights of a passing car could pick him out.

He gazed at the steel fence enclosing his target. Pointed spikes topped the spear-like pickets. No surprise there; he cased the place this morning, complained about it to Snake.

"So?" Snake replied. "You gotta get a grip on the end post and launch yourself over the top. We've done this zillions of times. It's no big ass deal."

"I just don't want to puncture my balls."

"Hell, the fence ain't much taller than you are. You can be up and over it in one second. No floodlights, no security guard. Piece of cake. In, out, you'll be gone."

Funny how the fence looked higher in the dark of night than in the daytime. But Snake was right. It was no big ass deal. They'd scaled taller obstacles.

"What are you, Dink? Scared?"

Scared? No, of course not. Well, okay, maybe a little, but he would never admit it.

Dressed for the mission he wore flexible-soled athletic shoes for climbing the fence, a ball cap to shadow his face, and dark green cargo pants to hold the spray paint cans. Those were so hard to come by. He bought them from an older kid who charged a lot for them. Merchants kept them locked up and wouldn't sell them to minors. Shoppers said it was the fault of taggers which was unfair. They should blame the huffers. Dink figured you must be pretty desperate to try to get high off of sniffing paint fumes. He could imagine screwing up and getting paint up his nose.

Time to move. He darted over to the fence and pulled himself to the top, careful to avoid the sharp-pointed spikes, swung over, and dropped down. At a crouch, he crossed the parking lot. He dragged a trash can close to the wall and mounted it. Dink gave the paint can a mighty shake. He wanted good coverage: no spurts, no skips. In blood-red paint, he inscribed "DIE ARABS" in tall bold letters across the wall's white stucco surface.

Mercedes laid down the pencil, spent and dazed. She had written

without pause as if entranced. Her handwriting now filled pages of the
Moleskine notebook not with a sketch of the woman in the suit, or the
man in the shirt, not even the breakfast-making mom, or sheet-folding
granny, but a tale of vandalism. The suspicious teen at the bus stop had
disturbed her more than she realized.

The *Lead in Her Head* no longer burned, though, so maybe now
she could sleep.

Sluggish from a night spent writing instead of sleeping, Mercedes
slogged along the sidewalk, struggling to reach her target heart rate.

Maybe different scenery would energize her. She made a left onto
Orange Tree Street. She shook her head. The developer of this subdivi-
sion had either been fanciful or deluded, naming the streets after fruits
that would never grow here unless cultivated indoors.

Fresh mulch covered the flower beds in the front yard of the house
at her left. She opened her nostrils wide. The fragrance of the wood
chips painted the picture of a log cabin in a pine forest. She'd never
been in one, but she figured it would smell like that.

The homeowner probably wished his neighbor would mow his
lawn. Grass that last week reached Mercedes' knees had grown waist
high and was topped with feathery seed heads. Too bad she didn't have
heat vision; she could sear the overgrowth to a more reasonable height.

She turned onto Pulaski Avenue, anticipating coming up on what
was one of her favorite sights along this route, which was odd since it
rarely changed from day to day. A plain masonry building, its pitched
roof tiled with composition shingles, it could be a preschool, a community center, even a pool hall. Three features distinguished it as a house
of Muslim worship. One was the timid lettering over the front door
identifying it as the Islamic Center. Another was the interior shutters.
Carved in intricate arabesque patterns, they appeared handcrafted and
called to mind illustrations in Sinbad the Sailor storybooks from child-
hood. And then there was the dome. Swelling out of one wall in an
otherwise rectangular structure was a windowless half-cylinder-shaped

bay topped by a golden dome. No matter what time of day or from what angle Mercedes passed it, the dome always glowed in whatever light there was.

Mercedes assumed the dome was a requisite of mosque architecture, but she wondered about the rounded bay and what it looked like on the inside. Did it house their altar, she wondered. One day she would go into the Center and ask to see. Except, no one ever seemed to be there. The parking lot always stood empty. That didn't surprise her; church parking lots were jammed on Sunday mornings and vacant every other day of the week. Mercedes didn't know anything about Islamic practice except that worshippers prayed several times a day and always facing toward Mecca. Maybe services were held at a time of day when she didn't happen to jog past, or the center's members prayed at home or work or school.

Anyhow, assuming she got in, how thrilled would they be about a visit from a nosy college student-slash-barista?

Something jarring caught her eye, and she slowed. What was that? Had someone graffitied the mosque?

She gave the markings a second glance as she passed. Perhaps they weren't graffiti, but instead some Arabic slogan or prayer.

Mercedes continued down the block, but her steps slowed. She realized she knew the writing on the mosque wasn't Arabic script. She turned and doubled back.

She arrived at the mosque, stood on the sidewalk, and studied the scrawls through the metal fence. Like dripping blood, streaks streamed down from huge red capital letters. She stepped back to take it in. Seen from the new perspective, the loops and whorls became legible.

No doubt about it. This was graffiti all right but not a tagger's emblem or gang's brand. Someone defaced the mosque with a hate message on the clean white wall: DIE ARABS.

Just as in her story. It had been the mosque that Dink vandalized.

Did she make this happen?

Her breath stuck in her throat, and despite the warmth of the day, she felt chilled.

In a few weeks, the anniversary of 9-11 would come around.

Mercedes was too young when it happened to understand then, but the incident left a scarring legacy. Middle Eastern terrorists had caused so much fear and death. Much as she might try to resist racial profiling, she was as fearful and angry as anyone else.

Still, vandalizing a house of worship? She would never have wanted that. *Where had that idea come from?*

The spring in her step snuffed, she trudged home, cleaned up, and headed for work.

Mercedes missed Kaffeteria's night shift. Its fast pace left her little time for clock-watching. But over the summer she came to enjoy the somewhat more relaxed day shift. Actual lulls gave her a chance to straighten the stockroom, something she knew the harried night staff would appreciate. Though autumn was weeks away, the coffeehouse had already laid in seasonal supplies of pumpkin-spice this and pumpkin-spice that. At first, she found the nostril-filling scents of cinnamon and nutmeg refreshing, conjuring up the energizing crispness of chilly morning air and the snuggly comfort of sweaters. The novelty wore off, and by the time the calendar actually flipped over to fall, she would have enough of all things pumpkin-spice, but that was okay. By then they'd be stocking peppermint- and eggnog-flavored items in preparation for Christmas.

The day shift also gave her opportunities to practice her latte art. She learned the free pour as a trainee; all the Kaffeteria baristas had to pull that off. The advanced technique of etching drawings into the foamed milk with a coffee stirrer opened up the chance to try more ambitious designs. She'd been perfecting grinning ghosts and leering jack-o-lanterns.

But today Mercedes couldn't focus, couldn't prepare a cup of black coffee much less pull off a flat white. You had to be quick on the draw at the espresso machine to make one of those. The intrusive specter of the lurid red letters throbbing against the white wall of the mosque kept breaking her concentration.

Had she made it happen? It was too great a coincidence to think otherwise.

Car after car advanced down the street. Mercedes had never seen so much traffic. Well-traveled during the morning and evening rush, at other times Pulaski Avenue presented less cross traffic to look out for and fewer exhaust fumes for her to breathe during her jog.

Except this morning. *Was it because with the day off from work and the fall semester yet to start she was out much earlier than usual?*

As she moved along the sidewalk, she realized the commuters were turning into the parking lot of the mosque.

She slowed, jogged in place a few yards from the mosque's gate, and watched traffic pour into the parking lot. A bearded man wearing a skullcap and a lime green safety vest over long white tunic and trousers directed the arrivals to available spaces. People exited their cars and moved toward the mosque's front door, and Mercedes found herself enthralled. The men were outfitted in long-sleeved knee-length tunics over plain loose pants, not a pair of jeans in sight, and they too wore skullcaps. Every one of the women, even the little girls, wore a filmy floaty tunic and billowy pants in ice-cream colors. They looked like fantasyland fairies. Was that how they typically dressed for services, she wondered.

Sure, she was aware the city had Muslim citizens. She even had the occasional classmate who wore a hijab, although Mercedes never did become acquainted. A whole crowd of Muslims, though ... that could arouse her wariness if she didn't feel like she had stumbled on a set from a production of *Aladdin*. The outfits were as non-threatening as they were exotic, and the gathering radiated pride and delight as brilliant as the gold braid trimming their clothing.

Mercedes couldn't help seeing that as they neared the entrance the arrivals glanced at the graffiti. An attempt had been made to whitewash it, but the red paint soaked through. The worshippers' steps slowed, their shoulders slumped, and their heads drooped, their gaiety deflated like air escaping a leaky balloon.

Despite being aware of her unpresentable, maybe sacrilegious sweat-soaked ball cap and "Save Water, Drink Tequila" graphic tee shirt, Mercedes drummed up the courage to approach the parking lot attendant. "Excuse me. I jog past this practically every day. I've never seen so many people. Is it a wedding or some special observance?"

He smiled. "A special observance. We're celebrating Eid." He held out his arm, his hand at a right angle, to pause an oncoming vehicle.

"Thank you. I see you're busy. I won't keep you. Have a ... happy one," she said, at a loss for a suitable Eid greeting.

She finished her run and slowed to a cool-down walk. She unhooked her smartphone from her waistband, launched a browser, and entered the search term "Eid." Apparently, there were two. One marked the end of Ramadan. Mercedes had a vague awareness of that. It was a month-long fast. The end of Ramadan would certainly warrant a celebration in her book.

Today's Eid commemorated an event with which she was more familiar: Abraham's willingness to sacrifice his son to God, a remarkable Bible story that creeped her out as a child but which she now saw as man's first acknowledgment of God's divine sovereignty.

She read that while Muslims could offer daily prayers wherever they happened to be at the appointed time, worshippers were to say Eid prayers in the mosque as part of a congregation, women as well as men. That explained the throng at the Islamic Center this morning.

Mercedes thought about how the congregants were dressed, so different from what most people wore, even when in their Sunday best. How foreign they seemed as if beamed directly from Mecca.

Today's worshippers would have had to ask for time off from work or school. She bet they took a personal or vacation day for it. Eid wasn't like Christmas. Everyone got a day off for that.

It must be difficult to practice a religion so alien, particularly one so feared and reviled, some would say with good reason. Yet, here they were. Mercedes would have to say that she was impressed.

Two men entered the Kaffeteria and strode to the Order counter. One of them looked familiar. The Kaffeteria had its regulars but not this man.

Still, Mercedes was sure she saw him just the other day. As he drew closer, she realized he was the man from the Islamic Center, the one who had been parking cars. No white skullcap today, or tunic; he wore a regular long-sleeved button-down shirt and slacks. His companion wore a sports coat over a polo shirt. An ID card hung from a lanyard around his neck.

Mercedes took their orders. Before they moved to the pickup window, she said, "Excuse me, aren't you from the Islamic Center?"

His expression wary, his posture defensive, the man in the sports coat replied, "Yes."

"I don't mean to be nosy. Well, okay, I do. Like, I jog past the mosque, and I couldn't help but notice the graffiti," she said.

Furrowed with worry and anger the man's brows pinched tighter. His companion's lips pressed together.

"Do you have any idea how it happened or who ...?" she asked.

The taller of the two men, the one who had directed traffic, said, "A little. Why do you ask?"

"I just ... it like really upset me. I just can't imagine who would do something like that."

The jacketed man said, "One kid."

Mercedes gulped. She knew that.

The tall man said, "We have security cameras trained on the parking lot. Courtesy of a most generous donation from Mr. Argent here, one of our members."

Mercedes glanced at the decal on Mr. Argent's ID badge, which read Argent Security along with the image of a silver padlock on a shield.

"It was dark," Argent said. "The footage doesn't show much. One figure. Small, probably a teenager. Not much to go on."

Mercedes' chest tightened.

He turned toward his companion. "Sorry, Imam. I know it's closing the barn door after the horse has been stolen, but who knew we'd need more protection?" To Mercedes, he said, "I'll be exploring ways to beef up the system."

"Oh, you don't have to explain to me. I just thought it was tragic."

"We reported it to the police of course," said the other man whom Mercedes now understood was the Islamic Center's leader. "There isn't much they can do."

"No?"

"The damage is so minor, and we have so little evidence to provide to them, it is not worth it for them to follow up."

"Not worth ...?" Mercedes glowered. "But the message. It's a hate crime. Doesn't that warrant some action?"

The Imam sighed. "The police have all they can do with more violent crimes--domestic abuse, rape, murders."

"Doesn't it make you angry?"

The Imam took a deep breath. "Yes. But I know anger does not solve anything. It can, however, destroy everything. A strong man is one who can control his anger."

Mr. Argent patted the Imam on the back. "Come. Let's sit. I have some ideas to run past you."

"Sirs, your coffees," Mercedes said. She slid their orders across the counter, an espresso and a latte on which she had swirled a peace symbol.

Mr. Argent reached for his wallet.

"No, sir, keep your money," Mercedes said. "The coffee's on me."

"That is very kind." The Imam smiled. Mr. Argent stuffed some folding green into the Tips jar.

Mercedes tried to read, to watch TV, but her attention wandered. The vandalism at the mosque bothered her all day, and it still did.

She wouldn't say she held any special affection for Islam, not that she actually knew a whole lot about it. *But freedom of religion, any religion, wasn't that what this country was founded for?*

Defacing a house of worship? Why would someone do that? The Imam was right. It accomplished nothing except to incite resentment, maybe vengeance.

The spot behind her ear flared. Perhaps if she wrote about it, she could understand it. Could settle down, go to sleep ...

Buoyed by success, Dink leaped off the trash can and sprinted back to the fence. Yes, he thought as he vaulted over the top, die, you Arabs. Dink hadn't been born yet when the stinking ragheads attacked the country, his country, but his uncle was. His uncle saw the 9-11 assaults on TV, described the horror to Dink as if he had been right there in New York when the Twin Towers went down. Dink's uncle didn't think the U.S. military was doing enough to safeguard America. "They should blow Afghanistan off the map," he would grumble.

Dink hoped his message would be a warning, that Snake and the other guys would get serious about bombing or burning this Arab hang out. That would be a start on making life safer for real Americans.

Mercedes paused. She had asked why someone would deface the mosque, and now she had an answer, but she was still agitated. The *Lead in Her Head* flared. There must be more to the story.

Dink dropped onto the street side of the fence and raced up the street. Around the corner was an apartment complex. He could lose the spray can in their Dumpster. That way, no one would ever be able to tie the tag to him. He raised his arm ready to toss the can into the trash container, but the metal ball inside made a muffled sound as if the can wasn't completely empty. Spray paint was so hard to get, he didn't want to waste any. Dink gave the can a shake and aimed at the Dumpster, but nothing came out. Maybe the nozzle had a clog. He moved near a streetlight, held the can close to his face to examine it, and pressed the nozzle. Red paint fanned out. The bill of his cap shielded his eyes, but the spray covered his cheeks, chin, mouth, and even got up his nostrils.

"Goddammit," Dink muttered and scrubbed at his face with his shirt sleeve.

The next morning, his face still tinged with red, Dink skipped breakfast and left before his uncle awoke. He didn't want to stay home, his uncle might find some crappy thing for him to do, but he couldn't walk the streets all day either. He texted Snake to see where he was hanging out.

The mall, of course. It would take a pocketful of quarters, but the bus could get him there.

The bus stop, it was damn close to the mosque. *What if someone had seen him, recognized him? What if someone saw his paint-stained face and put two and two together?* Rather than take a chance he walked to a distant stop.

At the mall, Dink strolled along the wide corridors, pretending interest in the shop window displays. Young mothers pushing strollers, old ladies with big purses, and power walkers in cropped pants passed him too preoccupied with their own selves to pay him any attention. He found Snake in the arcade.

"Let's head over to the food court. I skipped breakfast and want something to eat." He had a little change left. He could buy a hot dog, load it up with free relish. And a forty-eight-ounce drink, that would fill him up.

Dink strode up to the vendor and placed his order. He garnished the hot dog with condiments, stuck a straw in the drink, and turned to join Snake only to bump right smack into a mall cop.

"Young men, you should come with me," the officer said.

Dink shrugged and moved to edge around the man's bulk. The officer clasped Dink's upper arm.

"Hey! You almost spilled my drink."

"Yes, well, I think, and you and your drink and your buddy better come along."

Snake glared at Dink. "You loser," he hissed. "You got me in trouble. Just you wait, you prick. I'm gonna hurt you for this." He reached out to grab Dink's throat.

Dink dodged his grasp, circled behind the cop, and trudged along on the officer's opposite side.

At the security office, they learned they were being detained on suspicion of inhalant abuse, a Class B misdemeanor, pending the arrival of a police officer.

The End.

Mercedes laid down the pencil. Wrung out, she rested her head on her folded arms. Her first fevered Blackwing writing sessions had left her feeling the way a hard run did: exhausted from the effort but euphoric with achievement.

Until she discovered they had ramifications, that she had made manifest something that previously existed only in a dimension of possibilities. With her words, she brought that into reality. It didn't always turn out so well. Like the very first time with the pencil when she wrote about zombies. It wreaked havoc, which to this day, no one could explain.

No run this morning. Exhausted by her late-night writing marathon Mercedes had overslept leaving only enough time to grab breakfast and dress before work.

Between swallows of coffee and bites of toast, she thumbed through her emails and texts and scanned the headlines in the daily digital news digest courtesy of the local paper. The school district had hired a new director. The high school football team was not doing well. The city planned to raise water rates. Great, Mercedes thought. No doubt a rent increase was in her future.

She scrolled on. A headline grabbed her attention.

"Youths Arrested in Tagging Incident"

She clicked on the link to the story. Two boys detained at the mall had been arrested for possible inhalant abuse. Police suspected connections with the defacing of the Islamic Center. The suspects had been released into the custody of their parents and guardians pending further investigation. The names had been withheld because of the age of the alleged perpetrators.

Yes! Apprehended and soon to be punished, just as she wrote. Nabbed for inhalant abuse was a fitting punishment for the spray-can-wielding hate monger. If that would have come about otherwise was hard to say. The Imam and the man from the security company didn't seem to think it likely.

So why didn't she feel relieved? The spot behind her ear was still warm, tender as if not quite done with her. *Was there more to the story?*

If there were, it would have to wait. Mercedes clicked off her phone and started for the door, then turned and slipped the notebook and pencil into her apron pocket.

In the Kaffeteria's cramped storeroom, Mercedes studded orange-frosted cupcakes with licorice candy drops and twizzles, making approximations of smiling and grimacing emojis, but her mind lingered on the young man arrested for tagging.

He should answer for his actions, but she felt uneasy. Her head drummed as if with the echo of his anger. *And what had the Imam said about anger? That it solved nothing but had the power to destroy?*

Had she laid the groundwork for more destruction?

The buzzing in her head, that wasn't the boy's rage, it was the *Lead in Her Head*. She cleared a space on the counter for her notebook and opened to a clean page.

Dink got off the bus but didn't head for home. Wait until his uncle heard. The man hated cops. He would be insane about Dink involving him with the police and the courts and all. The time Dink spent in the holding cell would give him serious street creds that might be worth the beating he was in for.

He couldn't ask Snake for help. Along with the court dates they got were instructions to stay away from each other.

Dink figured he'd better keep his head down until he figured how he was going to get out of this mess.

He drifted down the block, his brain turning over what should be his next move, not watching where he was going until he realized he was almost at the mosque. Goddamn ragheads. This was all their fault.

What kind of church was this anyway? No one was ever here. They must be off somewhere plotting how to bomb buildings.

He stood outside the fence, admiring his handiwork. Someone had tried to clean it, cover it up, but Dink had used the good stuff, stuff that wouldn't wash off easily or fade.

"You wouldn't know how we can remove it, would you?"

Dink spun to face a tall bearded man wearing a long tunic and a snug white cap.

Dink made to run, but the man stepped in his path.

Dink glanced at the paint job. "Looks like that's gonna be there a while. Anyway, whaddaya askin' me for? I don't know nothin' about it."

"Oh, I think you do." The man stuck out his index finger and almost tapped Dink on his nose, still unnaturally pink.

"Well, so what if I did? Ain't nothin' you can do about it." Dink crossed his arms over his chest. "I already been arrested." He tried to sound tough, not scared, but the man was big. *Would he throw a punch? Pull out a sword and cut off his head like his uncle said Arabs did?* Dink took a step back toward the street, but the man stepped forward and closed the space.

Try touching me, Dink thought. I'll scream, call you a pervert. He could try to dart through traffic, run across the street and lose himself in the neighborhood but at the moment Pulaski Ave. was empty of cars.

"Yes, we know. The police informed us. You are in a lot of trouble. Criminal mischief like graffiti is a misdemeanor. You could be fined, even do jail time."

Dink didn't know that. He tried not to gulp. Street cred was good; jail, not so much.

"The fine could be as much as $30,000 since you marked up a place of worship."

Oh, crap, Dink thought. His uncle would freak out.

"And a hate crime." The man glanced over his shoulder at the marked-up wall. "Well, there are laws and penalties, especially for that." He turned back to Dink. "The question is, what are you going to do about it?"

Dink didn't know. While he tried to think of something, the man asked, "This is your first offense?"

"Yeah." The first he'd been caught at, anyway.

"Much of what you will be charged with depends on the amount of damage that you caused, the price tag of our loss."

"Yeah? And what are you going to tell them?" Dink snorted. "It's just paint."

The man lifted his chin and gazed off into space, thinking. "Paint that you said was hard to remove. Unless you know how to remove it."

"What if I did?"

"Then we would have less damage to report." The man tapped his bearded chin. "You might get let off with a warning."

The tightness in Dink's stomach and shoulders loosened. Maybe there was a way out of this. "What's the catch?"

"The catch?"

"Why would you do that? You must hate me. Aren't you angry?"

The man nodded. "I was angry at first. We all were." He frowned and pressed his lips together, and Dink thought he might still be.

The man closed his eyes and took a deep breath, then said, "But what did that accomplish? What should we do? Strike back at you? Then your homies seek revenge, and then we retaliate and then we are at war. Is that what you want?"

"Yeah. Yeah, I do."

The man cocked his head to one side. "Why? You don't even know me."

"Cause you're an Arab. Cause you Arabs blew up those buildings in New York. You killed a lot of people."

The man nodded. "That was a bad thing. That was done by men unable to control their anger. They were angry, but they were not strong. No, they were weak. It is a strong man who can control his anger."

Dink thought about his uncle, about how he would pitch a fit when he got mad, and throw stuff and break things, and smack Dink. Afterward, his uncle had a bunch of broken stuff he had to fix or throw out, and all that did was piss him off more.

"Are you a strong man? Or are you a weak man who lets his anger tell him what to do?" the man asked.

Dink hadn't thought about it that way. "I'm strong."

"You make the decisions."

"Yeah. I decide what I'm going to do."

"So. What have you decided about this?" The man waved his arm at the building. "Are you going to let an act of anger ruin the rest of your life? Or are you a strong man?"

Dink peered past the man at the side of the building. He thought about the stone-face cops who hurried him along and told him to do this and go there like he was some kind of animal. And being in the holding cell with Snake who would have killed him if they weren't surrounded by cops. And the beating he was in for from his uncle.

"My, uh, friend. He got arrested too, and he didn't have anything to do with this. Can you do something about that?"

"We can try. If he is innocent, then he should not be punished."

Dink shrugged. "That paint? No problem. I can fix that."

"Good." The man put out his hand.

Dink took it, and they shook on it.

Mercedes lifted her head, startled to find herself in the Kaffeteria's storeroom. Her stomach growled. A tray of orange-frosted cupcakes grinned up at her, and she devoured one in a single bite.

The spot behind her ear no longer stung and though enervated, she also felt serene. Like leaving a movie theater having shuddered through a nail-biter of a horror film with a cathartic ending.

She slid the notebook and pencil into her apron, straightened her cap, grabbed the tray of cupcakes, and hurried back behind the counter.

Mercedes worked up a sweat by the time she reached the mosque, and she was more winded than usual. It could have been the heat of midday; Indian summer held them in a stuffy overheated grip.

She had stayed up till one a.m. and slept in to recalibrate her circadian clock in preparation for a return to the night shift. She arrived at the mosque later than usual to find a few cars in its parking lot, albeit nothing like the horde that thronged it for Eid.

And off to one side, a slim figure wearing a bandana and a ball cap stood on the platform of a metal scaffold. A hoodie jacket lay draped over the scaffold's railing. Like a wizard waving a magic wand, he directed the spray from a pressure washer onto the wall making the graffiti vanish.

Mercedes' racing pulse soared, and she whooped. The painter half turned. Mercedes waved, gave a thumbs-up, and charged down the sidewalk.

Could the Man of Steel have felt any more empowered bursting from that phone booth, his cape streaming from his shoulders, she wondered as she flew down the street, her feet barely touching the ground?

So, she didn't have X-ray or heat vision. But she had powers, superpowers. She could make things happen with her words. Okay, not just her words. Her words and the notebook.

And the pencil, the Blackwing pencil.

Maybe it was the way she had been inoculated.

She pressed a finger to the *Lead in Her Head*. She would always have it with her. She was Blackwinged.

Blackingwinger.

Blackwingman.

No, Blackwingwoman.

She chuckled. That wouldn't work. Emblazoned on her chest, it would run under her armpit.

Ms. Blackwing then.

No ... Lady.

Lady Blackwing.

—**END**—

ABOUT DEVORAH FOX

"What if?" Those two words all too easily send Devorah Fox spinning into flights of fancy. Best-selling author of award-winning books including The Bewildering Adventures of King Bewilliam literary historical fantasy series and several thrillers, she also penned Fantasy/Science Fiction and Mystery Mini Short Reads and contributed short stories to popular fantasy anthologies. Born in Brooklyn, New York, she now lives on the Texas Gulf Coast with rescued tabby cats ... and a dragon named Inky.

Visit the "Dee-Scoveries" blog at http://devorahfox.com

and subscribe to receive the free email newsletter at:
http://eepurl.com/LrZGX.

facebook.com/DevorahFoxAuthor

twitter.com/devorah_fox

instagram.com/devorahfox

HUMMING

BY R.M. DEMEESTER

I clocked out, gathered my jacket and keys and headed for the door, absently brushing my hand through my hair and adjusting my collar before exiting my office for the night. On the bench outside the front door were two men, both dressed in black. A cold shiver ran down my spine, and my eyes darted away. I could feel my heartbeat increase. Behind me, I could hear the scrape of boots as the two shadowy figures rose to follow me. I gulped. I didn't want any trouble. My car was just a few blocks away on Miller Street.

There was a back alley about half a block up, which was the most direct route to my car. I used that shortcut all the time, but tonight was cold and dark. Did I want to risk it with these two following me? A knot formed in my throat. The two figures were hot on my tail. What did they even want? Did they want to rob me? Or were their motives more sinister? I couldn't help that trouble seemed to find me.

I reached the alley, turned, and sprinted as fast I could. They chased after me. I ran faster, glancing back every few seconds. My heart thumped in my chest, and my movements were slowed by improper clothing. I glanced back and tripped over a heap of dirt before falling face first onto the ground.

"Shit!"

I tried to get to my knees, but a heavy boot on my back prevented me from standing. I tried to wiggle out, but one of them kicked me in my side. I groaned. My body struggled to move. From the opposite side, the other man kicked me in the stomach, and I exhaled a labored breath. Curling up into a ball, I cradled my gut. An intense throbbing pain circulated throughout my entire body. I tucked my head toward my chest, trying to protect myself from further strikes.

Were they going to take my car? That'd make picking up Natasha difficult.

Another strike kicked the wind out of me. Everything around me became one big blur. I blinked my eyes and saw four of everything. This wasn't good.

I found the strength to turn my head slightly and make eye contact. "What do you want?" My voice was shaky, almost unrecognizable, even to me.

Their response was another sharp kick.

"Shut up!"

I tried to block the blow, but my efforts were rewarded by intensified pain in my stomach. I squeezed my eyes shut. All I wanted to do was get to my car, pick up Natasha from work, give her the biggest hug, sweep her off her feet, and tell her I loved her. Instead, I vomited.

With no strength left in my body, it wasn't difficult for the two men to turn me over onto my back.

"Let's see what this guy has on him."

One of them placed his knee on my chest and reached into my jacket pocket. Maybe they'd take my money and leave.

Please, not my keys. I don't want to leave my girlfriend stranded.

He pulled out my wallet and cell phone, and I forced my gaze to meet his. He looked at my screen, which was a picture of Natasha and me on vacation a few months ago. He smirked before turning the screen toward me.

"Cute girl. Would be a shame if something happened to her, wouldn't it?" His voice was full of venom. "Don't look so glum."

"Please, don't hurt her..." I begged, swallowing my pride. I pathetically reached for my phone, but I stopped as my insides threatened to explode. I was in no position to do anything.

The man dangled the phone in front of me. "Is this what you want?"

I didn't respond. A vision of Natasha formed in my mind. I imagined hugging her and staring into her seductive eyes. All I could do was tell myself she would be okay and everything would be fine.

"Hurry up!" the other man snapped.

"Just keep lookout," grumbled the man with my phone before turning his focus back to me. He licked his lips like I was Sunday brunch. "I'm not done with you, not by a long shot."

"What do you want?"

He raised his fist, ready to punch me, but stopped.

He laughed sadistically. "Should see the look on your face. Scared wittle puppy, hey. Hey?"

I didn't respond. What was the point?

He frowned. "Not laughing. I'll give you a reason not to laugh." He plunged his fist toward my face, and I flinched.

"Hey! What are you doing?" A voice called from a distance.

"Let's run!" the man screamed, as he stood up and relieved the immense pressure from my chest.

"Not so fast!" The voice yelled. Whoever the voice belonged to was getting closer.

I opened my eyes to see a woman. She had long blonde hair and wore a bubblegum pink dress. A glowing aura surrounded her, and she was humming. The two men tried to run, but couldn't.

"What the...?" one man shouted, "what is this?"

As the woman floated past me through the air, the humming intensified. Suddenly, the two men vanished. I was seeing things. I had to be. This wasn't happening.

She turned and floated back toward me.

"They won't bother you anymore, Thomas," she said, hovering over me.

"What?" I asked. "Who are you?"

I really needed a doctor because I was seeing things.

"Relax, young Thomas. Help is on the way. When you wake up, you won't remember me at all. If I could erase this entire experience for you, I would. Soon you'll understand. But for now, I must go."

"Wait!" I whispered.

She hummed something else, and I felt my eyes close. For a moment, my mind separated from my body, then everything went dark.

My eyes fluttered open. I glanced around for a good minute before I could comprehend where I was. I was still in the middle of the alley. I rolled onto my back and an acute pain shot through my insides.

"Shit!" I recoiled.

Everything was cloudy, and I couldn't move without my body retaliating. I felt helpless. Then Natasha popped in my head. I needed to call her and make sure she was all right. I was very warm, and my heart was pounding in my chest. I reached into my pocket only to find my phone and wallet missing.

"Damnit!" I cried. A car sped past the alley. I needed to get to the sidewalk and find someone with a phone. It was my only option.

I tried to get up but quickly collapsed back to the ground. I felt shaky. What was I going to do? Natasha entered my mind once again. I promised to pick her up, and I didn't. Acrid bile rose in my throat again. I felt so ill. How could I allow myself to be robbed? I checked my coat pocket again. My keys were still inside. Thank god; at least they didn't steal my car.

Every so often, another vehicle drove by. But no one turned down the back alley. Every few minutes, I gathered the strength to haul my body through the alley one notch closer to the street. Every time I scrunched my face in anticipation of the pain in my stomach, searing pain shot across my face. I couldn't catch a break.

A few feet from where I had been beaten up, my body finally gave out and dropped to the ground. I lay there waiting for someone to come find me. I drifted in and out of consciousness. The primary thought in my mind was of wrapping my arms around Natasha. I wanted to cuddle her and run my fingers through her curly hair. She'd smile at me with her freckled complexion and daring brown eyes. I was so lucky.

A fluorescent light filled the alley. I turned my head toward it to see a car halt in front of me. Someone exited the vehicle, but my vision was too obscured to make out who it was.

"Are you all right, sir?" a man asked, flashing a light at me.

I jerked my face away from the blinding light and cried out in pain.

"Are you all right?" he asked again.

As he came closer, I made out the logo of a nearby business. I stammered something in response, but my throat felt dry. It hurt too much to talk.

"Hold tight, sir. I'll call for help."

"My phone..." I somehow found my words.

The man walked passed me and bent down to retrieve something off the ground.

"Missing a wallet?"

I nodded slowly.

He opened the wallet, looked inside, and looked at me. He reached over and put the wallet back in my pocket. "Sorry, I don't see your phone. But I'll call for help."

He pulled out his cell and made a call. I felt some mild relief, but not enough. Those men threatened to hurt Natasha. I needed to talk to her.

The man came back over. "Help's on the way."

I forced a weak "thanks." Any further talk was out of the question.

The sound of sirens approached. A police car arrived, and the business owner went to speak to one officer, while another approached me.

"Sir, are you all right?" he asked.

Do I look all right? I wanted to ask him. "No."

"Can you tell me what happened?"

"They followed me."

The details of what happened were a blur. Everything felt like a blur. "Sir, who followed you?"

"I-I don't..." I vomited again. A burning sensation stopped my line of thought. I heaved, trying to catch my breath.

"Is there anything you remember?" he asked.

"I was jumped."

An ambulance arrived, and a paramedic came out the back. He came to my side. "Sir, can you tell me what happened?"

I blinked a few times. "I got the shit kicked out of me." I tried to laugh a little to lighten the mood.

The paramedic loomed over me. "Can you tell me your name?"

"Thomas."

He nodded. "Okay, Thomas. Can you tell me what year it is?"

"2018."

"Good, good." The paramedic smiled.

I didn't particularly feel very good at that moment, though.

"Okay, Thomas, we're going to put on a cervical collar."

"Okay," I whispered. For all I cared, they could do whatever they wanted to me. They drilled me with a few more questions, and I did my best to answer. After what felt like forever, they finally loaded me into the ambulance.

On the way to the hospital, the paramedic hovered above me and inserted an intravenous needle.

"You had quite the night, huh?" he asked, noting my vitals.

"Yeah, you could say that," I said, trying to make light of the situation.

He pushed on my stomach lightly. "Does this hurt?"

I gasped and weakly affirmed that it did.

I wanted to tell him to stop, but I didn't have the strength. I was at his mercy. What the hell did I do to deserve this?

The ride felt like it went on forever. All I wanted was some painkillers and a phone. I could pay for a cab for Natasha. I didn't want her to wait alone in that part of town with all those seedy, horny men and drug addicts running around. I worked in a decent area, but that didn't prevent *me* from getting jumped. She would stand no chance. The mere thought sent a wave of nausea through my body. I was helpless.

Soon the ambulance rolled to a stop.

"We're pulling in," the paramedic said.

"Thanks," I mumbled.

As they rolled me down the platform and into the emergency room, I closed my eyes.

"I'm glad you're all right."

I recognized the voice, but I didn't know where from.

"Who are you?" I asked.

I opened my eyes to find myself surrounded by hospital staff. At least half a dozen of them were staring down at me.

"How are you feeling?" one nurse asked.

"Fine."

But my head kept going back to that initial voice, that woman's voice. It seemed so familiar and so real, but I knew it was in my head. I had to have a concussion. There was no other reason why I would be hearing things. At least, none that I could explain.

I just lay there like a dead log, trying my most darn to keep it together.

"What time is it?" I finally asked.

"Almost ten, sir."

I swore to myself. I hoped and prayed that Natasha made it home all right.

My mind drifted in and out of consciousness.

"I know you don't remember, Thomas, but you'll be all right."

"Who are you?"

"The answer will be clear soon. I just want you to know you did well tonight. It may not seem like it right now, but you saved a life."

"Show yourself…"

There was a faint humming in the distance as a woman with blonde hair and a pink dress slowly came into focus. I knew her. I knew her from somewhere. She was someone I had met recently, but I couldn't remember where. She hummed and smiled.

"Who are you?" I asked again.

"I'm a power, a strength within. Now rest, Thomas. You must rest. You won't remember this conversation. It's for the best."

"Wait!!!!"

Without another word, she floated past me and vanished into thin air.

I opened my eyes and looked around. I was in a different room. My body felt like I had been repeatedly run over by a dump truck.

A nurse was checking my vitals.

"What's going on?"

"You lost consciousness."

I took a deep, painful breath. "Then what?"

"You had some bleeding, which turned out to be nothing serious. A doctor will be in later to talk with you. Get some rest."

A few minutes later, my mother walked into the room with a cup of coffee and a magazine. What was she doing here?

She ran over and gave me a loose hug. "Thomas, you're awake! How are you feeling? I was so worried."

I looked behind her for a moment. "Where's Natasha?"

My heart stammered. My mind raced back to the alley. Those men knew what Natasha looked like. They took my phone and god knows what kind of information they could get from it. They threatened me. Even though they were likely just trying to get a rise out of me, I couldn't be sure Natasha was safe unless I saw her with my own two eyes. "Did Natasha come with you?"

Mom frowned. "No, she didn't come."

I noted the disdain her voice. Surely she could put her differences with Natasha aside for this one night.

"Did someone try to contact her?" I asked, "At least to let her know I'm here."

"No, it's four in the morning, son. You've got to take it easy, honey."

"I need a phone." I adjusted my position in the bed, carefully untangling the IV cord.

Mom placed her hand on my arm. "Let me get a nurse."

I shrugged her away. "No, I need a phone. Give me a phone."

"You should rest."

Mom had never cared for Natasha but now wasn't the time. "I need to talk to Natasha. Either you get me a phone, or I'll get up and find my own."

Why didn't anyone call her? I knew I should have updated my next of kin. I was always forgetful. In returned I gained a controlling, over-bearing mother.

"All right, son. Please take it easy. You've been through a lot." She reached into her purse and handed me her phone.

My limbs shook uncontrollably as I dialed Natasha's number. *Please answer. Please answer.* It went straight to voicemail. I hung up and redialed her number. My throat grew itchy. Did those goons find her? God dammit! I hope they didn't find her. Maybe she went to bed. Maybe she was angry that I didn't pick her up. That had to be it. I hope that was all it was.

"Thomas Tinsley."

I jumped slightly. My mother stepped out of the way of a nurse, who shut the door softly behind her. I handed my mother back her phone.

"How are you feeling?" the nurse asked with a smile.

"Fine!" I snapped at her louder than I expected.

"Any pain?" She jotted something on a clipboard.

"My stomach."

"Here, let me take a look."

She pulled down the sheet.

Mom gave me a little wave. "I'll be right outside if you need me."

When she was out of sight, the nurse stared at me. "I'm going to lift the gown, okay?"

I nodded as she pulled up the gown. A large bruise in the shape of a footprint covered much of the lower quadrant of my stomach. They had kicked me there too many times for me to count. I still wished I knew what they wanted.

"Are you experiencing any nausea?"

"No."

"How about double vision?"

"No!" I exclaimed, "I feel all right, except for some pain in my eye and my stomach."

The nurse nodded, jotting something down.

She retrieved a disposable thermometer. "Open up."

I opened my mouth, and she took my temperature.

"Vitals look good. I'll be back in a few hours to check up on you. Ring me if you need anything."

"Okay, thanks."

Just as she left, Mom walked back in.

She sat on a chair beside the bed. "Natasha called back."

"What did she say?"

"She's on her way."

"Go pick her up." The face of the man who had dangled my phone above my beaten body appeared before me over and over again. I didn't want Natasha to get hurt. "She isn't safe."

"Don't worry. She's taking a cab."

"Okay."

I turned and faced forward. An awkward silence filled the room, but I felt better knowing Natasha would be here soon and wasn't on a bus somewhere.

"Thomas?"

"Yeah, Mom?"

"What happened?"

"I left work around eight. Two men followed me into an alley and beat me up."

"What were you doing walking?"

"The parking lot is under construction. So I had to park a few blocks away." I sighed. "Can you wake me up when Natasha gets here? I have a headache."

"All right, son."

I closed my eyes. Mom meant well, she really did, but sometimes she worried too much. She still saw me as this helpless child. She had always been the sort of helicopter parent that no child wanted.

"Thomas?" I heard my mom say softly.

I opened my eyes. "Yeah?"

"They were lucky to have found you. When I walked in here, I cried. I had to leave, in case you woke up and saw me in tears."

I hadn't even seen my face yet. I imagined it didn't look too pretty. "Do you have a mirror, Mom?"

She looked into her leather purse and pulled out a small mirror. It was similar to the mirror Natasha used to put on her makeup. She handed it to me.

As I expected, I looked like shit. I sported double black eyes, both slightly swollen. *Watch, tomorrow I won't be able to see out of them.* My cheeks were puffy. A bandage was wrapped around my forehead, and gauze covered the bridge of my nose.

I handed her back the mirror, as I lay there. I knew I should sleep, but Mom probably wouldn't let me. All I wanted was for Natasha to show up.

In the corner, Mom was looking at something on her phone.

"Hey, son," she said, showing me the screen, "breaking news. They say two men who were wanted on suspicion of many robberies had been captured. They said they heard voices in their head, telling them to confess. The lengths some people will go to get out of trouble, huh?"

I reached out, but a dull pain radiated up my arm all the way to my shoulder. I stared at my mother. "Can you scroll down?"

She did. There wasn't much reported, except for a video of a man being escorted into a police car. For a brief second the figure turned and stared at the camera. It was him—one of the guys who robbed me.

"See, I told you you'd do good tonight." It was that voice again. So familiar. Like I should remember but couldn't quite. "Fifteen victims. You found justice for fifteen people."

Then there was that humming. I recognized the humming. It was from the back alley. I couldn't remember who she was, but there a woman had been there just before they found me.

"Thomas?"

I shook my head. "Huh?"

"Are you all right?"

"Yeah, Mom."

I faked a smile. I had to be losing my mind, but that voice was so clear. I was sure the voice was looking over me. I was convinced of it.

Code Blue. This is an announcement for Code Blue.

Mom and I stared down the hallway as a fleet of medical personnel flew by at full tilt. I hoped whatever was going on would be all right.

"I need to get a refill. I'll be right back."

"Okay, Mom."

She left the room, and I closed my eyes once again. I was hoping to find out more about this voice in my head.

"Okay, I'm alone. Who are you?"

There was silence.

I sighed.

Still no response.

Code Blue lifted. I repeat Code Blue lifted.

"You did good," said the voice in my head.

"Huh?"

I sat there startled as Mom and Natasha walked into the room. Relief washed over me.

"Natasha, honey, I'm so glad you're here!"

She ran over to me, and we hugged. She held my hand. "I'm sorry this happened. I-I was so scared."

"I'll be right back," Mom said, as she left the room.

"You're all right," I breathed with relief, "they didn't find you!"

"Find me?"

I shook my head. "I'm so glad you're here. You're safe!"

A load had been lifted off my shoulders. Natasha was all right. She was still whole. If my memory served me, the two men who did this to me had been caught. Still, the mysterious voice lingered in my head. *"You did good."*

The only question was what to do now.

"I love you," I told Natasha.

"I love you too. I'm so glad you're alive."

"How did you get home?"

"I called a cab. I had to wait before I could get into the hospital."

I looked at her concerned. "Why?"

"There was an emergency. Police sirens and a man on a stretcher being carried in."

A gleam of sweat formed on my forehead. That must've been the code blue. It could've been me.

"It could have been you, but it wasn't," the voice returned, "But I think you know who it was. You've met him before."

"Who?"

"The man being rushed to the hospital."

Natasha tapped my shoulder. I jumped. "Huh?"

"Who are you talking too?" she asked.

I clutched my arm to my chest. How could I explain the situation to her when I don't even know what's going?

"I think I got a concussion. I've been hearing things. Almost like my guardian angel is speaking to me." I paused to take a deep breath. "I-I know how ridiculous this sounds." I broke into a cold sweat. My body shook. "The guys who jumped me. They were caught. My mother showed me the article saying someone caught them right after I got here."

A quiet voice in the back of my head was telling me I was losing it. Natasha stared at me as if I was nuts. Maybe I was nuts.

"Say something!" I blurted out.

Natasha rubbed the back of her neck. "You've always had a way of changing your luck. Call it what you want, but I always believed in karma."

"What do you mean?"

Natasha stood. "Do you remember that time when we were sledding in the middle of the night like dummies?"

I grinned. "Yeah, and I crashed right into a tree."

Natasha smirked. "But remember when that guy did the same thing, flipped into the air, and crashed face first into the tree."

I bit my lip. "Yeah, I remember." The guy's head had been gushing blood, and he wasn't responding, but then something came over me. I told the guy everything was going to be all right. For some reason or another, he walked away from the scene shortly after the paramedics arrived.

"You remember when you told me about that head-on collision you and your family were in years ago?" Natasha asked.

My skin tingled, and my heart raced at a thousand miles per minute. A sudden coldness struck me at my core. I was ten when the drunk driver swerved into our lane. Dad slammed on the breaks, but couldn't avoid the oncoming vehicle. We rolled three times before landing in a ditch on the side of the road. The next thing I remembered I was waking up in the hospital. I was praying for my family. Later, I found out that they left the scene with only some minor scratches. I had broken my collarbone and tibia. Even the first responders on the scene that night couldn't believe it.

I bit my lip. It all made sense. My misfortune led to the positive fortune of others. But that didn't explain the voice in my head. It was a woman's voice. How did she fit into all of this?

"Thomas?"

I glanced over at Natasha. Mentally, I wanted to jump over the bed and hug her. She put all of this into perspective. Her arrival was almost out of nowhere as if she could read my mind.

"Yeah?"

She smiled. "I guess that means you have some kind of secret powers."

I laughed. "Like a superhero?"

The dread evaporated from the room.

"I guess so."

My mother returned to the room with a cup of coffee in hand. "How are you feeling, honey?"

"Better," I said, smiling at Natasha.

Mom glared at Natasha. "Why don't we let him rest? What do you think?"

Natasha's eyes darted away.

"Mother," I said.

She grinned at Natasha. "What do you think? Why don't we let him rest? The sooner he feels better, the sooner he can get out of here."

Natasha reluctantly turned to look at me. "I'll be back."

"Get some rest, sweetie," Mom said.

I gripped the edge of the bed frame. I didn't want to rest, even though I should've. I wanted to talk to Natasha. All I had to do was send Mom home and tell her that I loved her, but reassure her that I was okay now that Natasha was there. That was what I'd do when she got back into the room. I'd tell her that I would be fine.

Out of nowhere, a woman with blonde hair, wearing a bubblegum pink dress surrounded me with a familiar aura. She hummed. Every-thing came rushing back all at once.

"You were there. I remember now."

She smiled. "I was, but now it's time for me to explain."

"Okay, start with who the hell you are?"

The woman floated around me before stopping above my head. "I'm you."

"Just stop with the mind games. Who are you?"

"I'm your conscience, and your ability to correct others' misfor-tunes. It all began the day you were born. You broke into a fever, but, that same night, a lady on the other side of the hospital woke up from a coma. Just like tonight, you solved the case and got justice for all those people."

I shook my head. "No!"

"But, it's true Thomas. Why don't you go into the hallway?"

"I-I can't."

She hummed a few familiar lullabies. "But you must. You have a gift. A superpower that no one can explain. Now, I insist you go out into the hallway."

Before I could respond, she disappeared.

I found myself getting out of bed, carefully steadying myself. My legs wobbled as I gripped the IV pole and walked toward the door. Every muscle in my body screamed, and my head spun. I didn't realize how much pain I was in until I began walking. I needed to make it to the hallway. It was the only way to prove to myself that I wasn't crazy or that I actually had some sort of power.

Mom and Natasha were nowhere in sight. I held onto the wall to balance myself. What was I looking for? A nurse walked by without saying a word to me. I wanted something to tell me what I was looking for. I waited a moment, feeling defeated and stupid for believing the voices in my head. I turned to leave when something caught my eye.

A man came walking down the hallway in a hospital gown.

"Sir, you really need to rest," a nurse called as she chased after him.

I remembered him. He was the man who found me tonight—the one who called the ambulance. He saved my life, but why was he here?

The man stood short of me and smiled. "I'm glad you are well. They did a number on you," he smiled, "but I had quite a night myself. I got hit by a car and almost died twice, but here I am, walking. I never felt better."

"You need to get back to bed, now, sir."

"Nice talking to you," he said, as he carried on down the hallway.

The nurse looked at me. "You get back to bed too," she said.

I stood there, at a loss for words.

It was real.

ABOUT R.M. DEMEESTER

WRITING AS MELODY ASH

R.M. Demeester lives in Saskatchewan, Canada. She is the mother of three young children, and owner of a rescue dog, a chocolate lab, Gainer. R.M. Demeester has been writing for as long as she could hold a pencil. She writes women's fiction, new adult, and sweet romance primarily. She has two women's fiction novels set to be released in 2019, along with several short stories.

facebook.com/RMDemeester

twitter.com/rmdemeester

instagram.com/rmdemeester

TABITHA BISHOP: RELUCTANT HERO

BY C.M. LANDER

Tabitha arrived at Il Punto five minutes early. The name was scrawled in brown lettering across a cream background affixed to the building's pale concrete façade. Alfresco tables dotting the sidewalk remained unoccupied as the sky threatened rain at any moment. With no awning to hide under, a decision had to be made immediately: stay or go? The interior restaurant's candlelit tables glowed through the tinted windows. She paused outside, looking at her phone, praying for a last minute cancellation text. She normally declined blind dates, but this one seemed genuine. Pauline practically fell over herself recommending this guy to Tabitha. So, against her better judgment, she relented. Pauline set the reservations and advised the two where to meet, but a quick peek inside told her there were no single men waiting. Every occupied table already sat two or more people. Her hand paused on the antique bronze door pull. She could just leave. She could go and say he never showed. Pauline would believe her.

But she was already there and dressed and hungry. She might as well give it a try. Just as she began pulling the door open, a man's voice bellowed behind her. "Excuse me," it said. The tone was condescending. It grated on her nerves as she turned around, holding the door for him.

"Please, after you," she said with a sarcastic bow.

The man brushed past and waltzed straight up to the hostess. "I have a reservation under Green. Eric Green." He smiled a wolfish grin, bearing his teeth in an almost obscene gesture. There was a sense of false bravado in his speech. He seemed to be playing a part. Why choose to play the jerk? Tabitha walked in after him and, upon hearing his name, called out, "Eric?"

He turned, annoyed. "Yes?" he asked.

"I'm Tabitha." His face paled, becoming almost transparent. "Tabitha Bishop." She held her hand out, and he took it reluctantly. She ensured that her grip was uncomfortably tight so that he immediately released hers. She obviously was not what he was expecting. Her light brown skin complemented her blonde-dyed curls which bounced near her chin whenever she took a step or turned her head. She was slim, toned, and taller than him in her four-inch stilettos. Her dark eyes looked out through mascara-thickened lashes with a cool, smart, confidence Eric would never be able to replicate.

"Nice to meet you," he said, pretending he didn't need to nurse his hand.

"Charmed, I'm sure," she said, following the hostess to their table in the middle of the restaurant. She was thankful for the better lighting in the middle. The booths around the perimeter of the dining room were practically in the dark. She wasn't about to subject herself to some self-righteous man in the shadows of the restaurant.

He followed close behind and sat before her, flattening his tie against himself and adjusting his jacket to better flatter his form. The hostess helped push in her chair and left the two to talk, but he became quickly consumed with his menu and failed to look up to exchange niceties. He was handsome. Pauline wasn't wrong about that. His skin was remarkably smooth and creamy, and his chestnut hair was perfectly coiffed away from his face in a wavelike swoop. His suit was tailored and expensive, judging by the way he picked at it. He moved his neck back and forth as if it needed to crack, but he just couldn't get it.

She placed her phone on the table and timed how long it would take him to look up and notice her. Three minutes. For three minutes she sat there staring at him, willing him to make eye contact, after which he eventually mustered the social consciousness to mutter, "What are you going to have?" over the top of his menu.

"Haven't picked yet," she said, finally opening up the black leather menu book and scanning its contents. The rain began all at once as if a water tap had been turned on. It pelted the roof and the windows in front with its diagonal downpour. The sound calmed her: the fire that burned at each snub, each injustice. She chose a niçoise salad—what better first date food than hard boiled eggs and anchovies?—and laid her menu back down.

A waiter came by with a crisp, white apron tied over his uniform: black slacks, a white button-down shirt, and black tie. Eric finally looked up from his menu. "Let's start with the steak tartar, Oysters Rockefeller, and two glasses of the Bella Serata Pinot Grigio. I'll have the filet mignon, and she will have the osso bucco."

Tabitha's eyes widened at his temerity. "Uh, no. I don't eat veal," she said. The waiter shifted uncomfortably.

"I just thought you needed a little help since you hadn't picked yet," he shrugged, nonchalantly.

She folded her menu and rolled her eyes imperceptibly as she couched the gesture in a general look around the room before returning her attention to the waiter, "I'll have the niçoise salad and water is just fine, thank you," she cooed, handing her menu to the waiter and casually checking where the nearest exit was in case she had to make an emergency escape or risk committing first-degree murder.

Eric adjusted his jacket for the fourth time since they sat down

Tabitha looked across the table at her date, the Fortune 100 CEO who made it very clear that she was lucky to be out with him in the first place. She couldn't tell the color of his eyes as he failed to maintain eye contact for longer than three seconds before turning his head, looking at other women, and, in short, participating in all sorts of boorish behavior typical of a man of his financial stature. She lamented her choice to wear her classic red dress that cut just at her mid-thighs and hugged her hips just so. She adjusted the straps over her shoulders as he went on about the struggles of working with such incompetent people, the joys of firing his assistants, and how much money he spent on his last vacation.

Tabitha made a mental note to refuse any future dates. If this is the type of guy that Pauline thought was perfect for Tabitha, perhaps there was a deeper problem in their friendship.

In all of his grand gestures to draw attention to his ten-thousand-dollar watch, a gift from his parents, he failed to notice that his sweeping movements blew out the flame that formerly shimmied in the votive between the two of them. Tabitha looked at the candle. She concentrated on it, and then the flame burst back into life.

Eric stopped. He hadn't noticed the candle go out, but its sudden reignition caught his attention.

"Did you see that?" he asked her.

"See what?" she replied, feigning ignorance. It was the first question he had asked her all night, and she was certainly going to enjoy herself for the remainder of the dinner if this was how he wanted to behave.

He dropped the subject, of course, brushing it off to his tired eyes, wearied from a day's hard labor and continued on some involved story about how he actually invented the first social medium, but he was seven years old and didn't have the start-up capital to see it through. Tabitha struggled to keep her eyes open. She had worked all day at the credit union as a loan officer. Her favorite part of the day was when people came in to tell her about their plans for the money they were borrowing: young couples buying their first homes together, new parents adding rooms to their houses for their growing family, people taking out a second mortgage to invest in their new company and follow their dreams. So many beautiful stories that she got to be a part of. Thankfully, she wasn't part of the heartache when those dreams didn't pan out. Her days were long, but fruitful and meaningful and at night she preferred to spend her time in the company of kind people. Not over-dressed buffoons who wouldn't know class if it slapped them across the face.

That's when she felt it: the seizing of muscles, the domination of gravity. A waiter with his tray overloaded with carbohydrates and piping hot tomato sauce was about to spill his burden over a child, out to dinner with his parents. She was at the next table before Eric even knew she was gone. She steadied the tray with her left hand and grabbed the waiter with her right. The waiter thanked her profusely as the family nibbled on their meals, clueless to the disaster averted right before their eyes.

Tabitha smoothed her dress and headed back to her seat where Eric had finally noticed she was missing. He turned around to watch her return and sit down as if nothing had just happened.

"What was that?" he asked.

"Just helping out," she replied, picking apart a breadstick and popping a piece in her mouth.

He cocked his eyebrow at her. "I have to say this is the strangest date I've ever been on."

"Me too," she chimed in, placing the napkin back in her lap as she pored over the dessert menu. Chocolate would be required.

He glowered. "Who are you?"

"Tabitha Bishop," she said, extending her hand in greeting again. "Our friends set us up for some reason."

He could feel the sting of her words cut through him. He softened. "I'm sorry," Eric began. The words shocked her. She didn't think him capable of using the phrase "I've been acting like a jerk. I'm not good at dating to begin with since I work twenty hours a day and I really don't like blind dates. They make me uncomfortable. So I act like an idiot, hoping the girl will go back and tell her friend not to set anyone up with me again and—I'm sorry. You don't deserve this. I didn't expect you to be so interesting. Usually, I get the pretty ones with no brains in their heads, but you seem—well, you seem different, and I regret how I've treated you."

Tabitha weighed his response. She read his facial features for any signs of deceit but found nothing, but sincerity. "Well, it's not cute," she replied.

"Do you think we can start over?" he asked. "Like actually get to know *you* instead of me being an idiot?" Her first instinct was a flat-out refusal. Anyone who could treat a stranger so disrespectfully wasn't worth her time. But then she remembered how prepared she was to ditch her date before he even showed up and leave him sitting at a table by himself for the evening while she ate snacks in front of her television. Was that really any nicer?

She cursed her conscience as she stayed seated. "I'm not eating another dinner tonight," she declared.

"No. I mean, let's have dessert and talk like I don't have emotional baggage."

The joke caught her by surprise, and she snorted her water a bit. The two shared a chocolate cake and finally began a normal conversation as two humans, interested in getting to know each other. She told him about the most ridiculous loan application she ever processed where a fifty-five-year-old man was looking for a $2.5 million loan to start a bakery for dogs. The loan was summarily denied. Eric told her about his first board of directors meeting when he finally got the money together for his startup. He was so nervous to speak in front of them that when he stood and walked toward the front of the room, he released a string of squeaky farts that followed him throughout the conference rooms. He tried to blame it on his shoes, which everyone accepted on the surface, but knew deep down was not the case. Tabitha cackled at the story, and he laughed along with her.

With dessert done, Eric picked up the check against the protestations of Tabitha to split the bill. He assured her that he had to make amends for his earlier behavior, and she relented. The two rose and walked out of the restaurant, still sharing stories and laughing together. Moonlight shone down and lit the streets where the streetlight's glow could not reach. "I have a car coming," Eric interjected, "Can I take you home?"

Without missing a beat, Tabitha answered, "You and your driver can drop me off at home and then take you to your own home if that's what you're asking."

He laughed. "Yeah. Sure thing." And she smiled, a little sad that the night was ending.

A black sedan pulled up, and he led her by the small of the back to the car's door. A shiver spasmed through her body, and the smell of danger hung in the air. Her pupils dilated, seeking out the source and before Eric could finish taking his last step toward the car, Tabitha had flung herself across the road, in front of an out of control taxi that nearly ran over the small child whom she had saved from being covered in pasta sauce inside Il Punto thirty minutes earlier.

"Today's not your day," she said, clinging to the little boy on the opposite sidewalk. The taxi sped off as she stood up, lifting the little boy onto his feet and walking him safely across the street to his parents who looked on with paralyzing fear. A cheerful smile spread across her face as she tried to comfort the parents who were certain they had just witnessed their child get hit by a car, only to see him returned to them unscathed. She tousled his hair and set him down next to his mother who he hugged immediately and returned to Eric, who stood by, watching the scene unfold. His eyes bulged slightly out of his head, questioning his own sanity. She hopped into the car, not acknowledging Eric's slack jaw. When his consciousness finally caught up to him, he blinked away his disbelief and followed her into the car.

He stared at her, positive that she would disappear in a puff of smoke before his very eyes. She smoothed her skirt once more, trying to avoid his gaze as it burned into the side of her face.

"Orchard and Broome," she called out to the driver who hadn't even seen the almost-accident unfold. He nodded in the rearview mirror and set off to his destination. Tabitha pressed her lips together and looked to her left, continuing to avoid Eric's adamant stare.

They sat together in silence for a block and a half before Eric was able to muster a voice. "What? Wha-- What? What was that?" She turned her head slowly to meet his befuddled gaze. She searched for an answer. She always hated this part. Generally, boyfriends didn't find out about her powers until—well, none of them knew about her. They just knew she was stronger and faster than them. To be fair, none of them asked if she had any superpowers.

"I used to run track," she answered. Which was true. She ran track all through high school and college, holding back her true speed so that people wouldn't notice exactly how fast she was. Her parents were the only people who knew the truth. The day she was born, doctors told her mother, Rhona, that there was a problem. That her daughter may never walk. Her muscles seemed to be detached from the whole of her body. The truth was that they developed far faster than her skeleton initially. Everyone was baffled. By six months old, Tabitha was running. Her pediatrician wanted her to meet with specialists conducting research on "exceptional children." Rhona didn't want that life for her daughter. A life of being different or made into an experiment. Tabitha was hell to keep up with as a toddler, but Rhona kept her hidden at home so that no one could take her away. It was a chore for Tabitha to get her mother to sign the permission slips to join track, but Rhona couldn't keep her daughter a prisoner. Rhona was the one to tell Tabitha to hold back in her heats, to slow down, so she wouldn't win by five miles rather than one.

Eric's narrowed eyes told her he wasn't buying her story. She smiled a toothy, awkward smile, hopeful that her adorable charm would overshadow the superhuman demonstration she put on back there...multiple times.

She sighed, "I'm fast." He kept glaring. "I'm very, very fast."

"Yeah, no kidding," he grumbled, finally breaking his gaze and looking away. He felt lied to, and she felt guilty. Had she not messed with him in the restaurant, she could have explained away the quick reaction as an adrenaline fluke, but the fire and then the waiter and now the kid were pushing it too far. She looked down at her lap and picked at the hem of her dress. They arrived at her building in silence. Eric got out and opened the door for her, walking her to the front door.

"I had a nice time," she ventured, walking up the concrete steps of her stoop to the well-cared-for brownstone she called home.

"Yeah," he muttered, following a step behind, morose.

She fumbled with her keys a bit, the desire to apologize welling inside her. "Listen," she began, "I—"

Whoosh. Crash. The metallic percussion of an air conditioner falling from three floors up directly on top of Tabitha practically stopped Eric's heart. He didn't hear it coming. The wind of the unit's fall only hit him after the great heap of metal hit Tabitha, landing on her back. She stood before him, holding the unit twice the width of her body, up on her shoulders, utterly unfazed by the impact. She looked like a metallic bobblehead.

"Sorry," a haggard voice called from above them. "Oh, it's you Tabby!"

"Hi, Ms. Durmott," Tabitha called up to the little old woman who popped her head out of the empty window above them. She had an oblong face too wide for her body, and her eyes were permanently scrunched from wrinkles and exhaustion. Her gray hair was pulled into a tight bun. Her oversized eyeglasses hung from a chain around her neck. She picked them up and held them away from her eyes as she gazed down at Tabitha.

"Oh, you brought a boy home." Ms. Durmott erupted in a fit of giggles. "Come up! Come up!" she called down to them, waving her hand twice before disappearing.

"Do you mind?" Tabitha asked, turning her back to Eric so that he could take the air conditioner off her back.

Before he could even think, he grabbed the machine off her back so that Tabitha could open the door. He struggled immediately, his knees almost buckling. Either he was badly out of shape, or this unit was not meant to be in a window. The key clicked in the lock, and the door opened onto a black and white checkered floor with a set of dark wooden stairs directly ahead of them. A little table sat at the side of the staircase with a bouquet of fresh flowers that Ms. Durmott bought once a week. The home was ornate and eccentric, highly reflective of its elderly owner.

"What is your life?" Eric breathed as he lugged the air conditioner in the front door.

"Come in! Come in!" Ms. Durmott's voice could be heard throughout the home, but it was dark: the only light available was from the streetlights shining in through the few uncovered windows in the hallway.

"Do you want me to take that back?" Tabitha asked as they approached the stairs.

"No, I got it," Eric wheezed. He strained up the stairs, breaking a sweat before he made it up the first step.

"I could—" Tabitha began as they approached the first landing.

"Nope. Got it," Eric croaked.

Up they crawled to the third floor where Ms. Durmott's door was wide open. Early jazz music played in a distant room, but the light in the kitchen drew the couple in. She appeared instantly at the doorway. "Come in!" Eric's knees were giving out. He took the last few steps across the threshold before dropping the air conditioner with a crash right in her foyer. He reached out his arms attempting to stretch the pain out of his muscles to no avail. He crossed them in front of his chest as Ms. Durmott, whose head did not reach past his chest, pushed him into a nearby chair.

"There's water on the boil," she called over her shoulder, bustling around her apartment like a trapped house fly. The living room where he sat was an assortment of peach and floral decor. The overstuffed couch he sat on hosted a garden of roses in its design so intricate that it nearly set off Eric's histamine enzymes. Art supplies littered her coffee table. It seemed this week's passion was decoupage as every magazine she had received over the past two years was cut up and strewn about the room. Little address labels marked, "Ms. Olive Durmott," littered the floor. Around the room were teacups and cat figurines. Abstract paintings leaned against the wall on the floor, waiting for years to be hung. It was a wonder the old woman didn't break her neck with the mess of the place, but anything less would not properly represent the chaos of her mind.

"I'm sorry. You don't have to stay if you don't wa—" Tabitha began, but a jolt of pain shot through her body. She doubled over at once and, before she knew it, was also seated in an armchair as Ms. Durmott had pushed it into the back of Tabitha's knees to force her to sit.

"Are you okay?" Eric asked, jumping to his feet as he saw her countenance shift.

"It's fine. I'm fine. Don't worry."

"You just got hit by a giant air conditioner. I think we should go to a hospital."

"It's not that. I just need to lay down." Tabitha stood, clutching her left side with both hands, her shoulders slumped forward and a grimace on her face, which she attempted to cover with a fake smile.

"Are you going?" Ms. Durmott appeared again. She had fastened an apron over her house dress and was covered head to toe in flour.

"Yes. I'm sorry we couldn't stay," Tabitha apologized.

"But you haven't had your tea!" Ms. Durmott held two blue handle-less teacups aloft on mismatched saucers, which she pulled seemingly out of nowhere.

"Let's take a rain check," Eric replied. A smile drew across the whole of Ms. Durmott's face as she was still for the first time since they arrived. Her eyes lit up, and she began dancing.

"Yes! A rain check. I like this one, Tabby!"

Tabitha draped an arm around Eric's shoulder as he helped her out of the apartment and back into the hall. She hobbled down the stairs to her second-floor apartment where he supported her as she fumbled with the lock. Another click and the door swung open into a relatively modest apartment, given the ornate decor outside. The door opened into her living room, painted a warm gold, where a brown couch was her final destination. Its supple leather was more high-end than Eric would have ever credited her with. His hand lingered on it as he set her down, gently helping her recline down to a prone position. She grimaced a bit but managed to relax into it.

"Are you sure I shouldn't call an ambulance? That thing was heavy. You might have ruptured something."

"No, it's not that. That's not the first time she's dropped an air conditioner on me," Tabitha replied matter of factly

"What?" he asked, though less taken aback than he would have been ten minutes earlier.

"Yeah. She's in her own world. TVs, air conditioners—one time it was a whole espresso machine. I genuinely don't know if she does it on purpose or not."

This new information whirled in Eric's mind. He became light-headed, overcome by this strange world he found himself blindly wandering deeper and deeper into. "So," he began, sitting down by

Tabitha's legs, "Does she hate you. Is she—is she your arch nemesis?"

Tabitha laughed. "No, she's just eccentric."

"Does she know about you?" His eyes flicked side to side as if the walls were listening.

"I don't think she even knows what year it is."

"Does anyone else know about your...powers?" The word felt silly, inappropriate. Eric cringed a bit at the suggestion.

"Aside from my mom and dad, no. It makes life easier that way." She grimaced again, clutching her side and pulling herself almost fully upright as another attack gripped her insides.

"Is it your appendix? Do you have an appendix? Oh my God, are you human?" His voice rose at the end of his sentence with a mixture of fear and incredulity tuning his pitch. The realization dawned on Eric all at once. Who did he just have dinner with? An alien?

She laughed at the question "Yes, I'm human. Yes, I have an appendix, and it's not that either. I'm just stronger than most people."

"And faster," he added.

"And faster," she acquiesced.

"And that candle?" he asked.

"Yeah. That was me."

He settled in at her side. "Then why are you hurting?"

"It's, uh," she began, but a groan of pain burst from her mouth before she could continue. She clenched every muscle in her body until the pain subsided once more. "It means there's danger nearby."

Eric's eyes bulged and darted around, looking for where the danger could come from. The sight made Tabitha laugh and then grimace again. "Not in here. Just...close by. It only hurts because I'm not there."

"It hurts because you're not in trouble?" he questioned.

"How do you imagine heroes are always close by when crimes happen? They can feel the danger. It's like another sense."

"Do—Do you know other superheroes?" Eric asked, practically salivating at the prospect.

"Yeah. We have lunch every Friday."

His mouth dropped almost to the floor. "Really?"

"No. I'm the only freak I know." Tabitha cast her eyes to the floor to avoid his expression. "One time I did respond to the wrong fight. I saw one guy beating up this scrawny dude and started swinging. Turned out I had shown up to the end of a fight. Ended up fighting the good guy and let the bad one get away. That guy definitely hates me now. Pretty sure I broke his jaw." Eric wasn't sure how to respond. Should he touch her? Pat her head? How do you comfort a superhero?

After a moment of silence passed between the two, he hoped enough time had elapsed to appropriately ignore the raw emotion that he was not yet ready to feel for this strange woman. "How can I help you?" he asked, placing his hand over hers on her belly. With concern etched in his face, Tabitha could see his desire to help was genuine. She shifted on the couch, uncertain she wanted to share the answer.

"It'll go away on its own," she said, not looking him in his eye.

He understood. "Once the crime happens."

Silence once again fell between the two. His hand slipped from hers.

"So you just let crimes happen?" he asked. "How many criminals have you let slip away?" He couldn't control the pitch or volume of his voice. He erupted with the accusation.

Anger flashed in her eyes, but she tempered it with a deep breath. Calmly, she replied, "How many crimes have you stopped."

"Well, none, but I can't. I don't know they're happening," the answer was fortuitous in its advent. He didn't actually have a reason why he hadn't helped more people. "I don't know how to stop them."

"So in your world, a doctor pioneers a certain operation should stay up all day, every day performing that operation on everyone who needs him?"

"What?" No," Eric began, but Tabitha cut him off.

"Even if it means people die?" she asked.

"Of course not," he began, but she wouldn't let him finish.

What about every policeman? Why aren't you mad at them for not spending every waking moment fighting crime? Don't *they* let criminals get away by taking a break? Having a single night off?

"I work hard all day. And yes, to answer your question, sometimes

I do step in. If I'm not exhausted from the day, and I'm not on a date," she said, gesturing to him. "But I can't be everybody's hero. Sometimes I have to be my own hero and remind myself that it's enough. It's enough to donate to charity when I can. It's enough to help when I can. It's enough just to be a good person. I've lost out on so much just for being different. Do you think guys want to date a girl who can bench press more than he can? No. The second they get a whiff of my abilities they take off. There have been so many times I've stepped in and saved someone when I should have been at a friend's wedding or meeting a date and do you think people thank the skinny girl who can lift the bad guys over her head? Not once. They're afraid of me. They run away from me!

"Do you think I can go into my job and sleep at my desk because I was out 'til three a.m. making sure some lost tourist got back to their hotel, okay? Would you let one of your employees behave that way? At the end of the day, it's a business, right? And you need people that don't sleep on the job. How much do you think I get paid to step in? I'm not independently wealthy. Should I risk homelessness to save other people? My superpower isn't staying awake all night and being fine the next day. I'm human. Superhuman, but human, nonetheless. Who saves the hero when the hero falls?"

Eric bit his lip. He wasn't sure how to respond. She was right, after all. She's human just like him, and she still does more than he ever has. Why should he expect more? "I'm sorry," he said, humbled by her words. "I never thought of it that way."

The anger seeped out of Tabitha with his words. She closed her eyes, another shock of pain reminding her that the world isn't perfect. She looked at him again. "Do you want to go?"

He sighed, "Are you going to be all right? I'm not comfortable leaving someone when they're in so much pain."

"No. I mean, do you want to come with me? We still have time to stop it." She started to sit up, planting one foot on the ground and then the other. The decision to act seemed to alleviate the pain.

Eric's eyes lit up. "You mean—you want me to come? What would I even do?"

"I want you to see what I see," she answered as Eric helped her up from the couch.

He helped her stand. "So what do we do?" he asked, excitement gripping his voice.

"Let me get changed and we'll head over there." She slowly disappeared into her dark bedroom, emerging moments later in a grey tank top and black leggings, white ankle socks, and multicolored sneakers. She seemed sprier. Her hair was pulled up into two pom-poms on either side of her head, giving her an even more youthful look.

"Oh, uh, is that what you're wearing?" Eric asked, looking her up and down.

"Yeah," she said, confused. "This is what I'm wearing," She gestured to her leggings and tank top.

"Don't you have a—like a bodysuit or something?"

"Listen, I don't know what you're into, but I would not even know where to go about acquiring a bodysuit besides hitting up a lingerie store, and I'm not walking around the city in fishnets. This is comfy, and I can move in it." She walked through the apartment to her front door, grabbing her keys from the dish on her table.

"But—aren't you going to wear a mask or something? Like, won't someone recognize you?" he asked, catching up to her.

"Probably. But for one thing, no one wants to admit they got beat up by a girl, so no one's going to report me to the police or anything and for another, have you heard about facial recognition software? Social media can recognize you by your big toe at this point. At least this way I don't have to mess up my hair. You ready?"

The reality of throwing himself into a dangerous situation dawned on him. "Maybe I should just stay here and make sure Ms. Dermott is okay."

"You're so keen on me fighting crime and whatnot, don't you want to see what it's like?"

"But—isn't it dangerous?" His face flushed a bit as his mind calculated the various risks involved. He could get injured or killed, or recognized and lose his company. There was a lot at stake, but the same stakes applied to her.

"Yeah. Exactly! Good enough for me. Good enough for you."

She bounded down the stairs, Eric struggling to keep up with her. "Sorry," she said, turning around to wait for him, "I've never brought someone along with me. I get into a mode and tend to forget about everything else." On their way out the door, Eric motioned to his driver who had dutifully waited outside. He waved him on to head home as he walked side by side once again with Tabitha. As the car pulled away, Tabitha picked up her pace again. Eric practically trotted to keep up with her. Once he accepted that he was going to charge into battle beside a woman he barely knew, he became overcome with a sort of stupid bravery that steeled his nerves. The prospect of crime-fighting turned him into a child once again as he galloped down the street, unconcerned with how people would perceive him.

"If I could have any superpower," he began out of nowhere, "I would want to fly. No! Read minds. No! Control time."

"You don't get to choose," she replied, turning her chin in his direction, but keeping her eyes fixed straight ahead. Her focus could not be deterred. They walked together in silence, down the city blocks, neither one looking at the other. Eric sweated profusely through his suit as he desperately tried to keep up. The streets were still bustling with people, mostly drunk ones, spilling out of bars on Delancey. The city was still very much awake and pulsing with the simultaneous potential for a fun night out and a near-future of victimhood. Tabitha wasn't shy about pushing past people, though she still passed mostly unnoticed by anyone. He was more of a standout in his full suit after midnight.

The sky was empty. Streetlamps were the only light source, and even their narrow radii illuminated only a small percentage of the sidewalk. The neon signs of bars and clubs cast off a preternatural glow on the immediate walkways outside their premises. Everywhere else was blanched by the lamplight or shrouded in shadow. Light could not bend into the cracks and alleys of a city built on sin—and Tabitha felt it. Each passageway between buildings pulsed with the threat of danger, but they weren't the one she sought. The pain of inaction had subsided and given way to the divining rod of danger innate within her. The nearer she reached, the faster she approached until Eric fell back a whole block behind her.

She stopped across the street from him, cars flying by, unconcerned with the presence of pedestrians pouring out from every direction. Eric jaywalked to her, beating out a taxi by a mere breath. No horn blared, but the annoyed hand wave of a perturbed cabbie. Tabitha stood there, stock still, outside a corner market that sold poorly dyed flowers in the front and a random assortment of goods inside. She closed her eyes and breathed deeply, preparing herself. Eric broke the silence, "Isn't there some faster way to get there?"

"You want to run there? I can't fly."

"Don't you have a special car or something?" He was jogging now. Panting through his words.

"Where the hell am I going to park a car in this city?"

The sounds of a scuffle caught their ears and Tabitha raced off, leaving Eric behind. He heard the squelching sound of fist meeting face. Eric rounded the corner and saw Tabitha in action. She was a blur of limbs thrown in every direction. She moved so quickly smoke began issuing behind her as her victim crumpled to the floor. In the alleyway, next to the dumpster a young woman stood, frozen in terror. With the baddie fully incapacitated, Tabitha turned to the young woman, a college student coming home from a late night at the library.

"You," Tabitha roared, "What in the world do you think you're doing out this late? It's dangerous," she yelled, gesturing to the man who had become a bloody mess on the ground. The young woman stood shivering in place, unsure of whether to cry or run or pee her pants. She was paralyzed save for her eyes, which darted from Tabitha to her assailant and then rested on Eric. He gave an uneasy shrug and a half-smile, a most inappropriate gesture given the circumstances, but he was at a loss, having never been in a crime-fighting position before.

"And you," Tabitha yelled, wheeling around to face the criminal, "What do you think you're doing attacking people in the middle of the night? Do you know what time it is? I'm tired! Do you think I have time to just be running around the city at all hours of the night, chasing after every dumb-dumb like you who thinks he's some big shot? No. I have a job. I have bills to pay. If you need to get beat up so bad, I'm happy to schedule a day with you in advance so I don't have to be up this late. Because if you're going to be running around, acting a fool like this, I'm gonna be out here protecting college dummies like this one and damsels in distress late at night, and I'm not gonna be happy about it. And that doesn't bode well for you."

The assailant lay broken on the ground, moaning and whimpering, unable to clutch the parts of him that hurt. Unable, really, to pinpoint which part hurt the most. He was awash with excruciating malaise. The girl had tears streaming down her face. Her sympathetic nervous system seemed to kick in finally as she ran, full speed, away from the scene.

Eric looked at Tabitha. She was beautiful, even with the splashes of blood bespeckling her lithe limbs. Her biceps were taut and larger than he had noticed before, though not out of proportion. She was absolutely lovely in a frightening way. She could beat him up without even trying. It was a strange feeling.

Without warning, Tabitha turned from the ailing assailant to exit the alley. Eric chased after her. "What now?" he asked, excited and giddy and a little bit nervous.

"What do you mean?" she asked, looking at him finally.

"I mean, like, what next? Do you call the police captain or something?"

She stopped. "No. And no one can know either." Her eyes locked on his. He'd never known a sterner stare than hers.

"Oh, yeah. Of course."

"No. I mean it. No one can ever know. That would mean danger for me. Life-altering things. Death or something much worse."

He met her gaze, its fire frightening him more and more as he felt the fury that lay beneath it. "I'm sorry," he answered. She bit her lip and carried on her path down the street, past more drunk people loitering outside of bars in clouds of smoke: vape, cannabis, and cigarettes all blown into one. A melting pot of vice. Eric chased after her. There was a change in her gait as if she were feeling the effects of gravity more so than anyone around her.

He grabbed her arm, a bold move considering her strength and emotionality at the moment. She turned instantly before he could even register that he was looking into her dark eyes. The sheen of her eyes gave it away. There were tears—just two—in the corner of each eye.

"What's wrong?" he asked.

"You don't see what I see."

"What do you mean?" A wave of people flowed past the two stationary objects on the sidewalk. Cars blew by. The entire world kept going on around them as Tabitha and Eric's lives changed in that very moment.

"What did you just see?" The question felt like an interrogation. As if Eric was somehow to blame for the attempted crime.

"You kicked that guy's ass!" he answered, excitement creeping into his voice.

"You saw a crime stopped, right?"

"Yeah!"

"You saw someone getting what they had coming to them?"

"Exactly!"

"Me attacking that man and him attacking that girl are no different. It doesn't feel good at the end of the day. I worry about whether I'm going to paralyze the guy. Whether I'm going to break his nose into his brain and kill them. I can't control myself in the heat of the moment. At the end of the day, I'm hurting someone. I'm volunteering for it. They are worse off than before they ever met me."

"You're saving people!"

"By hurting others. Believe me, the sugar-coating wears off. It doesn't feel righteous. I don't feel vindicated. I worry. I worry about the people I've hurt. I wish that I could just talk them out of this shit, but the fact is, most of them are doing it because they don't have another choice. Life dealt them blow after blow whether it was poverty or absent parents or whatever other sob stories there are out there. They're people, and they're trying to survive, just like we all are. It's not right what they're doing, but it's not right for me to kill them in response."

A lump formed in Eric's throat. Had she killed someone before? He wanted to ask. The question nagged at him, ricocheting around in the back of his mind until he thought he would go crazy if he didn't ask. But he didn't. It wasn't the right moment. He didn't know her well enough, and she didn't seem ready to talk about it anyway.

He opened his arms and enveloped her in an embrace that was warm and comforting and exactly what she needed at that time. She sobbed gently into his shoulder, but quickly found her composure once more and pulled away. "Thank you," she said.

"Anytime." Tabitha wiped the corners of her eyes to ensure her mascara wasn't running down her eyelids.

"This can't happen again," she said.

Eric's heart sank. He was looking forward to more. More time with her, more adventures, more possibility. "Oh. Can I ask why not?" Had he been too forward? Too weak for her? The rejection stung.

"Because it's not fair. It's not fair to you to worry about me. It's not fair to me to worry about you." She shook her head to punctuate each sentence crescendoing to a sullen shoulder shrug at the end.

"So what's your plan? To live by yourself forever? Never finding someone to make all the battles worthwhile?" His voice caught a bit in his throat as an almost desperation set in. This wasn't fair to him. Never giving him a chance.

She quirked an eyebrow. "What makes you think you've already won me over?"

The declaration gave him pause. His face grew hot. He was blushing. He couldn't remember having ever blushed. His heart beat simultaneously slow and fast in his chest. Eric searched for words but found none. He became in tune with his surroundings, hearing for the first time the rhythm of the rock music issuing from the club to his left and the shouted conversations of drunk college kids, sloshing away any memory of class from the afternoon. He looked at her, gazed at her. At this woman he never imagined could exist. This gorgeous, smart, funny, hardworking, and moral woman that he didn't have the creativity to even dream up. And she didn't want him. It was a blow he felt instantaneously.

She felt his sadness. And she felt his kindness, his understanding. She could sense the type of man he was: someone who valued loyalty above all else. Someone who knew on a cellular level the difficulty of being different. He was almost her complete opposite, but they complemented each other in such a wonderful way. He could learn from her and she from him. She could see the memories they would share already. And they were lovely.

A smile pulled up the corner of Tabitha's lips. She stifled a laugh before throwing her arms around him. His panic was the sign she needed. She kissed him right there in front of the drunk twenty-some-things and the cabbies who didn't give a crap.

"We just have to figure out a way to not get you killed," she said, laughing.

He draped his arm around her, turning to the sidewalk that would lead back to her apartment. "So, what about that whole fire-starting thing?" Eric asked. "How many powers do you have?"

"Oh, enough to blow your mind." She giggled once more, a bounce in her gait.

And the two walked off together into the night, each one strengthened by the other.

ABOUT C. M. LANDER

C. M. Lander is an emerging voice in the fantasy and science fiction genre. She holds a bachelor's degree in Creative Writing from Hofstra University where she focused on her first love—poetry.

She has been featured as Tumblr's Poet of the Day, placed 2nd in the Bartleby Snopes' Dialog-Only Contest, and has been published by Newsday and ProtestPoems.org, among other publications.

Ms. Lander is currently a student of law and is devoted to marrying her love of writing with philanthropic causes.

Keep an eye out for her next novel, The Witch of Ildra Lac, due out in March 2019.

You can follow her on the social media sites below!

facebook.com/AuthorCMLander

instagram.com/authorcmlander

PERSIMMON

BY MELISSA E. BECKWITH

Liam tore out a sheet of paper from his notebook and crumpled it up. "Do it again!" he challenged as he threw the ball of paper onto the grass just starting to turn green after a long winter.

"We have to get this report done by tomorrow, or we'll be in big trouble." Persimmon continued to write in her notebook and when Liam said nothing else, she looked up at him and drew her brows up in a question. He made a pathetic looking sad face and pointed at the crumpled ball of paper.

"Come on, Persi. One more time." She sighed, but then a grin slowly curled across her cocoa colored cheeks. She turned her brown eyes to the crumpled paper, her smile fading as she concentrated.

Suddenly the paper ignited into a yellow ball of flame. Liam hooted and clapped his hands. His red hair shining in the sun as they sat on a bench in the cool, spring afternoon sunshine outside her dad's auto repair shop.

As the fire grew, Liam's blue eyes widened, so Persimmon held out her clenched fist and quickly opened her fingers, sending a small deluge of water from an invisible source to put the fire out. The fire hissed as a puff of white smoke curled into the air. "That's amazing,"

Liam exclaimed in awe like it was the first time he had seen her do that. Of course, it wasn't. Persimmon chuckled.

They had discovered Persimmon's new "gifts" on one colder than usual morning while they were walking along the Blue River that had frozen over a few nights before. Persimmon had talked Liam into walking across the ice. He was hesitant but eventually followed her. They were in the middle of the river when the ice had given way with a sickening crack and Liam was thrown into the water. She had watched her friend disappear into the frigid water, his knit cap bobbing for a few seconds before it too was sucked under the ice.

Overcome with panic, Persimmon cried out and stretched her gloved hands toward where Liam had disappeared. The ice gave an eerie groan, its deep moan echoing off the naked trees. A hole opened in the ice, and a spout of blue water pushed Liam up and out and onto the bank of the river, and he landed with a thud on the frozen ground.

Persimmon ran toward Liam who was coughing up water and trying to catch his breath. She slipped on the ice and fell, her knees jarring with pain. She got up and ran to her friend landing on her sore knees in the decomposing leaf litter. Puffs of white mist came from his mouth as he choked.

"Liam, I'm so sorry!" she cried as she turned him over on his side.

Finally, he caught his breath and looked up at her, "How'd you *do* that?"

She sat down hard on the damp ground, the cold seeping through her muddy jeans. "I don't know," she whispered as she took off her jacket and wrapped it around Liam. His lips had gone blue, and he started to shiver violently.

After that day that had almost ended quite tragically, they had discovered that Persimmon could also create wind and fire and manipulate them, and shortly after that, they found that trees, plants, and rocks would heed her call as well. It was a stunning revelation that Persimmon couldn't explain and even now tried hard not to think about too much. She had gone over it in her head until she felt like she was going to explode, but she could never make a connection between something significant happening in her life and the emergence of her strange powers unless it was that moment when she was so over-whelmed with fear that she had lost her best friend.

"Enough playing around, we really need to get this homework done, or we won't be able to go to Big Four Burgers for supper."

Liam sighed, "Since when did you get so nerdy?"

She could tell he was kidding, but it miffed her anyway. "Since I have to get into college in a few years."

"College? You could own the world with the powers you have." He brushed a clump of bright red hair out of his eyes.

That time his reply did sting. He was right, of course, but she wasn't about to tell anyone else about her powers, and she certainly wasn't going to use them to get rich!

Just then she heard raised voices in her dad's shop. A man was yelling in anger, and her uncle was calmly replying, seemingly trying to de-escalate the situation. She couldn't exactly hear what they were saying, so she jumped up and went to one of the windows of the building. Liam quietly followed along. She peered through the dirty window at her dad and uncle as they both held out their hands, palms down as if they were trying to calm a skittish horse.

Three men were facing her dad and uncle. One of them was yelling and animatedly waving his arms. It would have been almost comical if the tension in the air hadn't been thick with certain danger. His shaggy, dirty blonde hair fell to his shoulders and shook with agitation. He had an equally bushy beard growing on his thin face. The clothes the men were wearing looked to be expensive despite their lack of grooming. One of the other men wore his black hair in a pony-tail and had a goatee covering a wide chin. The other wore his light-colored hair in a buzz cut, his angry, hate-filled face was cleanly shaven.

Persimmon frowned in exasperation; she couldn't make out what they were saying. She looked over at Liam and touched a finger to her lips, then crept around to the open garage door. They peered around the corner, the men's backs were now facing them. The man who was still yelling at her uncle and father had a slight accent—probably from New York. Her uncle had lived there for several years and had only come back to Indiana a month earlier. She figured her uncle knew these jokers.

The man was demanding that her uncle pay him back some money that he apparently owed. His voice was sharp and echoed angrily across the shop. Persimmon's stomach clenched in fear. These guys didn't look like they'd be put off with an IOU. She knew her dad had been reluctant to hire her uncle when he showed up unexpectantly at their front door one night. Her uncle Robert had been involved in some shady things in the past, and she knew her dad was afraid he would bring trouble with him. Now it looks like he was right.

"If you're unable to pay us, I'm sure your brother here would be happy to clear your debt," the man with the ponytail said nonchalantly as he stepped closer to her dad. Cold metal bit into her fingers as she gripped the metal garage door opening. She could hear Liam let out a long breath behind her. The man took an exaggerated look around her dad's shop. "You have a lot of nice equipment here. I'm sure you could scratch together what your brother owes us." He reached out and set his hand on her dad's shoulder. Her dad gave the man a sharp look, and he removed his hand with a dismissive chuckle.

These men were intent on something, and it seemed like it could be more than just some owed money—unless it was millions of dollars— and who in their right mind would loan her uncle that much money? No, she thought there was something more to their threats.

"My brother has nothing to do with this," her uncle said nervously. "I haven't said nothin to nobody."

"You ran outta time, my friend," said Shaggy as Buzzcut grabbed her uncle by the arm. "I think we'll just take you both back to my boss, you know, just to keep you safe," Shaggy said to her father with a grin.

"You guys are going to have to leave before I call the police. I don't want trouble here, this is my place of business, and you're not taking Robert anywhere." Her father grabbed a pry bar that had been sitting next to one of his tool chests and thumped it in his hand as if to show the men he meant business.

With shocking speed, the man with the ponytail grabbed a gun from the waistband of his jeans and pointed it at her dad. She heard

Liam suck in his breath as a scream escaped Persimmon's lips. Her hand shot out, and a frigid gust of wind caught the men up into the air in a whirlwind and threw them clear of the shop. They cried out in shock and landed with a thump in the driveway, but she didn't waste her attention on them. The gun had gone off, and Persimmon ran to her father who was sitting dazed on the concrete floor of his shop. Her dad and uncle had been thrown to the floor in the burst of wind.

"Are you okay?" she cried as she patted down his arms and shoulders looking for a gunshot wound.

"I'm okay, Little Bird," her dad said as he grabbed her arms. She could see the fear in his dark eyes.

"Were you shot?" Tears started to stream down her cheeks.

"No, I'm okay." He stood and took her in his arms. Beside them, Liam gave her uncle a hand and pulled him from the floor. When they looked back at the men she had blown out of the shop, they were gone. Persimmon's Uncle Robert cautiously walked out to where they had landed in a heap on the driveway and looked around. Her fists were balled up at her side as she followed her uncle out, her eyes carefully scanning the area, but they were gone. When she glanced back at her family and Liam, they were all looking at her. Liam's blue eyes suddenly fell searching the floor. Her dad and uncle both looked at her as if they were expecting her to speak. Perhaps they were waiting for an explanation, or if she was lucky, they didn't realize she was the one that swept the dangerous men from her father's shop.

"...so, what happened to them?" her uncle asked hesitantly, breaking the silence as he looked around at all of them. Liam was still avoiding eye contact.

"I have no idea," her dad answered, but didn't take his eyes off Persimmon. She had a sinking feeling he knew her secret.

"We should call the cops." Persimmon raised her chin and spoke up.

"Well, I don't think they could do anything now. Something scared those guys off. I don't think they'll be back."

Persimmon's dad looked at his younger brother. "I think we should

call them anyway. What if they do come back? They have a gun."
Persimmon saw the fear flash across her uncle's face.

"Now, don't overreact, Brian, I don't think they'll be back. They
won't bother us anymore," he said, his voice trailing off in shame as he
looked down at his ratty shoes. He was hiding something, Persimmon
was sure of it. Her dad let out a sigh, and she knew he wasn't going to
call the police.

He was always making excuses for his little brother. Their father
had gotten shot many years ago when they still lived in Louisville. Her
father had just been a teenager then, and her Uncle Robert had only
been ten. Her Nana Shell had taken the boys and moved them out of
the city and across the river to Jeffersonville—a smaller, safer town.

It was in Jeffersonville High that her parents had met. Her mom
had been an only child, and Persimmon's grandparents had recently
moved into Jeff from Mitchell, a tiny town up north. Her mom and
dad, both new in school, became friends instantly. They were married
two years later and two years after that Persimmon was born. Her
grandparents had left Indiana soon after her mom had died five years
ago. She visited them once a year, but she had always been closest to
her Nana Shell who still lived in that little red house down the street
from the large Federal Census building where Liam's mom worked.

Later that night Persimmon sat in her upstairs bedroom texting to
Liam. Her dad had quickly closed up his shop and took her home after
dropping her uncle off at her nana's where he had been living since he
got back from New York. Liam had asked if her dad had questioned
her about how the men ended up blown out of his shop. She texted him
back, reassuring him that her dad had said nothing about it at all. After
dropping her uncle off, they rode in silence down Dutch Lane and then
around the corner to their little house on Mary Street. She had wanted
to go inside and visit with her nana, but her dad said he wanted to get
home and he wouldn't let her stay there without him. He wanted to
keep her near—safe. But how safe was she, really?

Sure, she used her powers to throw those men out of her dad's shop
after one of them pulled a gun, but could she actually hurt someone?
Her stomach knotted when she recalled how frightened she had been

when she thought that her dad was going to be hurt. If something happened to him, she would be crushed. She couldn't go through the pain of losing another parent. She was close to Nana Shell but losing her dad would kill her. She wished her Uncle Robert would just go back to New York and leave them all be and then almost immediately she was overcome with shame. He was in need, and they couldn't turn their backs on him. He was a likable guy, but he always carried a shifty energy around him— she could never completely trust him.

She clenched her fist up and closed her eyes taking in a deep breath, then let it out slowly. Opening her eyes, she held out her right hand, and a small flame sparked and started to dance on her open palm. She felt a tiny bit of heat, but it didn't burn—in fact, it felt good. She reveled in the power she held, yet didn't fully understand. Her eyes grew soft as she followed the tongue of fire. It seemed to whisper to her. A calm confidence washed over her as she contemplated how destructive her powers could be…if she ever used them for evil.

Persimmon pulled herself out of her trance and curled her fist shut, snuffing out the flame. She would have to come to some kind of agreement with herself. Perhaps she should just ignore her powers and agree never to use or even think about them again. That would be an option except, of course, Liam knew about them and wouldn't let her just forget. She rubbed her temple, the first little twinge of a headache was starting to bloom.

Her gaze drifted to a picture of her mother in a silver frame sitting on her bedside table along with a smaller picture of her dad and Nana Shell holding Persimmon as a baby. A book she was halfway through reading also sat on the table, and a small figurine of a calico cat Liam had given her a few years before. He had given it to her to cheer her up about not being able to have a real kitten. She had found out she was allergic to cats when they had gone to a fellow classmate's birthday party a few days before.

Persimmon carefully picked up her mom's picture and ran a finger over the cool glass covering her mother's beautiful face. Her mom's name was Terra. Her skin was a few shades darker than her own, and her eyes had been a haunting green color. Her mom had once told her she had gotten her eye color from one of her grandmas. Persimmon smiled when she thought about all the times she nagged her mom to tell her all about how she had been chosen to be the Queen of the Mitchell Persimmon Festival in 1998 when she was only fifteen years old. She had been the first black girl to be crowned Queen of the Persimmon Festival—in fact, the only one still, as far as she knew. They had been the only people of color in the whole town. But her mom hadn't felt intimidated. She fearlessly made friends with all of those white girls. They had no chance, really, after they fell under the charms of Terra Johnson.

Persimmon laughed softly. Her mom had loved persimmons so much that she gave the name to her only child. Her mom the cheerleader. Her mom the social one. So different than how her daughter had turned out. Her mom had told her that when choosing the right persimmon, you had to be very cautious since some of them were so bitter they could scare the taste buds right out of your mouth! It was only the special ones that were sweet. Her mom had always called her daughter her special little persimmon.

She let out a lonely sigh and returned her mom's picture to her bedside table. She walked over to the window and pushed it open, the old wooden sash squeaking as she muscled it up. A cool spring breeze wafted in smelling like potato chips from the Krunchers production plant nearby. She sat in the broad window sill and looked up at the dark sky. There were too many lights from downtown Louisville, just over the river, to see very many stars but she saw a few.

She wondered if she would ever make it out of Indiana. She was hoping to get into a college in California, but now that she had suddenly developed these strange powers she wasn't sure what her future would hold. What was she supposed to do with them? Did she have a moral obligation to use them for good—she certainly wouldn't use them for evil! She supposed that she could just never use them. Her mind circled back to Liam. That wouldn't work either. Besides, she would always be worried about using them without a thought in a moment of fear or danger like today. And then what? People would seek to manipulate and exploit her powers if they found out that she had them. It was just sheer luck that those men didn't come back and question her or her family about what had happened at the shop today. Who knows, maybe they still would? And then what would she do?

She felt so alone as she turned from the window, put her long soft nightshirt on, and slipped into her bed. She turned off the lamp, but a yellow glow from the street light outside still let in enough light for her to stare at the ceiling until she fell into a deep sleep, dreaming of persimmon festivals and a strange pale-haired little girl.

The next day after school, she and Liam sat at Riverfront Park on one of the grassy strips used for seating carved out of the small hill sloping down to the banks of the Ohio River. A floating stage drifted on top of the dark water barely moving in the afternoon sun. The forecast had called for rain, but it had cleared without a drop. The sun was deceptively bright and cheerful but the day was chilly—warmer weather was still a month away for southern Indiana.

"So, your dad didn't say anything about what happened yesterday?" Liam asked, narrowing those bright blue eyes at her.

"Not really. He just said my uncle owed some guy in New York some money, and that he'd probably end up paying his debt, so those guys wouldn't come around anymore." Persimmon shrugged and looked back over the water, still thinking there was more to that story.

"He didn't say anything about...you know?"

"No."

"Good. I know you're pretty close to your dad, but I think that'd be hard to try and explain..." His voice trailed off as he picked a blade of grass and rolled it between two fingers.

"I don't want to have to tell him unless I have to."

Liam looked over at her again, but she didn't look back at him. "You'll have to tell him eventually."

She shrugged again. "Maybe not." Suddenly her skin prickled, she felt someone's eyes boring into her back. Casually she looked behind her up to the street. A man with a shock of blonde hair was standing at the railing peering at her between the thin trees lining the street. He quickly looked down at his phone and casually turned around. He might have just been texting or even playing one of those virtual games for all she knew, but her intuition told her to be cautious. He looked out of place.

"What is it?"

"I just thought someone was looking at us. It's nothing." She turned back around and looked west up at the Big Four Pedestrian Bridge. It was full of people slowly making their way over the vast expanse of the river from Indiana to Kentucky or vice versa. People were out enjoying the sunny day after being trapped inside over a long winter. The tall buildings of Louisville reached into the blue sky on the other side of the water. The arc of the domed Mercer Tower and the shorter, dual red peaks of the Galt House Hotel drew her eyes.

Next weekend was Thunder Over Louisville, and millions of people from all around the world would descend upon the area, all partying as they kicked off Derby Season. She had lived in Jeff her whole life and, even though she liked the excitement of Derby Season, she never really understood the attraction of horse racing. She watched a flock of geese fly in and gracefully land on the water, letting out a few honks that echoed across the river. Her quiet little town over here across the river would soon be crawling with people. She got an uncomfortable feeling.

Suddenly she heard screams and the loud whining of a car engine coming from behind her. She and Liam jumped up and turned around. The blonde man who had been there a few minutes before was now gone. Persimmon could hear Liam suck in his breath as a car busted through the railing at the top of the small embankment and flew out toward the floating stage. Towards them!

Without thinking, Persimmon threw out her arms, her silver bracelets falling together with a chime, and a huge muddy arm of water reached out from the Ohio River catching the car and gently guiding it down on top of the slightly pitched roof of the stage. Rivulets of hundreds of gallons of spent water ran from the roof of the stage in a hurry to get back to the flowing river, now that its job had been done. The motor of the car was still winding out at full throttle as it teetered on the roof, then tipped forward and quickly dove head first into the water slowly sinking as the current pulled it west down the river.

Persimmon and Liam jumped down the two levels of grassy seating and ran up to the railing at the edge of the river. People started gathering all around them. Her eyes desperately searched through the dirty windows of the car, but no one climbed out, and after a minute or two, the vehicle completely disappeared under the water as it made its way to the Falls of Ohio.

Two police officers ran up to the crowd and started asking people to back away. Persimmon followed Liam's gaze up to the walking bridge where a police side-by-side was speeding from the Kentucky side to Indiana. She knew Liam wondered if his dad was one of the officers, but they were too far away to tell. Liam's dad was a Louisville Metro cop and still lived in Louisville. He and Liam's mom had gotten divorced several years earlier, and she moved her family over the bridge to Jeff. That was when Persimmon and Liam became friends.

Liam grabbed her hand and pulled her through the murmuring crowd and up the ramp and stairs to the street above which was now clogged with lookie-loos. He quickly guided her across the street as more police showed up and across a parking lot and through an opening in the thick floodwall where they finally stopped. He turned toward her gently grabbing her arms. His red hair was shining in the sun, and he wore an expression of palpable concern.

"Are you okay?" he asked apprehensively.

"Yeah." She nodded but couldn't look away from the fear in his eyes.

"They were after you." It was a statement, not a question. At that, she did pull her eyes away and cast them to her feet. "They're trying to kill you!" he cried as a cold breeze gusted along the wall stirring her tightly curled hair she wore long.

The emotion in his voice caused her to look back up at him. "I don't think so." Liam sighed and let her arms go. She pulled her jacket tighter and tried to tame her hair by carelessly running a hand over it.

"They drove a car at you!" He threw his hands up in the air.

"I don't think they were aiming for us," she tried to explain.

"You think it's a coincidence that some shady guys tried to kill your family yesterday and now someone almost mows us over with a car?"

"No—"

"Someone is trying to kill us...*you*."

Persimmon took a deep breath trying to stop her hands from shaking. "The trajectory of the car was off. They wouldn't have hit us. It was going to plow into the stage."

"Why would someone want to take out the stage?" He held out his hand in the direction of the river which was now blocked by the thirty-foot-tall concrete flood wall that sheltered them from the scene a block away.

Persimmon peeked around the corner of the opening in the wall. The crowd had gotten larger, and now two police cars were parked on the street with their lights flashing. She looked back up at Liam. "Maybe they were testing me," she said quietly and looked around suspiciously, expecting the men from yesterday to appear at any moment.

The blood drained from Liam's face, making him even paler as understanding washed over him. "Testing your powers..." he whispered, the sprinkling of freckles on his face standing out even as a cloud sailed over the sun. "Persi, we need to tell someone. My dad?"

"No!"

"You need protection. My dad knows people....the Mayor..." his voice trailed off as even he could hear how weak of an argument that was.

"The Mayor of Louisville can't help me." She looked down and rubbed her temples with dismay. "No one can." She started to cry, and Liam took her in his arms.

"It will be okay, Persi," he whispered into the mass of her shiny black hair.

The rest of the week Liam stayed close to Persimmon, and they were very wary of their surroundings, but she couldn't shake the feeling someone was watching her. She had wanted to tell Liam several times, but she thought she was just making a big deal out of nothing—just being a scaredy cat—so she said nothing. Her dad had forbidden her and Liam to hang out at the shop after school, and he reassured her that the men had not returned, but still, she couldn't shake her uneasy feeling.

She and Liam knew that car crash had not been a coincidence. The police had pulled the soggy vehicle out of the cold water, but there had been no one inside. Liam's dad had told him someone had rigged the gas pedal to stay depressed, so it would drive itself into the river. No one had apparently asked how it had completely missed the hulking structure of the floating bridge and made it into the water—or if they had, Liam's dad over in Louisville hadn't heard about it.

Persimmon tried to force her nerves to calm down, but she still jumped at every loud noise and had woken up once in the middle of the night during a particularly bad dream. As the days crept by she and Liam tried not to talk about it and fell back into a little bit of normalcy. They were looking forward to Thunder. Liam's dad had been hesitant to allow him to go after the car incident, but, as always, security was going to be very high, and Liam had persuaded him to let him go.

That Friday Liam and Persimmon left her nana's house, each with a handful of homemade cookies. "Thank you, Mrs. Cook!" Liam called, waving as they started toward Persimmon's house.

"Love ya, nana!" Her Nana Shell kissed her fingers and blew her only granddaughter a kiss. Her plump face curled into a smile as she waved. At sixty, Shell hardly had any wrinkles to confess her age. Persimmon chuckled as she turned around, she loved her nana as much as she loved her dad.

Nana Shell's parents and grandparents had all been sharecroppers, and her great-grandparents had been slaves in Mississippi. She could sit and listen to her nana tell stories for hours. Life must have been harrowing back then for her great-grandparents and their parents. She chewed on her chocolate chip cookie contentedly feeling grateful that they had survived and she was even here today, walking down this street in Indiana with the sunshine on her face.

"You have the sweetest grandma, Persi," Liam said as he shoved a whole cookie in his mouth.

She laughed at his puffed out cheeks that barely contained her grandma's cookie. They excitedly discussed Thunder. Liam's mom was going to take his two little sisters down to the Great Lawn early to stake out a place to watch the air show and the multi-million-dollar fireworks display after the sunset. Liam and Persimmon would join them later. They stood on the sidewalk and watched as two fighter jets streaked overhead leaving them holding their ears as the deafening noise of the jet engines echoed across town. They were practicing for the air show. Persimmon smiled when Liam let out a loud, hysterical laugh. He was a big kid when it came to the air show. She was too, and she was thinking about funnel cake and fireworks when they said their goodbyes and Persimmon walked down her quiet street and into her little house.

As evening crept in and the sun set behind the big trees in her backyard, Persimmon grew worried when her dad didn't come home from work. She called her dad's cell phone and the shop phone, but there was no answer. As it got darker and he missed dinner, she really began to worry. Nana Shell called and asked if her Uncle Robert was there. Her stomach dropped, but she reassured her nana that they were probably just out running errands. Persimmon knew it wasn't true but didn't want to alarm her nana.

As soon as she hung up with her nana, she texted Liam. Her hands shook as her fingers flew over the glass display on her phone. He texted her back right away and said he'd be over as soon as he could. It was only ten minutes later when Liam pulled up on a scooter and parked it in her empty gravel driveway. She flung the door open before he could knock and he quickly came in. "Oby let you borrow his scooter?" she asked skeptically. Oby was Liam's twenty-something-year-old cousin who lived down the street from him who had gotten his license taken away for too many speeding tickets.

"I told him it was an emergency." Liam sat the helmet he had been carrying under his arm down on the coffee table. "You still haven't heard from him?"

"No. I'm really worried."

Liam took a deep breath. "We'll give it a little longer and then we'll have to call the cops, Persi."

Persimmon sighed. "I know, I just—" suddenly her cell phone started to ring. It was her dad. Relief flooded over her as she quickly answered the phone. "Dad, where have you been? I've been so worried!"

"Hey, Little Bird. I'm sorry, I didn't mean to worry you..." his voice trailed off.

"Dad? Are you okay?"

"Persimmon, I need you to listen to me very carefully."

Persimmon started to shake. The only time her dad used her full name was when she was in trouble, or something terrible had happened. He used that same tone when he told her how sick her mother had fallen just before she died. "Dad?"

"Run to the police sta—" her dad screamed into the phone, and then there was a big crash, and someone yelled the background. Persimmon whimpered and felt Liam's hand on her shoulder.

"What is it?" Liam hissed.

"Dad!" she cried into the phone. After a while, it went silent on the other side. "Dad!" she called again.

"Persimmon, your father can't come to the phone right now, and if you ever want to see him again, you'd better do just as I tell you." The man's voice on the other side was dark and filled with malice.

"Who are you? Where's my dad?" Desperate, she looked at Liam who was standing very close to her, searching her eyes. He grabbed her free hand and squeezed it softly.

"Miss Cook, believe me when I tell you that your father and uncle will both be dead by the morning if you don't do exactly what I tell you to do." The man's voice was calm like he kidnapped people all the time.

"W-what do you want me to do?" Persimmon was barely keeping it together.

"Tomorrow you will go to the Ferris wheel over at the event in Louisville at nine pm. I will meet you there. I hope I don't need to tell you calling the cops will mean you'll never see your family again. Nine o'clock at the Ferris wheel tomorrow, Miss Cook." The line went dead.

Persimmon set her phone down on the coffee table next to the helmet. She began to shake as tears rolled down her cheeks. Liam took her in his arms, and she began to sob. "What did he say?" he asked softly.

"He has my dad and uncle..." she said between sobs. "He's going to kill them if I don't meet them at Thunder tomorrow."

"What? Why? There's going to be a million people at Thunder tomorrow. Why do they want to meet you there?"

"I don't know...to blend in, maybe...I don't know," she cried.

"There's always so many cops there. I don't think they'll be able to get away with anything."

She leaned away from him, wiping her eyes with the back her hand. "I don't know what to do, Liam."

"Maybe it's time to call my dad."

"No! He said he'd kill them if I called the cops." Her voice sounded desperate even to her own ears. Her stomach was upset, and she was trembling with fear. She didn't know how she was going to make it through the night, let alone all day tomorrow.

Liam gently gripped her arms until she looked up at him. "Don't worry, Persi. We will get them back, and no one is going to get hurt... except maybe them. Remember, you have your powers. What can they do to you?"

"They can kill my family!" Tears rolled down her cheeks, leaving shiny streaks. She felt trapped, and she started to struggle to take in enough breath.

Liam guided her to the couch and helped her sit down. "I'll get you some water. Take some deep breathes. Everything is going to work out." He went into the kitchen and returned shortly with a glass of water and handed it to her. "I'm going to stay with you until we have to leave tomorrow," he said and sat next to her.

She took his hand in hers and looked into his eyes. "Thank you, Liam. I don't know what I'd do without you."

"You're welcome, Persi. We'll get through this. Your dad and uncle will be just fine."

"I hope so," she said, but didn't believe it was going to turn out all right at all.

The next night Persimmon stood at the foot of Skystar, the giant Ferris wheel, brought in and erected every year for Derby Season. Liam was somewhere out in the crowd. He reassured her he'd be close. She forced herself not to look for him, so she wouldn't draw attention to him. She felt exposed. Her hands shook, and she shoved them into her jacket pockets. The weather had turned gray and cold. As she had walked through the crowd on the Great Lawn earlier, she heard several people complaining how disappointing the air show had been due to the weather, but her mind was on one thing: freeing her dad and uncle.

Her stomach was in knots when she ran through all the possible things these guys might want from her to free her family. It just didn't make sense. Her dad didn't have a lot of money, and she surely couldn't liquidate all her dad's equipment at his shop to make a ransom payment. She was a sixteen-year-old girl! What did they expect of her?

Her dark brown eyes scanned the crowd milling about waiting for the fireworks to start. She knew they must have seen her use her powers when they tried running that car into the River Stage. That thought chilled her to her bones.

Suddenly an explosion went off behind her, and she spun around ready to bolt. She looked up to the dark sky, but the firework show had not started yet. The Skystar shuddered, and a loud creek echoed across the crowd. Several people screamed, and everyone near her ran for cover as the giant wheel started to list. Persimmon was frozen in place as she looked up at the rocking baskets full of screaming people. The wheel started to lean, and she had no time to think; she had to act!

She threw her hands out toward the wheel and instantly thick, brown roots shot up from under the grass and entwined themselves around the base of the wheel and up around the structure throwing clods of dirt and pieces of grass all over the area. Vaguely she was aware of someone recording her on their phone, but she didn't have the time to pay them much attention.

Police started to flow into the area. They were all wearing looks of shock as they gazed up at the Skystar being held up with thick, massive roots. From seemingly nowhere, Liam was standing next to her. He took her hand in his. It was warm and solid. "We need to get outta here," he said and pulled her away.

"But I need to stay to get my family back..." her voice trailed off in hopelessness.

He guided her around the back of a funnel cake vendor and stopped in the shadows. "Do you really think they'll show up now? They're probably the ones that caused that."

Persimmon knew he was right. Just then her phone started to ring. She fumbled trying to pull it from her jacket pocket, and it dropped with a crack on the asphalt. Quickly she grabbed it up scraping her knuckles and then bringing it to her ear. "Hello? I'm here!" When she heard someone on the other side of the phone, a wave of relief washed over her that it still worked.

"Look at the video I sent you. You have thirty minutes to make it to the Black Cat before I send this video to the FBI with your address. And don't bring any cops."

He hung up, and Persimmon heard the chime that indicated she had received a text from her dad's phone. She touched the message window through the crack in her screen. It was just as she feared: the video of her using the roots to save the people on the Skystar. She looked up at Liam who had watched the video with her. His eyes were as round as an owl's. His face etched with alarm. "What does he want?"

"I have to meet him at the Black Cat in thirty minutes."

"The Black Cat? That old arcade that's been shut down for fifteen years?"

"Yeah. I'm sure they don't have working surveillance cameras installed." She looked around as if trying to find the answers to her problem milling about in the crowd.

Liam rested his hands on Persimmon's shoulders until she looked up at him. "We *have to* call my dad now."

"Absolutely not!" She sliced her hand through the cold air cutting off any suggestion to involve his dad. "He specifically said *not* to tell the cops…again."

"Persimmon, this is too dangerous. They almost killed everyone on that Ferris wheel, plus anyone that it might have fallen on! And besides, kidnappers *always* say not to involve the cops."

She pinned him with a deadly look. "I have something more dangerous than bullets or jails," she said very quietly.

Liam took a deep breath and let it out slowly nodding his head. "Then we need to get going. Traffic is crazy."

Twenty-five minutes later they pulled up to the Black Cat on the borrowed scooter. The building was dark, the parking lot empty. They crept through the shadows toward the building, the hum from the interstate was in the distance as crickets, newly emerged from their winter sleep, chirped into the night. This part of town was completely empty. Those who weren't at Thunder were relaxing in their warm homes. A light rain started to fall. Persimmon ran her hand over her wet curls trying to push them from her face.

They went to the front doors, but they had been boarded up tightly. The words "No Copper" were spray painted on the plywood covering the glass doors in hopes of deterring thieves. Persimmon looked at Liam and jerked her head toward the side of the building and took off around the corner. They slunk down the alley sticking to the wall in the darkness, hopping over piles of trash that had blown to rest against the building. They rounded the corner and crept toward the back door. A cat with saggy orange fur darted out from an overflowing dumpster and ran down the alley.

When they reached the door, Persimmon wasn't surprised to find it sitting slightly ajar. She moved to go in, and Liam grabbed her arm. She looked back up at him. His eyes looked black in the dark. He silently pleaded with her to reconsider. She shook her head, and he dropped his hand in defeat and followed her in. The inside of the building was completely dark. Persimmon couldn't see her hand in

front of her face. She went to reach for her phone to turn on the flashlight, but suddenly she felt a pinch on her neck. She heard Liam yell
just as she lost consciousness.

———————

When she woke up, she was lying on a thin cot on a hard floor. She
brought her hand to her head and rubbed at her pounding temples. Her
stomach was sour, and she was so thirsty. Slowly she sat up, the room
spun. She was in a concrete room. A camera was hanging from one of
the corners, and there was a large one-way glass window cut into one
of the walls. A round speaker was also cut into the wall above the
glass. A stout looking door was on the next wall.

She sat on the thin mattress and took a few long breaths, trying to
calm her nerves. There was a pitcher of water and a glass sitting on the
floor at the head of the cot. She reached out to pour herself some water
and discovered metal bands around both of her wrists. Embedded in
the bands were large green stones, one on each wrist. The bands
weren't quite uncomfortable, but they were tight. Trying to push their
use from her mind, she poured the water and drank deeply as if she had
never had water before. I was cool and tasted wonderful. She drank
until her stomach couldn't hold anymore.

She sat back on the mattress and folded her legs up while she
looked around. There was a pretty large vent up on the ceiling, but she
couldn't reach it. She didn't even bother with the door—she was sure it
was locked. She fought back the tears when she thought about where
Liam might be and where her dad and uncle might be—if any of them
were still alive.

She closed her eyes and breathed slowly, clearing her mind. After a
few moments, she opened her eyes and held her hand up. She pulled
her brows down in concentration and narrowed her eyes, but the fire
would not answer her call. She tried it again but nothing! Icy fear
gripped her stomach as she looked at the pitcher of water, willing the
liquid to jump from its container, but the glassy surface remained still.
She laid her head in her hands and did cry this time.

"You'll find your powers no longer work, Miss Cook."

Persimmon jumped at the crackly voice as is blared through the speaker. She frowned at the glass angrily scrubbing the tears from her cheeks. A few choice words popped into her mind, but she didn't let them slip—her dad would have been disappointed. "Where is Liam?" She demanded.

"He is safe, with your family."

"I did everything you asked. Let us go. We have no money for you."

The voice on the other side of the speaker laughed. "You still think this is about money?"

"What then? What is it about?" She was losing her patience, but realized, with a sinking feeling, without her powers there was nothing she could do about it.

"My dear, you are a very valuable commodity."

Now she was even more terrified. She tried to calm herself and hoped he couldn't see her trembling. She didn't want to give him the satisfaction. "I want to see Liam and my family!" She tried to sound confident.

"You will, shortly. I just needed to make sure the Volirite bracelets worked at neutralizing your powers before we let you out of your cell." She looked down at the metal rings encircling her wrists. "Volirite is a remarkable piece of space rock. It was by accident that I discovered its ability. A gift from the stars." The voice hissed. He was clearly insane. However, he was right. Something had taken away her powers. She sighed in defeat. She had to keep her wits. An opportunity to escape would present itself sooner or later. She just had to wait.

It seemed like hours later, but finally, she heard a key twisting in the lock of the door. It swung open with a squeal. Persimmon quickly stood as that man with the blonde hair from the other day walked in. He had a smug look on his face. His pale skin was poked by some kind of disease he had once had. His blue eyes were so light they were almost white too. They were cold and soulless. She repressed an urge to shiver under his gaze. "Come on." He motioned with his hand for her to follow him. Without sparing her a backward glance, he walked out of the cell—she had no choice but to follow.

They trod through some dimly lit hallways and then passed through another thick door into a huge room with several cages or pens made of chain link. A dozen people were in the cages! "Persimmon!" She heard her dad call out. Quickly she scanned the faces of people in the cages and found some familiar ones at the end of the row. She ran to them.

"Dad!" She grasped the chain link in her hands trying to pull it down, but it didn't budge. Just behind him stood Liam and her uncle. They all looked uninjured for the most part, but her uncle had a bruised and swollen eye, and they all looked disheveled.

"Are you okay, Little Bird?"

"I'm fine, Dad. What happened to you?"

Her dad threw an angry look at the blonde man standing several feet away from them. "We were ambushed at the shop. We were told you wouldn't be hurt if we came with them." He glanced at the other people in the adjoining cages, who were all silently watching them, then back to her. "We were brought all the way here. I didn't know they had you until they brought Liam in."

"Where are we?" she whispered.

"I think we're in New York. We were thrown in the back of a van they drove all night and through the next day... Then last night Liam was brought in. I was so afraid they'd hurt you, Little Bird." Liam moved up to the fence and touched her fingers gripping the chain. She saw raw fear in his bright blue eyes once so filled with silliness and joking. Her heart was crushed. She was powerless to free them.

Footsteps echoed in the silent room as someone approached. Persimmon fought the urge to spin around ready to defend herself. She didn't want to give them the satisfaction of seeing her so frightened. The footsteps stopped, and she could sense someone standing behind her. "They'll be fine as long as you do just as I say, Miss Cook." That same voice from the speaker.

She turned to him and pinned him with the most ferocious stare she could muster. He was of middle height and had balding hair just turning from brown to gray. He wore a short beard. His clothes were impeccable, and his shoes looked more expensive than her dad's car. She looked back up at his gray eyes with contempt. "I've already done everything you've asked," her voice was barely above a growl.

"Careful, Miss Cook. I hold all the cards." As if to make a point he looked from her to Liam and her family then back again. "You will do as I say or I'll have them all killed in front of you. Then, I assume, the fight will fade within you like a dying flower."

She wanted to punch him. Hard. "What do you want me to do?"

"Nothing major. I just want you to follow orders, that's all. Now, say your goodbyes and follow me."

Persimmon turned around and put her fingers through the chained link again. Her dad touched one hand and Liam the other. There were tears standing in her dad's eyes, and it made her own tear up. "Stay strong, Little Bird. I will come for you."

She looked at Liam, and he gave her a little smile with no humor behind it. "It will be okay, Persi," he whispered with a wavering voice.

She followed the man out of the massive room down another few hallways twisting in what Persimmon was sure was the belly of a huge building. She thought it was strange that she was probably in New York. She wondered how long she had been out. He led her to another large door that the blond man unlocked and swung open. The balding man held out his hand, motioning her to enter. She took a deep breath and entered the room.

This room was a bigger cement cell than the last one she had been kept in. It had a good-sized window that let in a shaft of bright sunlight. With a sense of discouragement, she noticed it was barred from the outside. There were four cots in the room, a little more substantial than the one in the previous cell she had been in. These had thin mattresses resting on what looked like cheap wooden frames, but at least there were pillows and blankets.

There were also three other teenagers standing in the room, all staring at her.

She spun around. "What is this?" Her fists were balled up, and she would have called up the fires of hell upon him if she could have. Oddly the metal bands around her wrists warmed up slightly.

"You four are going to make me a very, very rich man." And then the door was slammed shut.

She turned around and looked at the others. There were two other girls. One looked to be around her age. The other was maybe eleven or twelve. The boy was maybe a year or two older than she was.

The youngest girl was Hispanic, her dark hair was braided and fell down her back. She was wearing a filthy dress made out of a thin material and wearing a jacket that was clearly too big for her. Her heavily lashed, round eyes were completely terrified.

The other girl was probably about Persimmon's age. Her blonde hair was straight and cut into a bob that fell just above her shoulders. She was dressed in a sweatshirt, muddy jeans, and black combat boots. She looked like she was about to start a fight.

The boy was also white. He had thick, curly brown hair and eyes the same color. He was tall and thin and looked defeated. They all wore identical metal bands on their wrists embedded with those strange green rocks.

"Does anyone know what's happening?"

"We're prisoners, obviously!" the blonde girl snapped, her green eyes were sharp and cut into Persimmon.

Persimmon frowned at her. "Thanks, Captain Obvious, do you know why?" the girl's mouth hung open as if she was surprised Persimmon would talk back to her.

The younger girl hesitantly walked up to her and touched one of the bands on Persimmon's wrist. She turned her large brown eyes up to Persimmon. "This," she whispered.

The boy let out a loud sigh and sat down on one of the cots that creaked under his weight. "He wants us for our powers. He'll probably make us start robbing banks or something. He has our families, you know, so we have to do what he says." His voice was sad as he looked forlornly out of the window.

Persimmon looked around the room. There was a vent way above their heads in the ceiling, but again, she couldn't reach it. There was also a camera hanging up in one of the corners, but no observation window with two-way glass. The floor was all cement, and there was a small door on the other side of the room probably leading to a bath-room—she hoped. She went to the door and opened it. It was a tiny bathroom with a vent none of them could fit through. No way to escape there. She came back into the room and started to pace. She had to think. There had to be a way out.

"Relax, I've been here for probably over a month now. There's no way out," the blonde girl said.

"A month?" Persimmon felt weak and quickly sat on one of the cots. "You been here over a month?" She felt her throat tighten and she swallowed painfully. She felt the tears start to prickle behind her eyes. Her Nana Shell surely would have called the police by now…that is, if she was still alive. At that, she did start to cry. Huge, warm tears ran down her cheeks as she tried to hold in the sobs trying to escape her lips. The young girl quietly sat beside her and put her little hand on Persimmon's shoulder.

That night she lay awake, staring out the window. She could scarcely make out a waxing moon. It would be full by the end of the week. She had taken her jacket off and rolled up in the thin blanket that they had provided, but it didn't take away the chill that was in her bones. The smothering fear she had deep down inside. The police would never find her; if they were even looking for her and her family. Sure, Liam's dad was most definitely looking for him, but he's just one cop in Kentucky.

She was about to start crying again when a whisper floated through the room. She bolted upright and looked at the sleeping figures of her co-prisoners. The boy, she had learned his name was William, was softly snoring. Jessie, the older girl, and Torri were both sleeping peacefully.

She was about to lay back down when she heard her name echo through her mind. She jumped and stifled a scream. She looked over to the others, but they still slept. Again she heard her name unravel through her mind like a ball of yarn. She clapped her hand on her ears, hoping to drown out the voice that was calling to her. Her heart pounded in her chest. She was sure she was going crazy. Finally, the whispers faded like a summer wind, leaving Persimmon shaking. "It's her. It's Beth," Jessie said then curled up and went back to sleep. Persimmon stared at her for a long time after that, wondering how she could be so relaxed about someone talking into her head.

The next night just as Persimmon was drifting off to sleep, she heard her name being called again. A soft voice tinkling in her head like wind chimes. Persimmon rolled onto her back and stared up at the ceiling far above her. *Who is this?* she demanded. Haunting laughter fading in the darkness.

My name is Beth, pleased to meet you, Persimmon Cook.

We haven't met. Why don't you show yourself?

Persimmon felt a thread of unease. *My father would not want it.*

Who's your father? Do I know him?

Of course, silly. He brought you here—all of you. Hesitation. *He's going to sell you.* A deep sense of shame and sorrow washed over Persimmon, and she gasped at its depth.

Can you get us out? When there was no answer Persimmon called out, *Beth, your father has my family. All of our families. Do you think he'll keep them alive after he's sold us?"* Persimmon sent a shot of desperation and fear through whatever communication line Beth was using. She also sent a picture of all those people in the chain linked cells in that huge, cold room. Suddenly Persimmon was alone with her dark thoughts again.

In the morning after they ate and one of the original men that confronted her dad in his shop came to take away their dishes, Persimmon asked Jessie who Beth was.

"Sinclair's daughter," she answered coolly.

"Has she been talking to you, too?" William asked. His eyes were wide, and then they slipped to the camera up in the corner of their cell.

Persimmon sighed. Well, if they had the room bugged it was too late. "Yes. She hasn't said much, though."

They can't hear us." Tori said as she sat down next to Persimmon in a dusty shaft of sunlight. "Beth told me so when I first got here."

"So, you've all talked to her?"

"In a manner of speaking…or *not* speaking, that is." Jessie smiled at herself for being so clever. William gave her an admiring look.

"Do you think she can get us out of here? Or call the cops or something?"

"She's too afraid," Tori said. "I can *feel* it when she talks to me."

"Sinclair uses her to find others like us." Everyone looked over at Jessie. She looked pleased to be so important suddenly.

When Jessie wouldn't elaborate Persimmon sighed in frustration. "How?"

"I don't know. Why don't you ask her?"

Persimmon thought their powers must give off some kind of signal that Beth was able to locate. That must be her power. "So, what are everyone's powers?" she asked.

"I can translocate myself," said Tori proudly.

"Well, that's pretty cool." Persimmon smiled at the younger girl.

"I melt things," Jessie said shortly.

"What kind of things?"

"*All* kinds of things." Jessie pinned her with a look that suggested she wanted to melt her.

"What can you do, William?"

At first, she didn't think he would answer, but everyone's eyes were on him. "I'm a shapeshifter."

"Wow. Impressive. So you can turn into animals?"

"Anything biological."

Persimmon looked down at one of her metal bands and ran her finger over it. "All this power in one room and we can't even use it."

Jessie stood up and walked up to the window. She closed her eyes and tilted her face up into the warmth of the sunlight. "If Beth is right, I suppose we'll get to use our powers all the time after we've been sold."

"Why would he sell us if he could just use our powers for himself?"

"I guess it would take too much effort to keep us compliant," William answered

"She's right," said Jessie. "Sinclair can't keep all of our families indefinitely. It would be much easier just to sell us to the highest bidder and let them handle *our security*." She used air quotes. "After he's made his billions he can have *daughter dear* just find him more of us to sell."

"He's made secret videos of all of us using our powers. That's what Beth told me. I'm sure those are his marketing tools. I wonder who the highest bidder will be? Russia? North Korea?" William ran his hand through his mop of brown hair, anger evident on his face.

The situation was looking hopeless. "You know he's going to kill them." There was a hitch in her voice even though Persimmon fought to keep the emotion from showing. Tori started to silently cry, and she placed a reassuring hand on the girl's arm.

Jessie turned from the window wiping tears from her face. "Those bastards will burn."

That night Beth came to her again just as she was drifting off. *Beth, you must help us!* She pleaded as soon as she heard her name being called in the watery depths of her mind.

I can't, she sadly responded.

If you don't help us, they will kill our families and sell us to bad people. Persimmon wasn't sure how old Beth was, but she got the feeling she was a little younger than Tori.

Go into the bathroom. Her voice was just a light whisper, and Persimmon wondered if she had even heard it at all. She threw off her blanket anyway and padded across the cold floor to the bathroom. When she entered, she was shocked to find a luminescent figure of a little girl, maybe ten years old, standing quietly in front of the sink. The little girl had large eyes, the exact color was lost to Persimmon in the bright glow of her apparition, but they looked pink. Beth's hair was white, as far as she could tell, and almost as curly as her own. It bushed up over her head in an unruly mess. She was wearing a nightgown that fell to her ankles.

Persimmon approached her cautiously. "Hello, Beth. I am Persimmon."

"I know," the ghostly figure said.

"It's nice to finally meet you."

"You too." Beth smiled a brilliant smile.

"You have quite an extraordinary power. Being able to talk into people's minds and appear out of nowhere."

She giggled. "I can make people do things, too." Persimmon must have looked terrified because she quickly said, "but not others like us. I have no power over the special ones."

"Oh..." was all she could manage to say.

"...and I can't make the mundane ones do anything they wouldn't normally do anyway. I mean, if they couldn't kill anyone deep down, I couldn't make them do it. I just give their mind a little nudge in the right direction."

Persimmon was horrified, but she fought to keep it from showing on her face. "Oh, well, can you nudge someone to let us out of here?" She looked sad all of a sudden. "Father keeps the iron bracelets on me when he lets me out of my room—when I'm not working. I can't make the men let you out. I am sorry." Her voice was small and sad.

"It's okay. We'll just have to find another way to escape before he sells us." She felt like she was drowning in despair and running out of time, fast.

"Father said the auction is tomorrow afternoon," she said matter-of-factly.

"That doesn't give us much time." Persimmon fought not to dissolve into a blubbering mess.

"I did get you this." She hadn't noticed until then that Beth had something gripped in her hand. She reached over and placed it on the counter beside the sink. It was then she realized the little girl's image didn't show in the mirror. Before she could question how an insubstantial image could leave behind something solid she swiped the object off the counter. It was a tiny black square that looked like it had some computer components embedded into it.

"That's a key for your bracelets. But you must be careful. Father has many men guarding you and your families."

"Oh, they won't stand a chance," Persimmon said and smiled.

"Thank you, Beth." She turned to leave the bathroom but then turned back around. "You should come with us."

"Leave?"

"Yes. Your father is a bad man. He'll just make you hunt us down again."

"But, I can't leave. Even if I wanted to, I'm locked in this room all night."

"We'll find you. Where in this building are you?"

Suddenly she looked afraid. Persimmon wasn't sure at all that she'd reveal where she was being kept. "I'm in a safe room on the top floor. In our apartment," she said hesitantly and then disappeared, leaving Persimmon in the dark.

Persimmon took a deep breath and held the key to the small opening in the iron band on the inside of her wrist. It made a sharp beeping sound and then fell off clanking as it hit the hard floor. She wanted to cry with relief but stayed quiet and quickly removed the other one. She clasped her hands together, trying to keep them from shaking. After a minute she opened the palm of one of her hands and, with no effort at all, a tiny flame appeared in the darkness casting the bathroom in a wavering yellow glow.

Persimmon cracked the door opened and peeked out. The others were still sleeping. "Jessie," she called just loud enough for the girl to hear her and hopefully wake up. She was the lightest sleeper of all of them. Jessie rolled over, but didn't wake. "Jessie," Persimmon called a little louder. This time the girl went completely still for a few seconds, then slowly rose her head from the pillow to look toward the bathroom. She gave Persimmon a questioning look.

"I've got the key for our bands." Jessie started to rise from her cot. "No! Pretend you're still asleep." Jessie fluffed her pillow and curled up as if she was going back to sleep. As Persimmon walked back to her cot, she said, "Wait for several minutes before you go in. It's a tiny black square than opens our bands. I've left it on the counter in the bathroom." She lowered herself back down onto the horribly uncomfortable cot and pulled her blanket over her.

By that time, she could tell the other two were awake also. "One at a time," she whispered. "Make sure you leave like a half an hour before the next one goes in, so we don't alert whoever it is that watches us all night."

"Okay," Tori answered.

Less than two hours later they were all back snuggled in their cots, their iron bands left in the trash can in the bathroom.

"We need to make a break for it," Jessie hissed.

"We need a plan. Can any of you remember the quickest way to get back to our families?" Persimmon turned over as if she were having a restless night's sleep.

"I remember. I have a photographic memory," William said. The thoughts: *of course you do, smarty pants...* and *thank goodness...* simultaneously popped into Persimmon's head but she was too wound up to feel ashamed of her judginess.

"Can you burn a hole in that door, Jessie?"

"I can melt that door," she stated confidently.

"Okay. You burn through it as quickly as you can, and I'll shoot whatever is left with water to cool it down, so we can get out. Then we make it to our families as fast as we can." Before Persimmon even quit talking, she could feel heat start to rise from the door bathing the room in an eerie glow. She knew they'd realize soon enough there was an escape happening. "You know, we might have to hurt someone to make it out of here." She stated a fact they all knew. No one replied.

The heat from the melting door that was now glowing brightly and was so hot that she was sure the whole room would burst into flames. Suddenly an alarm started to sound, and a red light started to flash through the room. They all jumped out of their beds, no time to get their shoes on. What was left of the door, melted onto the floor in a puddle of lava. The acrid smoke made her choke, but she threw out her arms dousing the area in frigid water. Steam rose and threw them all into a hot cloud.

Tori suddenly appeared next to her and gripped her arm. She wasn't sure at all the magma was cooled off enough to run through it barefoot, but they had to get out. "Come on!" she yelled above the scream of the siren.

Suddenly a giant Golden Eagle screeched and flew out of the room, they all followed the flapping of William's massive wings. Persimmon was grateful that the hole Jessie had melted through the door, and part of the adjoining wall was big enough for William to fly through. Without hesitation, she stepped into the wet mess that was left on the floor. She slipped in the warm liquid, and it squished between her toes, but it didn't burn her feet, so she ran on.

They had run down two halls already, when they turned the next corner the two men that had come to her dad's shop that day came running toward them holding guns, yelling for them to stop. William let out an ear-splitting cry and attacked them. One of them shot at him, but the bullet buried itself in the wall. William gouged out eyes. The other man turned his gun on them as they stood frozen in the hallway. Persimmon screamed and flung out her arms, and a gust of wind blew him off of his feet and through a metal door, leaving scraps of fabric from his clothes hanging on the jagged hole his body had made.

William flew around another corner, and they all followed him, stepping over the sightless man who was now rolling on the floor moaning in agony, blood smeared all over his face. In a few more turns they were at the door that would lead them to their families. Jessie did her thing again, and in less time than it took for her to melt the last door, nothing was left except a pile of glowing hot liquid that Persimmon doused again with ice water filling the hallway with sharp-smelling steam.

By the time they got into the room, Tori was already in one of the cells in the arms of her mother and grandmother. Jessie went around melting the locks from the doors and letting everyone out. "My Little Bird," her dad cried as she ran into his arms. "Are you okay?" he breathed into her unruly hair as Liam wrapped them both in his arms while her uncle stood behind them smiling.

"I'm fine, Dad," she pulled herself out of his arms. "You have to get out of here."

He grabbed her hand. "I am not leaving you!"

More men ran into the room and shouted for them to stop. There must have been a dozen men starting to surround them. They were completely outnumbered. Persimmon had to do something, or their families would all die.

She flung out her arms and four of the men were swept away in a massive blast of air so strong they were smashed into the far wall and lay on the floor in a crumpled heap. They lay silent and unmoving.

Another man shouted in alarm, and they all started shooting. Everyone hit the ground except the kids leaving them standing in the din of the red flashing lights and the relentless scream of the sirens.

The men's horrific screams carried across the opening above the shriek of the alarm as their feet melted, followed by their legs, and finally, their bodies caught fire. Soon they were just a puddle of fluid slowly spreading across the floor. The sounds of someone vomiting washed over the group as the cloyingly sweet smell of burned flesh filled the large room.

"I told you they'd burn," Jessie said not taking her eyes from the empty space where the men had just been standing a half minute before. Goosebumps rose over Persimmon's flesh.

Tearing her eyes from Jessie, she looked over at William, who had assumed his human form once again. "Lead them out of here. I have to go get Beth."

"It's too dangerous. We'll call the police when we get out." William tried to reason with her as his family surrounded him eager to be away.

"They'll be long gone, and I told her we'd come for her."

Her dad grabbed her arm again. "Persimmon I forbid you to go. We're leaving, now!"

He tried to pull her toward the door, but she ripped her arm out of his grasp. "Dad, I have to go save the little girl who helped us escape. If it weren't for her, you'd all be dead, and we'd be sold off to the highest bidder." At first, her dad's eyes were hard and unyielding but eventually, they softened as he realized his little girl had grown up.

"I suppose you're more dangerous than they could ever be," he finally said, standing up tall. "Go save her, Little Bird."

William started to lead everyone out of the building, and Liam appeared at her side. "Who are we going to go save?"

She looked at him and smiled. "I should have known I couldn't get rid of you."

"Are you kidding? I'm already going to be grounded for the rest of my life, I might as well have an adventure while I'm in New York," he said with a twinkle in his blue eyes.

"Okay, just be careful, these guys are serious douchebags."

"I don't think your dad would approve of such language, young lady." She laughed and led him into the hallway where they ran around for what seemed to be forever until they found the stairwell. The alarm made it hard to think, but they ran up floor after floor of stairs until they finally reached the top. They stopped on the landing to catch their breath and ease their sore legs. It seemed they had been climbing all night.

Persimmon looked at Liam who was clearly fatigued. "Are you ready?"

He nodded his head, his red hair falling into his eyes. "Yes."

"This might get bad, Liam."

"After seeing those guys melted in front of my eyes into a puddle of goop, how could it be any worse?"

"Good point," she said and slowly opened the door to the top floor of the building. She looked inside but didn't see anyone so nodded her head at Liam and entered.

For some reason, the sirens and red flashing lights were not going off on this floor, but the noise could still faintly be heard as they made their way down a wide, very elegantly decorated hallway. They crept toward a set of double doors complete with highly decorative moldings and what looked like expensive tables placed on each side of the doors holding copious amounts of flowers.

Persimmon tried the door handles, but they were locked. Knowing that they had lost their element of surprise long ago, she held out her arms, and both the doors blew off their hinges landing inside the apartment with a thunderous crash.

With her nerves pulled tight she ghosted into the apartment with Liam close behind her. This place was fancier than anything she had ever seen. The apartment was completely illuminated, so she knew someone had to be awake. No one could have slept through those alarms. Sinclair had to be in here somewhere.

It must have been getting close to dawn because Persimmon was able to make out other buildings all around them. They were obviously in a huge city. She remembered her dad and Liam thought they were in New York.

Carefully stepping over debris from the ruined doors in her bare feet, they entered an opulent living room with over-stuffed furniture on which a plethora of pillows rested. Large paintings hung on the walls, and dramatic sculptures dotted the whole room. More flowers exploded from brightly colored vases almost as tall as Persimmon.

"She's in a safe room."

"I don't know how we'll find her in this place. It's huge!" Liam said, in dismay.

They entered a library filled with hundreds of books and well-appointed furniture that looked overwhelmingly comfortable. Persimmon was reminded of her aching legs that threatened to cramp up at any moment. They continued into a hallway and followed it around a corner and there, standing in the doorway of what looked to be a quite spacious bedroom, stood Sinclair. He was fully dressed— even had his shoes on. Either he knew they were coming, or he never slept—maybe he was a bot. She had to suppress a totally inappropriate laugh at that thought. She must be going hysterical from lack of sleep.

"Miss Cook, I see you have found the penthouse." He was all poise and confidence on the outside, but the slight tremor in his voice told her he was scared. Scared she had come for him.

"Where's Beth?" She wasn't going to waste time conversing with this sicko.

For a moment his smug, condescending expression slipped. In a flash, though, it was back, but this time with a contemplative smile. "Ah, she's talked to you, has she? Isn't she a marvel, Miss Cook? A real miracle. With her, I can find and build an army. Or, like I was going to do to you and your friends, sell you to governments for billions."

He was insane! "Where is she?" Persimmon asked again.

Suddenly Sinclair pulled a gun he had been hiding behind his back and pointed it at them, but Liam was just as fast as he was and shoved Persimmon into the wall with a thud. She felt the bullet whizz by them. Angered, she stretched out her arms, and he burst into a ball of flame. They stepped back from the intense heat and threw their hands up to cover their faces.

A vase next to the door exploded from the heat sending water and flowers flying down the hallway. Sinclair let out a wail so haunting Persimmon knew she would never be able to forget that sound. He turned and ran back into the bedroom and Persimmon and Liam followed just in time to see him crash through the balcony door, run full speed until he hit the balcony railing, and flip, falling in a streaking fireball out of sight.

Liam made a strangled noise next to her, and she looked over at him. His eyes were huge, and his mouth hung open. She walked in front of him and gently put her hands on his shoulders. She could feel him trembling. "Are you okay?"

Liam tore his eyes away from the balcony where Sinclair had jumped to his death in a ball of fire and looked into her eyes. She saw fear in them, but not of her, thank goodness. "I'm good," he said in a thin voice.

"Good, we need to find Beth and get out of here. I'm sure the cops are on their way up by now." Persimmon turned around and went back into the hall, careful not to step on any piece of the broken vase with her bare feet.

"Beth!" She called out over and over as the minutes ticked by. She was expecting to hear the police announce themselves at the front of the apartment at any moment.

They made their way past an enormous kitchen and even bigger dining hall and then into another sitting room, calling out the girl's name as they went. Finally, she heard the girl whisper her name into her mind. *Where are you? We have to get out of here!*

Look behind the painting. Beth's words were as soft as silk as they slipped through her head.

Persimmon quickly scanned the room and saw an enormous

painting on the back wall. "Come on!" she ran toward it with Liam right behind her. "The safe room is behind this painting," she said as she felt around for a latch.

"I found it," Liam announced and swung the six-foot-tall painting open to reveal a knobless door with a keypad on the side.

"Oh no." She couldn't blow the door off its hinges or set it on fire without possibly hurting Beth. She wished Jessie had come with them.

8270. The numbers floated softly through her mind.

Thank you! Persimmon's fingers flew over the keypad, and a green light flashed across the screen as the heavy door beeped and swung open slowly.

Persimmon and Liam walked into the room and looked around. The whole room was white! From the walls to the furniture to the plush carpet. No paintings hung on the stark walls nor were there any flowers like there had been in the rest of the apartment. A white desk was piled with books and papers and pens.

In the corner of the room, sitting on a white bed, was Beth. She walked up to the little girl and smiled at her. "Hello, Beth. This is my best friend, Liam." Persimmon turned to Liam. "Liam, this is the girl who saved all of our lives, Beth."

"Thank you, Beth! You saved twelve innocent people from losing their lives today." She looked up at him with those pink eyes and smiled.

Persimmon was thankful the girl was already dressed so they could leave quickly. "Come on, Beth we need to leave as fast as we can."

She stood up but didn't move. "Is he gone?"

Persimmon took a deep breath. "Yes, Beth, he is gone and will never hurt you or anyone else anymore."

Beth started to cry. Soon her body was wracked with sobs. Liam walked over to her and very gently took her into his arms. "You're safe now, Beth. We'll always be here to take care of you." He picked her up, and they walked back out into the sitting room. "Beth, you wouldn't happen to know of a quicker way down than taking the stairs, do you?"

"The secret elevator is in there." She pointed to a bookcase that was standing open slightly. She wondered how they had missed that before. Persimmon pushed the down button and the same pin she had used to free Beth and then the elevator doors opened. They quickly boarded the small elevator, pulled the bookcase closed behind them and pushed the bottom floor button just as they heard voices calling out in the apartment. The cops must have finally made it up to the penthouse. The elevator doors shut and in no time, they were flying down to the first floor.

The elevator dropped them off in a small room at the back of the building where a long set of steps lead them into a tunnel and out a couple of blocks from the building. They couldn't find out how to turn the lights on, so Persimmon created a bright ball of light that floated in front of them showing them the way out.

They emerged from a small utility shed as the sun tried to climb above the huge buildings surrounding them. Persimmon and Liam were filthy, she didn't even have any shoes on, and Beth was just as sure to draw looks with her snow-white hair and pink eyes. How would they get out of this giant city without notice?

"They are in the park down the street waiting for us," Beth said quietly.

"Are you talking to someone?"

"Tori," was all she'd say.

Liam looked at Persimmon with relief. They had both been worried they wouldn't be able to find her dad and uncle. "Okay, let's go."

Liam was still carrying Beth, and they walked as fast as they could down the street to the park. They hobbled onto the grass too exhausted to walk one more step. Liam set Beth on the grass and flung himself down on the soft lawn. Persimmon sat and watched as Tori, her family, and Persimmon's dad and uncle appeared out of the trees and walked up to them.

Tori knelt and wrapped Persimmon in a strong hug. "You did it! You saved Beth."

Persimmon grabbed Liam's hand and gave it a squeeze. "*We* did it. I would have been a goner if it weren't for Liam."

He turned his head and looked up at her from his bed on the grass. "We make a pretty good team."

"Where are the others?" Persimmon asked as she looked around the park.

"Jessie and her family left as soon as we got out of the building." She looked down the street toward where they had come from, police sirens still blared, echoing through the tall buildings. "And William and his family left soon after we found this park. He said they shouldn't find us together."

Persimmon sighed. "I guess he's right." She looked over to Beth and affectionately patted her shoulder. The girl looked at her with those startling pink eyes and smiled. "We have Beth to help us communicate with each other now." The girl beamed, seeming to glow in the sunlight with her pale hair and almost translucent skin.

Tori's mom and grandma walked up to her and stood close. They seemed afraid to let her wander off too far—as they should, after what they had all been through. "Victoria," her mother called. "Vamos cariño, tenemos que irnos ahora." *Come on sweetie. We must go now.*

Tori hugged Persimmon again and then, more carefully, hugged Beth. "Thank you both." She looked over to Liam, "And you, too." She stood, then walked away holding hands with her mom and grandma.

Persimmon laid down on the cool grass beside her best friend and looked up at the morning sky that had turned a happy blue—much happier than it should be on this day, after so much carnage. She tried to push the events of the last week from her mind, but she knew there'd be scars—for all of them. She brought her grubby hands up and looked at them. They held great power—more power than she wanted or even thought she could wield responsibly. She was a sixteen-year-old girl! She should be thinking about the junior prom, not the haunting screams of Sinclair as he jumped from his penthouse while being consumed by flames.

She took a deep breath, trying to calm her nerves and rested her hands on the spiky blades of grass. She followed puffy, white clouds as they slowly drifted through an untroubled sky. This was her reality now. She would have to learn how to deal with it one way or another.

She turned onto her side toward Liam, and he did the same. He reached out and took her hand. His skin, as dirty as it was now, was still so pale to her own brown skin. His bright blue eyes didn't hold any more fear. She saw hope deep within the blue pools of his eyes, much like that stubbornly optimistic sky. She smiled at him. "Let's go home now."

Persimmon sat on the shifting brown sand and watched Beth play in the cold water of the Pacific Ocean. Liam walked up, flinging salty drops of water onto her as he dropped his surfboard onto the sand and flopped down on a towel next to her. He was very awkwardly learning how to surf. School just had just let out for the summer, and she planned on spending every day at this glorious beach.

It had been a little over a year since that horrible night in Sinclair's building when they all came so close to losing everything. But now they sat on a warm beach in southern California enjoying life.

When they had all got back to Jeffersonville, Persimmon and her dad sat with Liam and his family and told them everything. His mom had been so worried, but his dad was furious that they hadn't come to him for help. After a while, he understood why they made the choices they had and realized it was the only decision they could have made.

Liam's mom and little sisters immediately fell in love with Beth, and she was now a part of their family. Beth had done her weird mind nudge stuff on the appropriate officials, and her adoption was promptly completed. They also gained access to Sinclair's extensive finances, which allowed them all to disappear.

They now lived in the dry hills of Capistrano Beach in California. Liam's parents even recently got back together. Something none of them thought would be possible. Liam and his family lived a block over from Persimmon and her dad. Her Nana Shell lived next door to her and her dad, and her Uncle Robert lived down the street.

Her uncle had told him that he had worked for Sinclair, but when he had kidnapped Jessie and her family and found out what he was really up to, that's when her Uncle Robert had left and come back home to Indiana. Those men hadn't been looking for money, that had been an excuse. They were going to kill them both that day. It was just luck they had come upon Persimmon. After Beth turned her attention to the Midwest, she was able to confirm that Persimmon was one of the "special ones" as she called them, and Sinclair grabbed them all.

But now they were all safe. Jesse, William, and Tori, and all their families had moved and were now safe and sound in their new towns as well. Beth kept track of them all, as well as a few more she had found over the last year. Persimmon had no doubt she'd meet them all someday.

A seagull effortlessly floated on a cool breeze calling to his mate who soon joined him as they made their way down the beach looking for snacks. Sandpipers ran up and down the sand trying to outrun the spent waves on their long, skinny legs. Yes, this was the best place in the world to hide out.

ABOUT MELISSA E. BECKWITH

Melissa has been writing books since before she had learned to read, in the form of picture books, and planned to be an author at age 4. She spent her youth penning short stories, poems and writing in her diary. At nineteen she married her high school sweetheart and started her family. She has spent her adult life raising her three children and teaching herself the business and craft of writing. Born and raised in beautiful Southern California she and her husband now live along the Ohio River in Indiana to be near their beloved grandson, Bryar.

Melissa enjoys the outdoors and nature, especially camping. She has an interest in the natural world, particularly the wonder of birds and bugs. She can't grow plants to save her life, though she likes to try. She loves art and paints a little herself. She has a great interest in history and plans on trying her hand at historical fiction in the future. Someday she hopes to travel the world starting with Scotland, Ireland, Africa, and Australia.

Melissa loves to listen to heavy metal, Irish rock, and Celtic music…well, anything Celtic really. She loves dangly earrings, big rings, bright clothes, the color red, yellow roses, orange cats, and little dogs, like her fuzzy Shih Tzu, Abby.

Most days you will find her tapping away at her keyboard, researching her next great novel, or catch her with her nose stuck in an epic fantasy or historical fiction story.

facebook.com/AuthorMelissaEBeckwith

twitter.com/M_E_Beckwith

instagram.com/author_melissa_e_beckwith

LET THERE BE PEACE

BY BOB JAMES

President Bensen swiveled in her chair as she turned away from her desk and rose to look out the window behind her. She crossed her arms as she scanned the trees, hoping to see some of the birds that often flitted through the trees behind the Oval Office. Today, the birds were absent, adding to the somberness of her mood. She looked down at the ground and spotted a rabbit hopping along the bushes. She watched as it hopped toward the underbrush closer to the White House. Watching wildlife calmed her in difficult times. The rabbit, not very interesting on a normal day, was the most exciting thing she saw in her brief break.

She sighed and sat back down, turning back to look at the work in front of her. "Agriculture Reports." She snorted and flipped the folder to a pile to be read later. "Jobs Report." She rolled her eyes. She was so distracted by the border dispute in Washington that nothing caught her attention. She looked at her computer screen and couldn't find the report she wanted to review before the ambassador arrived.

Before she could pick up the phone to call him, Jackson came through the door with a folder in his hand. "Madam President," he said as he handed her the folder, "Here's the hard copy. The latest update is in an email from Ambassador Rodriguez." He stood at attention and awaited her next thought.

President Bensen smiled as she shook her head. After the Discovery, the Constitution had been amended to prevent any Extranormals from holding political office. Extranormal staff were allowed, but she didn't have many. Steve Jackson had worked with her since before the Discovery. When she thought about it, his telepathic power was evident even back in the days before. Since he could now practice his telepathy openly, he was even more effective in helping her. "Thanks, Steve," she said. Then she laughed nervously. "I'm still a little unnerved by your power."

He bowed. "I'm sorry, ma'am. I don't mean to be that way. I can tone it back if you like."

She shook her head. "Nope. Be yourself. Your ability to know my desires saves too much time, even if I don't think I'll ever get used to it."

He chuckled. "I knew you were going to say that."

President Bensen laughed with him. "I wish you could tell me what's going to happen in our border dispute."

"I stay tuned to you, ma'am. Besides, my powers don't extend beyond five hundred meters."

"I know. I need to read these reports before Ambassador Rodriguez arrives. Protect me from anyone who might want to come in and let me know when he gets here."

He bowed and nodded before he turned and left the room. She watched him leave, wondering how people had gained powers like that. She opened the folder and glanced at the historical overview. She'd lived through the incursion that happened right after the Discovery. A group of Canadian Special Forces had moved to take out the Extranormal families living close to the border. They were worried about the security threat the Extranormals might pose. Sneak attacks don't work well when telepaths sense every move of the attackers and the Canadian forces were surrounded and captured. The standoff had lasted five years as the Canadians disavowed any knowledge of their forces.

As the first president from Washington, Bensen wanted to put an end to the issue. She'd been raised about fifty miles from the Extranormal village in Washington and people saw her as a bridge between the Normal and Extranormal world who could help end the standoff. A sigh escaped as she opened the email from the ambassador. Ambassador Rodriguez was one of the best negotiators in the State Department. Ever the optimist, he sounded discouraged in his email. The Canadians were demanding protection from the Extranormals. She laughed a bit as she said, "Well, of course, untrained novices using their powers had captured some of their best forces," out loud, as if the ambassador could hear her.

She stood up and walked over to one of the couches. She leaned on the back and said, "The Canadians used to be peaceful and reasonable. Now they're being stubborn and obstinate. We need to find a way to break through." She practiced her lines for her discussion with Ambassador Rodriguez. She hadn't seen Steven walk in.

"Very good, ma'am," he said clapping quietly. "Ambassador Rodriguez is on his way up."

"Thanks, Steve," she said while trying to hide her embarrassment.

"No need to be embarrassed ma'am," he said without cracking a smile. "And, if I may…"

"Not now," she said. She'd been wondering if he had any ideas but didn't want to ask him for fear that he had some.

"I understand, ma'am," he said. "I'll head back to the reception area and wait for the ambassador." He turned and headed out the door to his desk.

The president shook her head. She turned and looked out the windows again as she muttered, "He drives me crazy when he does that."

"Who does what, Kris?" Ambassador Rodriguez asked as he walked in. He shut the door behind him to avoid interruptions.

The president turned back to look at him when she heard him. "Oh, it's nothing. My aide has a knack for being a step ahead of my plans. Sometimes he finishes my sentences before I do." President Bensen was careful not to hint that he was an Extranormal. Some of the old school politicians weren't keen on working with them.

The ambassador looked at the president and nodded. "Maybe," he hesitated a bit, "maybe he's part of the gifted community?"

"The what?"

"The gifted community," he said as if he wished he hadn't said that. "Most people use the term *Extranormal*. According to the group in my hometown, they prefer to be called *Gifted* instead."

The president stared at him, pondering how to deal with his response. "Gifted, huh? I've never heard them called that. Why do they prefer that?"

"First, gifted is easier to say," the ambassador responded with a chuckle. "Some have said *Extranormal* makes it seem like people see them as being better than other people. They're humble and don't want others to think that way."

She decided to feel him out. "So you've worked with extr....er....gifted people before?"

The ambassador reddened slightly and seemed nervous. "Yes, ma'am."

President Bensen picked up on the nervousness. "How long have you worked with people in the gifted community?"

"No repercussions, ma'am?" the ambassador asked. When she waved him to continue, he took a deep breath. "About fifteen years."

President Bensen's jaw dropped. She raised an eyebrow and asked, "Fifteen years? So you knew about them seven or eight years before everyone else?"

"Permission to speak freely, ma'am?" the ambassador asked.

"This isn't the military, Mr. Ambassador. We throw ideas around her freely all the time." She realized after she said it that it might have seemed a bit harsh.

"Yes, ma'am. I just want to remind you that you asked how long I've worked with the gifted community. I've known of them for much longer."

President Bensen smiled. "Are you gifted, Mr. Ambassador?"

He smiled wryly. "If I were, the negotiations would have finished long ago, assuming I received the right gifts to be an ambassador." He changed the direction of the conversation. "Perhaps we could speak of the negotiations."

The president laughed and indicated a chair near her desk. "Of course, Pablo. You just got me thinking about Extranormals, or the Gifted as you prefer." He stood by the chair until she sat down. Then, he took a seat also. "Do you have any hope for the negotiations?"

The ambassador stared at the floor. "I fear that we're at an impasse. Although we hold the Ace in the Hole, the Canadians aren't budging on their demands."

"And the only people more stubborn than the Canadians are the Americans, correct?"

"That's my calling, ma'am."

"I know, Pablo. You're my favorite stubborn negotiator." President Bensen sighed. "I fear, though, that we might need to take a different tack."

The ambassador coughed and stood up wringing his hands by his waist. "I understand, Kris. How soon do you want my letter of resignation?"

President Bensen was stunned by those words. "How about never," she sputtered. "I think you misunderstand. I was fascinated that you've worked with the Gifted because I think we may need to include a gifted person on your team now."

Ambassador Rodriguez laughed. "With all due respect, ma'am, that might cause an end to the negotiations. The Canadians would see that as an insult."

"They might. On the other hand, when we reveal her gift, they might be more open to us including her on our team. We would, of course, allow them to expand their team as well."

"Do you have someone in mind? Or did you want me to pick someone gifted off the street?"

It was President Bensen's turn to laugh. "Have you ever heard of Kimberlee Thompson?"

***

Fifteen Years Earlier

"KimberLEE THOMPSON!" It wasn't the whack of Ms. Fox's ruler on the desk that woke Kimberlee up. It was the gentle nudge of the interpreter who glanced at Ms. Fox with a terrified look while she got Kimberlee's attention. Her eyes were wide open as she signed Kimberlee's name by signing a K dissolving to a T in the air in front of her chest.

She yawned as she woke, not realizing how loud it was, causing Ms. Fox to rage even more. The interpreter couldn't keep up with her. "Young lady, you will not fall asleep in my classroom ever again! Do you understand that? I'm not going to let you fail because you stay up all night playing video games or whatever it is that you do. You will stay awake, and you will pass so that in a couple of years when you get to high school, you can learn to use your gift to help our world!" Kimberlee avoided laughing when she saw the teacher wipe some spit from her lips before the interpreter caught up.

"No gift," she signed when the interpreter finally caught up to the teacher. "High School's no big deal for me." Then it dawned on her. She'd fallen asleep in class. That only happened when... She looked down at her seat. The red time hadn't begun yet. She looked up at the clock and realized that she still had an hour before she got out of school. The red time had started soon after she woke up from a daytime. When this happened at home, it was the weekend, and she had cleaned herself up both times with no one finding out. At school, it would be a disaster. *Why couldn't this have waited one more day?*

She'd ignored her interpreter who had to tap on her shoulder again. "Stand up," she signed with a head nod toward the teacher.

Kimberlee rolled her eyes. "Why?" she asked the interpreter.

The interpreter thought better and decided to answer the question instead of voicing it. She always hated dealing with Kimberlee when she got in trouble. "Ms. Fox thinks it will help you stay awake."

Kimberlee tried to hide the growing panic as she felt the wetness beginning. She might be able to hide the blood if she were sitting down. Standing up, she'd end up dripping for all to see. When the cramp hit her, she decided to ignore Ms. Fox's directive. "I'll stay awake now," she signed to the interpreter. "I don't need to stand up." The cramping got worse, and Kimberlee could feel the blood beginning to leak.

Ms. Fox was furious. "I'll decide whether or not you need to stand up young lady! And I say," she looked down at Kimberlee and suddenly realized what was happening. She couldn't hold back the gasp which drew everyone else's attention.

When the interpreter stopped signing and looked down also, Kimberlee knew what had happened. The red time had begun. Her cheeks flushed as she looked around the room and saw the laughter begin. She lost it and ran out of the room crying. She turned right and headed out the nearest door and saw just enough to dodge any objects in her path. There was a forest on the other side of the fence around the schoolyard, and she headed that way. She slipped through an opening in the fence on the side and ran parallel to the fence until she reached the forest. She was breathing heavily as she ran along the edge, looking for a path.

She didn't look back to see if any of her classmates were trying to catch up to her. She was looking for a path, any kind of a path into the forest. She wished she'd paid attention when the other kids talked about the forest, but the forest terrified her, and she didn't want to know about it. Now, it looked like sanctuary – if she could only find a way in. She was so focused on finding a way in, that she didn't notice that no one was following her. Because of that, she took the first narrow path she saw into the woods and dodged most of the branches in her needless flight. Branches scratched at her face, and she wiped the blood away and ran. She ignored the rips in her clothes, twisting so she could get passage through the underbrush.

The trees thinned out, and she wiped her eyes as she looked up to see a small clearing. She sniffed a bit, thinking, *Maybe I can rest there.* She took a quick glance back and didn't see any signs of followers, so she slowed and approached the clearing as her eyes darted from side to side looking for anyone close by. She was surprised to see a bench sitting at the far end of the clearing. *I wonder why that's there? Do people come out here often?* Her head told her to get away from here, but she was drawn to the bench. It was a place to rest, and she was so tired. She kept looking but didn't see anyone. She took the chance and sat down when she got to the bench.

The flight, especially during the red time, had worn her out. She closed her eyes and drifted off to sleep, falling down on the bench. She didn't know how long she slept, but it was dark when she opened her eyes, only to find herself staring at a woman, or was it an angel. There was a bright aura behind her and Kimberlee rubbed her eyes to make sure that they were fully open. She pinched herself as she sat up and the pain told her she was awake, then she wondered if she would feel pain in a dream.

"Yes, you're awake," the being signed.

Kimberlee's eyes widened. *How does she know sign language? How does she know I'm deaf?* She examined the lady in front of her. The aura made her brunette hair sparkle and her flowing blue robes shimmer. She was a little taller than Kimberlee. Her smile radiated joy, and in spite of her better instincts, Kimberlee felt at ease. "Who are you?" she asked as her hands flew faster than her normal conversation speed. "How did you know I needed sign language?"

The glow from her smile lit up the clearing. "You may call me, The Huntress. I know all my children. I've been expecting you."

"Expecting me? Why?"

"You're supposed to come here during the first month after your flow starts," The Huntress replied. When she saw the puzzled look on her face, The Huntress pointed at the red stains on her pants. "Your monthly flow," she signed.

Kimberlee blushed and hid her face. Then she turned her head and signed, "I can't help it." A tear rolled down her cheek, and she wiped it away with the back of her hand. "I'm sorry."

The Huntress teared up and wrapped her arms around her as she sat beside her on the bench. She held her, patting her back, as Kimberlee started sobbing. The Huntress shook her head and voiced quietly, "No one told her. No one let her know what was happening. No one prepared her."

Kimberlee looked up at her comforter and signed, "I'm sorry," again.

The Huntress stood up, taking pains to support Kimberlee as she did, then she signed, "I love you. You don't need to be sorry." And then, The Huntress took the time to explain to Kimberlee what was happening with the changes in her body and how to take care of herself during this time of the month. She talked about how she would change emotionally and physically in the upcoming years.

When she finished, she looked at Kimberlee, giving the young girl time to process what she'd seen. She waited until Kimberlee responded by asking, "So I didn't do anything wrong?"

The Huntress smiled and signed, "No, child. No." and then she hugged her one more time. Then she pulled away and asked her another question. "Do you know that you came here to understand your gift?"

Kimberlee laughed. "I ran here to get away from the other kids who were laughing at me. I don't have any gift."

The Huntress frowned. "There is so much they haven't told you, my child." She reached her hands out as if to hold her head. Then she stopped and signed, "May I?" When Kimberlee nodded, she put her hands on each side of her head.

Her gentle touch soothed Kimberlee, and the last of her tension faded away. A smile began to cross Kimberlee's face as she felt peace overwhelming her. She looked up at her benefactor and saw a frowning face locked in concentration. Her head jerked in little tics as if she was involved in battle. But her hands never lost that gentle touch. Then, that face of grim determination melted away as a smile replaced the frown.

"I was concerned about your delay in coming," she began, "but the delay has served its purpose. We have granted you your gift." She looked at her with a sense of awe. "This is a gift that I've never seen before. You have a special calling."

Kimberlee stared at her, her head shaking from side to side. Then she burst out laughing. "Me? Special? Ha! I'm short, fat, and not too good looking. My family can't talk to me because I'm deaf. What kind of gift could I get that would make me so special?"

The Huntress recoiled. She hadn't expected this outburst. She held her hands up to calm Kimberlee down. When Kimberlee stopped ranting, The Huntress signed. "What you are now, is not what you'll become. In days of strife, all become one."

Kimberlee shook her head. *Now I know it's a dream.* "That makes no sense," she signed. Her face showed the disgust she felt

"It will. But," she continued, "You've been here a long time. Your father is worried about you. You must go home and talk to him to understand your gift."

Kimberlee shuddered. "How long?"

"Five hours past school time. You slept long."

She sighed. "Dad's gonna kill me. Not only have I been gone so long, I've ruined these…" she looked down at her pants that were now clean. "How?" she signed looking at the place The Huntress had been. She was gone.

Kimberlee scanned the clearing, expecting to see her, but she had vanished. She stood up. Her eyes wide open trying to see in the now-darkened clearing. *Ok. This must have been a dream.* She ran her hands down her pants to feel the sticky wetness; only there was none. She looked, and there were no stains.

She shook her head to clear it. There was only one thing to do. *I need to get home.*

Kimberlee didn't hear the frantic voices of people calling for her. If she had known they would do that, she would have had a good laugh. She walked through the streets at night with a bounce in her step after her meeting with The Huntress. She'd never felt so positive in her life. Then, as she began walking toward the front door, she gulped. She could see Ms. Fox in the living room with her father. Both looked furious. Kimberlee couldn't hear them, but she was certain that they were yelling at each other. *I'm in so much trouble.*

She took a deep breath and walked through the door. They didn't hear her as much as they were alerted by the motion when she shut the door and walked toward the coat closet. They turned and headed toward her. She couldn't tell what they were shouting, and their mouths were so exaggerated from yelling that she couldn't read their lips. She looked behind them and saw the interpreter from school was trying to get around them so she could tell Kimberlee what was happening. Kimberlee smiled, blessing her deafness that didn't allow her to be affected by the yelling.

When she smiled, the atmosphere in the room changed. The tension dissolved. Ms. Fox did something Kimberlee had never seen: she smiled. Her father turned off the anger and turned on the joy as he reached out and hugged Kimberlee. He couldn't bear to break the embrace and squeezed her for over a minute. When he broke away, he looked at Ms. Fox and said something. Kimberlee looked over at her interpreter whose jaw had dropped open in amazement. She realized Kimberlee was watching her and apologized quickly before signing, "Your dad just told Ms. Fox that he'd call the police and tell them you'd come home." Then the interpreter looked around and asked, "What just happened?"

Kimberlee's eyes opened wide, and she smirked. "I don't know. I just got here. You tell me."

"Seconds before you got here, Ms. Fox was laying into your dad about not preparing you for..." her eyes dipped toward the floor, "well, you know. She mentioned how embarrassed you were when your period started and that was why you ran into the woods." She stopped and looked around at Ms. Fox and Mr. Thompson, who seemed to be working well together, not paying attention to this conversation. "Didn't anyone tell you about...you know." She averted her eyes momentarily.

"Not until today. The Huntress explained it to me."

"Wait! The Huntress? She's real?"

"You've heard about her?"

"The kids talk about her. Every girl who's started her monthly flow has seen her in a dream. Every boy that's reached physical maturity has seen The Hunter. I think that's how people here get their gifts." She stopped and stared. "Did you really meet The Huntress in person? Did she give you a gift?"

Kimberlee shrugged. "I'm pretty sure I was awake. I kept pinching myself. She hugged me." Kimberlee blushed. "My pants are clean." Then she changed the subject. "Why didn't you visit The Huntress?"

The interpreter glanced back toward Ms. Fox. "I'm not from here. There aren't any interpreters in this town. I don't know anyone except people from this town who have these gifts. It's strange. And you didn't answer my question."

She shook her head. "She said that I got a gift, but she didn't tell me what it was. Said that I'd have to discover it by talking to my dad." Then she glared at the interpreter. "Now, tell me what happened here!"

The interpreter rolled her eyes. "It's been a war zone here ever since school let out. She grabbed me and brought me over here in case you came home. She lit into your dad like nobody's business."

"Why dad? I'm the one who ran away."

"I can't remember everything, but she was talking, er, yelling about him not preparing you for your monthly flow. He kept asking how he should know how to do that. Well, they went on and on about that and a few other things."

"The whole time? It looked like they were fighting as I walked to the doorway."

"They couldn't agree on what kind of pizza to order." The interpreter stopped. "Hey, you must be hungry. Do you want some pizza?" When Kimberlee nodded her head, the interpreter motioned her to follow, and they went into the living room where two pizza halves were laid out next to each other.

Kimberlee looked at the pizzas and laughed. "My dad got the all meat pizza, didn't he?"

The interpreter chuckled as she signed, "And Ms. Fox got the veggie delight."

Kimberlee shook her head and picked up a paper plate next to the boxes. She took one piece from each pizza. Then, she used a fork to take some of the meat off the all meat pizza and put it on the veggie delight and then transferred some of the veggies to her slice of all meat. Then she raised her eyebrows as she looked at the interpreter and took a bite.

She hadn't noticed Ms. Fox watching her. When she looked up, though, she saw her beaming face. It looked like she was saying something, so she looked over at the interpreter who signed, "I approve. That's a great idea!"

Kimberlee turned back to Ms. Fox and signed "Thank you."

Ms. Fox called to the interpreter and mimicked the sign Kimberlee had made. "What's this sign, dearie?"

"That's *thank you*, ma'am," she responded.

"And how do I say, *you're welcome*?"

For a split second, she wanted to embarrass Ms. Fox. But then she thought about how much she had fought for Kimberlee today. "Just make the same sign back."

Ms. Fox signed "Thank you" to the interpreter and then repeated the sign toward Kimberlee.

It was a simple gesture, but after the day Kimberlee had gone through, she had to wipe a tear away when she saw her teacher taking a step toward understanding her. Then she nodded and smiled.

Ms. Fox headed toward the door and motioned for the interpreter to come along. "I need to get you home, dear," she said. "It's way too late."

The interpreter rolled her eyes. She was twenty-two, although she looked like she was seventeen, and Ms. Fox always treated her like she was twelve. Still, she got up and followed her out after hugging Kimberlee and waving at Mr. Thompson.

Kimberlee looked at her dad. One of the first signs he had learned was *Sorry*, and he signed that now as he rushed to hug his daughter.

Kimberlee looked out the car window, not making a move. Mr.

Thompson nudged her to urge her to get out of the car. At first, the nudges were gentle. Then he became more insistent. Kimberlee looked back at her dad. She snarled until she saw his face. She shook her head and exhaled when she saw her dad's "puppy dog face." She knew she wouldn't win, so she slapped his shoulder playfully and got out of the car. She stood there, looking at the car as he drove away.

She sensed the motion behind her and turned to see Ronnie coming up to her. She gulped. No one had teased her more than Ronnie. She made it known that she though Kimberlee was too fat, or too short. When they both hit sixth grade, Ronnie had been merciless, and Ms. Fox hadn't noticed, because it was all done wordlessly. She couldn't run, so she stayed there ready to endure what she could when Ronnie teased her about last Friday. *Dad, why couldn't you have let me stay at home for about a week, or a month even.*

Her eyes narrowed when Ronnie motioned to her to follow. Then, her jaw dropped when Ronnie signed "Sorry." Kimberlee cocked her head down but took a chance when Ronnie motioned her to follow again. She followed Ronnie as they entered the school and joined a group of her classmates in Ms. Fox's room. She looked around and saw the interpreter, with five of the girls, all who had teased her often, and Ms. Fox.

"What's happening?" she asked.

Ms. Fox answered after the interpreter voiced. "After you left last Friday, these girls said some ugly things. Then I found out that they'd been bullying you all through sixth grade. We had a little talk, and now they want to apologize."

There was an awkward silence, and no one moved. When Ms. Fox gave Ronnie the eye, she rolled her eyes and signed "sorry" again. She elbowed the girl next to her, and each of the other four girls apologized the same way.

"And these girls are going to be your friends. Aren't you ladies?" Ms. Fox glared at them.

They all looked down at the floor as they nodded.

Ms. Fox looked back at Kimberlee. "If they give you any trouble, you let me know."

Kimberlee looked at the interpreter and nodded.

"We're all agreed now?" Ms. Fox asked as she looked around at everyone. "Good. Ladies, you'll work with the interpreter to learn how to talk with Kimberlee. Communication is vital." She looked straight at Kimberlee and said, "Smile, child. Everything's going to be all right."

When Kimberlee smiled, Ms. Fox grinned. "Great, now, let's take on the day."

The five girls watched her go, and then came up to Kimberlee, each trying to outdo the other in reconciling their past differences. The warning bell letting them know that school started in ten minutes. The girls all went out to their lockers. As other class members wandered in, they had no clue about the meeting. The atmosphere in the classroom changed, though. The five girls who had led out in bullying Kimberlee, as well as others in the class, stopped their bullying and began supporting their classmates.

Kimberlee began enjoying school. Her grades started improving. Ms. Fox handed back a test with a 93. "I'm so proud of you, Kimberlee! Your grades are getting better, and it's so nice to see you smiling so much. Your face lights up the room."

Kimberlee blushed. "Thank you, Ms. Fox. You've helped a lot."

"Your interpreter has too. She's taught those kids a few signs." She patted the interpreter's shoulder gently, not wanting to interrupt her signing.

Kimberlee nodded. "It's nice to have some other people to talk to."

"So much of this happened after you met The Huntress, but you've never told me about your gift. What's your gift?"

Kimberlee's face darkened as she shrugged. "She said I'd find it when I talked to my dad. When I came home, you were talking to him. When you left, we never did get around to talking about that."

"I think we were both so relieved that you were home safe that we didn't ask you about The Huntress."

"You knew I was there?"

Ms. Fox lifted her eyebrows and said, "It was time, and you headed into the gifting forest. What else would you be doing?" Then she shook her head. "You were there longer than most. Did she say anything to you?"

Kimberlee nodded, then frowned as she thought back to that day.

"Think about it. I'll be right back," Ms. Fox said. She headed to the other side of the room and started talking to two boys. She didn't seem happy.

Kimberlee looked at the interpreter who said, "Those two boys started arguing about something."

"What? I don't know. You know boys. They'll fight about anything."

They both laughed and then Kimberlee went back to her encounter with The Huntress in her mind. *What was it she said?* She remembered that it was something cryptic. Maybe her dad hadn't told her because she hadn't told him what The Huntress had said.

She racked her brain trying to remember the words. She looked back at Ms. Fox who was still dealing with the two boys who kept fighting.

"We haven't seen this much strife in a while," the interpreter said.

Kimberlee nodded, then her face lit up. "Strife," she said. "That's it. The Huntress told me 'What you are now, is not what you'll become. In days of strife, all become one.'"

"That's interesting," the interpreter said. "What's it mean?"

"I wish I knew." Kimberlee pursed her lips and shook her head. She looked up and followed the interpreter's eyes. She'd been distracted by the sound, and Kimberlee saw the two boys still scuffling. She shook her head and laughed, asking the interpreter, "Why is it that boys are always like that?"

"Who knows?" the interpreter responded. "I think that's how they establish their pecking order."

Kimberlee giggled. "Ah, I see. I should want to be with the guy who wins, right?"

The interpreter nodded. "Yep. You want to be with the loser who wins this fight, not the loser who loses the fight." Their laughter caught the attention of a few people in the room, so they made stern faces as if to say that they hadn't laughed, and then had a harder time stifling their laughter. They didn't notice Ms. Fox come back.

"What's so funny, ladies?" she asked.

Kimberlee watched and nodded as the interpreter explained verbally and in sign language. She saw Ms. Fox rub her chin. Then Ms. Fox responded, "I think you ladies are beginning to understand boys." The interpreter almost didn't finish interpreting the sentence before she started laughing again. Then Ms. Fox asked, "Did you remember what The Huntress told you?"

Kimberlee nodded. "She said, 'What you are now, is not what you'll become. In days of strife, all become one.'"

Ms. Fox reached up and twirled her hair as if thinking. Then she said, "That's an interesting prophecy. If The Huntress told you to talk to your dad about that, you need to do that."

Kimberlee agreed. "I hope it isn't too late to do that. Maybe this gift has been taken away because I didn't find it fast enough."

Ms. Fox shook her head. "It doesn't work that way. The fact that your gift came with a prophecy though..." she stammered a bit. "I think that means that it's really different."

Kimberlee's face darkened as she looked down at her desk. "I don't think I can make any of this clear to him. Would you go with me and talk to him?"

"Just a second, hon," she said, then she shouted out to the class, "Settle down! I'm dealing with something important here."

Kimberlee chuckled as she looked at the interpreter cleaning out her ear in a mock gesture, having born the brunt of the volume because she was sitting so close to Ms. Fox. Ms. Fox laughed too. "Sorry, I didn't want to leave the conversation here." She looked at the interpreter and asked, "Can you join us also?"

The interpreter interpreted exactly what Ms. Fox said, and Kimberlee gave her a silly look. "She meant to ask if the interpreter can make it too."

The interpreter grinned and then raised her eyebrows innocently.

Ms. Fox interrupted their private joke. "I'm thinking you didn't voice everything Kimberlee said."

Innocence turned to guilt as the interpreter gulped. "Sorry, ma'am. I interpreted what you said when you asked, 'Can you join us also?' Kimberlee made sure I realized that you were talking to me." She hesitated. "Which I did, but I was just following my code of ethics. So, if you were asking if the interpreter can join you, I guess I pretty much have to."

Ms. Fox rolled her eyes. "So does the interpreter have a name, so I don't run into this problem again?"

The interpreter interpreted Ms. Fox's question precisely.

Kimberlee shook her head and laughed. "Why don't I go to the restroom so you two can talk without having to interpret for me." Kimberlee got up and went to the restroom while the interpreter was still voicing, leaving them no way to stop her.

Kimberlee opened the front door and flashed the lights to let her dad know she was home as she welcomed Ms. Fox and the interpreter into the living room. The lights flashing as they sat down on the couch startled them. Kimberlee snorted and signed, "My dad's coming. He's just answering me. What do you expect him to do, yell?"

Ms. Fox nodded when the interpreter voiced. "Thanks, Sharon."

The interpreter nodded in acknowledgment, then interpreted so that Kimberlee would know what was said. She spelled her name and then made an "S" with her hand and ran it down the side of her head as if drawing a picture of her long black curls in the air.

"So the interpreter has a name!" Kimberlee signed, obviously teasing Sharon as she repeated the name sign.

Sharon voiced for Kimberlee and signed and voiced, "All you needed to do was ask," as she shrugged her shoulders.

"Ask what," Kimberlee's dad asked as he came down the stairs. "Oh, hello everyone. Teacher, interpreter, and my child coming together. What kind of trouble is Kimberlee in now?"

Sharon signed her dad's words and Kimberlee narrowed her eyes and signed, "Dad!" so hard she left a red mark on her forehead.

Her dad's eyes opened wide as he shrugged his shoulders. "What? Something must be happening."

Kimberlee was grateful that he used the interpreter. Sometimes, his attempts at signing were painful. Ms. Fox answered before Sharon finished interpreting, though.

"The Huntress told Kimberlee that you'd reveal what her gift was. She never got around to asking about it because of the confusion."

Mr. Thompson rolled his eyes and pursed his lips. He didn't need to say a word. His face showed his bewilderment.

Kimberlee looked at his face and turned away, giving a short, disgusted laugh. She looked at Sharon and signed, "How would he know. Ever since mom died, he's…" she stopped when she realized that Sharon was voicing her signs. Her eyes widened in fear.

Her dad wiped a tear and shook his head dejectedly. "You're right, Kimmie baby. Ever since your mom died, I've been lost. I don't know how to take care of a girl. I've done my best, but that isn't good enough."

Kimberlee watched Sharon intently as she interpreted her dad's words. Then she bit her lower lip and turned to look at him. She could see the tears welling up in his eyes. All the hurt and anger of the last five years melted as she realized for the first time how much her dad hurt. She had lost a mother. He had lost a wife. She went over to him and grabbed him in a bear hug, her face on his chest.

They stood together, sobbing silently for a few minutes. Sharon and Ms. Fox moved away and sat on couches in the living room, giving them time. Mr. Thompson broke the hug as he looked Kimberlee in the face, used his finger to wipe away her tears, and then signed "I love you," before kissing her on the forehead.

Kimberlee wiped the tears that had rolled down her cheeks and smiled as she saw her dad sign. She returned the sign and the tension in the room dissolved. Her dad led her toward the living room to sit with the others. He led Kimberlee to sit with Ms. Fox and took the seat close to Sharon, so Kimberlee could see her.

Then he began. "About ten years before 'the gifts' started appearing, Lydia started seeing visions. We'd just gotten married and, quite frankly, they scared me a little bit. She had a few that made me realize they were real visions, and then she got the one that changed our lives. She believed we were supposed to move here."

He laughed and shook his head as he reflected on the memory. "I'd just been hired by a corporate law firm with a nice office in Chicago, Illinois, and she wanted me to move to Okanogan, Washington – population 2,500. We argued for a couple of months. Then one day she looked at me and said, 'Walter, we need to move now. Either you move with me, or I move alone.'" He shrugged and wiped away a tear that had escaped. "I decided I loved her more than I loved Chicago. I quit my high paying job and came out here to hang my shingle."

He looked at Kimberlee and smiled. "We didn't have much, not many people need a lawyer here, but as your mom said, 'God took care of us.'" He looked at the floor and bit his lips. "Then about five years later, you were born." He gestured toward Kimberlee. As he looked at her, his eyes welled up again. "I never realized that you had your mother's eyes."

"You were the joy of our life. Your mom realized it first, though. You didn't respond to sounds. You didn't react when we fought. When you were six months old, doctors confirmed that you were deaf." He looked at Ms. Fox, then glanced back at Sharon who was finishing interpreting his last sentence. "Lydia worked at learning sign language. Me, I was getting a little more business as farmers began fighting banks and the government when the fields didn't produce. I didn't have time." He shook his head. "No, I didn't make time to learn sign language for the second most important person in my life."

He saw Kimberlee's frown and shrugged, "Your mom was always first."

Ms. Fox nodded. "As it should be."

Mr. Thompson paused, bit his lip and continued, "When you were about five, the giftings began. Parents didn't know what to do. Some had physical gifts. Fred Smithson gained super speed. Teachers thought it was funny because he'd always poked along, last in everything. Some had gifts that were mind oriented. Do you remember Steven Jackson?" When no one showed recognition, he laughed. "That guy couldn't remember anything. He got some kind of mental telepathy power."

"But I digress. Parents didn't know how to deal with these powers, these gifts. Lydia talked to each parent after their kids met the Hunter or the Huntress. Your mom knew. I asked her why she did this, and she said, 'That's why we moved here. Parents needed someone to explain.'"

"She knew this would happen ten years before you moved here and didn't tell you?" Ms. Fox was amazed.

"She told me she had a special call to be here, and I hadn't seen any evidence until this happened. Her job was to put the parents at ease, and she had a special gift for that."

"That's great," Kimberlee interjected, "but what does that have to do with my gift?"

Mr. Thompson grimaced. "I don't know. I don't know what to tell you about your gift. I was hoping that telling you about your mom might help you understand your gift. Did The Huntress say anything to you in your dream?"

"We don't think it was a dream," Ms. Fox broke in. "We think she had an actual physical encounter with The Huntress."

"That's different!" Mr. Thompson exclaimed. "Lydia always talked about the dreams. What did she say to you about your gift in person, Kimberlee?"

"I don't know what it means, but she said, 'What you are now, is not what you'll become. In days of strife, all become one.'" Kimberlee signed, and Sharon voiced with almost no lag since she knew the prophecy well by now.

"Nothing like a straightforward response," Mr. Thompson muttered. "I think your mother kept a notebook of things the Huntress said to the different parents. Maybe she heard it before and wrote it down. Excuse me a moment." Mr. Thompson stood up and looked around. "Where did she...," he began. Then he walked over to the staircase. He pulled out a box that seemed to have been there forever. He blew some dust off the top of the box and brought it back into the living room. "It may be here," he said as he put the box down on the table.

Ms. Fox looked at the box and wasn't sure if she could pick up anything without releasing a cloud of dust. Mr. Thompson looked inside and frowned. "More dust than I thought," he said. "Hold on a second." He went into the kitchen and brought back a hand vacuum. "I have to vacuum a spill or two when I'm working in there." He laughed sheepishly and ran the vacuum over the top of the books.

Ms. Fox and Mr. Thompson each pulled out a different notebook and began skimming. Kimberlee looked at them, and then back at Sharon. "What're they trying to do?"

Sharon was startled. "Sorry, I got so engrossed in what they were doing, I didn't interpret. Those are some of your mom's old things that they're looking through, hoping to find anything that can help them understand your prophecy.

Kimberlee looked shocked. "I didn't know my mom had anything like that."

Sharon shrugged. "What can I say?"

Before Kimberlee could respond, her father walked over to her. "I can't believe I forgot about this box," he said. "I'm so sorry." He looked back at Sharon to make sure she'd interpreted. "When we have time, we'll need to look at these together. The first book I looked at was your mom's memory book about you."

Kimberlee started to get up, and her dad held out his hand. "Later. I want to look at it with you. Please?"

She nodded and signed, "Okay. Later."

Ms. Fox put a notebook to the side. "This one's about you, Jason." Then she lifted an eyebrow. "You were quite the lover, weren't you?"

Kimberlee turned red as Sharon interpreted. Mr. Thompson blushed a little himself and walked over and took the notebook from her hands. "I'll keep that one, thank you."

Ms. Fox giggled and said, "Ok, but just remember that I'm single."

Jason glared at her as he put the notebook down and pulled another from the box. Ms. Fox tried to look innocent as she took the last note-book from the box. She opened it and smiled. "This could be it," she said. "The title is 'Meetings with Parents.'"

Jason's face softened. "This is a book about our time together in Chicago. Let's look at yours together." He walked around the table and sat next to Ms. Fox. They pored over the notebooks. She'd kept detailed records of each child and her meetings with the parents, but no one else had any kind of prophecy that she'd recorded.

Ms. Fox looked disappointed. "It sure would have been nice to see another prophecy like Kimberlee's, but given your wife's meticulous record keeping, I can't believe that anyone else got a prophecy that she didn't record." She turned in her chair and looked at Kimberlee. "You're one of a kind, girl." Then she got up and walked over to give her a hug. "Sorry, we couldn't find anything."

Jason had gone back to his side of the table and began looking through the notebook about their time together in Chicago. The three ladies watched as he walked back through the memories. At times he'd smile, at other times he'd sigh deeply and look sad. Once or twice he wiped a tear away quickly as if hoping that they hadn't seen him cry. Then, he stopped flipping pages and stared intently. The ladies saw him running his finger over the page. Then, when he turned the page slowly, his jaw dropped. "This is it," he said, and he waved them over.

They gathered around the table and looked over Jason's shoulder. Kimberlee's gasp broke the silence. Ms. Fox mumbled the words of the prophecy out loud as if speaking them would make them come true.

"In the future, there will be peace

Nations rejoice, strife will cease.

For accord to come, a smile will do

From the bringer of peace, which comes from you."

Jason turned back to the previous page and let the others look at it. Ms. Fox covered her mouth with her hand. Kimberlee's eyes widened. Then she looked at her dad and asked, "Why would The Huntress send the two of you to Okanogan, Washington? Wouldn't Chicago have been a better place for her to do her peacekeeping? It's already peaceful here."

When Sharon finished voicing, Jason responded. "Earlier, The Huntress had revealed to your mom that she was going to bring these powers to this small town and let those with gifts filter into society to make it better. We didn't argue about much, but it took your mom a while to convince me to move here. The Huntress kept urging Lydia to move here with or without me, so she could help the kids, and their parents go through their transition into receiving these powers. She needed to be here to bring peace to these families."

Ms. Fox shook her head. "You two don't get it, do you?"

"Whadda ya mean?" Jason asked.

Ms. Fox took a deep breath. "I don't think she had the power to bring peace. She was a prophet of The Huntress, and The Hunter, but she didn't have the power to bring peace. It wasn't her smile that would bring peace. It was the smile of someone who came from her."

Kimberlee cocked her head. Realization smacked Jason in the face. "That would make Kimberlee..."

"The bringer of peace," Ms. Fox finished his sentence.

Kimberlee protested. "I'm a 6th-grade deaf girl. You can't expect me..."

Sharon had stopped voicing and held her hand up to stop Kimberlee. "I think she's right," she signed and voiced at the same time. "Think about it." She paused as if trying to remember. "When you came home after meeting The Huntress, what happened?"

Kimberlee shrugged.

"We saw you and your teacher, and I stopped arguing," Jason said.

"You were just happy I got home," Kimberlee said as she scowled.

"We were," Ms. Fox said, "but the whole atmosphere of the room changed."

Kimberlee snorted as she laughed.

"Do you remember when we were talking with Ms. Fox today? The class was really good, unless you stopped smiling. When you stopped, Ms. Fox had to deal with those boys."

Ms. Fox nodded her agreement. "Ever since you talked with The Huntress, things have been much better in class. I don't think you need to save the world now, though. But sometime, Kimberlee, sometime."

"So when, Ms...er...mom?" Kimberlee still had a hard time calling her old teacher, "Mom."

"You can call me Sophie, or Sophia if you want to, Kimberlee," Mrs. Thompson said. "It shouldn't be that hard after all these years."

When her old teacher married her dad twelve years ago, Kimberlee wondered. They credited the marriage to her gift of bringing peace. *She did learn sign language well.* "I know, but still..." Kimberlee let that concern linger before she changed the subject. "What's going to happen to the Canadians?"

Sophie lifted her hands up as if to say she had no idea. "You know how government works."

"'Government works,'" Kimberlee snorted. "If they really wanted to work..."

"The problem with you, Kimberlee, is that as the peace bringer, both governments will have to make concessions they don't want to."

"Isn't peace worth making the right concessions?"

Sophie smiled. "Yes, but sometimes people would rather win than have peace."

Kimberlee shook her head. "You'd think these diplomats would understand history. People who win the peace cause the next war."

Sophie paused, then nodded. "Good point. What's the latest from the captives?"

Kimberlee stood up and walked toward the living room window where she stared at the street outside. Sophie waited, knowing her habits. After giving her a little time to think, she walked over and maneuvered so that she could see her and asked, "Is Carter ok?"

Kimberlee swatted her step-mom on the shoulder. "You make it sound like the only reason I go to see the Canadians is to see Carter."

Sophie put her hands on her hips and peered out over her glasses as she pursed her lips. "Well?" she finally signed.

Kimberlee signed, "Oh, Mom," and then walked away, laughing. She turned around. "Ok, I do go to see him, but that's not the only reason I went."

"At least not to begin with," Sophie muttered, forgetting to sign.

"What was that?" Kimberlee asked.

"I said, 'at least not to begin with.'" Sophie smiled.

Kimberlee eyed her suspiciously. "Are you trying to imply something?"

Sophie's eyes opened wide in mock innocence. "Of course not. You began with the purest of intentions."

Kimberlee snarled. She'd been the first from Okanogan to meet with the Canadians, trying to seek peace. The rest of the townsfolk were a bit more cautious, although the telepathic members of the community had been able to determine that the invaders weren't really bad. "They just suffered from misguided patriotism," one of them had written in a note he gave Kimberlee.

Her smile not only began the peace process between the town and the Canadians, it had won Carter over. It was hard to keep a secret with all the telepaths in the town, and soon their romance was the main source of gossip in Okanogan.

"You can't keep secrets in this town," Sophie said. "Everyone knows that you and Carter have plans."

Kimberlee glared at her until she agreed and started smiling. "So what's wrong with that?"

Sophie walked over and hugged her step-daughter. "Nothing, dear. I'm happy you've found love," she said as she broke off the hug.

Kimberlee's face glowed. "He wants to wait until after he's freed, but when that happens, he's ready to stay here and marry me. He's such a wonderful man."

Sophie bit her lower lip to keep from spoiling Kimberlee's mood. "So what will he do here in Okanogan?" she paused and then added, "Aside from being your husband that is."

Kimberlee paused. "He has a lot of stories he can tell. Maybe he'll be a writer?"

Sophie snorted. "In other words, he'll be living off of whatever you can make as a peacekeeper, eh?"

Kimberlee shook her head. "Mom, deaf Canadians do not add *eh* at the end of their sentences. That's a verbalist thing." She walked over to the window and stared at the tree-lined street. Then she turned back toward Sophie and signed, "besides, he has wonderful stories of his service to the Canadian government. People will want to read those stories."

Sophie's response annoyed Kimberlee. She just stared, shaking her head slightly.

Kimberlee waited for Sophie to sign something. The lack of motion was uncomfortable. "He's a wonderful man! He'll succeed!" she finally spewed out, signing far more emphatically than normal

Sophie let the words slip off her fingers before she thought. "If he's so wonderful, why was he trying to wipe this town and all the people off of the map?"

"Whatever," Kimberlee signed in disgust. She started walking away, ignoring any response from Sophie. Then she turned around, catching Sophie stomping on the floor to get her attention and signed quickly so Sophie couldn't respond "Isn't the president from Washington? Doesn't she have someone from Okanogan on her staff?"

Sophie stopped stomping and thought. "The President's from Washington. She lived about fifty miles from Okanogan when she was growing up." She scratched her head. I'll have to check on the members of her staff. Why?"

"Maybe that person can suggest my name to the President."

Sophie nodded. "She may not have heard about you, but I'm guessing she has since your reputation has spread." She paused. "That may be why it's taken her so long to call you."

"What do you mean by that?"

"You know those concessions we talked about earlier? I'm guessing she's afraid that she may have to give in more than she wants."

Kimberlee grimaced. "I don't see what she would have to give up. They invaded us. They tried to destroy our town."

Sophie shook her head. "They were scared. I hope now that these five have lived among us, they'll take a different report back to their government."

Kimberlee smiled and nodded. The flashing light stopped any further conversation. Kimberlee walked over to her videophone and answered. It wasn't a relay call. The president had called her directly.

Next to her stood a lady in a black dress, and next to her stood a Hispanic man in a light tan suit. Kimberlee took a deep breath and signed greetings.

Kimberlee could tell that the lady in the black dress was an interpreter as her mouth moved as Kimberlee signed. Then she saw the president begin to speak and realized that the interpreter had her work cut out for her. She interrupted the President, signing *slower, please. My eyes can't keep up.*

The president laughed at the interruption and Kimberlee breathed a sigh of relief. "I'm sorry, Kimberlee," she said. "This is an important issue, and I'm passionate about it. We've been negotiating with the Canadian government for about four years now, including both years of my presidency so far. This is Ambassador Rodriguez," she gestured toward the man in the light tan suit who nodded his head. "Every time we think we're making progress, we reach another impasse."

Kimberlee remained non-committal. "That's not good."

"No," the president said. "We've finally decided that you are the only hope for peace between the United and Canada."

Kimberlee nodded. "If it's taken this long without an answer, you're undoubtedly right. You should have called me sooner."

The president agreed. "True. We thought we could settle this quickly and it just got out of control."

Kimberlee looked stern. "And, you were afraid of concessions you'd have to make. Concessions will have to be made by both sides, you realize."

The president nodded. "We understand. We need to finish this."

"The Canadians need to know," Kimberlee insisted. "They distrust those of us who are gifted already. If they don't know that my gift is bringing peace before it happens, they'll cause problems once they find out." Kimberly paused. "Canadians can be reasonable. Our guests don't seem to want to destroy us anymore."

"If we tell them about your powers, the Canadians will back out,"

Ambassador Rodriguez tried to explain. "If they don't know about you, when both sides agree to the peace you'll bring, they'll realize it was a fair deal."

Kimberlee crossed her arms and glared at him. Then, a smile crept over her face.

"Maybe if we told them and offered a concession at the same time, it would work," Ambassador Rodriguez thought out loud. Then he shook his head. "You didn't." When she didn't respond, he said, "You did. That's not right." He frowned.

Kimberlee chuckled. "Think about how cheated you feel now, and we're on the same team. Even though the solution you came up with is logical, you think I tricked you. Am I right?"

The ambassador nodded. "I wasn't expecting to have to make any concessions in these negotiations. We're clearly in the right. They invaded us." He stopped in thought. "They were trying to destroy your town, and you seem more sympathetic toward the invaders than the Canadians themselves do."

"The people of the town and the Canadians have come to terms. They're no longer afraid, now that they know that we aren't looking to use our powers to gain political advantage."

The ambassador nodded. "And do you have a concession in mind?"

Kimberlee nodded. "This concession can benefit both sides. We allow a representative of the Canadian government to visit the invaders in our custody and debrief them without acknowledging, for the time being, that they were agents of the Canadian government."

"And how does that help the people of the United States?"

"When they talk with their agents, they'll realize that they have nothing to fear from those of us who are gifted. The agents can explain how well treated they were by those of us living in Okanogan."

The ambassador cocked his head as he looked at her. "You have the supernatural gift of bringing peace, but you have a natural gift of putting people at ease as you explain. While I'd prefer not to play it your way, I think we'll have to do that."

Kimberlee giggled. "My way, Mr. Ambassador? Those were your words I was explaining."

Ambassador Rodriguez opened his mouth to protest, but no sound came out when he realized the truth of what she had said. * After a short pause, he asked, "So how do we let the Canadians know of your status as 'gifted?'"

Kimberlee thought for a few moments. "American law prohibits revealing the status of the Gifted. You couldn't tell them ahead of time. I don't think it's right to hide my gift from them since it will play a material part in the negotiations. After you introduce me as the new member of the team, I make that statement. Then I make the offer that a representative of their government may visit the invaders as a gesture of good faith."

Ambassador Rodriguez nodded. "This might work." Then he chuckled. "You might as well take over the leadership of the team. You've made more progress with me than the Canadians have. And, you're willing to come up with creative solutions that I hadn't thought of."

Kimberlee bowed. "You have the experience. Many nations trust you. It's only because of your reputation that this plan has a chance to work."

The ambassador returned the bow. Then he looked at the clock on the wall. "Formalities will begin in about five minutes. Might I suggest that you engage in the most important preparation for negotiations that has ever been discovered?"

The interpreter didn't have to voice Kimberlee's quizzical look. The ambassador pointed at the restroom and said, "Always take care of necessary bodily functions before the discussion begins. It's embarrassing to pause negotiations to go to the restroom."

Kimberlee laughed and headed to prepare for the negotiations. The ambassador did the same.

Before they stepped out of the room, Ambassador Rodriguez warned Kimberlee about the Canadian ambassador. "Be careful with Ambassador Gagnon. He's one of the most skilled practitioners of diplomatic speak in the world. He may seem to make concessions, but when you parse what he said, you'll end up on the losing side if you agree with him."

Kimberlee gulped as she acknowledged the ambassador's words, then, the whole team walked through the doors of their ready room and into the main conference room. Kimberlee tried hard not to laugh, or even smile prematurely. *Diplomatic protocols are so silly.* She bit her bottom lip to keep from laughing.

Ambassador Rodriguez addressed the Canadian Delegation first. "Ambassador Gagnon, fellow laborers, allow me to introduce the new member of the team that we informed you about. This is Kimberlee Thompson." He waved an arm in her direction. "She would like to…"

"Please allow me to interrupt, Mr. Ambassador," the Canadian ambassador said. "But I see two new members." He pointed at the interpreter. "We only agreed to one. Was the lack of inclusion perhaps an oversight?"

Remember why. Kimberlee nodded. "It might seem that way, sir," she signed, "but as my interpreter, this lady will be my voice when I speak, and my ears when you do. She won't interject her own opinion." Perhaps it was a lie by omission when she failed to note that this was the President's interpreter. Kimberlee knew that she wouldn't tell the president anything that Ambassador Rodriguez wouldn't, though.

"And how do we know that she'll interpret accurately?"

"An excellent question, sir. How can we allay your fears?" Ambassador Rodriguez's subtle jab didn't go unnoticed, but Ambassador Gagnon made no mention of the diplomatic insult.

"We shall require time to find our own interpreter. If you had warned us of the need, we could have been prepared." He stood up as if to leave the conference room.

"Before you leave," Kimberlee continued, "I need to tell you one more thing and make an offer."

The Canadian ambassador stopped as he turned to look at her. "There's more I need to know?" He raised his eyebrows to punctuate his question.

Kimberlee nodded. "The president asked me to join the delegation because I am one of the Gifted, or the Extranormals may be the term you use. My gift is unique and should help to bring these negotiations to a successful conclusion."

Ambassador Gagnon's jaw dropped. He glared at Kimberlee, then at Ambassador Rodriguez. The burn on his face spread from his neck to the tips of his ears. "You knew this?" he shouted at Ambassador Rodriguez. "You knew this, Pablo, and you didn't prepare me?"

"I would have broken the laws of my country if I had informed you," Ambassador Rodriguez replied, not reacting to the anger. "We are not allowed to reveal the gifted status of any individuals. Ms. Thompson demanded that you know her situation so that we would be fair with you."

"You would have let her use her gifts to bamboozle us if she hadn't demanded that she be allowed to tell me her status?" the Canadian's veins popped out on his neck. "And what is this one's so-called gift?" he spat at the U.S. Ambassador.

"This one is first, a human being, Mr. Ambassador," Kimberlee signed. "My gift is that I'm a peace bringer."

"A peace bringer?" the Canadian Ambassador snorted. "You've destroyed the peace of these negotiations, and you expect to bring peace between our countries?"

At least he's talking to me. "My gift is best used when all sides have had a chance to express themselves," she answered. "I won't propose the peace plan. When my gift is used, all sides will make concessions. My country has decided that instead of winning the negotiations, it would be better if our countries were at peace again."

"I cannot believe you'd bring such a naïve child to these negotiations, Pablo," Ambassador Gagnon said in his most condescending tone. "If this is your plan, I can see no reason to …"

"But you haven't heard our offer, our concession," Kimberlee said, interrupting the ambassador.

"I'm not used to being interrupted, young lady," the ambassador said. Then he took a deep breath and remembered his position. "It can't hurt to hear your offer, though."

Kimberlee cocked her head. "Ambassador Rodriguez rightly said that you are a wise negotiator," she began. "I'm from the town of Okanogon." She saw the Canadian Ambassador's eyes show a spark of interest. "About five years ago, five men sought to come into our town to destroy the Gifted population. They didn't realize that the gifts of the people in the town were able to prevent them from fulfilling their mission and capture them. They claimed to be Canadians working for the government."

"I know the allegations," the ambassador said with an eye-roll. "That's why we're at an impasse. These men are not in the employ of my government."

"I understand your position, Mr. Ambassador. Up to now, my government would not let you talk with these men until you acknowledged that they were working under the auspices of your government. We'd like to show you that those of us who are gifted are not a threat to anyone, so we would make the offer that a representative from your government be allowed to question these men so that you can determine whether or not they're even Canadian and discover that we are not a threat to Canada. Your government would not be required to acknowledge the citizenship of these men, let alone their employment status in order to do this."

Ambassador Gagnon had regained his impassive attitude. "That is quite a new concession, indeed. I shall have to consult with my government on that offer. Ottawa will make that final decision."

"Of course," Ambassador Rodriguez replied. "While you're waiting for their reply, you can search for an interpreter."

With a slight nod, Ambassador Gagnon and the Canadian entourage left the room. As the American delegation left, Ambassador Rodriguez said, "That went well."

Ambassador Rodriguez led the American delegation into the conference room to await the arrival of the Canadians who had sent the message that they were ready to begin negotiations again. He cocked his head and looked at the team members to his right, and then his left.

He exhaled and said, "I was beginning to wonder if they were going to come back to the table."

Kimberlee looked shocked. "You didn't get my daily updates? I let you know what was happening during their visit to Okanogan."

The ambassador bit his lower lip. "I was … uh … unable to read those emails."

"The information was good."

"Perhaps, but from what you said in the first one, your telepaths listened in on their private conversations. That goes beyond the bounds of our relationship with the Canadians. They were entitled to private conversations with their citizens. If they were enemies, it might have been a different story."

Kimberlee screwed her face up in thought. Her eyes narrowed as she scratched her head. "But information is good," she said. "In this negotiation, they *are* the enemy."

"Sometimes friends get crossways," the ambassador said. "If they're willing to accept you as a member of the team, peace will come."

Kimberlee nodded. She was content, since the American government had transported the prisoners to the conference believing that an agreement would be reached, and they could be released to their government. Being able to eat dinner with Carter last night, and breakfast this morning had been a joy. *Once he's freed...* "If Ambassador Gagnon is ready to start, why is he late?" Kimberlee asked after looking at the clock. "Ten minutes is…"

"Ten minutes late is part of the game Ambassador Gagnon plays. He likes to keep the other side stewing. Patience, Kimberlee." He turned and faced the entrance the Canadians would use, removing all emotion from his face.

Kimberlee sighed and adopted the same posture.

When the door opened a few minutes later, the American delegation sat a little taller. "Ah, my friends, I apologize for the delay. Our national government always has one last round of instructions." He put his briefcase down on the table and smiled. "I would guess that you run into the same problem occasionally, eh my friend?"

"One never knows with governments," Ambassador Rodriguez replied. "Especially when there's a change in leadership."

"Well, then, let me inform you of the status of my discussions with Ottawa." He opened his briefcase and pulled out a single sheet of paper. "We are prepared to accept the presence of one of the Extranormals," he coughed, "excuse me, the Gifted on your team. Our Prime Minister spoke to your President who convinced our Prime Minister that she would be fair. You have already seen Celeste, our interpreter, in action."

Kimberly looked at the American interpreter and asked, "Is she good enough?" When the interpreter nodded, Kimberlee replied, "I believe this interpreter has the skills to participate in this work. If I may be so bold, I will expect her to interpret your words, and Leslie, our interpreter, to voice my words and interpret the remarks of the American delegation."

The Canadian Ambassador nodded his head in agreement. "We have also interviewed the men who made the incursion onto American soil. While we admit that they are Canadian citizens, we still disavow any prior knowledge of their actions."

Ambassador Rodriguez stifled a grin. "Did they explain to you why they invaded my country and sought to kill my countrymen, including this esteemed member of my team?" He gestured to indicate Kimberlee who looked straight at the interpreter to avoid any kind of facial reaction.

"They were concerned that these gifts, if used improperly, could be used to force their will on other people in the world." Ambassador Gagnon rubbed his hair back over his ear and scratched his head. "To be honest, my friend, there are many in Canada and around the world who have the same fears."

"I have lived with and worked with those who are gifted from the beginning of the giftings, my friend. In the fifteen years since the giftings began, they've made no such efforts." The ambassador looked to Kimberlee. "Would you like to add anything?"

"Anyone can misuse power, Mr. Ambassador, whether it be superpowers like I and my people have, or political power, such as exercised by those in office." Kimberlee bit her lower lip before she continued. "Let's not forget that Canada is one of the few countries that let Bingo become an example of abuse of government power." She bit her lip to keep from laughing or even smiling. "Gifted people have no desire to abuse their power. If so, your five men would be in much worse shape than they were when you saw them."

Ambassador Rodriguez pursed his lips, then wet them with his tongue. He took a deep breath.

Ambassador Gagnon chuckled. "Well played, madam. Well played. I assure you that while they are Canadian, they are not 'our men.' It is good to see that you know your Canadian history, though."

Rodriguez let out a soft sigh. Then, his face hardened, and he spoke. "The position of the American government remains that the five men were agents of the Canadian government sent to invade American territory. We're adamant about that. We intend to keep these men in American custody as Prisoners of War for violating the territorial integrity of the United States with intent to commit acts of war."

"You have not budged, that is too sad," Ambassador Gagnon said. "Given the proof that these men are Canadian, based on our discussions with them, I will restate my government's position. While we had no prior knowledge of the incursion, we will confess that five rogue Canadian citizens crossed the border with the United States intent on doing harm to the people known as the Gifted. We demand that they be extradited to Canada to stand trial under our laws."

"Five years of negotiating, and only that one small concession, Mr. Ambassador. We are at an impasse that calls for the peace-bringing skills of Ms. Thompson. Will you agree to allow her to work?" Ambassador Rodriguez gestured toward Kimberlee again.

"And what if we don't agree to the solution she offers," the Canadian asked.

"I offer no solution," Kimberlee said. "My gift, my superpower, is to restore relationships. The two of you will reach an accord. There will be concessions on both sides. My gift works without my direct action."

The Canadian huffed. "And how do we know that you won't

manipulate the results? How do we know that you won't impose an unjust peace?"

"My friend," Ambassador Rodriguez said, "she doesn't impose peace. She just said that. Her power restores relationships."

Ambassador Gagnon wrinkled his nose. "I don't trust this *gift* of hers." He folded his arms and stared at Rodriguez.

"If I were going to impose a peace on you, Mr. Ambassador, I wouldn't ask your permission to begin. I don't know how to manipulate the outcome of my gift. I just know how to initiate it."

"And what hocus-pocus do you use to bring peace?"

Kimberlee looked down as she bit her lip once again. "It seems that when I smile, those around me seek ways to bring peace. If you think back, I've avoided smiling during this whole time."

The ambassador looked at the other members of his team. They met his questioning glance with their own. None of them had any response. "That was not something we looked for since you kept that part of your secret to yourself," the ambassador responded. He glared once again at the American Ambassador.

"I had no idea how she brought peace, either, my friend. After all these many years, though, aren't you ready for peace?" The ambassador pleaded with his adversary, hoping to end the negotiations.

"Why should I fear true peace?" Ambassador Gagnon shrugged as he made his comment. "What do I need to say to make you smile?"

"Just ask," Kimberlee said. "And you must do so also, Mr. Ambassador," she said looking at Ambassador Rodriguez.

"Then go ahead and do that voodoo that you do by giving me a big smile," Ambassador Rodriguez said.

Ambassador Gagnon laughed. "What he said. Smile pretty, Ms. Thompson."

"Let there be peace," Kimberlee said with a smile.

The light flashed over Kimberlee's video phone. Sophie rolled her eyes and shook her head. She walked upstairs to Kimberlee's room and pounded her foot on the floor outside the door to let Kimberlee know that she was outside the room. When she didn't notice any response, she tried the door. It was still locked.

She pounded on the door, hoping that Kimberlee might feel the vibrations, or notice things falling off the wall. She took a breather after knocking and was just about to start again when the door opened. "Finish!" Kimberlee said. "Enough."

"You've got to get out of your room!" Sophie didn't get this emphatic with her signing often. "The president keeps calling to thank you."

Kimberlee teared up. "No thanks are needed," she said and then wiped her eyes. "Not wanted either."

Sophie took a deep breath. "How many times have you said that the only way to get to peace is if everyone gives up something?"

"I didn't think that meant me, mom. I'm the bringer of peace, not a participant in the negotiations." She wiped her eyes again. "Well, not usually anyway."

"And you brought peace and ended the dispute with the Canadians. They aren't afraid of the gifted people now since they won't be allowed across the border. The invaders have gone home never to bother us again. The Canadians acknowledged their role in the invasion."

"But why did they all have to leave, mom? Why all of them. I thought Carter and I would…" she broke off and grabbed Sophie, hugging her and crying on her shoulder. "Why couldn't he stay?"

ABOUT BOB JAMES

Bob James is a native of the Chicago area, growing up in Oak Park, Ill. He currently lives in Corpus Christi, TX. He retired after twenty-five years in the education business – one year as a sign language interpreter followed by twenty-four years as a teacher in the fields of Special Education and Technology. All of his unpublished work can be accessed through his new site, Bob James – The Author. He writes daily devotionals, Science Fiction and Thrillers, and is also working on a book about the journey that he and his wife went through during her battle with breast cancer. Bob has been married to his wife Lucy since 1979. They have two sons, one daughter, one granddaughter, and one grandson.

facebook.com/BobJamesauthor

twitter.com/rockyfort

THANK YOU

We hope you have enjoyed our anthology. It would mean the world to us if you had the time to leave a review! Reviews are what keep us writing!

FOLLOW FICTION-ATLAS PRESS FOR INFORMATION ON FUTURE PUBLICATIONS.

FICTION·ATLAS
PRESS LLC

http://fiction-atlas.com

facebook.com/fictionatlas

twitter.com/fabookbargains

instagram.com/cl_cannon

youtube.com/clcannonauthor

ABOUT OUR SELECTED CHARITY

100% OF ALL PROCEEDS FROM THIS ANTHOLOGY
WILL BE DONATED TO ALEX'S LEMONADE STAND!

About Alex's Lemonade Stand Foundation

Alex's Lemonade Stand Foundation (ALSF) emerged from the front yard lemonade stand of cancer patient Alexandra "Alex" Scott (1996-2004). In 2000, 4-year-old Alex announced that she wanted to hold a lemonade stand to raise money to help find a cure for all children with cancer. Since Alex held that first stand, the Foundation bearing her name has evolved into a national fundraising movement, complete with thousands of supporters across the country carrying on her legacy of hope. To date, Alex's Lemonade Stand Foundation, a registered 501(c)3 charity, has raised more than $150 million toward fulfilling Alex's dream of finding a cure, funding over 800 pediatric cancer research projects nationally. In addition, ALSF provides support to families affected by childhood cancer through programs such as Travel For Care and Supersibs.

For more information on Alex's Lemonade Stand Foundation, visit AlexsLemonade.org.